THE
BURNING
WITCH

Volume 3

Delemhach

To those of you fighting and working to overcome what holds you back.
Keep being your wonderful, kind selves and doing your best.
You can get through this, and you should be proud of how far you've come.

Cover design by Kate O'Hara

ISBN: 978-1-0394-4849-0

Published in 2024 by Podium Publishing
www.podiumentertainment.com

Podium

THE BURNING WITCH

Volume 3

CHAPTER 1

SURPRISES AT SUNRISE

Katarina Ashowan awoke groggily.

She squinted at the ceiling as pale winter sunshine poured into her eyes, prompting her to stretch her arms above her head and let out a small groan. She shifted in the bed, feeling blissfully relaxed. The sheets were soft, the world was quiet, all was well.

Her mind proceeded to lazily drift through her thoughts until . . .

She happened to remember that she had just gotten married the night before.

To the future king of Daxaria.

To Eric Reyes.

Sitting upright, her eyes wide, Kat found herself staring at the very prince who happened to be her husband. Eric was already awake and sitting at the small round table in their room at the inn the Troivackian king had arranged for them for their wedding night. Eric had been in the middle of raising a steaming blue mug of what Kat guessed to be coffee to his mouth, when she startled him into motionlessness. He sat dressed in a fresh white tunic untied around his throat and chest and untucked from his brown trousers. His wavy dirty blond hair appeared a little damp as though he recently had run wetted hands through his tresses, and his hazel eyes shone with more green than brown . . .

The two locked gazes.

Kat blushed and squirmed, then threw her gaze at the footboard away from him.

"Good morning," Eric greeted with a small chuckle. It was his turn to take stock of his wife's appearance.

Given the drunken state she had been in the night before, he had only removed her blue uniform vest, left on her tunic and trousers, and removed the pins from her hair.

As a result, her hair was mussed and set ablaze, as were her golden eyes, in the sunshine of the day from the window on his left.

The prince stood and casually stepped back over to the bed. "I . . . am a lucky man."

Kat lay back into the bed and drew the covers over her head. "Are you trying to be annoying?" she shouted through the thick quilt.

Eric grinned. "What? I can't tell my young wife how beautiful she looks the morning after our wedding?"

"You sound like an old pervert when you put it like that!" Kat accused from her hiding place.

Eric peeled back the blanket and stared down at her scarlet face, still smiling.

"I hate to tell you this, but I'm now *your* perverted old husband."

Kat scowled, then rolled over and buried her face in the pillows.

Deciding he had a lifetime to torment the redhead, Eric let her off the hook and changed the topic.

"I ordered tea for you, but I'll have to leave for the castle soon, so we can't share a breakfast together." The prince reached over and tousled the hair at the back of Kat's head, making her grumble.

He turned toward where he had discarded his boots the night before and set to pulling them on, which prompted Kat to finally look at him again.

"We didn't . . . Last night, we didn't . . . you know . . . Did we?" she wondered with a wince.

Eric straightened and tilted his head over his shoulder with a look of incredulousness.

"Do you really think I'm the type of scum to do that sort of thing to a woman who was drunk and unconscious?"

Kat sat up and rubbed her face in her hands. "No, I don't. I just wondered if I . . . perhaps . . . persuaded you while in that state . . . I can't recall how much you imbibed last night either."

"I didn't drink."

Kat looked at Eric more seriously.

"Why does that make you concerned?" he asked wryly. "I didn't because I had the feeling that Faucher and his sons were waiting for the opportunity to poison me."

Kat considered his words, then nodded in understanding. "They're more likely to stab people, not poison. Though Conrad is oddly good at hiding crossbows in places you wouldn't suspect."

"Noted." Eric blinked, then proceeded to watch Kat again. His heart started skipping several beats. "Well . . . I better get going."

His gaze met with hers, and the look in his eyes made all words die in Kat's throat as he slowly moved back over to the bed.

Leaning down, his left hand rose and gently tilted her chin up before he brushed a kiss on her lips.

He pulled away a mere inch, but when he saw the dazed look on her face, he was unable to resist kissing her again.

The gesture was turning hungry and heated rather quickly, and Eric was becoming wholly convinced that he could arrive later than planned at the castle, when a sharp knock on their door interrupted them.

Frowning, Eric straightened and made his way over to the door. Opening it a crack, he stiffened when he saw Prince Henry's ashen face waiting.

"You both need to come back immediately," Henry whispered, his voice warbling.

Eric glanced over his shoulder and saw that Kat had risen and had already tucked in her tunic, so he opened the door wider.

Kat gave a small bow to Henry but looked at him with furrowed brows.

"Your Highness? What are you doing here—"

"Duke Finlay Ashowan arrived this morning and has been asking to see you. We don't have any time to waste. We've kept him waiting as long as possible"

Eric felt the room swim around him, and dread filled his being. His grip on the edge of the door tightened.

Kat's face drained of color. "Oh."

"Come, Kezia is in the carriage with a dress for you, Lady Katarina. Prince Eric, I brought a horse for you so that you can ride ahead."

Eric bobbed his head in thanks, and after swallowing, turned back to the room and seized his coat from the hook by the door.

Managing to only spare a moment to share a wordless nod with his wife, he then took a swift exit without a second look back while Kat did her best to braid her hair, then snatch up the last of her belongings.

So much for a leisurely morning . . . the redhead lamented anxiously.

She left the room expediently and closed the door, her stomach clenching in between barrel rolls, making her feel all kinds of terrible as Prince Henry followed behind her.

Henry and Kat departed from the inn that was already rowdy with Winter Solstice celebrations and made their way to the carriage that sat waiting in the snowy alley. While the vehicle felt as though it may as well have been death's carriage to Kat, she did her best to assure herself that everything would be alright . . .

But she was having a hard time making herself believe it.

Finlay Ashowan paced the solar, while his familiar, Kraken, lay flopped over in a sunny patch on the floor.

The house witch felt he had been waiting far too long, and he noticed how panicked the king and Alina had been upon his arrival . . .

Something was definitely going on.

Had they banished Kat to some remote building? Was she sick? What if the king had imprisoned her for one of her pranks? Perhaps she was scared to leave her chamber after having met the devil?

His mind raced with what could possibly have warranted their behavior, when the door behind him opened.

Spinning around and preparing himself to demand that he be taken to his daughter's chamber at once, found he didn't have to bother, as Katarina, dressed in a navy blue gown with long loose sleeves, cut in a deep V over her chest, appeared. Her gold bracelets adorned her wrists as usual; she seemed to glow with health. Kat ran over to her father, smiling.

"Da! You're here!"

Throwing her arms around him, she buried her face in his chest and breathed in the comforting aroma of garlic and flour . . . How was it possible that after weeks of travel he smelled like he had just come from cooking dinner?

"Oh, thank the Gods! I thought something was wrong when they kept me waiting!" Fin breathed a sigh of relief as he squeezed his daughter.

Stepping back, his hands still gripping Kat's upper arms, he surveyed her more closely.

"Sorry about that. It's been busy the past little while, so I slept in," Kat explained while doing her best not to appear shifty or suspicious.

"Tired? You? How hard are they making you work?" Fin asked while only half jesting.

"O-Oh, well . . . you know I've also started learning swordsmanship, so there's been training as well as council work," Kat reminded while the father-daughter duo made their way over to one of the sofas and seated themselves.

"Yes, but your training was only supposed to be conducted with the purpose of it being used as a last resort. They shouldn't have worked you too strenuously."

"Oh, but I love it! It's everything I wanted and more! I've gotten really good at it, Da! I'll have to show you later what I can do," Kat gushed hurriedly, already anticipating with an internal wince how quickly her father was going to find out about the sparring matches she had won against seasoned warriors . . .

Fin stared at his daughter with a frown. "Well . . . if you're doing it because you enjoy it, that's fine as long as you aren't getting into fights . . . But Kat, you know this whole ordeal with the devil isn't something you need to face alone, right?"

Kat nodded while letting out a small sigh and pointedly ignoring his comment about getting into confrontations. "Yes, yes. But, Da, tell me about home! How is Mum?"

Fin eyed his daughter another moment before he leaned back into the couch. "Only you could be cavalier about the son of the Gods having an interest in you. As for your mother . . . she should be joining us soon actually."

Kat balked. "W-What?"

"She left a week or two after me . . . I thought we had agreed she'd stay behind, but we've been so worried about you that she decided to join me."

"Who's taking care of the keep?! Or all your work?! By the way, why in the world did you become a duke?! I thought you absolutely refused to ever be ennobled a third time!"

Chuckling, Fin stared at his daughter lovingly. "I'll tell you about it when your mother gets here . . . though I do have a surprise for you."

"A surprise? Really? Where? I— Oh, hi, Kraken! I didn't think you'd ever come, what with having to get on a boat— WAIT! You can talk to my familiar, Pina! Everyone is so excited to hear what she's saying, but—" Kraken lifted his head up sleepily when Kat called his name.

Fin reached out and gently clasped Kat's hands, quieting her and drawing her golden gaze back to him. "Kat, is everything truly alright? Aside from the devil? After your last letter about finding your familiar, you haven't written or told us much."

She swallowed.

Kezia and Henry had explained that telling Kat's father everything was important, but they suggested it be done as a group with the king, queen, Eric, and Faucher . . .

"Oh, I'm . . . Yeah. Yes. You know me, I'm always great!" Kat smiled, but she could tell her father wasn't buying it entirely.

"You've only been gone four months, but you seem . . . almost like a different person." Fin's studious gaze was making Kat start to sweat along her temple.

"W-Well, I've never been apart from my family before, and this is a brand-new place, so it only makes sense that I—"

A knock at the door stopped Kat's attempt to ward off her father's uncanny insight.

She looked over her shoulder with a frown. No one was supposed to interrupt them. Kat had been instructed to catch up with and calm down her father, and then she was to escort him back to his chamber to rest while she was to attend a council meeting with Alina. They apparently had the results regarding what powder Sir Seth Herra had been attempting to throw in her face at the end of their sparring match.

"Ah, it sounds like they brought your surprise." Fin rose from his seat and made his way over to the door.

Kat stood as well, curious as to what her father could have brought for her.

When he opened the door, however, she felt her knees buckle, and she half wished she were in a nightmare.

There . . . standing and smiling at her was . . .

"Likon."

The young man who had been in love with her for years stepped through the doorway, his light brown eyes aglow as he drank in the sight of the redhead.

"Hey there, Kitty Kat. Did you miss me?"

CHAPTER 2

OBTRUSIVE OBSERVATIONS

L-Likon, what are you . . . Wait . . ." Kat turned from her childhood friend to her father. "If you're here, and mum is on her way . . . Did you leave Tam to handle everything *alone* back home?!"

Fin winced and reached up to rub the back of his neck, while even Likon scuffed his foot against the stone.

"I mean . . . Clara stayed behind to help . . . I think? Did Annika bring Clara?" The duke looked to Likon uncertainly.

Likon nodded while continuing to grimace before looking back at Kat.

"Ah . . . well . . . He'll be fine. He's learned a lot in the past year!" the young man attempted to soothe both his and the duke's guilt. "Now, don't I get a hug?"

Kat sighed with a small smile and embraced her old friend. Likon picked her up as he usually did after not seeing her for months at a time, but was forced to put her down more quickly than he was accustomed.

"Oof! You're heavy now!" Likon laughed as the two pulled apart.

Kat nodded vaguely. "It's the winter, not much to do but eat . . . So, I heard that traveling here was a lot more difficult than it normally is!"

Likon raised an eyebrow and looked at Fin.

"I know. She's acting odd." The house witch confirmed Likon's wordless question while his earlier concern returned to his face.

"Or it could be that you two are the ones that keep making it strange," Kat grumbled while stepping around Likon and closing the solar door behind him.

"Oh, I don't know. You've got some muscle on you; you aren't as . . . loud, or expressive . . . Overall you seem pretty different to me," Likon observed while Kat led them back over to the couches.

"I'm in Troivack—of course I'll have toned it down," Kat reminded while seating herself.

"I know your mother taught you that, but it's odd that you're taking it so well," Fin cited while sitting down across from his daughter and resting his elbows on his knees.

"Alright, well how about we circle back to this mystery of how I'm different later on? You were delayed a long time coming here, Da." Kat stared at her father somberly. "I really hope you didn't have to take too many risks."

Fin met his daughter's stare head-on. "I'm sorry it took so long. Apparently the storms this year are unlike anything any captains have seen before. Though I can see even here in Troivack there is a good deal of bizarre weather happening given that there is snow on the ground outside."

Kat nodded. "That's been a topic of concern here, yes."

Fin sat back and looked at Likon again, whose stare lingered on Kat before turning to meet the duke's gaze.

Neither of them had ever heard Kat sound so . . . mature . . .

"Well, all that matters is you both got here safely. How is His Majesty doing with both his children being gone?" Kat asked while leaning forward. She knew Eric would want to know, but most likely wouldn't get the chance to ask the house witch for a while . . .

Fin pondered the question, his unnerving attention remaining fixed on his daughter. "King Norman Reyes is handling it better than anyone guessed he would. I think at least knowing where they are has helped. How *is* Eric doing here?"

Kat's heart leapt to her throat, and she tried to smile vaguely. "Oh, I hear he's . . . he's doing fine. Haven't seen him too much the past month."

It wasn't a complete lie! She'd been training and he'd been off investigating Duke Icarus until the past day or two.

"Mm. Well, I guess that's good then. Is Alina adjusting well?" Fin questioned next.

Kat barely suppressed a sigh of relief when the topic changed. "She is. She's definitely the change the court needs here."

"That's reassuring to hear. How she would settle in Troivack is something her father is still very worried about. I'm surprised it has been so quiet though . . . Other than Eric's kidnapping, I would've thought they'd aimed for Her Majesty's own life."

"S-Sure . . . I mean . . . that . . . that is a fair . . . fair thing to imagine." Kat cleared her throat and Fin's eyes narrowed.

"Kat, is there a thing or two perhaps you could've mentioned in your letters?"

"You both must be tired. I can show you to your quarters and see about getting a meal sent up. Despite today being the solstice, there is an emergency council meeting I must attend now with Her Majesty." Kat stood back up quickly, her hands folded over her skirts.

Finlay rose as well, but the hard set of his mouth told his daughter that he was not letting her off the hook, until she raised her hands in defense. "Alina is going to tell you all about certain events herself."

The duke's features darkened. "Kat, your safety is tied to Alina's. What happened?"

Her mind racing, Kat tried to think of some way to throw off her father, some way of getting out of the interrogation, when lo and behold . . . another knock at the door interrupted them.

Fin didn't move, and Kat remained frozen in place, leaving Likon to go see who had come in during the tense silence.

"Ah! Lord Finlay Ashowan! I'm so happy you're here!" Alina entered the room, her face pale but a polite smile already drawn over her features.

Fin finally tore his attention away from his daughter to bow to the Troivackian queen.

"Your Majesty, it is good to see you in fine health. It's great timing that you're here, in fact. My daughter here is dancing around the matter of attempted assassinations and informed me you wished to tell me about everything yourself."

Alina faltered for a single breath, but she regained her composure like the queen she was.

"Ah, I do want us to have a long talk about certain events, but I am afraid that the reason I had to interrupt your reunion is that the council is waiting on Kat to begin the meeting."

Fin slipped his hands in his pockets. "Why is Kat's presence in the Troivackian council meeting so imperative?"

While Kat was falling to pieces internally, Alina held her ground. "Because Kat is the only one I trust to take notes for me during the meetings. Now, I am terribly sorry again, Your Grace, but we must be off. A steward will show you and Likon to your chambers."

Alina turned to Kat, who nodded gratefully back, and the two made an expedient exit from the solar.

Once the two men were alone, Fin looked to Likon. "We're going to wait until the end of the day, but if they don't tell me everything, then I want you to turn over every stone in this castle to find out what it is they're hiding."

The young man bowed.

He was in complete agreement, as there was a funny bad feeling that was tickling his own stomach.

"Have I mentioned I love you?" Kat gasped to Alina as they rounded the corner of the solars corridor.

"Yes, but you need to say it a lot more often because I just about fainted from that. Gods, I've never been on that side of your father's intensity," she replied breathily.

"It's awful, isn't it? We're going to have to tell him everything sooner rather than later because otherwise he'll tear it out of me and that won't go over well."

Alina nodded in agreement as the two women made their way down to the council room.

"By the way, how are you *feeling* this morning?" the queen asked casually with a mischievous glint in her eyes.

Kat looked at her friend incredulously.

Alina noticed this and, with a smile, rolled her eyes. "Good Gods, you teased me to the high heavens about *my* honeymoon. Am I not allowed to do the same to you?"

"You do remember *who* I married, right?" Kat asked flatly while ensuring to lower her voice.

Alina hesitated then. "Fair point. It *is* unpleasant when you put it like that . . . Though you were quite out of it last night, so I'm guessing nothing of consequence did occur between you and my brother."

"You are correct about that." Kat gave a small laugh.

"Well, from now on, you two will be sharing a chamber, so don't be too upset about it."

Kat blinked as she processed this information, and they descended the last few steps of the grand staircase. "I forgot about that."

Alina looked at her friend, bemused. "You forgot that being married means you live together?"

"Completely."

The queen couldn't help it, she snorted in laughter at Kat's stricken expression.

The two had reached the council room, however, and so she was forced to cut off her guffaws quickly as the guards eyed them.

"Alright, shall we enter?" Alina looked at Kat, who had miraculously managed to become appropriately serious.

"Yes. I want to know what that arsehat tried to do to me."

Instead of uttering her agreement, Alina turned to the guards, who proceeded to open the doors for her while she released Kat's arm.

The two strode in, their masks of impenetrability in place as the long table filled with Troivackian men awaited them.

Kat noticed that many of them were regarding her with interest as opposed to disapproval compared to the last time she was there, and she was feeling quite good about the fact, until her gaze landed on Eric.

While he didn't smile, he did force himself to avert his eyes as Kat could feel a telling blush begin to warm her face.

Brendan sat waiting patiently, and once his wife and her new sister-in-law were seated, began the meeting.

"We should all be celebrating the solstice with our families, so I will make this meeting quick. It has come to our attention that the powder that Sir Seth Herra attempted to throw at Lady Katarina is in fact dried up and ground Witch's Brew. In its new form, the drug is even more potent, but it requires less of the mushroom to create," Brendan informed everyone darkly.

Duke Icarus was impressively calm as he listened to the news while feigning concern.

"But . . . *why* would they want to dose Lady Katarina? It seems an odd time to want to incapacitate her what with us all there as witnesses," Viscount Sanchez queried from farther down the table.

Brendan shook his head. "We don't know yet. Sir Herra is holding his silence thus far in the interrogations, but we will extract the information from him one way or another. It has been a bit difficult, as Sir Cleophus not only knocked a few teeth from his mouth but also concussed him. For now, everyone should be on the lookout for the powder; it still has its distinct smell, so it isn't likely that it'd be easy to add to any of our food. Even so, members of the elite knights are guarding the kitchens to ensure everyone's safety."

The room filled with murmurs.

"Now, on to the obvious matter of ending Lady Katarina's exile from court."

The men quieted back down. "She not only won the sparring matches against her peers, but even against one of our best-trained men. Does anyone object to her return?"

No one spoke, and so Brendan nodded in satisfaction, until a younger noble raised his hand. Kat recognized him from the first banquet she had attended in Troivack, Lord Edium, was it?

"With Duke Ashowan here, can we assume that Lady Katarina will be leaving for Daxaria in the near future?"

Brendan lifted an eyebrow. "That has not yet been decided. Our original agreement was to have Lady Katarina join our court for a year, but in light of the threats to her life, that agreement may come under review. However"— Brendan leaned back in his throne, his features gentling ever so slightly—"today is a day of celebration, and so this meeting is concluded. We will discuss the details at length another time. Just be on guard now that we know there was some kind of master plan Sir Herra had with drugging Lady Katarina. Captain Orion has been temporarily detained as he, too, will undergo extensive questioning. Leader Faucher will be assuming his duties until further notice."

Many men tensed at the last bit of news, but eventually they all began to rise, save for one red-faced nobleman (who had most likely already been sampling some of the festive beverages), who raised his hand.

"Your Majesty, what are we going to do about the women who now wish to learn self-defense?"

Everyone froze.

Brendan only gave a brief tilt of his head before he looked at Kat.

The redhead almost scowled in response.

He was entirely too calm after such a question . . .

"Lady Katarina is the most appropriate teacher for them, in my estimation. She can hold lessons until she finds a replacement." Brendan stared at Kat as though daring her to object.

Underneath the council table, Kat's index finger was rapidly tapping the knuckles of her opposite hand.

"I wouldn't mind helping, Your Majesty," she responded while withholding agitation from her voice.

Brendan merely nodded in response, then looked back to his council.

"That is all that needs to be said on the matter for now. Go, and enjoy your solstices."

Without any other unnecessary pomp, Brendan stood, offered his hand to his wife, and led her out of the council room. The lords all rose in suit, pushing in their chairs, then bowing to Kat and Eric as the throng gradually drifted out of the council room.

The couple loitered at the back of the crowd, casually drifting closer to each other.

When they were within two feet of each other, Kat noticed a swell of tingling fill her being, demanding she go even closer to Eric. Awareness of his nearness was making her thoughts stumble over one another.

"How is your father?" Eric asked quietly, his left hand "accidentally" brushing against the back of Kat's hand.

"Um. Good. Yes . . . My mum is apparently coming as well and will be here in a week. They also . . . They brought Likon."

The two exited the council room, and Eric risked a small side-glance at her.

Kat looked at the ceiling to try to distract herself from the potent impulse to reach out and touch her husband. "Da's already suspicious."

Eric slipped his right hand in the pocket of his brown trousers.

Despite the festive day, he wore simple clothes. A black coat, and a white tunic with no other finery . . . though at the very least the pieces were of superior quality; Kat thought he looked rather dashing.

"Try to last until this afternoon. There is the luncheon we have to get through first."

Kat nodded but felt a burr of stress reappear in her chest before she risked looking at Eric's profile.

She was irked to see he appeared completely calm.

"Why don't you seem as worried as I am?"

Eric looked at her with a bemused closed-mouth smile. "I know how to bluff. You really are your father's daughter."

Kat looked ahead of herself again and grumbled.

"I thought everyone was upset because I *could* hide my nonsense."

Eric's smile turned genuine as the two continued walking.

"You know how my father is . . . and it's not like I'm hiding one or two little things," Kat reminded the prince when they reached the end of the corridor and stopped.

The two turned and faced each other as servants filed past carrying fresh tablecloths and silver pitchers in the direction of the throne room.

Eric clasped his hands behind his back and locked eyes with Kat. His mild mannered expression faded to gentleness, the adoration in his hazel eyes were making the redhead's nerves work themselves to a fervor.

"I do know how your father is. In fact, I've known him longer than you have." Eric leaned in slightly, his voice lowering.

Kat put her hands on her hips as she worked to regain control over the urge to kiss him right there in the hall.

Days ago, she had been able to hold a conversation with him without any issue . . . How was it that after two nights and a simple wedding, she felt so extraordinarily drawn to him?

"You know, *husband,* I look forward to seeing how you handle him since you're such an expert on Finlay Ashowan." She matched his quiet volume, but her tone was no less haughty.

However, the look in Eric's eyes when she called him *husband* made her knees weak. His gaze lowered to her mouth, and she began to have trouble recalling why an empty corridor was *not* a good place to kiss him . . .

"Kat! There you are. Did you—"

Likon rounded the corner, apparently at first he had only seen the red-head, but once he'd pulled into view, realized she wasn't alone.

Kat turned her face away from Eric briefly, taking the chance to try to collect herself, and Eric turned and faced her childhood friend while giving a greeting nod.

Likon stared at the pair, momentarily stricken by the peculiar air around them . . . then remembered he was in the presence of royalty and bowed. "Happy Solstice, Your Highness."

Eric inclined himself in return. "Same to you. Lady Katarina and I were on our way to the luncheon. The council meeting has just concluded, but I'm sure you two would like time to talk." He looked at Kat, who was still struggling to meet his gaze. "Good day, Lady Katarina."

He bid farewell to her politely and coolly, then strode off regardless of Kat belatedly remembering she had to give a small curtsy.

Once the prince was out of earshot, Likon stepped closer to Kat warily. "What was that about?"

"We were talking about the council meeting is all. So tell me, is my brother actually going to be alright managing the new dukedom on his own?"

Likon casually avoided her coy grin as he then offered her his arm.

The gesture caught Kat off guard, and so her face fell and her gut twisted, but when Likon looked back at her, she tentatively accepted his offer to escort her.

"You know how smart your brother is, he'll sort it out," Likon dismissed breezily, his face brightening at her touch.

Kat nodded while trying to ignore the discomfort that overtook her at being so close to a man who wasn't Eric . . . Every part of her wanted to release Likon's arm and move farther away but knew she couldn't.

Likon glanced at her briefly, his pleased expression turning momentarily calculative.

There had been something odd in the way Kat had been talking to the prince . . .

She had had a look that Likon hadn't seen before, and it was troubling him a great deal . . .

Giving Kat's arm an extra squeeze, they continued toward the throne room for the solstice luncheon and settled into making easy small talk along the way, though the two childhood friends had far more on their mind than either of them wanted to let on.

CHAPTER 3

A FATHER'S FURY

Kat fanned herself with her hand as she sat in the council room for the second time that day.

She had been completely thrown off when Likon had appeared during her conversation with Eric, and as a result had forgotten that she had to be on guard the entire time during the solstice luncheon due to the Troivackians that wished to speak with her about her duels the previous day.

Luckily, she had managed to lock her father into conversation with Brendan and Alina for most of the meal, and she was able to distract Likon thanks to Sir Cas, but the time had come . . . to tell her father *everything*.

Eric sat at her side, looking a mite green, which did help Kat feel a little better, as she saw that she wasn't the only one feeling utter terror over the storm that was about to break out.

Alina and Brendan may have looked like the calmest people in the room, but beneath the table they were tightly clasping hands. Faucher sat on the other side of Kat with his arms crossed.

While he knew that things weren't ideal, he wasn't sure he understood what had even the king on edge . . . He had never met the infamous house witch, but he'd glimpsed the tall redhead at the luncheon and, aside from noticing where Katarina inherited a large amount of her looks from, didn't see anything all that alarming or intimidating about him.

After what felt like both a too short and an excruciatingly long time of waiting, Fin entered the council room.

He had changed from the clothes he had initially arrived in, wearing a black coat with gold edging, a white tunic, and cream-colored trousers. Fin eyed the small group, his gaze already sharp, and his expression stony.

He made his way over to the table, and after issuing the appropriate bows, seated himself down at Brendan's left, directly across from Eric.

Fin locked eyes with the Daxarian prince and his hostile aura slipped as he straightened in surprise.

"Eri— Your Highness. You're looking quite well!" Fin openly marveled at the changes in the prince that had taken place over the past four months. The prince had made himself scarce during the luncheon, and so it was the first time since they'd spoken in Daxaria that the house witch had laid eyes on him.

Eric's hair was neat and tidy, his complexion healthy, and he no longer looked haggard and thin, but strong. Though there were touches of exhaustion around his eyes . . .

"It is good you are in fine health as well, Your Grace. Congratulations on your dukedom." Eric lowered his chin in respect and forced himself to meet Fin's shimmering blue eyes that, powerless or not, still revealed he had been blessed by the Goddess herself in the Forest of the Afterlife.

Fin nodded, his stare appraising, and a small tentative smile lifted his mouth before he looked to Brendan.

"I take it we are all gathered here so I might learn about what my daughter has not been sharing with me?"

Kat felt like she was going to be sick.

Alina began, "That would be correct. We were unaware of how much Kat had or had not chosen to share with you, but in light of the political climate here, decided discussing it as a group would be worthwhile."

Fin nodded along to what Alina was saying thoughtfully, before his eyes cut to Eric, and then Faucher, who held his gaze evenly.

"Is there a particular reason, Your Highness and . . . ?"

"Leader Gregory Faucher of the first rank, Your Grace."

Fin raised an eyebrow but bobbed his head in greeting.

Then he looked back to Brendan and Alina expectantly. "So, is there a reason for Leader Faucher and the prince to be here?"

Alina tried to smile reassuringly at the duke but wound up appearing as though she were grimacing instead.

"Both Leader Faucher and His Highness's presence today will make more sense as we talk."

Fin didn't react, but after another moment of quiet when no one started speaking, he leaned back in his chair and folded his arms patiently.

Awkwardly, Kat shifted forward in her seat.

"Well . . . there was a bit of trouble on our way here to Troivack," she declared slowly. Risking a glance at her father, Kat immediately regretted it and lowered her face back toward the table. "When we arrived, we found out there was an assassination planned for Alina, and so, His Majesty decided to split us all up to confuse whoever intended to harm her."

Fin stiffened as he regarded his daughter with stern concern.

"After our first night traveling, I was poisoned."

"What?"

Kat winced at the sharpness in her father's voice.

"Y-You know poison doesn't affect me much, so it was fine, a-and Faucher took care of the people that night, so—"

"You killed people in front of my daughter?" Fin looked at Faucher, who remained the calmest out of everyone present.

"Lady Katarina had gone to bed when I handled the assassins, and I cleaned up the scene before she rose the following morning."

Fin took in a deep breath, his dislike over the idea of several deaths apparent, but his initial agitation settled. "I should have been informed of this as soon as possible. Had I known, I would have at the very least sought aide from the Coven of Aguas to help guard everyone."

It dawned on everyone then . . . that the duke was unaware that there was just a tiny bit more to the events leading them to the present moment . . . He looked as though he were already relaxing under the assumption that that was the worst of the news.

"Er . . . Da . . . that . . . that was the first attempt."

Fin's face drained of color and his expression tensed once more.

By everyone's next breath, they could all sense the dangerous ire brewing in the house witch. He looked to Brendan who, impressively, remained unperturbed . . . At least that's how he managed to make it seem.

"How many attempts have there been?" Fin asked quietly, though the ominous note in his voice was not lost on anyone. When no one volunteered to speak first, the duke fixed his attention back on his daughter, who was starting to sweat far more noticeably. "Kat. How many times were you in danger?"

"L-Like I said, with poison, I don't really get affected. You know how my magic is, Da."

Fin rose to his feet and pressed his palms against the table.

Kat's heart felt as though it were about to explode. It was racing so quickly . . .

"How. Many?"

"Poison, twice. T-Then there was the third attack on the carriage, but nothing happened because Faucher and the knights defended us. But uh . . . The fourth time I got hurt, though, it wasn't as bad as last time, I swear!"

It was a struggle to remember in that moment that Fin did not have his magic as he straightened and the full force of his wrath directed itself at the king.

"My daughter was injured, and I heard *nothing?*" Then the duke registered the way Kat had worded the ordeal. "What did you mean when you said 'it wasn't as bad as last time'? What 'last time' are you referring to?"

While Kat couldn't bring herself to say the words, her father managed to figure things out faster than she would've preferred.

"Kat . . . are you telling me . . . you were *stabbed*? AGAIN?"

Everyone forgot how to breathe.

When the room once again fell silent, Fin addressed the king. "You have hidden the well-being of my daughter from me and placed her in jeopardy multiple times? Did you not vow to us that you would protect her? Where were you when she was getting poisoned and stabbed?!"

Brendan raised his chin when he addressed the duke, and only Alina noticed his throat bob before speaking. "Her Majesty and I were on a separate path than the decoy carriage. Lady Katarina was traveling with His Highness Eric Reyes and Leader Faucher."

Fin's head snapped toward Eric, who held his gaze.

Then the house witch looked to Faucher.

However, when he spoke again, it was still to the king. "You will face dire consequences for this."

"Da, it's because I-I asked him not to say anything. I made His Majesty swear that he wouldn't. I really was fine! Faucher had men die trying to protect me, and His Majesty has been respecting my wishes and—"

"Katarina, he should have been respecting the wishes of your parents. We are your guardians. You were stabbed and poisoned, and we should have been made aware to decide whether you should return home!" Outraged, Fin paused his lecture to stare at the Troivackian king. "You will be hearing from His Majesty King Norman Reyes about the penalty you will face."

Brendan said nothing, but he did lower his chin once more.

Fin rounded on Kat. "Is that everything?" His acid tone hurt deeply. She knew it was coming from a place of fear and love for her . . . and pain. She knew he was mortified over the jeopardy she had been placed in . . .

"Da, if I had been truly afraid any of those times, you would have known! I just—"

"Your sense of safety . . . I've been afraid for a long time to say this . . . but your sense of safety and judgment is not to be trusted. Kat, I am beyond . . ." Fin trailed off, shaking his head and dropping his eyes—he couldn't bring himself to say the words.

He continued to silently process the news, his hands eventually finding his hips as he grappled with his emotions.

After letting out a long shaking breath, without being able to look at his daughter who was battling tears, he asked, "What else is there?"

Fin's voice was hoarse. When he did meet Kat's eyes again, she could see his anger had merged with his anguish as the two emotions filled her father's face.

Her voice died in her throat.

"This meeting started with me being told Leader Faucher and His Highness's presence were important. I'd like to know why."

Clearing his throat, Faucher had to confess he *was* starting to feel affected by the stress in the room. He was not used to such . . . vulnerable displays.

"My presence was requested as I have been Lady Katarina's sword instructor and guardian for the past few months."

"What do you mean, 'guardian'?"

Faucher responded carefully. "Lady Katarina was exiled from the court temporarily due to some of her questionable conduct, though that was more so what was said for the sake of the other nobility. In truth, after her encounter with the devil, we believed it'd be safer if she were far from those plotting to harm her."

"That is the first piece of relieving and reasonable news I've heard yet." Fin remained standing but nodded at Faucher to continue.

"She is an exemplary swordswoman and surpassed everyone's expectations. My sons have aided in her training, as has Mr. Kraft, the Coven of Aguas leader, and she has learned to hone her magical abilities to her benefit."

Fin looked a little troubled by hearing about the intense nature of Kat's training but jerked his chin down in understanding again.

"There were two troubling incidents at my keep."

Fin's look of exasperated alarm renewed itself.

"The first event was when one of my students attempted to haze Lady Katarina, only he ended up committing a far more dangerous error. He offered his life as penance, however, Lady Katarina mercifully forgave him and instead has had him vow a life of servitude to her."

Faucher plundered on not giving Fin a chance to ask any incriminating questions about the situation with Broghan Miller. "The second incident, a stone golem attacked the keep and a magical being attempted to bind Lady Katarina's magic. She was able to successfully evade them, and we returned to His Majesty's castle while my keep undergoes repairs and investigations are carried out."

Fin licked his lips before speaking. "Thus far, Leader Faucher, your decisions have been of the most sound judgment. I thank you for taking care of my daughter, though I would like more details about the incident that led to Kat obtaining an indentured servant."

"Broghan Miller has really become a lot more likable; I'm sure he and Likon will get along well," Kat interjected, her voice weakly optimistic as her father's mood tentatively settled back down.

However, when his eyes cut to his daughter, she could see that he was far from finished lecturing her, but that was the least of her worries, as in the next moment, he addressed Eric.

"Why is it that Your Highness is a part of this meeting?"

It was Eric's turn to let out a long, drawn out breath. He swallowed, then lifted his face to the duke, his former friend.

"Fin, I . . . I want you to know, none of what happened was done out of malice, or drunken stupidity."

The house witch frowned. "What're you talking about?"

Eric's hands curled into fists atop his thighs under the table.

"Fin . . . Kat and . . . and I . . . We—" Fin's expression turned murderous, and Eric had to take another quick breath to force himself to finish the sentence though he never broke eye contact.

"We got married."

The silence was deafening.

Fin stared at Eric blankly, his entire mind and being consumed in shock . . . and then white-hot rage.

He turned to Kat, who was trembling in her seat.

The house witch then stared at the king whose expression had turned apologetic.

"Katarina." Fin's voice was like ice. "You need to explain yourself. Right now."

Kat was struggling to stave off tears as her heart fluttered in her throat.

"Eric . . . and I . . . developed a relationship, and . . . we are now married."

Fin's eyes were wide and unblinking when he stared at his daughter.

"Why?" His attention snapped to Eric, who looked completely chastened. "Why . . . are you two not courting, or merely betrothed?" His voice was faint, but everyone knew his quieted words weren't going to last long.

Kat didn't say a word, and so Fin addressed Eric. "Did you . . . *bed* my DAUGHTER?!" The roar rang out, and the walls seemed to quake . . .

Even though Eric had the keen premonition he was about to be slaughtered where he sat, he replied.

"Yes."

Fin rounded the table and seized Eric by the front of his tunic and threw him to the ground with impressive strength.

"Da! Stop!" Kat was on her feet, her aura gently flickering from her skin.

"I knew we weren't as close as we used to be, but how *dare* you do that to her." Fin seethed at Eric who, after recovering from the fall, gradually brought himself back up to standing.

"Fin, I'm sorry. I really . . . I really didn't do it to hurt you or because I was being—"

"You have been in and out of a drugged or drunken haze for four years, and you come back and do *this*?"

Everyone in the room stilled instantly.

Alina looked at her brother in alarm, while Faucher winced.

Kat moved in front of her father, blocking him from Eric.

"Da, I already know about everything."

Fin stared at Kat furiously, then at Eric over her shoulder.

Eric gently touched Kat's shoulder, silently requesting she step back away as he moved to place himself directly before his old friend.

"I know, Fin. I know very well your daughter is too good for me, and yes, I am a selfish drunk who has taken too much Witch's Brew in the past four years to remember every horrible thing I've done."

Alina gasped in her chair, but Brendan's hand covered her own, quieting her back down.

"I'm not pretending I'm anything better, but I love her, Fin. I promise. I've never broken a promise with you, have I?" Eric asked sincerely as the duke's fury was visibly replaced with agony. "I promise, I'm going to try. She can leave me whenever or however she wants, and she knows that, but Godsdamnit, Fin . . . I swear. I swear this all happened because she's—"

"Stop." The duke looked away from Eric. "I can't . . . I can't hear this right now."

"Da, I—"

Fin jolted back from Kat as she stepped forward and reached for him. "No, Kat. I . . . I can't look at you right now. I'm sorry, but this . . . I need some time."

He turned and started to move toward the doors.

"Da, it isn't—"

"Kat, you . . . you got married, stabbed, poisoned, and attacked, and . . . you're my daughter. You're part of my family that I love more than life itself, and I just can't . . . understand how you would think so little of me to not tell me any of this." Fin spoke the words without looking at Kat.

He hadn't even fully turned around to address her, and when he finished, he didn't wait to leave.

In his wake, his daughter succumbed to her tears and let out a soft sob while her hand came to her mouth to try and stifle it. Alina looked at her brother with disappointment and shock, and Eric stared at Kat's back and shaking shoulders with his heart shattering, regret crawling throughout his entire being.

CHAPTER 4

ROOM FOR REGROUPING

Kat and Eric sat with their backs to each other in the discreet bedchamber they had been permitted to use.

The room was small and cramped, but it was quiet and far from the festivities, which, after the conversation with Kat's father, was desperately needed. A bed large enough for two people with a dark blue coverlet, two night tables, and a single chest at the foot of the bed with a rug in front of it was all there was room for.

"I'm sorry."

Eric's voice was hoarse, his elbows braced against his knees as he stared at the wall before him.

"Why're you apologizing?" Kat's voice was thick from her tears. "He just announced to everyone about your history with Witch's Brew."

"I'm sorry because if I were a better person, we wouldn't be in this mess."

Kat turned to look at Eric's back, anger and a fresh wave of tears rising. "I swear to Gods, Eric, I need you to not say this is a mistake right now."

The prince felt the ache in his chest deepen.

"We've been over this. I know everything, and I love you, why—"

"Because I'm still a mess, Kat. Your father has every right to feel the way he does." Eric cut her off, his own emotions whirling closer to the surface. "Neither of us are . . . are ready for marriage. We have to be honest about that. If we were, Fin wouldn't have been as horrified, and we wouldn't be as shaken."

"I'm shaken because my da is disappointed in me. But you want to know something?" Kat paused, as the salt in her tears began to make her cheeks sting. "I've been proud of everything I've done here. I finally feel . . . accepted. Like I found who I wanted to be, and the people I wanted around me."

"Kat, you've done incredible things here. You have grown, but I—"

"You're going to put yourself down next, aren't you?"

Eric fell silent.

"Can you look at me, please?" Kat's voice was firm. So, after taking a moment to steady himself, Eric turned to face her. "Look . . . you're right. Neither of us are ready for marriage, but . . . I do think we are on the same page, and because of that, I think we can move in step with each other."

Eric's darkened eyes did not look at all convinced. "Kat, what if you do become pregnant because of that night? We got married so quickly because we had no idea when Fin was going to arrive. And . . . I know we jested, but . . . are you really alright with taking on the responsibility of ruling a kingdom?"

The redhead knew she shouldn't attempt to sound excessively optimistic, or it wouldn't come across sincere enough . . . which meant, as always with Eric, she was honest and open to a fault.

"Gods, no. I'm not alright with it *at all*. Your parents studied and trained for years before they took over! The only studies I've enjoyed have been swordplay. That said, I do want to protect people, but . . . I honestly don't think I should be ruling—and now that I think about it, it might be in direct violation of a witch's purpose. We are supposed to be medians, not leaders . . . I will most likely get expelled from the coven . . . It could brew bad blood . . . All this is . . ."

Eric didn't finish her thought though he knew exactly the choice curses he would use. Instead, he silently recognized the validity of her points.

"So . . . annulment?"

"Pfft. Not happening."

"Because of a potential child?" Eric wondered while shifting on the bed so that he was facing Kat more directly.

She did the same.

"No. We stick this out because my gut instinct says we made the right choice. It sounds ridiculous, and I have no idea how this will all work out, but . . . I know I love you, and I just . . . I just know I'm supposed to be with you. Married to you. Loving you . . . It isn't the easiest of things—I'm reckless, but not a complete idiot—I know this is going to be absolutely shit at times."

Eric succumbed to a slight smile at that.

"But are you going to fight at my back for this or not?"

The prince stiffened at the reference to their vows, and . . . he felt something inside himself solidify at the reminder.

"I will. I hate hurting you, Kat, and I hate that my past has made things like this with Fin, but . . . I do want you, and if you still say after all this you want me too, I will fight for it."

Kat nodded.

Her face and eyes were bright red and pink, tear-stained, and swollen.

Without thinking, Eric shifted on the bed over to her until he could pull her into himself and ease them both back.

He held her, and felt her relax in his arms, which prompted him to wonder why she felt so safe with him, though Fin's words observing her lack of sound judgment pertaining to danger rang in his head . . .

Eric didn't mention that to Kat though as he decided they had enough to worry about in that moment, and he should try to remember that he was wildly grateful that Kat *did* feel that way about him.

"I think we have to settle in for the long haul when it comes to getting Fin on board." The prince sighed into the top of Kat's head before releasing her.

"Probably . . . but . . . even if it isn't about us, I want to talk to him about everything else that's happened to me in Troivack."

Eric nodded seriously while gradually stretching his legs on the bed until they dangled over the side, and stared at the ceiling. Kat then followed suit.

"Something tells me my sister might want to have a word or two with me as well."

"Oh Gods, that's right . . ." Kat grimaced and looked at her husband's profile. "Are you going to be alright?"

Eric gave a small wince but gave a slight shrug. "I have it easier than you do, sorry to say. I'm at least showing signs of cleaning myself up at this point."

Kat nodded glumly to herself. He was right . . . Then a thought occurred to her.

"Do you still crave the Witch's Brew?"

Eric considered the question carefully. "At times . . . but it's usually when I have a moment on my own while stressed."

Kat's mouth twisted thoughtfully after his answer.

"I'm sorry." Eric turned and stared at the redhead's profile. "I don't know that it is ever going to go away."

Slowly, Kat reached for his hand and clasped his fingers in her own warm, calloused palm. "Well . . . you're already better than you were . . . so maybe you just keep getting better. And if you mess up here and there . . . well . . . we'll figure that out then."

Eric let out a long breath, then allowed himself a half smile as he then lifted Kat's hand to his mouth and kissed her fingertips before he looked back to the ceiling, pulling her hand to rest on his chest with his fingers still interlocked with hers.

"How long do you think we'll have before the hounds are at our door?"

"Kat . . . Lady Dana is in the castle; you need to specify if you mean actual hounds or not."

The redhead sighed while rolling her eyes, though she grinned as she did so.

"Alright. I'm going to go talk to my da. If he still says he doesn't want to see me, I'll go to Kraken."

Eric gave her hand an extra squeeze. "I'll see my sister. I need to find out if we are still announcing our marriage tonight."

Kat rolled over and flopped her face onto Eric's chest before letting out a muffled moan.

The prince's free hand came up and scratched the back of her head. "I know. I'd hoped for a few days of peace before more excitement."

Eventually, Kat hoisted herself off her husband and began to trudge over to the door to go talk to her father.

"Why are you still wearing a dress?"

Kat halted, then turned to look over her shoulder at Eric in confusion.

He stared back at her in equal bafflement, uncertain about why she was reacting so strangely. "Wouldn't it be more comfortable wearing pants to talk to your father?"

She rounded her toes back to point toward her husband and gaped at him for another long moment before uttering, "Have I mentioned that I love you?"

Eric snorted, then laughed while he pushed himself up off the bed.

"I know who I married," he retorted good-naturedly while making his way over to Kat. "I also know that whenever I have a particularly difficult task, wearing a uniform or armor helps give me the sense that I'm stronger. Even if I do not feel that way the rest of the time."

Kat let out a whoosh of air and nodded.

She stepped assuredly over to the chest that contained her clothes, which had been brought over to their room ahead of her other belongings, and while crouching down before it, began tugging at the ties on her dress.

She had nearly finished freeing herself from the garment when she realized Eric was watching her with a roguish half grin.

"Oh, for the — Get out, you pervert!" she hollered while clasping her loose dress to her body.

Eric chortled but sidled over to his wife and dropped a kiss on the top of her head. "Wondered when you were going to remember I was here. Alright, I'll go see my sister. Good luck with your father. I'll see you at dinner?"

Kat's chin tilted up to look at Eric's face above her. "Sounds like a plan."

Eric slowly bent farther down and brushed a gentle kiss on her lips before rising back up, though he gave a small grunt as he did so.

He rolled his shoulders as he strode toward the door, trying to work some stiffness from his body as he moved. He acquiesced that he should start doing more stretches if he was going to have any hope of keeping up with his wife.

Casting one final look at Kat's back as she opened the chest, a flutter of happiness and peace soothed some of the tension in Eric's chest. Smiling to himself, the prince took his leave, feeling far more assured of himself than he had all day . . .

Though it came as no surprise.

Things always became brighter around Kat.

Striding purposefully down the castle halls, Kat bore down the path toward the kitchens where she knew her father had most likely seduced the cook into letting him take over the space by baking or cooking something divinely tasty. The overall atmosphere around her was festive and cheery, but that didn't help Kat's nervousness that had risen again.

"LADY KATARINA!"

Looking over her shoulder, Kat was surprised to see Broghan Miller barreling toward her.

She waited for him to reach her with a raised eyebrow, her hand resting on her sword hilt instinctively.

"Lady Katarina, you need to come now; Lord Ball has Joshua cornered. You're the only one who outranks him! Come on!" He announced desperately, his brown eyes wide.

Kat hesitated for a single breath.

She really needed to talk to her da . . . but then the thought of Joshua's pale, terrified face the day they had returned to the castle.

"Godsdamnit, it isn't even an eighth, ninth, eighteenth, or nineteenth day to or from the new moon," she said before she took off at a sprint with Broghan at her side.

"Don't tell me you're starting to believe his superstitions as well," Broghan panted as he fell into step beside the redhead.

"He's always been right though," Kat argued right before the two of them leapt out of the way of an upcoming maid, who squeaked as they hung a sharp turn around the corner and half leapt down the stairs, which startled a good many more servants and even one or two nobles.

"Every time it's been those days, something bad has happened," Kat continued as she landed nimbly at the bottom of the steps onto the first floor, then waited for Broghan to catch up to her.

He was unable to speak by the time he reached her side as he gasped heavily.

She looked at him expectantly, but instead of telling her where the confrontation was taking place, raised his hand and pointed.

Kat followed Broghan's gesture that directed her toward the training courtyard, took an educated guess, and darted ahead of her personal guard.

Sure enough, in the hall right in front of the training grounds entrance was a huddle of people, with Lord Ball standing before Joshua, who was shoulder to shoulder with Caleb Herra, glowering darkly, while two knights and two nobles stood as onlookers.

Kat stopped running.

They hadn't seen or heard her approach, as they seemed intent on ganging up on Kat's fellow students who were wearing Faucher's uniform just like she was. She could see how terrified Joshua was . . .

Her eyes homed in on Lord Harriod Ball.

"Oyy! Lord Ball!"

When everyone's eyes had swiveled to Kat, she threw her shoulders back and strutted forward purposefully. She needed to draw attention to herself, but also to make Lord Ball act irrationally . . .

An easy feat for a proud nobleman like him.

"Lady Katarina," he greeted with a narrowed gaze and a slow, reluctant nod of respect.

It wasn't the bow he was supposed to give, and so Kat used the slight as grounds for her next response.

"I sincerely hope your cock is as thick as your head so that you have *something* to be proud of. Because it sure as hell isn't your honor that you should count on."

Jaws dropped.

"*What did you just—*"

"You're cornering two men who've done nothing to you unfairly and using your status as a weapon, but then don't respect what status indicates you should do when you see someone of higher rank. So. Shouldn't you *bow properly*? Possibly as an *apology*?"

Lord Ball struggled to overcome Kat's confrontation, as it was far more uncouth and aggressive than anything he'd ever heard from a woman before.

"Lewd comments such as that are—"

"I said *bow*," Kat's voice echoed down the hall.

The two nobles behind Lord Ball wasted no time in folding themselves in half.

Lord Ball didn't bow, but his pulsing vein did appear.

Kat waited, and when he instead stared down his nose at her, she smiled.

He opened his mouth to make a disgusted remark, when Kat pulled off one of her gloves, maintaining eye contact with the lord, then proceeded to slap him across the cheek with the leather, using enough force that the blow rang out, and he stumbled.

"For your rudeness, I challenge you to a duel."

"L-Lady Katarina, y-you don't have to—" Joshua was starting to step forward, but Kat shot him a quick wink and shook her head.

Lord Ball, clutching his bruising cheek, stared at Kat, hatred burning across his face.

She leaned forward, a small magical pulse running through her golden eyes. "Happy Solstice, Lord Ball. I'll send you the details of the duel shortly. Until then . . . stay away from my comrades. As the head of our unit, I will pursue the full letter of compensation if you try to antagonize them. I will even take this straight to the king should I need to."

A flicker of fear appeared in his eyes.

Kat held her ground and smiled, then waved him off.

Reluctantly, the group dispersed, leaving Faucher's students alone at last. Though the hateful glances that were cast back at them weren't all that submissive . . .

"Lady Katarina, you don't need to defend me." Joshua Ball's quiet voice called her attention to him.

She looked over to the young man with a frown. "That wasn't a fair fight. You know Faucher assigned me as the head of our class, meaning I'm responsible for you all."

"It's still *my* fight!"

Kat raised her eyebrows and stared in surprise.

Joshua Ball had never raised his voice before, but . . . she noted the determination in his dark gaze and the fist clenched at his side.

Even Caleb Herra looked surprised.

"I know it's your fight, but that doesn't mean I can't offer support. If you want to be the one to duel your brother, I'll name you as my champion." Kat stared at Joshua levelly, and she could see some of his anxious energy settle.

The thought of dueling with his older half brother made the young man hesitate . . . but . . . he straightened and nodded once, vaulting over his fear neatly.

Kat grinned. "I can't wait to watch you beat him. Now, if you all will excuse me, I need to go see my father . . ."

"Does he know you talk about men's cocks?" Broghan asked casually, having joined his peers sometime during the redhead's uncouth insult.

Kat shoved him but was glad to see both Caleb and Joshua respond with laughs, though the latter blushed scarlet.

The troupe gradually broke off to head in separate directions after exchanging a few more good-natured jests and jabs.

Oddly enough, the nasty exchange with Lord Ball had a bolstering effect on Kat's mood, as she was reminded just how much she really had accomplished in Troivack to be placed in charge of men-at-arms . . .

Even if it was one of the most ragtag groups of unwanted people in existence, in that moment, she was glad to be a part of it . . .

Now she just had to show her father that despite her unconventional choices, she was growing into someone he could still be proud of.

CHAPTER 5

AN ATTEMPT AT AMENDS

Kat waited in front of the kitchen door where two armed guards stood.
"So . . . you're saying Duke Ashowan *is* in there?"

"Correct," the guard on the right answered.

"But I'm not allowed in there because someone tried to poison . . . me?"

"Yes, my lady."

"Well . . . how did my father get in there?"

"Our cook has wanted to meet Duke Ashowan and speak with him since he was a boy."

"And you're saying my father banned me from entering?"

"He banned everyone from entering, Lady Katarina."

"This isn't even his kingdom!" the redhead exclaimed, throwing her hands in the air.

Neither of the guards responded.

Kat let out a small huff of annoyance.

She eyed the men while placing her hands on her hips, an idea coming to her.

"Have either of you met my familiar?"

Kat stepped into the kitchen while a chorus of *awes* rang out behind her.

Before her was Fin and the Royal Cook for the Troivackian king. The two were deep in discussion, while on the table sat what looked like an herb-crusted pork loin.

Her mouth began to water involuntarily.

The two men, after hearing her entrance, turned.

At first Fin looked normal, his face calm, his blue eyes intent in a particular way that Kat only ever saw when he was talking about food . . . but then he registered he was staring at his daughter. Anger flashed in his gaze until he noted her change of clothes, and he wound up blinking in surprise.

"How did you get in here?" the cook at Fin's side asked in surprise.

"My father isn't the only one in our family with charm," Kat responded with a small eyebrow lift. "Don't you have an entire feast to prepare for the Winter Solstice celebrations?" she wondered next while noting the empty kitchen.

The cook blustered, and Fin's hands found his hips as he stared at his daughter. She decided to get to the point of her visit sooner rather than later.

"Da, I'd like to talk with you. Could we go for a walk . . . please?" Kat's voice softened, as she felt her anxiety reestablish itself.

When he didn't answer instantly, Kat noticed that her heart was starting to race.

Fin slowly rounded the cooking table and walked over until he was in front of his daughter.

Looking over his shoulder, he addressed the cook again.

"I'll be back again, Christos."

The cook practically glowed.

As he and Kat left the kitchen, Fin was caught off guard by the sight of the two burly guards seated on the floor in front with one of them holding a kitten up to his shoulder like a baby while the other man scowled.

"She just prefers me over you!" the one guard announced to his comrade smugly.

Kat almost laughed, and without thinking, looked to her father to see his reaction.

Then she remembered that he hadn't met her familiar.

"Pina," Kat called out.

Hearing her witch, the small kitten squirmed in the guard's hands, his triumphant grin falling to sadness. Even so, he gently released her, and the tiny feline trotted over to the redhead.

Bending down and scooping her up, Kat looked at her father with a shy smile. "This is my familiar. Pina Colada. Pina for short though . . . I tried that drink Captain Alphonse found in Insodam, and it was the best drink I'd ever had so . . . I named her after it."

Fin raised an eyebrow at the kitten, whose nose and whiskers twitched, and her eyes grew large as she stared up at him.

His face softened as he reached his hand out and let her sniff his fingers.

She gave them a tentative lick.

Fin gave a closed-lipped smile.

Kat felt joy and relief surge through her.

Maybe everything really would be alright!

That is, until Fin's attention drifted to her face, and she saw the grief in his eyes.

"H-Here, Pina you can . . . can play with these nice guards while my da and I go on a walk."

The men on the floor brightened back up as she set the little beastie down, then carefully sidled by the men with her father following closely behind.

The pair gradually made their way outside the castle, and coincidentally, into the private space Kat had used to train for her spars . . .

Absently, she thought how she would've preferred to do another twenty years of the grueling training than be faced with her father's disappointment, but she knew there was no other way.

Willing her feet to stop, her hand nervously found the hilt of her sword.

"Da, I'm sorry I didn't tell you about everything."

Fin's stare drifted over his daughter's head, and her heart ripped itself to shreds when she saw the tears in his eyes.

"I . . . I . . . just . . . I know for normal people none of these situations were safe, but I'm different. I can handle a lot more than others, and I want . . . I've always wanted to use my abilities to protect and help people. I never really got to try before, and I didn't want to lose this chance to actually see what I could do. And Da, I've learned so much. I can do incredible things, and even my magic . . . I'm not scared of it anymore! After killing Roscoe, I . . . was worried I was going to turn into a monster. That I would just one day snap and start killing people."

Fin finally looked at his daughter's face as fresh snowflakes drifted down around them.

"I now know that that isn't how my magic works. It feeds off intentions around me. Similar to how your magic feeds off the number of people who feel they are at home," she explained with a taut smile. "We're still working on how to disperse my magic without me having to forgo proper sleep for a month or starve myself, but with Mr. Kraft's and Faucher's help, I know that we'll—"

"You're going home, Kat."

She stopped, stomach twisting. "Da, I faced the devil, and I could've beat him! I'm not leaving an entire kingdom to—"

"You could be carrying the heir to Daxaria; you can't face the devil again." Fin's voice was hoarse, and his eyes fell to the ground, making Kat's heart sink with them.

"We don't know that! We can at least wait and find out! And why do you get to make that choice? Da, this is why I didn't want to tell you about everything! You keep setting my limits for me!"

Fin's hand rose and pressed against his eyes. "Kat . . . do you know why I accepted the dukedom?"

Startled by the sudden shift in topic, Kat frowned and shook her head as her father's hand dropped from his face and he looked back to the sky, his jaw flexing.

"I did it . . . because you said you wanted to live unmarried for the rest of your days. I was going to give you the viscount house and your brother the dukedom."

Kat's face drained of color, and her eyes grew wide.

"I never wanted to stop you from doing what you wanted, but you don't take care of yourself." Fin looked back at his daughter, tears rolling down his cheeks. "Do you understand what you're signing up for? You are saying fighting against the son of the Gods, using your magic, and marrying an addict is now what you want."

"Eric is more than just an addict," Kat countered roughly, though it was a battle to get the words out.

"You are choosing a life of struggle. He might disappear someday, just like he did to Alina and their father. And what about if there are children? Are you really alright knowing that one day he might choose the drug or drink over helping you or them?"

"Of course I don't want that, but we'll take it a day at a time! He's already improved a lot since coming here!"

"You've only known him for four months, Kat."

"And how long did you know Mum before *you* bedded and wedded her?" Kat snapped angrily.

Fin's shock at his daughter's words sparked his fury back to life.

"Your mother and—" the words abruptly died in his throat as he stared at Kat.

Kat watched in mild concern as realization washed over her father's face.

"You're exactly like your mother."

Whatever Kat had been expecting, it wasn't that.

Fin looked back to the sky as though he expected to see the Gods appear and confirm his conclusion.

He gave a small laugh of disbelief.

"Holy . . . Gods . . . how did I . . . not see it? You are . . . *exactly* like her."

Absolutely baffled as to what was happening, Kat started to wonder if her father's mind had frothed over.

"Er . . . how . . . ?"

Kat didn't get a chance to finish her sentence as Fin stumbled past her, muttering to himself.

"Thinks getting stabbed isn't a big deal . . . Wants to fight . . . Recklessly makes a terrible choice of husbands . . ."

Kat would've been insulted if it weren't for the strangeness of it all.

After her father had disappeared into the castle, the redhead reached one very important conclusion.

I don't think anyone other than Kraken can fix this . . .

Tilting her head with a frown, Kat struggled with the knot for the second time.

"We *aren't* announcing our marriage?"

"Not until your father stops threatening war. Which could still be tonight, but it's doubtful," Eric responded as Kat made another valiant attempt to tie the silk cravat at his throat.

"Then why are we allowed to still share a room? People are going to find out really quickly."

"That's what my sister is hoping will help push your father to settle down. It's better to stay in control of the situation than letting it spiral, and your father knows that. Therefore, Fin will either have to whisk you away or be forced to accept us."

Kat let out a low whistle as she worked on the silk. "Damn, Alina can be scary."

"She's like our mom," Eric agreed.

"You and your sister are still okay after everything . . . ?"

The prince gave a halfhearted shrug with a sigh. "We aren't exactly on the best of terms right now. She's furious with me for keeping it a secret, but also appreciates the efforts I've made to sober up." Eric winced at the memory of his conversation with Alina earlier that day and decided he'd rather change the topic. "Do you think your father will attend the ball tonight?"

Kat grimaced and shook her head. "Doubtful. I'm a little worried he might be having a mental breakdown if I'm honest . . . Son of a bitch, do you really have to wear this stupid thing?"

Eric chuckled. "I told you I can do it myself."

"I used to watch my mum doing this for my da and always thought it was a nice thing to do." She sighed while stepping back and putting her hands on her hips. She glared at the infernal bit of cloth that lay inconspicuously against Eric's tunic.

"I can show you how to do it again later," he consoled with a grin.

"Stop laughing at me."

Eric chuckled. "I'm not laughing at you."

"You just laughed!" Kat pointed at her husband accusatorily.

He did laugh then as he moved closer to her, his gaze drifting from her irritated expression down to the golden gown she had donned for the evening.

"W-Why are you looking at me like that?" Kat asked while trying to sound angry but instead felt her pulse quicken and her cheeks burn red. In the short time they had been together, she had come to learn what that look in his eyes meant . . .

Eric leaned closer, his hand slipping into his pocket, his warm breath tickling her right ear . . .

He smelled of the bath and its oils of sandalwood and . . . and . . .

"I think you know why I'm looking at you."

Goosebumps swept across Kat's arms and legs. "H-How can you be thinking of that?! After the day we've had? You talking with your sister and then the whole thing with my—"

Kat didn't finish her train of thought as Eric's warm mouth brushed against the side of her neck, and her knees went weak.

"Y-You know w-we'll be late if we—"

Eric pulled Kat to him, and that was about the time all other feeble attempts to stop her husband's advances were ended.

CHAPTER 6

AN UNFORTUNATE UNVEILING

Alina stared at herself in the mirror blindly as her maids quietly worked on arranging the most beautiful and unique dress anyone had ever seen . . .

For the announcement of her pregnancy, Brendan had arranged an exorbitant budget for Alina to look as impressive as possible.

The gown was a combination of a deep shimmering teal and emerald. While it was emerald by its loose gauzy straps, by the time it streamed down into the skirts, it changed to teal with tiny diamonds sewn into the skirts. When walking to the ball, Alina was to wear a fine white wolf fur mantle, and upon standing before her citizens to make her announcement, she would shed the cloak.

All this was Brendan's and her orchestration to be dramatic and shocking—typically elements to a night that would have Alina in high spirits—but after her conversation with her brother . . . her mind was far from the event.

A knock at the door had the maids backing away from their queen while bowing reverently.

The king entered the room, already wearing his all black finery and mantle, his crown atop his head. "Leave us."

The serving staff filed out dutifully.

Once alone, Brendan regarded his wife and blinked.

Alina couldn't resist.

She smiled.

Not many people could read her husband the way she could, and she could tell that he was in awe of how she looked that night.

Her hair had been partially tied up and treated to shine. Her crown rested atop her head, and golden earrings dangled from her ears. She wore her usual bracelets, and an upper arm cuff as well.

"You are . . ." Brendan trailed off and cleared his throat.

Alina blushed.

"How are you? I heard His Highness came to speak with you," the king asked instead, a faint tinge of color in his own cheeks that was almost entirely hidden by the short-cropped beard he sported.

At the mention of the meeting, the queen's content smile faded. She looked down toward the subtle swell of her belly and clasped her hands over her skirts, then fixed her attention back to her husband.

"I'm . . . worried."

Brendan nodded and waited for her to continue as his wife took a slow, deep breath.

"Eric is a recovering drug addict? He's married to Kat, and . . . the two of them are supposed to rule a kingdom. I just don't understand all this. I was able to accept their relationship in a way . . . especially when I started looking at all the clues. I remember Kat had mentioned she knew what happened between Eric and her father the night after my wedding, but she said she hadn't learned it from Lord Ashowan . . . I had been right in the middle of questioning her when Eric had shown up. Then there were so many other instances . . . looks they gave each other, the way she would avoid giving me straight answers about him . . ." Alina's brows lowered. "She knew about the Witch's Brew. She helped lie for him, and he helped lie for her, and those two are supposed to lead Daxaria?"

Brendan folded his arms patiently as Alina gently tossed her arms in the air, at a loss as to what to say. After a moment of still not being able to find any other particular words, she looked intently at her husband. "You knew, too, and lied to me."

The king stiffened.

"You did it to protect me, but we've been over this. The fewer secrets the better. Especially when it comes to family."

Brendan lowered his gaze, properly chastened.

"Despite knowing everything, why do you still support them? Is it really just to avoid scandal and war with Daxaria?"

The king considered his next words carefully as he studied his wife's weary face.

"I think . . . if your brother is to have any chance of ruling a kingdom, it *has* to be with Lady Katarina."

Alina blinked in confusion, and Brendan's eyes grew lost in thought in how best to explain.

"I'm more worried for Lady Katarina in their union, I'll admit. The prince's entire motivation to better himself revolves around her, and that is a heavy burden to bear for one person."

The concern on Alina's face urged Brendan to continue expounding on his thoughts.

"However, I think once the two of them are back in Daxaria, there will be enough support for the prince around him that it will remove some of the pressure on her, and eventually they will be on more equal footing. Though I do believe the future well-being of Daxaria rests solely on whether Lady Katarina can remain steadfast enough. If she can, and perhaps learn to reveal her weaknesses and concerns more openly to those they trust, then there is a great chance the two of them will lead successfully."

"Those are a lot of uncertain variables," Alina observed warily.

Brendan nodded. "But it's the best chance your brother has of coming back to himself."

Tears rose in the queen's eyes as she gave a nod of understanding.

She looked away to try and compose herself.

"Just . . . how did it go so wrong for him? He had everything. He was faultless . . ."

"Those who aren't familiar with darkness have a harder time finding their way out when they fall into it. Especially when they're already set in their views."

Alina considered this, her throat aching fiercely. "You think our mother's death prompted this?"

Brendan shrugged. "I cannot say. I know of your brother's present more than his past. What I do believe, from what I've come to see and know of the prince, is that he is an incredibly intelligent and shrewd man, which makes failures all the more frustrating."

"You speak from experience?" the queen wondered seriously.

Brendan nodded. "When I was seventeen, I started ruling more independently, and my first few failures in judgment were devastating."

Alina stared at her husband, her gaze turning tender as she carefully stepped down from the stool she had perched upon while being tended to by the maids.

She moved over to Brendan and grasped his warm hands in her own.

"Well . . . let's avoid dark thoughts for today. I've had enough of them, and we should be more excited for our news."

Brendan gave a small smile before his eyes darted to Alina's middle.

"As you wish, my wife."

Alina chuckled at her husband's formality, then lifted herself up to her tiptoes to brush a sweet kiss on his mouth. Maybe the rest of their night didn't need to be quite so dour after all . . .

"Godsdamnit, we are really late. I'm supposed to go to Alina's chamber to escort her," Kat said breathily as she finished readjusting her hair.

Eric was in the process of pulling the sleeves right side through his tunic while sitting shirtless on the bed.

Kat looked at him with a raised eyebrow.

He stared back. "I apologize for nothing."

"Perverted old man," she grumbled while turning to the door, though she felt her cheeks grow warm.

Eric rose and followed behind her to see his wife off.

"I'll see you down there," she called, glancing over her shoulder as she opened the door.

However, with her gaze turned away, Kat then proceeded to nearly crash into none other than . . . Likon.

His hand was suspended in the air as though about to knock. He was dressed in a fine forest green coat, black tunic, and pants, and in his hand was a small box wrapped in brown paper and tied with a silvery string.

Kat froze.

He smiled at her and marveled at her beauty until his eyes then registered Eric standing behind her, without his shirt on.

"Kat, what—"

Shoving him back, Kat hastily stepped outside the chamber and closed the door behind herself.

"Likon, I don't have time right now to explain; I need to go to Her Majesty's chamber." Kat tried to take off down the hall, but Likon seized her by her elbow.

"Kat, what the hell did he do to you? If he made advances toward you—" Likon's voice was starting to echo down the hall, and Kat stared around fearfully. If anyone overheard, things would get even worse.

"Likon! It isn't like that! I promise I will tell you everything later, I just—"

Likon ignored her and dove for the chamber door, throwing down the small gift that had been in his hands without a second thought.

However, thanks to her training, Kat was fast enough that she was able to grab him by the front of his coat and haul him back away.

"Stop!"

"Kat, you don't know about him! He's courting almost every noble-woman in this castle! Not to mention the stories I've heard of him around Daxaria . . . ! If you won't listen to reason, then I'm going to your father." Likon grasped Kat's hands on his coat, his eyes wild and furious.

If Kat were honest with herself, he looked as though he could kill some-one, and it was deeply startling to her . . .

But then he was starting to look over her head down the empty corridor, his sights set on going straight to Finlay Ashowan.

Overcoming her hesitation, Kat managed to blurt out, "No! Likon, my da already knows! Right now, I—"

"Fin knows?" The young man's attention snapped back to her.

"Likon, let go of my hands." Kat's stomach was reacting in that strange way again to his touch . . . It was roiling, telling her to get away from him.

"Kat, no. You can't court him! He's going to hurt you, and Gods . . . Tell me you haven't bedded him!"

"I really need to tend to the queen; Likon, you need to let go of my hands." Kat tugged, but his grip grew firm.

She was about to ignite her magic for the strength to successfully pull away from him when from behind her, Kat's husband's voice called out, "Kat, everything alright here?"

Eric appeared in the doorway of the chamber, fully dressed. While his stance may have made him appear lax as he tugged at his cuffs, the way his hazel eyes had darkened told Kat that he was far from calm.

"Eric, I just need to—" Kat tried again to pull her hands free from Likon, but instead he held on to one of them even more tightly and moved the hold to his side.

The prince's gaze flit to the clasped hands, then back to Likon's enraged face.

"Your Highness, you need to stay away from Lady Katarina from here on out."

Once again, Kat worked to snatch her hand back, but Likon thwarted her by yanking her down the hall with him.

"Kat?" Eric's voice rose.

He remained rooted to the spot, but his gaze sought his wife's awaiting the answer to the unspoken question.

"I—" She started to speak to tell him she would handle the matter, but Likon gave her arm another tug that had her almost stumbling.

Slamming the door behind himself, Eric caught up to pair right in time for Kat's magic to surge, her aura bursting from her skin as she at last wrenched her hand free.

"Likon! I said *stop!*" She breathed angrily, her golden eyes glimmering as Likon rounded back to stare at her, his frantic, murderous energy far from settled.

"Kat, I will tell you exactly why you need to stay away from—"

"Enough! Likon, just . . . listen! I can't explain everything right now. I have important duties that I need to attend to." Kat enunciated her words carefully while steadily holding his gaze and holding up her hands as though to warn him off making another grab for her.

Likon didn't say anything, but he looked at Eric, who waited nearby without moving a muscle. The prince's eyes were trained on the man, who he could already tell was carrying at least two knives concealed on his person.

"Kat, go tend to my sister," Eric said softly, making Likon round on him. That suited the prince fine as he addressed the younger man next. "If you try to stop her from leaving again, I will remove your hands myself."

The redhead didn't budge.

She didn't trust them to be left alone any more than she trusted Kraken not to take a bite out of an unattended dinner roll.

"You . . . are disgusting," Likon spat.

Eric said nothing in response, only looked at Kat. "Didn't you just say you were running late?"

Likon seized the front of Eric's tunic.

"You stay away from her, Your Highness. Or I'll personally see that you fall to ruin before the spring. Kat won't be tainted by someone like you."

"Gods, Likon, you need to—" Kat didn't get the chance to finish her angry retort.

Eric had Likon's hand peeled off him, but before Likon could deliver the uppercut to his jaw like he was already aiming to do, the prince dodged and instead landed a slap across the side of Likon's head that sent him crashing to the ground.

"Kat, go to Alina," Eric repeated.

"Likon are you alright?" Kat asked after taking a steadying breath without addressing the prince.

Her childhood friend didn't answer. He only glared up at Eric, who stared back, his face disturbingly unfazed.

"Just so you know, nothing I ever do will ever 'taint' Kat," he informed Likon lightly.

"Eric, maybe you should go ahead, I'll just—"

Her husband's gaze found Kat's, and that was when they proceeded to share an entire conversation with a single look.

Eric knew then and there Likon was in love with her, and he could tell that Kat was desperately trying to spare his feelings. But Likon was not calming down, and Eric had not liked the way the younger man had handled her. Not. At. All.

"Likon, I understand you are worried about Kat, but you will respect her wishes. She told you she would explain later," the prince informed his wife's friend, who was rising to his feet again, looking in no way any more receptive to what was being said.

"Well, did you respect *her* wishes? Or did you ambush her in her chamber and take your clothes off?" Likon seethed.

"Again, you are misunderstanding the situation."

Kat was shocked that Eric was staying as controlled as he was, but . . . she should have known it would not last.

"I don't think I've misunderstood anything! You were alone in a room together in a state of undress! You've bloody well gone and ruined her for the sake of relieving yourself wherever you damn well please."

"I am *not* ruined, Likon," Kat snapped furiously. "Look, I need to go. Why can't you—"

"You can say what you like about me, but you need to stop talking about Kat like that." The warning in Eric's voice was chilling.

"You can act like the hero all you want, and maybe you have Kat fooled, but I know what you are," Likon continued while pointing his finger in Eric's face. "No matter what you say, I know what I saw, and I know about your nature."

Eric tilted his head to look around Likon. "Kat, maybe Her Majesty shouldn't be angry at both of us at the same time."

Kat put her hands on her hips and her eyes narrowed.

However, things took a turn for the worse when Likon whirled around and grabbed Kat by the shoulders, making her hands fall from her hips, "Don't worry, I'll marry you, and everything is going to be—"

Eric seized Likon by the throat and hauled him off Kat and slammed him against the opposite wall.

"I've been patient, but that's enough. My *wife* shouldn't have to put up with this." The dangerous, hoarse rumble that came from the prince brought a brief spell of silence.

"Eric!" Kat shouted, then closed her eyes with a grimace.

Likon's eyes were bulging out of his head, but he no longer struggled against the prince's hold.

"Let him go," Kat ordered. While she was frowning, Eric could see the glint of relief in her eyes when he looked at her. He released Likon, and still in a state of shock, he crumpled to the floor.

Kat wasn't happy with what he'd done, but Eric raised an eyebrow, implying *What did you want me to do? I tried being nice.*

Likon gasped on the floor and looked up at Kat, his eyes bright with fear and horror. "K-Kat, it's not true . . . right? Y-You aren't—"

"I wanted to tell you in a better way, but you weren't listening! Look, I still want to talk with you, but I'm going to go now to help Her Majesty. I'll see you later, Likon. Eric? You come with me; I don't trust the two of you alone."

Eric looked around himself with feigned innocence.

As Kat began to stalk down the corridor, the prince cast one last look down at Likon, whose trembling hands were curling into fists on the ground.

"ERIC!" Kat barked.

He sighed and stepped over Likon. "Yes, dear."

"Don't call me that. You sound like you're patronizing me."

"You're already sounding like an old nag. Would you prefer me to call you that?"

The couple's bickering voices disappeared down the corridor, though Kat kept occasionally looking over her shoulder. She was unable to mask her worry.

Eric eyed her, and after a quick glance around them, reached out and gently grasped her hand.

"I didn't want to hurt him like that," Kat murmured quietly as they slowed their walk.

"He wasn't leaving us a lot of options," Eric countered, his tone turning firm. "Kat . . . I didn't like what I saw there."

"He's never been like that before, I swear," she assured quickly.

"Because you've always given in to him?"

"No, I . . . We never actually courted or anything, I just—"

"You didn't court anyone else though, did you?" Eric guessed.

The sound of footsteps coming up the stairs prompted Eric to release Kat's hand. It wasn't ideal that they were being seen together, but . . . then again it was roughly what Alina predicted would start fanning the flames to help Fin come to terms with things.

"I didn't, but that's because I didn't like anyone."

Eric looked at her skeptically but didn't voice his thoughts.

Especially about his true opinion of Likon. He'd seen all manner of men during his time traveling around Daxaria and even Zinfera, and Likon was making Eric's instincts prickle.

The couple were relieved when the footsteps sounded as though they were continuing to climb to the next floor.

"I'm going to Alina's chamber, and you're going straight to the ball, right?" Kat asked while turning to her husband and eyeing him up and down.

He wore his usual black tunic and pants with a white coat trimmed in gold over top. Kat noticed that he had left his cravat untied, making him look, in her opinion, all the more roguishly handsome.

"I suppose I will," Eric replied, though he looked back down the corridor they'd walked with an indiscernible glint in his eyes.

Kat reached out and tugged the front of her husband's coat, drawing his attention back to her.

"I'll see you soon. Please don't do anything else."

Eric wasn't hasty in nodding his assent, and so when Kat did finally leave, she couldn't help but feel her nerves grow more frazzled.

She knew that things with Likon were far from settled, but . . . if she were honest?

Some part of her felt relieved.

It was done.

She no longer had to fret about forcing herself to have feelings for him . . . Though the way her gut responded to his nearness and touch . . . she wondered just what had changed so drastically.

CHAPTER 7

BIT BY BIT

Fin stared at Brendan darkly, his elbows braced against his knees and his hands clasped together in his seat.

The Troivackian king sat across from the house witch, and while he may have appeared at ease with his hands loosely clasped in front of himself, his right bicep would occasionally twitch . . .

"What do we know about the devil?"

Brendan held the duke's ferocious stare when he answered. "From what we've been able to gather, he has ties with the most notable mercenary group here in Troivack. If we didn't know better, we would've assumed he leads it, but the group is actually headed by a man called Leochra Zephin." The king paused, his eyes lowering as his mind sifted through the information. "His Highness remembers the devil saying that he was hired to stop Her Majesty from taking the crown, but he was hesitant to become involved with Lady Katarina, as she was 'a mess of destinies.' Since the abduction, we hadn't heard or seen anything threatening or strange until the attack on Faucher's keep. If I'm honest, my theory is that the devil either retreated to disengage entirely from Lady Katarina, or he decided to carry on attacks at a distance. But there's more . . ."

Fin gradually pushed himself up to sit a little straighter.

"We think there is another witch here in Troivack that can open portals to the Forest of the Afterlife, but whether this person is on the same side of the devil is unclear. We are also suspecting this witch has something to do with the creation of Witch's Brew, as the devil made a few comments to His Highness about such a thing."

Frowning, Fin lowered his gaze thoughtfully. "First the ability to bind magic, and now Witch's Brew . . . The appearance of magical beasts . . . The involvement of mercenaries with ties to the rebellion . . . Do you think they are trying to take over Troivack as a joint effort, or are the devil and this other mysterious witch warring over it?"

Brendan shook his head slowly. "It's unclear. Furthermore, it could be that the rebels have their own agenda. While the devil's mercenaries did temporarily join them, they may have separated from their efforts, as we've noticed their activities have fallen quiet since the devil supposedly retreated. Which is another sign that Leochra Zephin and the devil are tied together somehow. Perhaps Leochra Zephin answers to the devil. That would make the most sense."

"Three warring parties in Troivack?" Fin let out a small breath. "And Kat's caught up in all this."

Brendan held Fin's gaze levelly. "Your Grace, please note that every decision I made pertaining to Lady Katarina was done after consulting her. Save for the exile—but given that it was primarily to keep her safe while learning the sword, she did not mind."

While Fin had been distracted by the mystery surrounding the shadow war that was brewing closer and closer to a boiling point, his expression hardened once more at the mention of his daughter.

"Speaking of my Kat's sword lessons; I thought I made myself clear that she was only to learn enough for an emergency situation, but she spoke with me today while wearing an official uniform."

The impenetrable mask the Troivackian king managed to pull on only made Fin become more suspicious.

"Lord Ashowan, I have come to learn a great deal about both my wife and your daughter since first meeting them, and one thing I have come to observe is that Lady Katarina's limitations cannot be defined by anyone other than herself. As unthinkable as they may be to most of us, I know when Leader Faucher allowed her to start weighing in on what was to be expected of her during her training that she not only made wise and safe choices, but she learned to hone her skills as we've mentioned before and seemed a lot more settled overall."

"Her ending up in a rushed marriage was a wise and safe decision?" Fin asked coldly.

The king took in and released a very long, drawn out breath.

"For now, I'm only discussing her swordsmanship. The matter with the prince is . . ."

"Imagine a daughter of yours marrying someone like Eric."

Brendan felt his voice die in his throat.

A face flashed in his mind . . .

A daughter . . . with Alina's brilliant hazel eyes and his own black hair . . .

Just the notion of what the duke was mentioning made his stomach burn.

"While I agree with you, Your Grace, at the time, we were trying to ensure Lady Katarina had as many options as possible available to her in light of her lapse in judgment."

Fin leaned back in his seat, his unblinking stare more than a little off-putting, but Brendan did his best to hold on to whatever measure of calm he could manage.

"His Highness Eric Reyes agreed that whatever she chooses to do moving forward, he will support fully."

Fin closed his eyes and rubbed the back of his neck. "Your Majesty, you are more worldly than my daughter, so you know that this union of hers . . . She most likely has an unrealistic expectation of it. She won't know the full burden of being with someone like His Highness . . ." The house witch trailed off, pain filling his features. "Regardless of everything, I do care about Eric. I just don't think this is a commitment that they are ready for."

Brendan bobbed his head in agreement. "I don't dispute that. However . . . we've become worldly, Lord Ashowan, because we, too, have made our own choices and errors. Children have to learn on their own eventually."

Fin raised an eyebrow. "I'm excited for the day I get to throw this conversation back in your face."

Brendan grumbled quietly.

He knew those days were not all that far away.

His only mercy was that the duke wasn't a citizen of his kingdom, and so hopefully he wouldn't see him all that often.

"I'll be blunt with you, Your Majesty. I think part of my shock about everything comes from the fact that you put so much stock in both my daughter and Her Majesty. For a Troivackian, you are being rather . . . open-minded. Or is it just that my daughter's choices benefit you?"

Brendan rose to his feet and made his way over to his decanter of moonshine.

"I won't lie to you. A lot of her choices and ambitions have gone along with what I wished, but . . . in my opinion, all parties are benefitting from this."

"I'm inclined to disagree." Fin joined the king in standing. "My daughter is in the middle of a war."

Brendan poured the clear liquid into two cups and handed one to the house witch. "From everything we've learned, Your Grace, the minute she was born she was entangled in this mess. Between her being a witch and your own connection to the Gods and Aidan Helmer, it's a miracle your son hasn't become more ensnared."

Fin blinked, his cup halting its journey to his mouth as he slowly lowered it back to stare at the king, a faint humorless smile lifting the right corner of his mouth.

"Given that you owe me a debt beyond what you could ever repay in this lifetime, I would like to know, what is it about my son that you distrust so much?"

The king had been in the middle of swallowing his first gulp of moonshine and instantly wished he had heard the duke's question *before*, as he desperately fought the urge to clear his throat.

"Your son," Brendan started to say, though his eyes were watering as he tried to remain in control. "Your son has been touched by darkness. I don't know if it's that he himself has dark things he wishes to do, or if he has simply experienced it, but in a way, it reminds me of His Highness Eric Reyes and myself. He has seen or lived something beyond the norm. What fuels my distrust of him? His secrecy surrounding his magic and the fact that he regularly hides his capabilities."

Something Brendan couldn't quite understand passed through Fin's eyes in reaction to his answer, and surprisingly . . . the duke didn't ask any further questions on the matter.

Brendan wagered it was safe to try taking another drink, though he decided while eyeing the house witch, who was at last taking a mouthful from his own cup, to ask his own question.

"Are you still going to threaten war?"

Fin brought his cup down after taking a generous gulp, though he stared at the contents remaining in quiet contemplation.

"I'm undecided. On one hand, I should have been informed of everything going on. However, Kat shares the brunt of responsibility for not telling me things she should've, and when I start to hear more about what Your Majesty is attempting to navigate, I admit . . . I'm more inclined to look at things . . . with a *bit* more understanding."

Setting his cup down, Fin fixed his ethereal blue eyes on the king once again.

"Besides, I really should talk with my wife before starting a war."

The king couldn't help but give a rueful smile at that statement, and afterward, he, too, set his cup down.

"Shall we rejoin the festivities?"

Fin nodded. "You've been away from Alina on this solstice long enough. With all that is going on, I can understand your hesitancy leaving her side."

"If Lady Katarina weren't there, I never would've agreed to a private audience right now," Brendan informed the duke seriously.

Hearing this, Fin looked to the king growing still once more.

"You've really changed your opinion of Kat that much?"

Brendan grimaced while reaching for the door handle of the study.

"I trust her to protect Alina. That isn't the same as trusting her to not start a fight with my courtiers or irritate me into lunacy."

Fin raised an eyebrow, and for the first time since the morning, a grin worked up his face. "I take it Kat has already realized she can refer to you as her brother-in-law?"

Brendan stared at the duke wide-eyed, let out a grumbling breath, then wordlessly turned and exited the room.

Giving a small chuckle, Fin slipped his hands into his pockets and followed the king out of the room.

At least my daughter hasn't completely changed.

Kat sat tensed at Alina's side as they eyed the nobles dancing, feasting, and mingling about the decorated throne room.

The king had gone off to have a private discussion with the house witch, leaving the two women to sit demurely by themselves, though there were guards lining either side of the stairs.

"They've been gone for a while . . . You don't think your da started a fight with Brendan, do you?" Alina murmured quietly so that no one else could hear.

The redhead at her side gnawed on her tongue for a moment before answering.

"No?"

Alina sighed. "Why is it that my husband has to endure so many protective fathers, I wonder?"

Kat winced at the reference to the time Alina's own father had launched a candlestick at Brendan back when Alina and him had been courting, knowing that she was the major cause for the drama of the day.

"You were late coming to my chambers. Care to explain why, now that we have a moment?" Alina looked at her friend out of the corner of her eye.

"Had a bit of an unfortunate situation arise," the redhead answered vaguely as she pointedly avoided a certain person who lingered at the right side of the room.

"Hm," Alina responded while sounding more than a little irritated. "So you knew my brother was . . . troubled . . . and you hid even *that* from me?"

"It wasn't my place to tell."

"Even though you knew everything I went through?" Alina asked, incensed, her head at last turning toward Kat, who flinched but met her stare head-on. "Are you the type of woman who abandons her friend all for a man?"

Her face draining of color, Kat frowned. "No. Your brother . . . He went through a lot, and I didn't want to scare him away again."

Alina gave a hard look at the redhead, then looked away. "It isn't just that though, is it? It's everything . . . I'm tired of feeling like I'm the only one who is open in our friendship."

Kat reared back in alarm, at first defensive, but then . . . she slumped forward.

"You have been patient with me, and I'm sorry I'm an immature mess, but . . . I know I was right not to tell you about Eric. I should've told you about the poisonings, and the stabbing though, I agree."

Alina barely glanced at the redhead again, her displeasure still intact.

Kat sighed. She had a hunch about what could be her olive branch . . . and so she braced herself for the uncomfortable conversation she was about to have.

"Likon has been in love with me for the past five or six years, and he found me and Eric in our chamber right before the ball."

Alina's head snapped back toward her friend, her eyes rounded.

Kat stared flatly back, her mouth already in a grimace. "It. Did. Not. Go. Well."

Alina's lips pressed together in a thin line. "Oh."

"Yeah." Kat stared out over the ballroom grimly.

"Did . . . Did the two of you ever court each other?" Alina questioned delicately, lowering her voice carefully and glancing around them to ensure no one was nearby.

"No. I never was able to return the feelings. I honestly didn't have strong feelings for anyone until . . ."

Kat trailed off. Her cheeks suddenly warmed, and annoyingly enough, she couldn't keep holding Alina's gaze.

"Until the tragic prince swept you away?" Alina's smile was slow and mischievous.

"Don't make me vomit."

"Oh, was he the *dangerous* type that you knew your father wouldn't approve of? And you, with all your rebellious tendencies, *couldn't* resist?"

"Oyy. Bit rich coming from the woman who chose the muscle-head who grunts more than he speaks."

Alina cackled. It was rare that she got the upper hand in teasing Kat.

"You know—"

"They're back."

Katarina had been just about to start issuing even more humorous observations about Alina's choice of husband, when the queen drew her attention to the ballroom doors where Brendan and Fin had just slipped back in.

Seeing that the two men actually appeared more relaxed than they had been going into the meeting, the two women let out sighs of relief. However, they were distracted a second time, when none other than Eric Reyes casually made his way over to them after having discreetly climbed the stairs from the side of the ball near the servant's entrance. Luckily, the guards that did notice could tell it would not be an issue for him to approach.

Kat's index finger began tapping as she gave a slight bow of her head while avoiding looking directly at him, and he in turn bowed to his sister, then her.

"Lady Katarina, would you care to dance?"

Kat's fidgeting stopped and she looked up at Eric, her hesitancy undisguised.

At first the prince didn't understand, but a small flick of Kat's eyes in the direction of Likon exposed her reasoning.

Eric briefly faltered, then understanding filled his face, followed by firmness.

"Lady Katarina, mind if we have a chat?"

Given that the two had yet again held an entire conversation without speaking, and with Kat's back to her no less, Alina watched them, feeling somewhat perplexed.

The redhead nodded nervously and accepted Eric's arm and stood.

As the couple stepped toward the side of the stairs that led down from the thrones, several courtiers noticed the exchange and instantly began whispering to one another.

Slowing their pace while descending the steps, Eric eyed the nobility and decided to use their temporary distance from eager ears to address Kat.

"You never danced at balls because of Likon." His voice was quiet but assured.

Kat blushed and, despite holding on to Eric's arm, felt her fingers briefly curl.

"If you don't want to dance with me, that's fine, but there isn't a chance in hell I'm having you turn me down because of Likon."

The future queen flushed. She felt angry.

"If I don't want to dance with you because it'll hurt someone, that's the same thing."

"Kat, he is a grown man and you have rejected him. It is his responsibility to deal with it. It isn't your duty to cater to his hurt, and furthermore, you are married. It's time for him to let go, and I'm not going to feel guilty for wanting to dance with my wildly attractive wife."

"I—" Kat began to speak out of a mixture of frustration and bashfulness. When they touched the bottom of the stairs, Eric immediately bowed to her, making all the nobles near them watch in interest.

His hazel eyes pierced her golden ones, a coy smile on his face, crinkling his eyes in the way she liked, his former sternness nowhere to be found . . .

"So, Lady Katarina, would you like to dance with me?"

CHAPTER 8

HONORABLE MENTION

Kat stared at Eric, awareness sending tingles throughout her being as everyone stared around them.

"F-Fine." She accepted his hand, making the prince smile more broadly and straighten.

The pair strode toward the brightly lit dance floor, but as they moved, they continued to cause more and more ripples of whispers around them.

"We're really backing my da into a corner," Kat muttered through clenched teeth as she pretended to smile and nod at some of the nobles she passed.

"What's wrong with dancing?" Eric asked flippantly as he, too, acknowledged the other Troivackian nobles to his left.

Kat couldn't think of a logical response, and by then they had reached the dance floor.

Gliding over to their place, Kat took a shuddering breath.

Even though she couldn't see Likon, she knew he was watching her.

"Just keep your eyes on me," Eric called softly to his wife as they walked, his good-natured expression fading.

Kat's golden eyes met with his. "I don't like being cruel."

"You aren't being cruel," the prince argued adamantly. "Seriously, Kat. You aren't doing this to be malicious, and he needs to start learning to take care of himself, like I said before. And you"—they had reached their spot, and Eric turned to her, bringing himself closer to Kat than the starting position required—"need to remember there is nothing wrong with dancing with your husband."

Taking a moment to catch her breath again, Kat watched Eric shift back to give a small bow before the music began. Her eyes narrowed. "We've been married for a day, but you sure seem to like throwing around the words *husband* and *wife* any chance you get."

The pickup note to the dance rang out, prompting Kat to curtsy, then gently grasp Eric's palm. He guided her around himself in a circle, then after clapping twice, his right hand was on her waist and his left in her own hand as they started their slow spin around the floor.

"Is there something wrong with enjoying our new titles?"

"I just don't want you abusing them."

Eric raised an eyebrow, his face intent. "I told you before. I love you more than is reasonable. Are you starting to see that?"

Kat blushed and battled a smile while looking away from him as they spun.

It wasn't until they were halfway through the dance that she could once again look at the prince.

"You must've been a wildly successful womanizer."

Eric chuckled. "Really? We're talking about *my* romantic past right now?"

Sighing irritably, Kat didn't respond as they once again moved in perfect sync with each other through another spin.

"By the way, I forgot to tell you, but Sir Miller got a gift for Pina. He wants to speak with you tonight about giving it to her."

Kat looked at Eric's barely restrained smile curiously.

"I'm relatively certain he knit her a sweater. He has a matching one."

Unable to help herself, Kat burst out laughing, though she didn't miss a single step.

As the couple continued dancing, they gradually began to forget about their spectators, however, that didn't change the fact that things were continuing to unfold around them.

Fin watched motionless as his daughter whirled around the floor, Eric's gaze fixed on her, his face lightened with peace and contentment. He hadn't seen such an expression on the prince in years . . .

Then there was Kat.

She was so obviously . . . happy. And together with Eric she looked . . .

"We have to make the announcement tonight, don't we?" Fin asked Brendan Devark quietly.

The Troivackian king stood at the house witch's side, equally as interested in watching the Daxarian prince and his wife.

"We don't have to, but . . . it'll be hard to stop rumors," Brendan responded while his dark gaze roved over the sea of courtiers, who were all becoming a little too excitable with the prospect of gossip about Eric and Kat.

Anyone who watched the couple could see they loved each other, and there was an intimacy and knowingness about their way around each other that would easily spark a variety of assumptions; some not entirely inaccurate either.

While Fin's hands were still in his pockets, they balled into fists.

"Annika's going to kill me."

Brendan looked to the duke in a rare show of sympathy. "Do I have your permission?"

Fin closed his eyes and let out a breath. "We don't have a choice now, do we?"

The king cleared his throat in response.

Then the duke's gaze slid over to Likon, who was almost hidden from sight as he pressed his shoulder into the crevice of one of the tall windows. Fin could see the agony and outrage in his eyes.

"Go tell Kat and Eric about the announcement, but don't start until I return."

The king looked quizzically at the house witch. "You're leaving again?"

Fin didn't spare the king another glance as he refused to look away from Likon. "I need a few words with our other family member."

Following the duke's line of sight, Brendan noticed Likon as well, and in an instant understood why the young man needed to be spoken to.

"Very well, but try to be quick."

Nodding, Fin casually made his way over to the boy he had adopted fifteen years ago . . . When he reached him, despite standing a mere two feet away, Likon still hadn't registered his presence.

"Care to go for a stroll?" the house witch invited, keeping his voice low.

Likon barely looked at him but pushed off from where he leaned and stalked toward the ballroom doors.

Fin followed behind, bracing himself for the conversation that was about to come.

Once the two men had made it out of the ballroom, Fin noticed that Likon wasn't slowing down or stopping, making him have to jog to catch up.

Fortunately by the time he did so, no one else was around the cold, dimly lit corridor.

"Likon, I might look young, but give this old man a break, will you?" Fin requested more to lighten the mood.

While Likon didn't respond, he did reduce the speed of his step.

"You knew?" he asked quietly.

"I found out earlier this afternoon," Fin answered ambiguously.

"Do you approve?"

"Not particularly."

"Then end it." Likon faced the duke, fury and pain still rife in his voice.

"It's already done, Likon. And it's what she wants." Fin's voice was soft and apologetic.

Likon made an aggravated grunt and turned away.

"He's going to hurt her," Likon snapped angrily with his back still to Fin.

"He might, but it's still her choice."

Likon swung back around to look at the duke squarely, and Fin found himself become somewhat taken aback . . . There was an air about his wife's protégé that put him on edge.

"Fin, how can you be so calm?"

"I wasn't calm when I found out, and I'm still not entirely at ease, but I can't force Kat to do anything. She is in charge of her own actions, just like I'm in charge of my own." Fin reached out and placed a hand on Likon's shoulder. "I'm sorry. I know how you've felt about her for a while."

The younger man's eyes momentarily rounded, but after overcoming the surprise of Fin's observation, he shook off his hand.

"This isn't about me, it's about Kat making a horrible mistake."

Fin stepped forward warily. "Right now, it *is* about you, Likon. As much as this is going to take time to get used to, there isn't anything we can do but try to accept it right now and go from there. Maybe take a few days to tour around Vessa, hm? Just get a bit of space to cool your head."

Likon didn't say anything else, a disgruntled breath instead escaping his mouth as he proceeded to storm off down the hall, putting as much distance between himself and the ballroom as possible.

Finding himself alone in the hallway, Fin worried about the young man he had come to think of and love like another son. He stared after Likon, his heart aching for the poor little boy that had only ever wanted to be by Kat's side . . .

Fin dropped his chin to his chest wearily.

Deciding that there wasn't anything else he could do in that moment, the house witch slowly made his way back to the ballroom. He knew his night was only going to get more difficult . . . There was already a large number of older Troivackian nobles who were glaring daggers at him for looking so much like Aidan Helmer . . .

Once back in the bright splendor of the party, Fin's eyes sought the king. He found Brendan Devark sitting in his throne beside his wife, and when the two locked gazes, the duke gave a firm nod.

Brendan looked to Alina, who gave a subtle smile, then he regarded Kat and Eric, who had placed themselves near the stairs of the throne with Lady Kezia nearby.

They were aware there was a chance that things could become a mite chaotic . . .

Standing from his seat, the king raised his hand, silencing the musicians and instantly drawing everyone's eyes forward.

"My people, on this blessed solstice evening, I bid you glad tidings. May our hearths be warm and our homes safe."

The nobility around him raised their cups and toasted with loud *hos* echoing around the room.

"It is with great honor that I deliver two pieces of joyous news."

Everyone fell silent, eagerly awaiting the king's announcement.

"By the early summer, the Devark family line is expected to continue!" Brendan's hand became a fist he thrust into the air, his voice booming triumphantly, making the nobility shout, stomp their feet, and cheer.

Alina bowed her head regally to the loud calls of "Gratitude to our queen!"

Brendan allowed the excitement to continue swarming the room for a while, basking in his vassals' exuberance for his future child.

However, once it had started to calm back down, he again gestured that he intended to speak.

Uncertain what could possibly compare to the exciting news of a future prince or princess, it was harder to settle his people's celebration down, but when they eventually did, Brendan lowered his hand.

"It also just so happens that I have the honor of officially announcing on behalf of His Highness Prince Eric Reyes, that he has in fact wedded."

It felt as though everyone in the room ceased to breathe.

No one could even look at Eric, as they were too stunned by the news to react.

"His Highness and . . ." Brendan had to take a quick breath in order to force his voice not to falter. "Lady Katarina Ashowan, daughter of His Grace Duke Finlay Ashowan, Viscount of House Jenoure, exchanged their vows earlier and are henceforth husband and wife. I ask that you all bow and show your well-wishes to the future king and queen of Daxaria."

The silence remained, and the only development was the unnerving number of eyes that swiveled to Eric and Kat.

The couple were trying their best to remain stoic, but Kat could feel her face start to become twitchy.

Luckily, Lady Kezia and Lady Wynonna stepped forward and curtsied before them.

"Long live the future king and queen of Daxaria. Congratulations," Lady Kezia called out loudly enough for everyone to hear.

When the two women rose and returned to their original places, the room at last exploded with another round of *hos* and apprehensive applause.

Though the din was quickly concluded, and in its place, a flood of conversations and exclamations filled the room.

Eric looked at Kat and offered her his arm.

The redhead noticed he had a faint tremor, but when she laid her hand on his sleeve, she found that she was also trembling.

The couple didn't get another moment of peace for the rest of the night to reassure each other, however, as they were descended upon by every noble wanting to ask a thousand questions.

From his place on the opposite side of the room, Fin stood with his arms folded and his mood an enigma.

Well, Kat . . . I guess we'll find out if you are ready to handle what you signed up for. Though this might pale compared to your mother's reaction when we tell her.

Eyeing the nobility and their reactions, it was then Fin noticed the man who had trained Katarina standing nearby with his sons; Leader Gregory Faucher. The four men were watching the crowd grow around Katarina, their postures tense.

The house witch studied the family thoughtfully.

At least it seems you've made some friends to help you, Kitty Kat. Maybe I'll try and get to know them a bit better.

Fin allowed a subtle smile on his face as he decided to lend a hand in dispersing the crowd from his daughter, and so he moved forward, sending several people scampering away from him. Even though he was only successful in breaking through the crowd because some of the nobles openly feared him, Fin didn't find himself feeling too bothered.

He had a lunch menu in mind for the following day that he was rather confident could persuade just about every soul present that the house witch was absolutely nothing like his vile father who had once brought a shadow to their shores.

CHAPTER 9

COMMUNICATION CAVEATS

The morning following the Winter Solstice, Kat awoke feeling unbearably warm . . .

She shifted in the sheets, wondering why in the world she was sweating when she wasn't wearing anyth—

Her eyes flew open, and she looked beside herself to see Eric fast asleep on his side.

She blinked.

Then she stared at his slackened features with a giddy smile that she then turned toward her hand clutching the sheet.

His face had a bit of scruff, and the faint lines around his eyes looked lighter than normal.

Kat gripped the sheet in her hand a little more tightly before she rolled onto her back and stared at the ceiling.

She was married.

And she was going to sleep beside Eric just about every night of their lives.

Kat let out a slow breath.

It was something she should have had time to process the first day she'd woken up after their wedding, but because of the arrival of her father and the fact it was a secret wedding, she hadn't been able to.

So in that moment, she relished the quiet peacefulness.

Awake, but not alone, and no maids would come unless she or Eric called.

A tension she hadn't noticed existed in her chest before eased, and with its disappearance, Kat found herself feeling tempted to fall back asleep . . .

And so she did.

She closed her eyes and slipped back into a dreamless slumber that she had never been able to achieve without exhausting her magic extensively.

In that moment, she didn't even care why that might be.

Fin stared at the food-ladened table in deep thought. He had to time everything just right, and it was quite a bit trickier when he didn't have his magic at his disposal.

"A-Are the ingredients not to your li—"

"Shh!" The Royal Troivackian Cook shushed one of the kitchen maids. "Let the man think."

Fin cast a kind smile at the maid who had tensed at the cook's outburst, making her relax once more and give a surprisingly shy smile of her own.

"Alright . . . I want you and you peeling the vegetables; Cook, please start simmering the broth; and I want you to add grated turmeric root. You and you, when those vegetables are peeled, I want the carrots chopped in quarters and the potatoes in cubes. We're going to start with a spiced vegetarian soup today, then serve the roasted chickens paired with green salad with an oil jam dressing. After that—"

The kitchen doors burst open, and in strolled Katarina, grinning ear to ear with her familiar, Pina Colada, on her shoulder.

"Good morning, everyone!"

The staff all jumped, then began bowing and offering their morning greetings to the future queen of Daxaria, who was dressed in her uniform from Faucher.

Fin raised an eyebrow. "Kat, you're interrupting our work."

While the house witch's ire had lessened compared to the previous day, it wasn't entirely dissolved. While he still needed time and space his daughter had never been the patient type.

Kat held up her hands apologetically. She couldn't fully quench her good mood despite sensing her father's reticence. "I've got some things to do today myself, but I was wondering if we could set up a time for Kraken and Pina to meet. I really want to know what she's saying!"

Fin eyed the sleeping kitten on Kat's shoulder and, with a short sigh, was forced to silently admit that he, too, would like to know the very same thing.

"Alright. He's in my chamber. Christos, I'm sorry for running off again, but I will be back by the time the broth is ready."

The Troivackian inclined himself to the duke, as did the rest of the serving staff, and then without further ado, Fin made his way over to his daughter's side.

Once they had left the kitchen, Fin briefly noticed that the guards outside the door were whispering amongst themselves and gesturing with their heads toward Pina . . .

"Your familiar has certainly made an impression," Fin observed casually as they walked.

Kat smiled as Pina pressed her nose to her witch's cheek and purred. "She's a sweet girl. Who can resist that?"

Fin tilted his head thoughtfully as they walked. "What duties do you have today?" he asked while glancing at his daughter's attire.

"Ah, I have to witness a duel between a classmate of mine and his brother, and I'll also be starting to recruit the women who wish to learn how to defend themselves."

The duke's lips twitched. "Someone mentioned you had something to do with that new subject being offered to the finer gender."

Kat smiled and pointedly avoided meeting her father's gaze. "A little bit."

"And then I also heard how someone tried to drug you during a certain sparring match."

Kat's smile vanished in an instant as she looked at her father wide-eyed and her heart skipped a beat. "I-I swear I didn't mean to leave that out, I just—"

"You forgot. Because it seems like something is *always* happening around you, or someone is attacking you." Fin's voice was hard, his expression stoic, but he kept his gaze ahead and didn't look at his daughter.

Kat wasn't sure there was anything she could really say to that, and so she opted to make the rest of the journey to her father's chamber in silence.

When they at long last had reached their destination, Fin pressed open the door, revealing a large room with a four-poster bed with a thick navy coverlet, chairs with matching cushions in front of the hearth, a table and chairs for dining, and plush carpets . . .

"I suppose being a duke has its perks," Kat observed while also looking around for any sign of her father's familiar.

"They give bigger rooms to house all the paperwork. I'll be making you help me while you train to be queen."

Kat turned to her father, her jaw dropped wordlessly in betrayal and dread.

Fin remained unmoved as he strode over to one of the chairs and put his hand on its back.

A fluffy tail dangled from its seat and swished.

"Kraken? Kat brought her familiar for you to meet and talk with."

Reaching up excitedly, her previous trepidation instantly forgotten, Kat gave a gentle squeeze to Pina's soft paw; she purred a little louder in return.

With a chirp, Kraken leapt from the chair, stared up at Fin, and meowed.

"I'll try to make sure it isn't a regular thing during your naps in the future." Fin sighed wearily while staring down at his familiar.

Kraken gave two shorter mews, then sauntered over to Kat and brushed against her legs.

Grinning, Kat crouched down. "Kraken, this here is Pina!"

The familiar stared at the kitten on her shoulder.

He went completely still.

Then, Kraken carefully leaned forward, his nose twitching.

Pina's eyes blinked open, and she proceeded to leap down from Kat's shoulder.

Kraken hissed in surprise and backed up, while Pina, on the other hand, went on her hind legs and straightened herself curiously.

"Awe! That's adorable! I've never seen her do that!" Kat whispered to her father.

However, Fin was watching the exchange, looking utterly baffled.

Kraken continued staring at the kitten, barely moving a muscle, when Pina dropped back down on all fours and gave a small mew.

"Well?" the house witch wondered interestedly.

"*I don't like her, witch.*"

Fin blinked and frowned. "Why not?"

"*I have no idea what she's saying.*"

"What . . . ?"

"What's she saying?" Kat queried, unable to contain her curiosity for a moment longer.

Fin held up his hand, prompting her to wait.

Pina gave another mew and Kraken growled before stalking closer to Fin.

"*She's speaking another language,*" the familiar explained briefly, though his hairs were still standing on end.

"Why are you hissing at her because of that?" Fin asked, confused.

"*She's not afraid of me.*"

"Well, she's a familiar, she probably isn't like other cats."

"*James Paws used to be a familiar too, but even he grew to respect me.*"

"Wait . . . the cat you said trained you? Who was his witch?"

"Da!" Kat interrupted the discussion her father and Kraken were having with a laugh. "What's happening?"

Fin grimaced as he tried to think of a way to answer, while at the same time trying to come up with a possible reason Kraken couldn't understand Pina . . .

"Kraken says she isn't using a language we know."

Kat looked down at her own familiar, equally surprised. "Is it because she's just a baby?"

Fin shook his head. "I understood Kraken perfectly fine when he was younger than her."

Kraken hissed again, and the two looked to see Pina inching forward while in a crouch.

"Careful, baby girl, he's the emperor in Daxaria."

"*I am the empurror of this entire world! I have met cats from all corners of the kingdoms—even Lobahl! But this kitten . . . I think she mocks me!*" Kraken hissed again and trotted back over to the chair he had been napping in upon their arrival.

"Kraken, there has to be an explanation," Fin tried to say to his familiar's fluffy haunches.

The emperor did not respond.

The duke sighed. "Sorry, Kat. I don't think things are going well between them."

Kat twisted her mouth in disappointment.

"I see . . . Come on, Pina. Let's leave him be for now. Maybe we'll try again later."

Scooping the kitten back into her arms, Pina gave a small heartbreaking whimper.

Hearing this, Kat looked at her father, her eyes wide and her mouth turned down into a pout.

Sighing, Fin looked toward the chair.

"*I don't care what you say! I'm done talking to that disrespectful creature!*"

Fin looked back at his daughter and gave a half shrug while shaking his head and rubbing the back of his neck.

Nodding in understanding, Kat made her way out of the chamber with her father following behind.

"I'm going to go back to the kitchen. I'll see you at the luncheon hour."

"Would you like to see me train?" Kat blurted out suddenly.

While it wasn't normally in her nature, she felt quite shy about how much she wished to show her father what she could do . . .

"Maybe later today."

Kat felt the last bit of her good mood drop her off into weary dejection, and it was written all over her face.

"Kat, look . . . I do still need time, alright? If you need me for something in an emergency—"

"You used to tell me that parents are always needed. Da, I . . . I'm really proud of what I've done here, and I couldn't have done it without Eric. Despite all the other stuff, when it comes to my swordsmanship, I really hope you . . . you can be proud of it too."

Without the fortitude to take any more disappointment for the day, Kat took her leave and didn't look back at her father, who stood in the corridor with a lump in his throat.

Fin idly wiped at his nose as he listened to his daughter's footsteps grow farther and farther away.

I want to be over it, Kat. I really sincerely do . . . Unable to finish the thought, Fin slipped his hands in his pockets and started back toward the kitchen. He hoped to distract himself with lunch preparations, and perhaps after completing a familiar task, he'd be able to let go of some of his pain.

Kat was merciless on her training dummy.

Her sword swiped up, down, across, then in reverse order. She switched her footwork, she moved faster, and faster, and—

A firm hand gripped her wrist.

Kat looked over to see Faucher.

"You're scaring the knights," he informed her dryly.

Kat only then noticed her aura flickering out, red streaks tearing through the normal orange-gold glow.

"Sorry," she mumbled with a small huff.

Faucher eyed her.

He didn't want to have to have a personal conversation with her, but . . . the stress in her eyes . . . and the way the duke had pointedly avoided looking at his daughter numerous times over breakfast struck an unexpected chord in Faucher as he found his thoughts turning to his own daughter.

He let out a sigh mixed with a grunt.

"Walk with me."

"Yes, sir." Kat sheathed her sword and, while passing the knights who were openly gaping at her, did her best to settle her aura.

When the two had made it out of the courtyard and began rounding the castle that would lead toward the gardens outside the terrace off the throne room, Faucher spoke again.

"Your father is . . . angry," he started slowly.

"Yes. Furious."

Faucher looked at his student and saw the guilt on her face. "Do you remember what I said back when we first returned to the castle? Firm up your allies."

"I'm trying!" Kat exploded, rounding on her teacher, her voice hoarse. "I've apologized! I've tried to explain. It just . . . He's mad about things that have happened, and I can't do anything about what is already done!"

The Troivackian regarded her without any outward reaction. "You are entitled to your decisions, just as much as you are entitled to the consequences."

"Faucher, I know! I'm not saying I don't deserve the repercussions . . . He has a reason to be upset! I get it!"

"Do you?"

Anger choked the words in Kat's throat, which was fine because it gave Faucher time to continue.

"Imagine the person you love more than anything does not feel safe or trusting enough to tell you the important pieces of their life. You shut people out of those moments, and they start getting the impression they are worth very little to you."

"He knows I love him! You're just repeating what he has already said. Why does everyone expect me to be an open book?! I don't think less of him, or think he is a bad father, I just—"

"Ashowan. I, of all people, understand not wanting to . . . Share your feelings, but"—he paused, his expression pained as he was forced to hold what to him was a lengthy conversation—"I knew about your wedding before your own father. I knew about your poisoning and being stabbed, and he didn't even receive a letter. What if your own child did that? Or if your husband or Her Majesty the queen had? It shows what type of relationship you wish to have with them, and it makes sense for a father to react as the duke has."

Kat couldn't say anything in response.

"You can live your life how you want, but that is why your father is behaving the way he is. Maybe you can't do anything, but at the very least, do your best to understand before deciding if that is the case."

Kat was battling her tears with everything she had.

Clearing his throat awkwardly, Faucher reached out and patted her shoulder.

"Your . . . Your feet were too far apart during your last set because you were overextending your backhand attacks."

Kat gave a burbled laugh before sniffling and placing her hands on her hips as she looked around. "Right . . . Right. Well . . . shall we go back and see if I can fix that?"

Her teacher nodded then gestured her forward.

"Thank you, Faucher."

He grunted, and that was it.

Kat could feel a small broken piece of herself tremble in fear as she realized what she should do . . . but . . . despite how terrifying it was, she was starting to see that she did *need* to do it.

Especially since her father of all people deserved any and every effort from her so that he knew just how much he meant to her.

CHAPTER 10

A SUFFERING OF THE SOUL

E ric stepped from the shop in Vessa and gave a cursory look around at the people drifting past; all of them were huddled against the biting cold. The occasional sunbeam pierced through the light gray clouds drifting along the sky, but the sparse break from the overcast weather was not enough to brighten the overall atmosphere of the outside.

Nodding to Sir Vohn, Eric then addressed the hunched over shopkeeper who had come out from the store behind him, bowing reverently.

"I thank you for your patronage, Your Highness. Glad tidings to you and your future queen."

Eric bobbed his head, making sure to remain as stoic as possible so the man wasn't made to feel uncomfortable by an errant smile.

Behind him in the front window of his shop, gold and jade glimmered amongst swells of black silk, twinkling at the crowds that drifted past prettily.

The prince then made his way back onto the street, his black cloak shifting a little to reveal the sword at his side, consequently inspiring a man carrying a hefty bag of flour to cross to the other side of the road. Both Sir Vohn and three other armed guards from the castle fell into step beside the prince as they walked.

"I have to admit, while I know I'm one of many who can't say they're surprised Lady Katarina had a whirlwind marriage, I *am* surprised you'd put yourself at the mercy of Finlay Ashowan," Sir Vohn observed quietly to his friend with a chuckle.

Eric cast the knight a warning look and continued walking.

"I wasn't speaking ill of her," Sir Vohn added cautiously.

The prince still didn't say anything.

The cold was already seeping through the fine seams of their leather boots, chilling their toes, and so the idea of hurrying back to the carriage to partake in a warm fire and heated cup of moonshine soon overcame all other thoughts.

Upon reaching the inconspicuous black carriage, Eric proceeded to climb in and close the door behind himself.

He eyed Vessa with its colorful roofs and black window frames, hinges, and doors idly.

That is until Eric felt an odd fluttering in his chest.

He ignored it.

Then it grew, and an icy twist in his gut made him look around the city scenery more scrupulously . . . He opened his mouth to shout to Sir Vohn to tell him to keep a lookout, only for the color in the world to suddenly fade and a creeping dread to spread through him . . .

He'd felt it before.

Slowly, with horrific foreboding and fear filling him, Eric turned and found the devil seated across from him in the carriage. Seemingly appearing out of thin air.

The man sat with his arms folded, wearing a fine black wool coat and his hair unbound and brushed to a silky sheen. His dark eyes fixed unnervingly on Eric.

"I hear congratulations are in order, Your Highness."

Eric's hand flew to his sword despite feeling every inch of him starting to tremble.

The devil sighed at the movement, completely nonplussed as he glanced out the window, his expression bored.

"Don't bother. I'm here to talk. It seems we now have a common enemy."

"What the hell do you want?" Eric demanded angrily, his pulse quivering in his throat.

The devil eyed the prince as the carriage began to move, no one outside seemed to notice the devil's presence . . .

After his intent appraisal of Eric, Sam settled back in his seat. "You're improving. For now, anyway. That new wife of yours is more of a boon to you than you'll ever know. Poor girl." He scoffed.

"Don't talk about my wife," Eric threatened hoarsely.

The devil gave a soft laugh. "Yes, yes. Now, aren't you curious about who this common enemy is? After all, unlike myself, they are interested in doing whatever it takes to get Katarina Ashowan out of Troivack. Even if it involves harming her."

"I'm guessing something to do with the witch behind Witch's Brew?"

Sam's eyebrows rose and he smiled. "Very good. I'm glad you all were able to work out that much. Though you got a small detail wrong . . . " he added more to himself.

"What about that woman?" Eric asked, the prickling fear in his mind ebbing away.

The devil looked around pensively. "She's closer to you all than you realize. She wants Lady Katarina sent back to Daxaria, but if she gets desperate, she could take it further, like I said."

Confused, Eric inched forward on his seat. "Why does she not want Kat here?"

"Hard to say. I myself am uncertain of her exact plans. I didn't even know she was bringing over creatures from the Forest of the Afterlife. It's risky, given they are loyal to me."

Eric tilted his head. "Why would the beasts be loyal to you if you are the one who killed the first witch?"

Sam laughed. "Because I think this world should once again be theirs. Witches and humans . . . they are not worthy of all this world has to offer. There are exceptions here and there, but those few people don't outweigh the amount of betrayal, greed, and undue pride in the rest. Back when the world was filled only with those beasts, humans were the weaker, new additions. Almost like their pets . . . But as time went on, it became clear that humans carried the capability of what they deem to be 'higher knowledge,' but with it came deeper depravity. The beasts are neither good nor bad; they are simply as nature intends. A greater wisdom lies within them. I didn't know how undeserving humankind was until my parents took the earth from our beasts and sent my sister and me here."

"So you have nothing to do with the sightings of the beasts here in Troivack the past few years?"

The devil didn't give an immediate answer. Instead he said, "I had nothing to do with the attack on Lady Katarina. That came because of that woman who wished to hide her presence from me. Which means Lady Katarina is *very* close with her."

Eric swallowed. "The witch is in the castle."

The devil raised an eyebrow and gave a mystifying smile. "I never said she was a witch."

The prince's alarm made his eyes widen.

"Now, I didn't come here to make things easy on you. If I meddle too much with the fates, my own existence becomes one headache after another until my death and rebirth, and it would be most inconvenient at this time."

"What do you want?" Eric asked darkly.

The devil took his time leaning back in his seat, eyeing the outside.

"I want you to tell me everything you learn as the king investigates. Only then can I have a hope of figuring out her plan."

"I don't suppose you could just tell us the identity of this woman?" Eric added dryly.

The devil's face grew serious. "I wouldn't need you annoying beings if I knew who she was. I only know she is a woman that needs to be kept in line, and she has grand plans that I cannot pinpoint as of yet."

It was the prince's turn to take his time responding.

"You know . . . I have to wonder . . ."

"Do you?" the devil drawled.

"You are a being that is condemned to live eternity on this earth, tormenting and tempting people into darkness and destruction. Do you just live from whim to whim, or do you yourself have a more grand objective?"

His brown eyes growing distant, Sam's mouth curved slightly. "Yes. And no."

"Is it that you wish to return to the Forest of the Afterlife? Or to destroy everyone wicked here in the world?" Eric theorized, his tone casual.

Sam's gaze flit to him, almost making the prince flinch. "While I do enjoy my whims and my games, I suppose in reality I'm waiting like many people do. Waiting to see what plan the Gods have in store for me."

Eric couldn't hide his surprise at being answered so honestly.

Then again, the devil was trying to convince him to be an informant . . .

"I'll agree to provide information if you tell me more about this woman and promise not to hurt anyone I care about or who is innocent—"

"You'll do it because this woman is a threat to your beloved wife." The devil cut off Eric, his expression lazy. "The most I can tell you about this enemy? She might be disappearing periodically for hours or afternoons at a time here and there. That is really all I know."

"How did she get her hands on Witch's Brew and connect portals to another world if she herself isn't a witch?" An edge entered the prince's voice when he realized the carriage was nearing the castle.

Sam's hand rested on the door handle. "She has connections."

"Alright, she doesn't want witches in Troivack, and she is trying to lure you out into the open. Why?"

The devil laughed, but . . . Was Eric imagining it? Or did the devil suddenly look tired?

"I don't know why she doesn't want witches here, but as for me . . . you don't worry about that. It's between her and me."

Eric frowned and opened his mouth to question how the devil could have such an intimate feud with a woman he had never met before, when the overwhelming cold and fear overcame him once more.

Sam exited the carriage that had pulled to a sudden stop as the driver seemed to be talking to a cart driver that was conveniently stuck in the road.

The devil abruptly turned back around, only his face and shoulders visible in the carriage window. "I'll give you one final gift as an incentive. I'll have it sent later this evening; it isn't any use to me anymore. Good day, Your Highness."

It took what felt like ages for the world to turn right again.

Even after the carriage resumed its journey to the castle.

In the interim, Eric focused on taking calming breaths . . .

He had learned a lot from his exchange with the devil, but he was too shaken up to get a sense of what he should do about it all.

Closing his eyes, he at last let out an aggravated grunt.

"When this is all over, I'm taking Kat on a three-month honeymoon, and no one except servants are allowed anywhere near us."

Eric stared at the kitchen door wearily.

He knew exactly where his father-in-law was likely to be working through his emotions.

However, the presence of the two guards added an extra deterrent to him going in and facing his former friend.

The guards glanced back and forth to each other periodically, wondering why the prince hadn't attempted to enter the kitchen . . .

Eric pretended to ignore this as he leaned his shoulder against the wall.

Then the door opened of its own accord, and out stepped the Royal Troivackian Cook looking incredibly pleased.

"Ah! Your Highness! I was just about to go retrieve a bottle of white wine for His Grace to finish preparing the sauce for the next meal. Did you wish to speak with him?" Christos bowed.

Knowing that Fin could most likely hear everything being discussed, Eric gave a resigned nod.

"Go right ahead." The cook then addressed the guards. "I have my most trusted aide in there, keeping an eye on things," the man added confidently.

The men-at-arms jerked their chins down in understanding, and Christos scurried past them toward the cellars.

When Eric stepped over to the Troivackian men, however, they each held up a hand.

"We have to inspect your pockets to be safe, Your Highness."

Raising an eyebrow, Eric proceeded to raise his arms without a word and allowed the guards to perform their inspection of his person without comment.

When that was all complete, he was permitted entry into the kitchen.

The sight before Eric took him back instantly to a time long before . . .

A time when a new redheaded cook stood behind a table and had greeted him warmly. The kind stranger had cut up fruit for him and listened to him talk about his training with a sword, and who had a kitten he could play with . . .

Fin was in the middle of whisking together the sauce that the Royal Cook had mentioned, while the aides were working quietly nearby, leaving the duke standing alone behind the cooking table just like when he had been the Royal Cook in Daxaria.

The room was already brimming with mouth-watering scents that could even make a full man's belly rumble.

The house witch didn't look up from his task as Eric approached.

"Hey, Fin."

The duke glanced at him briefly and continued whisking.

"Are we going to talk about this?" The prince kept his voice low.

At first, it didn't seem like the house witch was going to break his wall of silence, but just as Eric dropped his chin to his chest and started to turn back toward the door, he spoke.

"Eric, I loved you like a son or a brother, and I want you to live a good life, but you are not whole right now, and I know you are aware of that. So I can't understand why the hell you would drag my daughter into it." Fin slammed the bowl down on the table, the bang making the aides as well as the sauce jump.

The prince slipped his hand into his pocket.

"You were . . . are . . . You mean a lot to me too. Regardless of the past. Fin, I tried. I did. I did everything I could to stay away from her. She'd either find me, or some twist of fate would bring us crashing back into each other, and—"

"There is more than one way to keep your distance from someone," the duke interrupted firmly.

"You of all people should understand that it isn't always so simple," Eric threw back defensively.

Fin opened his mouth to make another argument, but the prince plundered on.

"Look, I know what I'm not. Better than anyone, I know what I'm lacking. But if I had to make the choice between being with Kat while I still figure out what my life is going to look like, and losing her? I have no regrets. I am sorry for the way it was handled, and if we knew you were going to arrive the very next day, of course we would've waited for your presence before any final decision would have been made. There just hadn't been any update on where you were for nearly a month."

Fin pressed his fists into the tabletop and stared levelly at Eric.

"Done is done. You two are married," the duke returned tersely before turning to the trays of warm dinner rolls and starting to cut small wedges in them before putting them back down on a platter.

"So you've given up on me completely? Written me off all over again?" The prince's throat tightened as old wounds rose back to the surface.

"I can't support what I know is a bad decision. I won't try to undo it, because it is not my place, but I won't pretend to be happy about it either."

"You know what else wasn't your place? Telling a room full of people about my issue. I kept quiet about all your family's under-the-table dealings ever since learning of them. I didn't even blame you for leaving me in that ruddy town all those years ago when I told you I needed you." Eric felt his eyes grow warm.

Fin chucked a bun down and rounded on the prince once more.

"I may be a witch, Eric, but I'm still Godsdamn human! I had a wife and two kids at home that needed me! I had offices to run, schools to inspect, *your father* to help! I'm sorry I had to leave you, I am, but it was the right decision! I can't . . ." Fin trailed off, his hands clenching into fists before meeting the prince's eyes. "I'm not a hero. I'm not the . . . the impervious person you always thought I was. I'm just trying to do the best I can like everyone else."

"You're asking for grace, but you won't give me an inch. You've judged me, abandoned me, and now when I'm starting to maybe turn things around, you drag me through the mud again for being human myself. Fin, I . . . I already said I'm not arrogant enough to know I won't have problems again. But I was hoping that maybe with the help of friends and family, I might have a shot of making an actual life for myself again. I guess I should've just died in a gutter and not bothered coming back, according to you, because"—Eric dropped his voice, an angry tear falling—"I guess an addict is all I'll ever be in your mind."

Turning away from the duke, Eric pinched the corners of his eyes and stopped any more tears from escaping. He stalked out of the kitchen without bothering to look back, passing Christos coming back from his trip to the cellar and leaving Fin alone with all their hurt and history laid out before him.

CHAPTER 11

A RESTFUL RECONVENING

When Eric opened his chamber door, he was greeted with the sight of his wife curled on her side, hugging a pillow, her golden eyes staring blindly at the wall across from her.

Neither of them had felt like eating the lunch her father had prepared, it seemed.

"I take it your day isn't going well either?" Eric asked while closing the door behind himself.

"Mm," Kat responded without taking her eyes off the wall.

Eric sighed and took off his boots, then crawled into the bed beside her, though he didn't make any move to touch her and instead lay on his back, looking at the ceiling.

"I tried to make peace with your father. It went badly."

"He told me he still needs time. Oh, and Kraken doesn't know what language Pina is speaking and thinks she's making one up to insult him."

Surprisingly, Eric felt himself smile over that last part. "The emperor *is* a bit prideful."

Kat let a breath out her nose.

"I heard you're going to be teaching some of the noblewomen self-defense soon," Eric prompted idly.

"Yeah . . . if anyone shows up, that is. By the way, weren't there any noblewomen who were upset about the announcement of our marriage? You were courting a lot of them."

Eric gave a small chuckle. "I thought there might be a bit of backlash from it, but most of them apparently had a good idea I wasn't being all that serious with them."

"Why were you courting so much anyway?" Kat rolled over onto her side to face Eric.

"I was getting information on their fathers."

Kat blinked in surprise and tried not to show her immediate feelings of relief and gladness.

"Oh."

Eric turned his head and raised an eyebrow. "You married me thinking I'd been sleeping with all of them?"

"Well, not sleeping with all of them! But . . . you know . . . other things," Kat blustered.

"What other things?"

"Things!" Kat snapped before turning back over to her other side to avoid staring at Eric's teasing smile.

He only briefly wondered how it was he could smile again so easily with her after such a wretched day . . .

He reached out and tickled her, making her shriek.

"You chose to marry me regardless of thinking I'd been sampling all the Troivackian women?! Gods, you must love me."

Kat couldn't answer as she jerked and twisted while laughing heartily as her husband continued to tickle her.

They proceeded to tease and wrestle each other in good fun, until at last, both with aching sides and lightened spirits, gave up and lay intertwined on the bed.

"You know, I think I have a new strategy on how to get my father to ease up," Kat announced while shifting to look at Eric as his thumb gently stroked the back of her hand that was resting on his chest.

The prince grimaced. "I'm sure it's a good one, but . . . I'll be honest, Kat . . . I don't think I have it in me to face Fin again. At least for today."

Kat's mouth twisted. She wanted to argue with him on the matter, but there was a quiet hurt in Eric's eyes that made her think that perhaps the exchange he'd had with her father was even worse than he was letting on.

With a sigh that turned into a yawn, Kat settled into Eric's side.

She suddenly felt quite tired.

"You used to barely sleep, now you look like you're ready for a nap," he chuckled softly beside her, making her hair flutter.

"Mm . . . I blame you. I think it's because my magic feeds off your old, tired arse."

Eric turned to look down at Kat's head. "Truly?"

Kat peered up at him, and when she realized that he was, in fact, alarmed, she pushed herself up to a seated position.

"I mean . . . possibly? You want to have a nap with me. Wouldn't it be logical that my magic senses that and feeds off it?"

Eric sat up, his eyes widening. "Kat, how much does your magic feed off others? To what degree do you absorb that?"

The redhead chewed on her lip thoughtfully, carefully considering the question. "We don't know. Mr. Kraft is worried about that as well. Especially if my magic keeps absorbing magical attacks. Look, I was mostly jesting about the napping bit."

Eric didn't look fully convinced.

"Mind telling me what has you so worried about my magic all of a sudden?" she asked with a raised eyebrow. She simultaneously shifted herself a little farther away from her husband on the bed.

"I know your magic feeds off intention, or magic power directed at you, but . . . I'm worried about what will happen if you keep feeding off my own feelings. What if it hurts you?"

Kat frowned. "Why are you suddenly even thinking about this?"

Eric faltered, but after a moment of studying his wife's face, his shoulders sagged forward.

"Alright. The devil visited me again."

Kat was on her feet in an instant, but Eric held up his hands to stop her from starting what was sure to be an elaborate tirade. "He didn't attack me. He just shared some information."

"Why in the world would you not tell me that sooner?! What information?! Why would you trust anything that the devil says?!" Kat spouted off, throwing her hands in the air.

Eric, still with one hand in the air to wordlessly plead that she not start shouting, pushed himself off the other side of the bed.

"He's never lied to us before, Kat. Just . . . listen." The prince waited to see if his wife was able to settle herself back down enough so she could actually hear him out.

It took a good while, but after a few moments of prolonged eye contact, she let out a huff and folded her arms over her chest expectantly.

"He said there is a woman close to us who is responsible for the recent altercations with the magical beasts. He said she wants you out of Troivack, though he doesn't know why. It seems it's all witches she wants banished from the kingdom, and unlike the devil who is now simply trying to avoid you, she isn't above killing you. I'm even wondering if she could maybe be the one who gave Aidan Helmer the dragon."

Kat frowned. "A woman who hates witches in Troivack? I don't suppose the devil was able to give us more details. You know, like a name? Odd mole placement? Perhaps a special pitchfork she likes to carry around?"

Eric shook his head. "The devil doesn't know who she is, but he knows she's plotting something and that she's the one bringing the magical beasts into Troivack through connections she has . . ."

Kat's index finger began to tap her arm. "That aside . . . Why are you suddenly paranoid about my magic consuming your intention?"

Eric's hands gradually fell to his sides. "The devil has always been pretty vocal about how I'd be the only one to benefit from our relationship. He has said numerous times that I'd destroy you."

"I see. And tell me. How is Mrs. Satan doing?"

The prince blinked in confusion.

"My point is, he sounds just like a bitter, angsty man who likes to judge other people's relationships."

Eric couldn't help laughing. "Kat . . . of all the . . . Really? Calling the devil angsty?"

"How is that man not angsty? *All humans are terrible. I'm going to hide in the dark and torment them. I like to make people scared because people are awful!*" Kat finished her performance, during which she had pitched her voice low and made Eric laugh all the harder.

It eventually devolved into the prince being forced to double over because he couldn't find breath to spare between his laughs. Even Kat struggled not to crack a smile.

"See what I mean though? He is judging people without living as a person, and he thinks it's his place to write us all off. Truth is, he *doesn't* know everything, or else he'd know the identity of this ominous woman. So don't go listening to his opinion on our relationship." Kat paused with a smile as Eric gradually regained control of himself. "I'm guessing he wanted something in exchange for telling us about this woman?"

Finally able to stand straight, though he was in the process of pinching the corners of his eyes where tears had started to accumulate, Eric managed to respond, "Yes. He wants information about what we are finding out about her. And I imagine the kingdom."

"He wants you to spy?" Kat's eyes widened.

"Didn't say spy—I would just talk to the king about it and see how he would like to proceed. More like an exchange of information. This woman is also close to Alina if she is close to you right now, so His Majesty *should* know about this," Eric pointed out.

Kat's hands moved to her hips. "I don't think we need to bother telling the devil anything. We now know we have to watch out for someone who dislikes witches and who . . . who . . ."

"Disappears for longer periods of time," Eric supplied with a small half shrug.

"Huh."

The couple fell into silence again.

"Do you know anyone who does that?" the prince prompted patiently.

Kat's tongue poked the inside of her cheek, and her gaze lowered as she ruminated on the description.

"Well . . . I know that Rebecca Devark certainly doesn't seem to be a fan of me, and she would have been around during Aidan's time here, which could explain the dragon, *and* she is probably the most well-connected woman in all Troivack."

Eric faltered in surprise.

"That . . . That actually makes perfect sense. Except for why she attacked you at Faucher's keep if it meant you being sent back to the castle. Unless it was the only way she could keep an eye on you." His mind began to whirr into action.

Kat nodded along, though something in her eyes stopped Eric from speculating any further. "You don't seem convinced," he said.

"My gut tells me I'm wrong."

"Are you sure you're not just hungry? You did skip lunch."

"Okay, I might be hungry. Can we go get something to eat before talking more?" Kat asked, a look of realization breaking through her cloudy mood.

Chuckling, Eric slowly rounded the bed until he stood in front of his wife. "Yes. We'll go eat at a tavern somewhere in Vessa, and then we'll keep trying to figure this out. Once we have something, we'll talk to the king together. Sound good to you?"

Kat nodded.

Eric offered her his hand.

She smiled and took it.

As Kat began to follow her husband toward the door, a thought occurred to her. "You know, I got into a lot of trouble growing up—"

"Oh really? I had no idea."

Kat shoved her shoulder into Eric's side right as he reached for the door handle. "But I have to say, getting embroiled with the devil really does set a whole new standard for me going forward. How will I ever top this?"

"You're going to be responsible for a kingdom someday. I don't think it'll be as hard as you think."

The two continued their typical banter mixed with conversation as they made their way down the castle corridor, and while their conversation may have surrounded completely real and terrifying situations, there was an air of comfort and quiet knowingness that eased any prickly anxiety from the day.

They each shared the sense that, while there was much more to come, they already were doing everything they needed to, with the best person fighting at their back.

She stared at Ansar with a partial smirk.

"The devil reached out to the prince?"

Her assistant remained bowed. "Yes, ma'am, he did."

Leaning back in her high-backed chair, her legs crossed, she licked her lips before fully smiling with a breathy laugh. "I'm making him nervous. Good."

"If the king becomes aware that you are close to the queen, it will be difficult for us to meet, ma'am," Ansar reminded carefully while drawing his shoulders straight.

She lightly clasped her hands on the massive desk before her. "That is to be expected. It doesn't matter much at this time. Everything is just about ready. I just need to wait for Sam to come find me. Though the longer it takes him, the better prepared I can be, so no need to help him along. I wouldn't mind a bit more information about the Ashowan family either, and waiting gives me the opportunity to learn more."

"Do you think we will be able to get Kraken the Emperor and Lady Katarina out of Troivack in time?"

She pondered this question with her head tilted over her left shoulder. "I was hoping her father would be a lot more forceful given her reckless behavior with the prince, but it seems as though the Troivackian king is doing everything in his power to fight against that. I doubt Katarina will want to leave Her Majesty's side now anyway." The woman paused. "Duke Icarus failed in getting her forced out, and my guess is the devil is now aware that the nobleman has turned on him to join me. Icarus is dispensable now, but . . . who knows. Maybe the chance of keeping his head will prompt him to be more receptive to taking a more active part in our plans."

She stood. "Give him more of the powdered Witch's Brew and clear instructions. Oh, and remind him that the devil doesn't simply leave alone those who abandon him. His days are numbered unless he succeeds and keeps me happy."

Ansar bowed to his mistress. "Yes, ma'am."

With a sigh, she stepped around her desk and headed toward the doors.

She wouldn't be able to return to her hideout in Vessa as of sunset, but that didn't matter.

Soon she would be rid of the devil once and for all, and then . . . well . . . she could finally live freely without the threat of his interference.

CHAPTER 12

FIN AND FAUCHER

Faucher leaned back in his seat.

His body, for the first time in years, was completely relaxed. Even his old war wound in his knee felt as though it never existed to begin with. He was full, and at peace.

The dining hall was pleasantly quiet . . . as though they all had found the same tranquility.

"Holy—"

"Gods."

"That was—"

"Unbelievable."

The soft back and forth conversation took place between Faucher's three sons as they stared at their emptied plates.

"I take back everything bad I ever said or thought about witches," Piers announced breathily.

Faucher was too content to respond. He felt his eyes closing, as though he were about to nap right at the table.

The luncheon had been an experience none of them would soon forget.

The sauce over the roast had been subtle, and yet the flavors lingered in their mouths . . . Rosemary? Garlic? Was there something else? Even the vegetables had been seasoned to complement the meat . . . Faucher belatedly regretted not giving the roast chicken a try as well.

Then, dessert had come, and despite Faucher not being someone who typically enjoyed desserts or excessively sweet things, found himself unable to turn away the blueberry pie.

It was unfussy, and yet it was perfect for the chilly wintry day. A slice of simple comfort, but with an extravagant flavor. Buttery crust, with thick crystals of sugar sprinkled on the top of the pastry, the filling tasting as divine and fresh as though made with summer berries . . .

Despite feeling as stuffed as a turkey, Faucher debated another slice of pie.

"Pardon me, Leader Faucher?"

Jolting back to his senses, the Troivackian military man opened his eyes and found himself staring into the pale blue eyes of Finlay Ashowan.

"I was hoping I might convene with you in my chamber."

Faucher didn't even have the energy to curse his bad fortune. He had just started to seriously consider succumbing to a nice afternoon nap . . .

He cleared his throat. "Very well."

Fin gave a gracious nod of his head and took his leave.

"Father . . . ?" Piers leaned over, his voice quiet.

Faucher looked at his son expectantly.

"Can we kidnap the duke and make him our own personal cook?"

Faucher gave a half smile and breathy laugh through his nose. "I'll consider it."

Piers grinned.

"I wonder if Lady Katarina can cook even a little bit as skillfully," Conrad speculated with a dreamy haze in his eyes.

"I imagine she burns food more often than produces anything edible," Dante guessed lazily. Even he hadn't been immune to the enticing serenity the meal had created.

His brothers all bobbed and tilted their heads in agreement.

"Well . . . good luck father." Piers yawned. "I am going to go rest in my chamber for a bit."

Faucher would never admit it, but he had to fight the urge to scowl in jealousy at his youngest son. Instead, he turned to his wife, only to find her staring blankly at her plate, as though debating whether she could get away with licking it.

Briefly forgetting himself and smiling at her wide-eyed wonder, Faucher gently touched her arm.

"I'll go meet with Lord Ashowan. What are you and Dana going to do this afternoon?"

Lady Nathalie jumped and began touching her hair as though trying to ensure her momentary lapse of focus hadn't rendered her an outward mess as well.

"Ah, we . . . we will most likely take the dogs we didn't walk this morning out for a stroll around the gardens."

Faucher nodded. "Remember, don't go anywhere without a guard or the dogs. A lot of people are angry with me for training Lady Katarina."

The noblewoman bowed her head. "I know."

Faucher reached out and clasped his wife's hand before then standing and leaving the banquet hall to locate the house witch's chambers.

He wasn't sure if he was supposed to feel worried about the upcoming discussion, but even if he was, he wasn't sure he would be able to force himself to feel that way regardless. The meal had done too satisfactory a job of lulling him into a state that bordered on meditative, but whether that would still be the case after the discussion with the duke remained to be seen.

Fin sat in front of Faucher silently, the table between them bore a copper teapot that sat over a small stand with a flame below, keeping the drink warm. The fire on Fauchers' right crackling sharply in the chill of the room.

"Thank you for agreeing to meet with me, Leader Faucher. I had a few things to ask you about, both in regard to my daughter as well as the presence of the devil. I believe His Majesty has already explained to you that you can be candid with me," the redheaded man started politely.

Faucher gave a careful nod. He could see in the duke's eyes that he was barely restraining a plethora of emotions.

"Fantastic. First and foremost, has Kat . . . has Kat hurt anyone while she's been here?"

The military leader pondered the question while resting his elbows on the armrests of the chair and folding his hands together.

"She knocked out one of her fellow peers during a spar in self-defense, struck me once while overtaken with magic, attempted to murder another student, and during her most recent sparring match against Captain Orion's chosen men, broke a few limbs of her first opponent under my direction. Her second opponent received a few bruises, and her last opponent received the most damage, though in all fairness, the brunt of that was from Lord Miller's eldest son."

Fin's face paled. "Why did no one stop her training after her first time trying to kill someone?!"

"Because it was mostly in self-defense. Her magic, we've learned, feeds off intention and any magical ability directed toward her. She does not harm the innocent, and also . . . it is dangerous leaving her abilities untrained when that is what she is capable of doing."

Fin swallowed with difficulty, his ethereal eyes slipping over to the hearth. "She says that she has been able to improve how she handles her power. Is that what you sincerely believe as well—that she is she getting better at controlling it?"

"Yes. She finds being physically active all day the most helpful for . . . what is it she calls it . . . ? Her magitch. That's it." Faucher grunted. "She has also been training on how to use her abilities in smaller doses so that they don't become pent up. Since she has been absorbing more magical abilities as of late, she has noticed that her aura has been burning more often, and she needs more releases for it. Mr. Kraft is of the understanding that we have yet to find the safest way for her to drain the power."

"What about Eric? How has he been about all this?"

Faucher froze. At first he debated trying to stay close-lipped about his whole experience with the prince to himself, but . . . given what the duke had revealed to everyone the other day at the meeting, and recognizing his fear as a parent, he relaxed his shoulders.

"Your Grace, permission to be blunt."

"Of course—and, please, call me Fin" The duke gave a weary chuckle.

Faucher nodded to himself and let out a long breath.

"His Highness . . . when I first met him . . . was little more than a drunk who cared for nothing. He would occasionally stand up for Lady Katarina when someone spoke poorly of her, but in general, that was all he was." Faucher paused, but when he glanced at Fin again and saw the tightness in the man's eyes, he forced himself to continue speaking. "I would say things began to change between Ashowan— Sorry. Lady Katarina," he corrected awkwardly.

Fin raised an eyebrow, and a mystifying smile sparked on his face at the accidental slip of casualness.

"Lady Katarina walked in when His Highness was having a soldier's spell."

The house witch's shoulders pulled back, and his eyebrows rose.

"She was able to calm him down and call him back to himself, though he is still unaware this happened. Since then, the two of them have gravitated toward each other, and there was an understanding between them that not even Her Majesty was apprised of. Once they arrived in Vessa, His Highness was her biggest protector and advocate. More so than anyone else. He even got the former queen of Troivack banished from the court on her behalf as you might have heard. Most people who spent time with them knew the nature of their relationship, and as they grew closer, His Highness has seemed to improve. From what I hear, he has deepened his bond with Her Majesty, he attends meetings, he works all hours of the day and night . . . He has impressed a good many people. Though I would be lying if I said he did not still imbibe heavily on occasion."

Fin nodded along, his gaze appraising the military man before him. He didn't say anything for a while, his thoughts and feelings unclear, but Faucher didn't fidget, and instead remained at ease.

"You think it's a good match?"

"I sure as hell wouldn't want my own daughter in it," Faucher informed the duke gruffly.

Fin gave a sardonic laugh in agreement.

"But I think it's better than the alternative of them ruining themselves trying to keep apart. For now, anyway."

The house witch leaned back in his seat, his legs stretching out before him, and his gaze once again moving to the fire.

The two men sat in companionable silence for a spell of time.

Faucher was just beginning to feel drowsy again when Fin suddenly reached for the teapot and poured its contents into two cups.

He slid one over to the military man, who raised his hand. "I can't say I'm someone who enjoys—"

"It's moonshine," Fin explained with a rueful smile.

Faucher gave a quick half smile of his own in response and accepted the cup with a rumble of approval and thanks.

"You more or less elaborated on things His Majesty has already said about Kat and Eric," Fin began. "As a father to a daughter, I have no doubt you can imagine my feelings and thoughts on the matter."

Faucher scoffed humorlessly. "I don't envy you, that's for Godsdamn certain."

The redhead shot the man a flat look that actually reminded Faucher a great deal of Katarina.

"Thanks for that," he replied sarcastically before taking a hearty gulp from his cup. "I don't want to be the villain to their happiness. Especially when there are greater things to be worried about right now."

Faucher remained silent.

"I know I also owe Eric an apology. Part of the reason he descended so far into darkness was that I failed him, and I seem to keep failing him." Fin's eyes saddened. "It was so much easier back when he was a boy and all I had to do was make him a raspberry tart, and he'd be right as rain again."

Chuckling to himself, Faucher found himself nodding along. "I understand completely. My daughter used to only ever need a puppy to cheer up. Now she wants to take part in the military."

"You gave her a puppy every time she was sad?" Fin laughed. "Gods, you must be overrun with them." He took another drink, having only been jesting in his response.

"She has twenty-five dogs. It's true."

Fin sprayed the moonshine out of his mouth and turned to stare in shock at Faucher, who had color rising in his face. The house witch wiped his mouth in the stunned silence and flopped back into his chair.

He kept his hand over his mouth.

Faucher eyed him suspiciously. "I know your daughter well, and you bear many resemblances. I know you wish to laugh."

Unable to refute the military man's accusation, Fin lowered his forehead to his hand and succumbed to his chortles.

For whatever reason, Faucher didn't mind.

When Fin had eventually settled back down, he looked over to his companion with a grin.

"Gods, there is nothing quite as humbling nor maddening as having a daughter, is there?"

Faucher wordlessly raised his cup in a toast.

Fin lifted his own, and the two drank.

The pair were once again partaking in the affable quiet, when Faucher turned with a raised eyebrow. "When is it your wife is set to arrive?"

All at once, Fin's relaxed expression seized. He then looked at the military leader wide-eyed.

"Gods . . . Probably in the next five days?"

Faucher laughed. "Another fate of yours I do not desire for myself."

Fin let out a groan and finished his drink. "You know, if you're going to be so smug about it, the least you can do is keep me company while I drown my woes for the day. I think I've had it with being serious—at least until tomorrow morning."

Faucher eyed the duke.

Usually such a request would send him bolting for the door with a growled excuse, however . . . Perhaps it was the fantastical food the house witch had prepared swaying his good senses, but . . . it actually sounded like a rather good time.

And so, the two men continued toasting and drinking well into the day, sharing stories of their families and life that had them tentatively forming what some could call a friendship.

CHAPTER 13

AN ATYPICAL APPROACH

Eric and Katarina returned to the castle after having consumed their weight (or in Kat's case, double her body weight) in hearty tavern food and fine spirits.

As the couple strolled through the front doors, nodding to the guards who bowed to them, the pair continued idly chatting about Kat starting to wield a dagger while sword fighting, when Poppy shuffled up to them. The young maid was wringing her hands and glancing around. While she was successful in keeping her expression calm, both Kat and Eric could see something was stressing out the maid.

"Your Highness, my lady." Poppy curtsied hurriedly, then double-checked their surroundings, making sure no one was within earshot before leaning closer to the redhead. "Lady Nathalie has requested you go to your father's chamber."

Kat raised an eyebrow, then glanced at Eric, who shared her look of confusion. "Is everything alright?"

Poppy gave a small, strained smile and nodded her head.

The redhead could tell there was no use in asking her maid any further questions, and so she set to making her way over to see her father, though feeling baffled about why Lady Nathalie was also involved.

Eric, while still not feeling completely comfortable with Fin, followed his wife out of curiosity—and in case there was going to be a fight between them she may need his support for.

By the time they reached the house witch's chamber, Kat could feel her heart pounding in her chest as she tried to brace herself for whatever she would find behind the door . . .

Was her da angry that she'd missed the lunch he'd prepared?

Did he have something else he needed to say about her marriage to Eric?

Or was it just that Kraken was less moody after a good nap and was willing to try talking to Pina again?

Letting out a long breath, Kat raised her hand and knocked.

Eric reached out and gave her other hand a quick, comforting squeeze as they waited.

Then the door opened a crack, and Lady Nathalie appeared.

The look on the woman's face wasn't one Kat had ever seen her wear before, making the redhead balk.

"Err . . . Lady Nathalie? Is everything alright?" she heard herself ask as she noticed the pink in the Troivackian woman's cheeks and the suspicious shine in her eyes.

"Ah, yes. Sorry to worry you, but . . . I gathered you may wish to be a part of . . . Well . . . this." The noblewoman opened the door, and revealed . . .

Kat's jaw dropped.

"What . . . the . . . fu—" Eric started to speak but was promptly cut off.

"ASHOWAN!" Faucher called out with a roar, the teacup in his hand waved out and sloshed a suspiciously clear liquid as he summoned Kat forward.

The man's face was red, his posture crooked, and partially sitting in his lap, with his arm around Faucher's neck . . .

Was Finlay Ashowan.

"Greeeg, sheee's now, got a dif'rent name, sso *I'm* ASSHowan," the house witch slurred with a smile.

Faucher bobbed his head dramatically while raising his teacup to his mouth and draining what little liquid had remained in it. "Right, right. But, yooou're Fin tooo me. Or Your Gráce."

Kat and Eric shared amazed glances before Kat looked to Lady Nathalie, who had come to be in her current state because she hadn't been able to stop laughing.

"They're drunk off their arses," Kat whispered while a smile climbed her face.

Eric was still at a loss for words as the two men continued drunkenly rambling and then burst out in a bar song that apparently Fin didn't know the words of but still tried his best to sing along with Faucher's off-key baritone.

Both Kat and Eric watched without saying a word while Lady Nathalie closed the door behind them.

"Conrad was wondering why Greg hadn't returned after the meeting, and so I came to check on them and found . . . this."

Finally able to look away from the comical scene of her stern and stoic teacher singing with her father more or less in his lap, Kat addressed the noblewoman.

"Has Faucher ever been like this before?"

The question made Nathalie's hysterics begin anew.

It was the first time Kat had ever seen Lady Nathalie do such a thing so openly, and she found that it made her seem twenty years younger and captivatingly pretty.

"Greg? Like this? Not at all. I have to say . . . I'd heard that your father had a peculiar effect on people, but I . . . I was not prepared for it."

"Oyy!" Fin called out suddenly toward his daughter and Eric. "You two!"

Fin gradually pushed himself up off Faucher, and after stumbling briefly, fixed his bleary gaze on the couple.

"Hi, Da," Kat greeted with a wave.

Eric didn't say anything, and instead moved his hand to his pocket and clenched it into a fist.

Fin closed his eyes and opened them wide again; evidently, he was having trouble focusing on his daughter and son-in-law.

Seeing this, Faucher also rose to his feet, though even he had to hold out a hand to find his balance before directly facing his student.

"Ashowan . . . or . . . Lady Kat, you . . . you come from good stock. Your father is—*hic*—surprisingly, a reasonable man."

Kat blinked and looked at her father, who proceeded to clasp a hand on Faucher's shoulder. "An' this man . . . is mos' impressive. Though I can't believe that uh . . . that uh . . . he's got so many dogs!"

Lady Nathalie already had her face dropped to her hand, her shoulders once again trembling.

"Right. Faucher, *I'm* surprised you let my da sit in your lap," Kat observed wryly.

Her teacher pointed an unsteady finger at her. "You . . . will tell no one. He fell."

"I will tell *everyone*. I don't care if he had happened to break an ankle and landed there! Everyone in this castle should know by morning." Kat grinned.

"Ashooowan," Faucher began with a growl before his knee started to give out and Fin was forced to catch him by wrapping his hands around his waist.

"You two make a darling couple." Eric eyed Fin borderline embracing the military leader, though the prince still had yet to crack a smile.

Kat noticed this and quickly deduced just how harsh of a discussion he and her father must have had earlier . . .

Faucher halfheartedly pushed Fin away as Lady Nathalie moved over to her husband, at last composed enough to lend her assistance.

"Come, Greg. I'll take you back to our chamber and— Oop!" Faucher's weight proved to be too much for the slender woman whose knees buckled almost instantly. Kat stepped in to help, throwing her teacher's other arm over her shoulder.

"Ah. Dear old Greg, come along!" she cheered with a brilliant smile.

"Don't call me that," Faucher murmured, his eyes already fluttering.

"I'm hauling your drunken arse to bed, so I get to call you what I want!" his student informed him as they made their way out of the chamber. A warming of Kat's aura helped her carry the man as his wife pulled free to try to regain control of herself as she once again began laughing.

Once the two women had closed the door behind themselves, leaving Eric and Fin alone, the jovial mood drastically cooled.

"You know . . . my mother did always say you brought out the unexpected sides of men when you drank together. Though I hope you realize the irony of me finding *you* in this state," the prince informed the house witch with his head tilting over his shoulder.

"Your mother . . . wass a great woman. The firs' night . . . The night of the ten fountains, your father—"

"Woke up to a parade of people informing him of his antics under my mother's directions," Eric finished the story he had heard countless times before.

"Yes." Fin gave a melancholy smile, his eyes growing lost to fond memories.

Eric turned to leave.

"I'm sorry."

The words made the prince freeze.

Eric turned to stare over his shoulder at the house witch after swallowing with difficulty. Fin was already leaning heavily against the armchair Faucher had just vacated, and his gaze was glassy.

"You're just saying that because you're drunk."

"I'm not. I wass . . . uh . . ." Fin rubbed the back of his neck sloppily. "I was goin' to do it tomorrow . . . but. Saw . . . Ssaw you now."

In his pocket, Eric felt his nails dig into his palm. "Guess I'll see if that's true by tomorrow, then."

The prince left without another look back.

After hastily exiting the chamber, he stood perfectly still, and closing his eyes, did his best to settle down his emotions before moving again.

He hadn't been ready to see Fin so soon after their last discussion.

Feeling the incredible urge to drown his sorrows in copious amounts of moonshine, Eric forced his mind instead to other matters . . .

Matters like Duke Icarus.

I better go talk to Eli. He must be scared given that they've locked him up in a secret location in Vessa . . . I wonder if I should take Kat with me to meet him.

Eric felt his thoughts settle to safer topics, away from his vices, and the tension in his chest loosened a little as a result.

Yes, facing his former friend again could wait until tomorrow. For the time being, there was a mountain of work to be done.

Kat stood and stared.

It was the second time that day she was too astonished to speak.

The king had requested her to take the names of the women interested in learning self-defense for him to present to his council to discuss the possibility of their participation.

However, Kat had not been anticipating a packed corridor filled with noblewomen and serving girls to greet her.

"Well . . . you certainly made an impression," Broghan Miller voiced faintly at her side while holding a board with parchment, an inkpot, and a quill he'd balanced on top. He looked down at the lone piece of paper he had brought.

"I think . . . I'll need more paper . . . and we might need someone to help us, or we'll be taking names past suppertime."

Kat swallowed and nodded. "Maybe see if Sir Cas or Lady Dana wants to give us a hand."

"Lady Dana is standing in line."

"Ah . . . Faucher is going to kill me."

"Probably."

"Given that you're supposed to protect me means that he'll have to go through you first at least."

Broghan fell silent.

He had forgotten about that detail . . .

"I'll go see if Ball or Herra want to join. I know the two were training for Joshua's match later, but this could be good to take his mind off that."

Kat nodded without taking her eyes off the eager faces before her. "Maybe see about getting chairs and tables as well."

Broghan inclined himself to her and handed her the clipboard. "You get started. Hopefully I'll be back before you fill up the page."

Looking to her personal guard, Kat accepted the materials, though her mind was still struggling with the sheer volume of women in front of her.

As he strode away, the redhead returned her attention to the women who all straightened their shoulders as though trying to stand out, all their eyes bright.

"Err . . . Right. If you all could line up two at a time along this wall in case anyone needs to pass by—" The scuffling and flurry of Troivackian furs and dresses was a small whirlwind that startled Kat back into silence until the women had reformed themselves and all stared ahead at her expectantly.

"Uh . . . Thank you." Kat cleared her throat. "Alright, the first two come up, and I'll take your names."

The two women who stepped forward were obviously nobles. The one in a lilac-colored dress that she covered in a rich white cloak lined with snowy wolf fur was eyeing the redhead rather intently.

"My name is Lady Selene Icarus."

Kat's eyes snapped up from the page in front of her.

The young woman was pretty. Wide, light brown eyes, a beauty mark above her left eyebrow, an oval face, and long, straight black hair. She was quite tall and broad shouldered for a woman, to the point where even Kat felt slight by comparison.

"Is your father aware that you're here . . . ?" Kat asked while trying to hide the hesitancy in her voice.

"Oh, I'm not here to sign up, I'm here to tell you that I'm not going to give up on Prince Eric becoming my husband."

The woman beside Lady Selene reared back to stare at Selene as though she had just pulled a weapon out.

Evidently the two did not know each other.

Kat's jaw dropped, and she stared at Selene while barely resisted the urge to laugh.

"Er . . . well . . . I'm *currently* married to him, so that might be a bit of a snag to your plans."

"I don't think you'll last long."

The woman at Selene's side began to back away from the scene, obviously not wanting to become embroiled in a possible fight.

Kat couldn't help it, she chuckled, though she tried valiantly to stifle it quickly. Selene raised a haughty eyebrow and crossed her arms over her chest.

"I bet he only married you because you crawled into his bed and your father made him do it!"

Kat started laughing again. This time she couldn't stop.

She wasn't even sure why it was more funny than it was enraging to her . . . Perhaps it was the young woman's unabashed approach, or how assured she seemed of herself.

However, Selene was becoming a mite more upset in light of Kat's reaction.

"You aren't saying I'm wrong. You're just laughing like a fool."

Unable to stop herself, Kat thrust the board at the young woman, making her grasp it instinctively.

This freed Kat up to continue laughing hysterically.

Perhaps after days of horrific stress, her mind had finally snapped, but her hands were on her knees as she doubled over, still squawking.

She knew she should put the woman in her place, but she first had to stop laughing.

"You really are—" Selene started to say something, but Kat held up a finger as she at last composed herself enough to stand straight while dabbing the corners of her eyes.

"Hoo . . . that was . . . Wow. You sure are something." Kat grinned at the noblewomen, who glared at her before rolling her eyes.

"Tell you what, Lady Selene." Kat took a step closer, her golden eyes shining a little brighter, making the noblewoman back up. "I won't report your disrespectful conduct just now to your parents, and perhaps even the queen if, and only if, you yourself sign your name on that there sheet in your hands."

Kat was prowling forward, her smile, while not intending to be menacing, was intimidating all the same.

"I-I would never sign! This is— Oh!" Selene's back was against the castle corridor, and to her left the crowd of women who had gathered to sign up to learn self-defense stood silently watching.

"Take a moment and think about what would be worse . . . upsetting your father . . . or getting exiled and possibly charged with slandering foreign nobility . . . followed by most likely upsetting your father."

Selene opened and closed her mouth, her hands beginning to tremble.

Gods, I know Rebecca Devark had indicated the duke's daughters weren't the brightest torches in the castle, but I didn't know they'd be this dense . . .

Duke Icarus's eldest daughter snatched up the quill from the board, scrawled her name, and hurriedly pressed the materials back into Kat's hands before stalking away with her cheeks burning red.

Kat, while still smiling, waved at Selene's back before muttering under her breath, "I get the feeling that I'm not finished dealing with that woman . . ."

CHAPTER 14

DATED DEFENSES

Kat had the chair she was sitting in pushed off onto its back two legs as Broghan pulled out a fresh piece of parchment while the next pair of women in line waited.

When he had returned, he hadn't been able to rope anyone else into helping, but he had at least found servants that were able to gather a table and chairs for him and Kat as they took down the names of a shocking number of women present.

They were not quite halfway through the throng of females, and the dining hour was drawing closer.

"At this rate we might have to finish this tomorrow. Otherwise, we'll miss Joshua's match," Broghan wearily noted as a shy young woman with her hair partially tied back finished scrawling her name on the sheet.

"Damn." Kat sighed. "I mean . . . it's a good thing this is the response my idea is getting. Though I have to admit that I'm surprised all these women aren't being stopped by their family members."

"Oh, we're only allowed to learn until we marry."

Both Kat and Broghan turned to face the young woman who had just finished writing her name down atop the fresh sheet of paper.

Under Broghan's direct gaze, she blushed. It wasn't the norm that a woman spoke without being first addressed by the man present in Troivack.

"You can only learn if you aren't married? Because your husband is supposed to protect you, I'm guessing?" Kat reasoned with a raised eyebrow.

The young woman nodded.

"A-Actually." The next woman in line, who appeared to be another noble, stepped forward nervously. She wore a plain beige dress with her black hair braided and pinned in a low bun. Her eyes were cast down demurely, and her hands properly clasped in front of her skirts.

"I'm already married, b-but I . . . I thought you . . . I thought you were amazing during your spars. I know I couldn't possibly ever beat an elite knight, but . . . you just looked untouchable, and I wanted to . . . to feel that way."

Powerful emotions surged in Kat's chest.

There were feelings of pride and happiness, and best of all . . . the feeling as though everything she had tried to prove had worked.

Easing the legs of the chair she was seated in back down to the ground, Kat was just about to open her mouth to talk to the noblewoman more interestedly, when a shout broke out overhead.

"ELYSE!"

The woman to whom Kat had just been about to introduce herself to flinched, her shoulders rounding.

Pushing herself up to stand, Kat peered over the noblewoman's head at none other than Lord Harriod Ball.

The man was red-faced as he glowered at the Troivackian woman, who slowly turned from Kat, her face tilted toward the floor. It didn't take her long to deduce that the lord must be Elyse's husband.

"I do not recall giving you permission to sign such a thing. Go back to our chamber. *Now.*"

It was instantaneous.

Kat's blood reached a boiling point in less time than it took to draw a breath, and she was around the table and standing beside the woman named Elyse before anyone could react.

"You stay out of this." Lord Ball's eyes flashed dangerously toward Kat, already sensing that she was about to weigh in.

"It's funny how you forgot to bow *again*, Lord Ball. I think I'll have to report this to His Highness Prince Eric and His Majesty today." Kat's golden eyes were glowing like a beast's.

Lord Ball, caught off guard by her comment, turned to face Kat more squarely. He had been anticipating her arguing with his order to his wife . . .

Her forcing him to bow while already furious was much, much worse, and she knew it.

He inclined himself to her. His eyes flashing dangerously as he did so.

"I'll have your apology now for your rudeness, or I can take it up with His Majesty. Your choice." Kat's voice was calm, but the heat rolling off her was a telltale sign that she was livid.

Lord Harriod Ball looked as though he were prepared to strike her.

The hall that had been filled with women talking excitedly amongst themselves fell deathly silent.

"I . . ." Harriod started, then needed to stop to swallow.

"Tell you what, Lord Ball. I'll forget about the apology, but you let your wife finish her business here," Kat interrupted him, and she observed a pulsing vein in his neck as well as at the center of his head, though this time she took no pleasure in seeing them.

No, she wasn't in any sort of gleeful mood.

The lord leaned in closer to her, and as he did, Katarina's former polite expression darkened to a glower.

"I can just as easily report you for your uncouth language the last time we spoke."

Raising a disdainful eyebrow, Kat didn't waver for an instant. "I suppose my husband would possibly have a few words with me about it . . . but you have far more to lose from the entire discussion that would be brought to light than I would. So, how do you want this to end today, Lord Ball? Keep in mind, I could just as easily challenge you to another duel right after your brother's. Will you be as confident in that case?"

Oh, how the man *loathed* her with every inch of his being.

Lord Ball's deranged gaze was fueled by the acid hatred that seared his insides.

"Elyse. Sign that damn paper and come with me. Now."

His wife, trembling in her shoes, shook her head, and sent her silent tears dripping to the floor.

"N-No . . . I-I only . . . only meant to speak with . . . Lady Katarina. T-That's all."

Kat hadn't remembered what bloodlust felt like in a while . . . but she felt it then. Potently.

Regardless of his wife's submission, Lord Ball was far from placated. He snatched Elyse's arm and hauled her alongside after him, making her stumble as she tried to keep up.

That is until a snarling hound lunged at the lord, making him half leap away.

Dana stood in the line of ladies, her dog Boots continued barking ferociously at him, and she made no move to stop him.

"Control your animal!" Lord Ball shouted at the young woman.

Dana didn't cower as many of the women around her did.

No.

She glared, and she looked a great deal like her father when she did.

"I will have you apologize for your dog, Lady Dana, or I will—"

"What seems to be the problem here?"

Everyone turned and found none other than Brendan Devark and Alina Devark standing before them.

No one had noticed the arrival of the royals amongst all the drama.

Everyone dropped into a curtsy or bow—incredibly, even Boots stopped barking and lowered his head.

"Your Majesty, I was asking Lady Dana to control her dog as he had just attacked me," Lord Ball informed his sovereign respectfully, though his face was still flushed in anger.

Alina looked at the dog, who sat down and peered up at her with a sweet head tilt.

"He seems well-behaved to me."

The lord didn't look at the queen at first, but the shift in Brendan's eyes had him rethinking that decision, and he bowed to her as well.

"You must have heard him barking—if not there are several witnesses here."

Lord Ball gestured to the wall of women before him.

"Oh . . . I don't know about that . . . Did anyone else here see anything?" Katarina's loud voice rang sharply in the tense air as she casually strode past the women that still stood in line.

No one said a word. While most of the women kept their gazes averted, however, Kat was glad to see a number of the young women staring furiously at the nobleman.

In fact, one face that surprised Kat in particular . . . was Lady Sarah Miller, who stood in line beside Dana.

Lord Ball grit his teeth.

"Is there something wrong with your hand, Lady Ball?" Alina asked.

While the queen's voice was soft, when her hazel gaze moved to Lord Ball's grasp on Elyse's arm, her expression turned icy.

Haltingly, Lord Ball released his wife's arm and instead grasped her hand.

"Y-Yes, I'm fine, Your Majesty, thank you for asking," the noblewoman managed to say despite still crying.

"Pardon us, Your Majesties, my wife and I were just on our way to prepare for dinner this evening."

Brendan studied his vassal carefully. "Lord Ball, I've wanted to have a discussion with you in my office at some point. Would now be a bad time?"

"Yes, Your Majesty, I'm afraid it would be. How about tomorrow morning?" Lord Ball was starting to look more in control of himself the longer he stood speaking to the king, whose indomitable presence didn't leave much room for disrespectful attitudes.

The king nodded his chin vaguely. "I will see if Mr. Levin can make time for you."

Lord Ball was about to bow and take his leave with his wife again, but Kat wasn't through with him just yet.

"Lord Ball, I look forward to resuming our discussion in the near future." She stood directly behind him and offered her hand to him.

He couldn't ignore her.

The gesture indicated he bid her a proper farewell.

He released his wife and seized Kat's extended hand, pinching her fingers brutally as he bowed and brushed his lips along her knuckles.

Which was precisely when Kat leaned in, lowered her voice to a hush, and said, "If you keep acting this way, one day you'll find yourself with crushed balls, and you'll be left regretting how you never took the chance to be a man when you could."

Lord Ball's gaze snapped up to hers.

Her expression told him she was fully prepared for him to snitch on her, and she was going to be sure to thoroughly drag him through every inch of mud she could if he did so.

He flashed a quick jeer at her, then turned around without another word.

However, Kat had seen it in his eyes.

Harriod Ball wanted to destroy her. No matter what.

Kat looked at the women present, and they all met her gaze in silent solidarity.

The witch nodded to them.

They nodded back.

Kat then regarded the king and queen who had just turned back after watching Harriod and Elyse Ball depart.

She bowed. "Your Majesties."

"Lady Katarina, we came down to hear if any noblewomen came to sign up to learn self-defense," Brendan called out to her while also moving closer with Alina clasping his arm.

"We have just about every available woman in the castle registering to join the lessons. These ladies here, we may have to resume collecting their names come morning, as we are running out of time and paper."

Brendan frowned, which in turn caught Kat off guard. Why was he unhappy?

"I see . . . Perhaps conclude the collection of names for today, Lady Katarina. Given that Lord Ball is not available for a meeting, now would be a good time for you and me to share a few words."

Unsure of what exactly the king could wish to speak to her about, Kat bowed in acceptance. When the royal couple turned back the way they came toward the nearest staircase, the redhead followed in their wake, though as she did so, she glanced over her shoulder at Broghan Miller, who still had rounded eyes from everything that had just transpired.

Kat shot him a half shrug as if to say *Guess I'll see you later* and continued walking, though she did also give Dana a quick wink that had the young woman smiling in return.

Once in the king's study, the trio seated themselves.

Alina leaned farther back in her seat than usual, however, with a wince.

"Back pain?" Kat asked sympathetically.

"Some," Alina retorted glibly while Brendan cast a loving glance to his wife.

After getting comfortable and sighing, Alina turned to Kat. "So what actually happened with Lord Ball?"

Taking a deep inhalation, the redhead did her best to calm her ire. "Lady Elyse Ball was wanting to sign up for my lessons, and he came storming in, frightened the wine out of her, and then started dragging her off."

"And you did nothing to antagonize him further?" Brendan asked with the unmistakable note of doubt in his voice.

"I pointed out when he was rude to me for no good reason and kindly offered that he didn't have to apologize if he let his wife finish her business."

Kat's direct answer and lack of playful mischievousness told the royals that not only was she taking the situation seriously, but that she sincerely believed she had done the right thing.

"Kat . . . listen, I know it's a hard thing to accept, but as things are right now? We won't be able to persuade noblemen who don't want their wives joining."

"I beg your pardon?" Kat looked at her friend stonily.

"The only reason we are starting to sway the noblemen about their unmarried daughters? They're trying to negotiate advantageous, hasty weddings. The men don't want wives who go through the training. It's up to the men to protect them, and the fathers of these women are more or less saying that they doubt any man can protect their daughters the way they can. It's sparking a competitive marriage boon."

Kat wanted to stand up and throw the chair she was sitting on.

"Then I won't actually train any of these women because it's all just to get them married? What even is the point to all this then?!"

"Not all of them are going to be able to get married. The ones who proceed with the lessons won't be looked upon favorably, and once they start training, most will never have any future marriage prospects . . . But Kat, even knowing this, many of the women still have chosen to go through with it," Alina explained with a hopeful note coming through her beleaguered tone.

Her hands gripping into fists, Kat stared levelly at her friend. "You knew this and didn't tell me?"

"We just figured out what was happening at the meeting," Alina defended herself wearily. Kat could see then that her friend was equally disappointed with the development.

"Let me guess. Duke Ick*arse* had something to do with it?"

Alina gave a brief snort of laughter and didn't even bother chiding her friend. "Correct."

"Regardless, this is a step in a good direction. The lessons bring into question women's rights to choose for themselves, and even laws pertaining to their inheritances for the ones who become unmarriageable. Some may not have brothers to inherit their fathers' titles," the king added with a subtle hint of optimism.

Kat stared at Brendan dejectedly before dropping her chin to her chest. "I hate politics."

"Good luck once you're crowned queen," Alina reminded her friend with an empathetic grimace.

Kat cringed and immediately shifted her thoughts away from the terrifying notion she still hadn't wrapped her head around.

"I'm more worried about Lady Ball." Alina looked at her husband. "I'm worried he'll vent his anger on her horribly."

Brendan surprised the two women before him then by shaking his head. "He won't. Well . . . he'll shout enough that I'm sure people will hear from the corridor, but to hurt one's wife is to indicate you cannot protect their well-being. Even if you're the one to inflict it, it shows a weakness of the mind. Lord Ball knows this."

Kat stared doubtfully at the king.

Brendan met the look and added, "Did you note his reaction when Boots lunged at him?"

"You *did* see what happened!"

"He moved his wife behind himself instinctively," Alina answered her husband, ignoring Kat's realization.

Brendan nodded. "He's angry, but he won't harm her."

"Well maybe not physically, but he doesn't have the right to yell at her either!" the redhead snapped.

The king regarded the redhead with an uncharacteristic amount of patience.

"Things *are* changing, but I understand it is frustrating that they are not happening sooner."

Kat fidgeted in her seat.

She still wasn't satisfied.

However, she could tell that everyone was doing their best, and so . . . annoyingly enough . . . the only thing she could do was wait.

Though that didn't mean she was through tormenting Lord Harriod Ball. Not by a long shot.

CHAPTER 15

AN ENCOURAGING ENTREATY

Cracking her neck, Kat strode toward the courtyard.

Her mood was grim, and her magitch was skittering under her skin like a thousand spiders.

She was craving violence after her earlier confrontation with Lord Ball, but she had acquiesced to Joshua's request that he be the one to spar with his brother. While this was perfectly understandable, it was still annoying to Kat, as it left her with next to nothing she could do to find an outlet aside from cheering on her peer.

Eric had also been absent from dinner, saying he had to tend to something, but he had left in such a hurry that Kat hadn't been able to question him further.

"Oyy! Reyes! Hold up!"

Kat continued stalking forward.

A laugh sounded behind her followed by a shout of "Ashowan!"

Kat halted and looked over her shoulder to see Piers jogging to catch up to her with Conrad and Sir Cas not far behind.

When the youngest Faucher son reached her, he proceeded to throw an arm around her neck and muss her hair with his knuckles as he had taken to doing on a regular basis.

"ARGH! Gods, do you do that to your wife?" Kat asked once Piers stopped and smirked at the bird's nest he had created in her hair.

"Not at all. She would have me neutered on the spot."

"Now there's an idea," Kat growled with a smile while reaching over to grasp and shake Piers's chin while his arm remained around her neck.

Piers gently shoved her away. "Not a chance. The only person permitted to be anywhere near the Faucher jewels are the wives."

Kat laughed. "Guess I'll just offer Nicole a hand when she decides to follow through on her threat."

"You didn't respond to your new name by the way." Piers changed the subject with a coy smile.

"My new— Ah . . ." Kat balked when she realized her last name technically no longer was Ashowan . . . Her father had mentioned that fact earlier that day, but she'd been so distracted by his drunken scene she had completely missed it . . .

"Just keep calling me Ashowan for now. I'm not ready for my name to change yet."

Piers sighed at the young woman's request but didn't say anything to argue with her as they once again started making their way to the courtyard. He'd heard she'd been having a hard enough start to her marriage.

As they walked, they noticed more and more clumps of serving staff and nobility standing around and talking amongst themselves . . .

Lord Ball hadn't wanted a large audience for his spar with his half brother, but word had already spread about the exchange, and so in the idle moments following dinner, the castle occupants took to gossiping amongst themselves.

"Do you think Joshua can beat his brother?" Kat asked softly.

Piers's normally flippant expression faded. "Hard to say. Harriod Ball used to be a decent swordsman, but I don't know how much he's practiced since taking over as marquess."

Kat made a grumbling noise in the back of her throat.

"If I were to guess? Skill-wise, assuming Harriod Ball hasn't been practicing, they may be closely matched. Except Harriod Ball has fifteen pounds on Joshua," Sir Cas interjected from behind as he and Conrad caught up to Piers and Kat.

After giving them a greeting nod, Kat continued speculating. "If Joshua loses, can I jump in and take over?"

Conrad was the one to shake his head in response. "If you do that, it'd cause all sorts of issues, but the one in particular that would most likely bother you is that Joshua would be mocked for the rest of his life for having had a woman save him."

Kat's right hand gripped into a fist at her side. "Before coming to Troivack, I really didn't give much thought to my sex. It's annoying as hell how much it matters here."

The three men shared a variety of sympathetic looks and shrugs.

"You're helping things along," Sir Cas reminded kindly with a smile.

"Not as much as I'd like. I just wish I could bash the heads of all the noblemen who insist on being arsehats."

While Piers grinned, Conrad leaned forward worriedly. "Lower your voice, Lady Katarina."

Unable to be irritated by the soft-spoken man, Kat bobbed her head apologetically. "I'm not naming names or anything . . ."

No one prodded her further on the matter.

Instead, the group fell into pensive silence as they reached their destination.

At the exit, Captain Orion stood with his arms crossed, blocking a small crowd of knights from going out.

"No one aside from His Majesty's and Lord Ball's associates are to be allowed to observe."

"Pardon us, but I believe we need to enter before the spar begins." Kat stepped forward, drawing everyone's attention. Her eyes were already flashing, daring the captain to fight her.

However, Captain Orion must've either been informed that it was in fact she who had challenged Lord Ball, therefore she was entitled to be there, *or* he knew that he was already on thin ice due to the investigation involving Sir Herra. And he understood that antagonizing the students of the man who was technically his superior as of that moment in time wasn't a great idea. Whatever the reason, he stiffened at her approach—with a clenched fist—nodded and sidled over to allow Sir Cas, Conrad, Piers, and the redhead past.

Kat was a touch disappointed, so she settled for sliding her sharp gaze to the nearby knights and glared. She didn't know if they were trying to attend the match to cheer for Joshua or his brother, but she didn't want to take any chances.

Once they cleared the doorway and were descending the long stone steps toward the roped off section, they noticed Joshua Ball sitting alone. He waited, his eyes blindly fixed ahead, his thoughts far from his surroundings, as he didn't move despite their arrival. Piers leaned over to Kat and slowed his pace.

"You seem like you're waiting for someone to pick a fight with you. What's going on?"

"Lord Ball pissed me off royally earlier today. I'm surprised Dana didn't tell you about it," she murmured back.

"I haven't seen her, my mother, or . . . actually, where *is* my father?" Piers straightened when he realized Joshua's teacher was nowhere in sight.

"Ah . . ." Kat's foul mood lessened as she vividly recalled the situation in which she had found the normally stoic military man earlier. "Would you believe me if I said he was drunk with my father this afternoon, and the two were wrapped around each other?"

Piers shot her a dubious look as they moved. "Careful with your jokes about my father."

"No, see . . . that's the best part. I'm telling the truth. Your mother was there, though Faucher may have sworn her to secrecy."

Piers was opening his mouth to question her outrageous claim, but they had reached the side section of the ring that Kat had entered for her own duel only a few days ago. Though the nearly empty courtyard had a far grimmer atmosphere compared to the day of her own match.

For one, only Joshua was present. For another, the young man looked as though he were about to face his death.

"Well, well, well, Joshua! Look at you saving our seats! You know, typically it's your friends and family that are supposed to do that," Kat crowed with forced jubilance as she plunked herself down beside the young man.

Joshua couldn't meet her gaze, but he gave a halfhearted effort at upturning the corners of his mouth.

Kat looked back at Sir Cas and Conrad, who collectively winced in light of Josh's reaction before shuffling around to seat themselves. Though Piers remained standing as he eyed Lord Ball's side of the courtyard.

"You can beat him," the redhead informed Joshua with an encouraging and resilient half smile.

The young man finally looked at her, the despair in his eyes concerning to say the least. "It's kind of you to say that, Lady Katarina."

"What is with this 'Lady' business? I'm Kat or Ashowan to you— Piers, I already told you I'm not ready to be called Reyes!" she barked over her shoulder, sensing that the youngest Faucher son was going to make an unwelcome quip. "And Joshy? I'm not just saying that you can beat him to be nice. Want to know why?"

Despite her continuing efforts to cheer up her peer, Joshua's shoulders slumped forward even more.

"You're going to win, because if you don't give your brother a sound beating, I might actually kill him. You heard from Broghan about what happened today with his wife, right? I need you to beat that turd with legs so I'll feel less inclined to murder him. I feel like it would put a whole damper on my newlywed life if I was imprisoned for manslaughter."

Joshua didn't respond, but he did nod vaguely as though he were only half listening despite maintaining eye contact with her.

"You're a student of my father." Piers stepped over the bench and sat himself down on Joshua's other side. "You should know you need to have more pride and confidence, or it's an insult to him."

Joshua still didn't give any verbal response.

In an act of desperation, Kat decided to slightly change her tactic . . . and it was one she had seldom used in the past . . .

She was going to be a mite vulnerable to someone.

Seizing the front of Joshua's tunic, Kat jerked him over to her so that he was forced to look at her.

"You're going to win because I'm the one who challenged him to a spar, and if something bad happens to you, I don't think I'll be able to live with myself."

All levity had left her face, and the men around her collectively stilled.

Joshua blinked numerous times as though snapping out of a spell.

He swallowed. "You're right. I made you give this to me. I need to . . . to try."

"No, you need to Godsdamn win. I will not accept anything less," Kat demanded without trying to hide the desperation in her voice. "Now, I want you to tell me three great things about the way you fight."

"I can't even fight with a real sword yet, I—"

Kat's free hand came up and flicked Josh between the eyebrows. "I said three great things, not three pointless things."

"Hey, the wooden swords have points!" Piers called out with a good-natured smile behind Joshua.

Kat didn't bother looking at him. She knew Piers was looking all too pleased with himself over his terrible joke.

"Let's hear it, Ball."

"I-I'm fast."

"Damn right you are. What else?"

"I'm good at bruising my opponent's fingers."

"Absolutely."

"I . . . I . . ." Joshua faltered.

"When your back is against a wall, you find a way, and you fight."

Everyone turned at the sound of Faucher's voice.

Kat beamed at her teacher, who, while vertical and donning his official military uniform, chest plate, cape, and all, was notably pale and perhaps even a little green.

However, his words distracted anyone else from making such an observation.

Faucher stepped over to the young man, who stared dumbly up at his teacher as though he were shocked that he'd even shown up.

"I do not accept just any student Captain Orion sends me. I pick the ones I think show the greatest potential, and I knew you had it when I found out how you had started learning the sword three years ago under self-study. And in the first year when your brother discovered what you'd been doing? I heard how he beat you to the point of being bedridden for a week. Yet you still picked up the sword and continued to learn."

Joshua's eyes started to mist.

"Joshua Ball, your mother told me all this, and that is why I agreed to teach you in secret. Your brother trapped you, and you fought and clawed your way out to make your own life. You want to be a knight, and you want to be free from your brother. Win or lose today, I can promise you will still have your first wish granted. You will still be free from the Ball household. As my student, regardless of the outcome, you have that. However, if you *win*? You will have begun to build a life that is entirely of your own doing that I have nothing to do with. Today will be the day you start grasping what you've always wanted."

Faucher clenched a fist in his student's face, his leather gloves creaking in the cold, but Joshua's attention was enraptured.

"Now, Ball, do you think you can win?"

His throat bobbed. "I do."

"I can't hear you," Faucher rumbled.

"I can win."

"Louder."

"I'm *going* to *Godsdamn win!*" Joshua was breathing heavily, and snot dribbled from his nostril from the cold, but the fire in his eyes, the hoarseness of his voice, and his tightened fists showed that he finally believed the words he was nearly shouting.

Faucher gave a brief half smile of approval. "Good. Now, we will discuss what I remember about your brother as a swordsman. Unfortunately, he doesn't have any injuries I'm aware of that we can exploit, but you might be able to make him sloppy by taunting him."

Joshua flinched.

"Faucher, what if *I* annoyed him from the sidelines?"

"You aren't supposed to make any sounds from the sidelines," Faucher reminded the redhead with narrowed eyes.

"We're still doing that? But Eric shouted at me from the sidelines during my spar!"

Her teacher blinked. "No one noticed."

He genuinely appeared to have no idea that it had happened.

Kat threw her hands in the air in exasperation. "I swear, I can never get away with anything."

Faucher ignored her and returned his attention to his student. "If you don't think you can insult him while fighting . . . aim for his joints. Small hits should help loosen the grip on his sword, and as you recounted earlier, you're fast. You should be able to avoid getting hit long enough to bruise his hand."

Joshua lowered his gaze thoughtfully as he listened and turned over the information in his mind. It seemed like a fitting plan . . .

Movement by the entrance to the courtyard to the group's left drew everyone's attention upward.

There, Harriod Ball strode in, a haughty eyebrow raised as he refused to look toward his half brother, and behind him, an array of knights and noblemen that they could assume were his friends.

Joshua's hands started fidgeting in his lap, prompting Kat to reach out and wrap an arm around his shoulder, pulling him closer to her so that her next words couldn't be overheard by anyone.

"Remember . . . I wasn't jesting. Win, or I'll have to kill him, and if I have to kill him . . . well . . . promise me you'll visit me in jail sometime. Oh, and if you need an insult? Point out that his name is technically Harry Ball."

CHAPTER 16

A BROTHERLY BRAWL

Despite the arrival of Lord Harriod Ball and his friends, as well as the king himself, the courtyard remained just as quiet as it had been when it had only been Joshua sitting waiting.

Though Lord Ball was whispering to his friends and casting a smug grin in Joshua's direction.

"You know . . . you actually have a big advantage here," Kat mused.

She had her legs stretched out and crossed in front of her with her arms folded over her middle as she scowled at the men across the sparring space.

"How do you figure that?" Piers asked on behalf of Joshua, whose earlier bravado had faded following his half brother's appearance.

"He's going to insult you and be a real pigarse during the match—most likely he's going to cheat—don't be shy about groin shots, Joshy," Kat added. "But, back to the insult thing . . . You're used to it, right? He's been insulting you since you were a child."

"Since my mother was pregnant with me," Joshua clarified bitterly.

"Since before birth! So you already have heard it all from him. That means it doesn't matter what he has to say; you can focus on fighting— Ooh. Or you could smile at him. That always works for me when someone wants to be annoying. Fools don't know that I'm the *Queen* of Annoying."

Joshua at least cracked a small smile at her musings. "You're going to be an actual queen too."

"No, no. Queen of Annoying takes priority."

He laughed.

Kat grinned when she noticed him letting out a calming breath. Then turned to look over her shoulder at where Dante stood while his brothers were seated with Sir Cas.

"Where are Caleb and Broghan?"

"They said they had to finish something before coming," Sir Cas answered innocently.

Kat opened her mouth to question the Daxarian knight further only to be interrupted by Lord Ball rising from his seat.

"Your Majesty, might I ask what we are waiting for?" he queried with his hand on his hip and his wooden sword tapping the stones impatiently.

Brendan looked at the lord without an ounce of emotion. It didn't hint at any form of anger, or kindness . . . but that just made it all the more unnerving.

"We are waiting on the rest of Mr. Ball's team."

The nobleman's eyebrows twitched, but he didn't complain and instead gave a shallow bow.

Without Alina at the king's side, Lord Ball was far more malleable.

However, Brendan Devark himself tended to be more impatient.

As the evening progressed, the courtyard fell into the shadows of the night, though at the very least the sky above them was a clear starlit backdrop as opposed to the oppressive clouds that had plagued the lands for more days than many wished to count.

Kat's eyes began to glow, and stewards came out to light the braziers.

"Ashowan, question for you . . . If you see in the dark as clearly as you do in the daytime . . . how is it you can see the stars?" Piers wondered thoughtfully while they all stared up at the glittering abyss above them.

Kat smiled. "You know . . . no one has ever thought to ask me that other than my brother."

"Ah yes . . . the mysterious other Ashowan . . . Interested to meet him sometime . . . Anyway, what's the answer?"

"If I want to see the stars? Everything dims so that I can."

"You mean you can control when you do or don't see in the dark?"

Kat's mouth twisted and she gave a small shrug. "Only with the stars. I can't any other time. I'm not sure why."

Piers stretched his mouth and nodded along thoughtfully when the door to the courtyard nearest their side of the sparring ring creaked open.

The first person to come out was the unmistakable shape of Sir Cleophus Miller with Pina already on his shoulder, her eyes gleaming in the night.

"I swear, I feel like she's more his cat than mine," Kat muttered under her breath to Joshua and Piers.

The two smiled in response, but Joshua was soon distracted by the line of men that followed the eldest Miller son . . .

"Wait, who are—"

"By the Gods." Faucher gave a scoff of impressed disbelief. "Ball, do you know who all those men are?"

Joshua shook his head.

Dante, who had joined the group shortly after his father, stepped forward, his brows knit together but his eyes wide. "They are . . . They are all illegitimate sons of some of the noblemen in court . . ."

Joshua's jaw dropped. "What?"

Cleophus had reached them then, with Caleb and Broghan behind him.

Kat peered at the faces that paraded in.

Some were men wearing humble clothes, others were knights . . . and then . . . there was Mage Sebastian.

"Sebbie!" Kat hollered brightly and waved.

The mage stared back at her flatly before rolling his eyes and ambling his way over to her.

"Lady Katarina," he greeted dryly. "Your hair is a disaster."

Kat blinked and her hand fell. She had completely forgotten that Piers had mussed it, and so she set to untying her hair from its ponytail in order to fix it while still facing the mage.

"I haven't seen you in ages! How've you been?"

Sebastian sighed. "Oh, keeping plenty busy. Though it sounds like you've been just as active . . . Congratulations on your wedding."

The redhead nodded along while she proceeded to finish retying her hair. "Yes, yes. Whose idea was it to have all the illegitimate sons here?"

"His Majesty invited them. Not everyone came of course, as not everyone was fine with publicly revealing their birthright, but . . . well, here we are."

"What if Joshua loses though?" Kat whispered as inconspicuously as possible.

Sebastian raised an eyebrow at her. "I think the point is to show that we aren't going to take our beatings quietly anymore."

Kat widened her eyes and bobbed her head in approval. "That's fantastic."

"Your Majesty." Lord Harriod Ball's voice rang out once more, this time his anger was far more apparent. "Are we going to begin now?"

Brendan raised an eyebrow, his dark eyes all the more ominous as the torches that were lit by his chair flickered in their inky depths . . .

"I believe it is indeed time." The king turned toward Joshua.

The young man gripped his wooden sword tightly in his hand and gulped.

Kat and Faucher each clasped a hand on his shoulder.

"Remember the strategy," the military leader reminded evenly.

"Remember I don't want to go to jail."

Faucher looked at Kat, who stared back without elaborating.

Taking a deep breath, Joshua looked around at the faces that filled his section of the courtyard.

The illegitimate sons of noblemen, just like himself . . .

They stood with their shoulders back and their chins held high.

He nodded to them, then turned to the ring and stepped in.

Once more, the courtyard fell into silence as Harriod Ball sauntered in as well.

The two brothers strode to the center of the ring, and it was then that everyone could see the family similarities . . .

The same wide brown eyes, the same shape of their brows . . . Though Joshua's face wasn't as long as his brother's and he stood two inches shorter.

"Thanks for giving me the chance to bestow a proper greeting, *brother*. It's been too long." Harriod smiled coldly.

"I think you should save your thanks for Lady Katarina. Without her slapping you, we wouldn't be here."

Harriod's lip curled in a jeer. "You don't have her to hide behind here."

"I'm not hiding. Though if you prefer to fight her instead of me, let me know." Joshua knew his voice warbled, and his brother looked as though he were going to smirk when he heard it, but his eyes happened to dart over Josh's shoulder. When he found Katarina glaring at him with her arms crossed and her aura flickering around her angrily, he swiftly returned his attention to his opponent. The woman looked fully prepared to snap his neck.

"Witches are demons. Glad to see you've sold your worthless soul . . . I'm sure our father would've been wonderfully disappointed."

"Not as disappointed as he would've been after he'd found out you've been married for five years without an heir."

Harriod backhanded Joshua in the blink of an eye, but the young man had been watching every twitch in his brother's body, and so instead of a full-contact hit, he leaned back and found himself only grazed.

Joshua drew out his wooden sword and backed up a step.

Harriod lifted up his own but remained in place. To some, the nobleman may have looked casual and unguarded, but the spacing and angle of his toes told the more seasoned audience members better . . .

Swinging his sword down with a substantial amount of his strength, Joshua aimed for his brother's exposed right knee.

Harriod didn't bother blocking it—as he proceeded to simply punch Joshua in the face.

However, he had underestimated Joshua's aim and let out a yelp while stumbling as the wooden sword cracked smartly against his kneecap. This in turn gave Josh a chance to recover from the blow.

Wiping the blood from his nose, Joshua readied himself again. For some reason, getting punched in the face made him feel more assured in himself, as though the hit wasn't as excruciating as he had been anticipating it would be.

He swung again toward the outside of his brother's right knee, but this time he kept his elbow up to guard his face.

Harriod used the opportunity to swing his own wooden sword brutally into Josh's exposed side, immediately winding him . . .

But not before Josh once again landed a hit on Harriod's knee.

"GODS—" the nobleman blurted as he half stumbled away, his leg throbbing in the worst way possible.

From the sideline, Kat grinned while Faucher didn't dare move a muscle as he watched.

He could tell Harriod hadn't been taking the match seriously but that the current state of his leg was making him change his outlook . . .

Joshua shifted the grip on his sword and noted that there was a small, sharp pain with every inhale he took radiating from the ribs his brother had just hit.

He did his best to shove that detail out of his mind. He needed to get two hits in. One to make sure he fully fractured Harriod's knee, and one blow to his brother's head to ensure a win.

Harriod turned his body, protecting his injured right side by leading with his left foot, meaning his weight was distributed differently, and his eyes had turned murderous.

Sensing what was happening, Joshua turned his position to match his brother's, and he didn't shuffle forward as he had before. Instead, he approached slowly . . . carefully . . . If he moved quickly enough at the last moment, he could at least throw Harriod off-balance . . .

Two heartbeats passed, Joshua's back foot planted itself and spread evenly in his boot to steady himself . . . then he lunged. He swung high instead of low, but Harriod had been prepared for either attack. He knocked the sword down to the ground with his own downward parry, which also pitched Josh forward.

With his body hunched forward in an unsteady position, Harriod wasted no time in crashing his fist against Josh's ear, then seizing him by the back of the tunic, dropping his own sword, and proceeding to punch his brother's groin.

Josh crumpled to the ground.

Panting, Harriod knelt his good knee on his brother's chest, pinning him on his back, and hit him again.

By that time, Josh was at least able to raise his arm up to block the initial punch, but Harriod seized his wrist and utilized his extra fifteen pounds, further incapacitating his half brother. The nobleman's left fist pulled back and crashed into the side of Josh's face.

Then he did it again.

The illegitimate sons on Joshua's side winced . . . It looked like a lost battle.

What had started as a duel ended up as nothing more than a brawl.

"To hell with this," Kat uttered breathily, her aura already rising.

Faucher turned to stop her, assuming she meant to jump into the ring.

"JOSH!" She shouted. Everyone leapt back as her magic surged out in a flare before dying back down. "PINA IS TOO PRETTY FOR JAIL!"

Everyone on Harriod Ball's side as well as the Troivackian king were too baffled to understand. What they couldn't see, however, was when Joshua's eyes snapped open at her call—a golden, magical ring that hadn't been there before encircled his pupils.

Harriod, momentarily distracted by this, was caught off guard when, with his free hand, Joshua reached up, seized Harriod's hair in a fistful, then used his entire body weight to throw his brother off him. In the next instant, he used his freed right heel to kick Harriod's damaged kneecap, but before the nobleman could even finish letting out another shout of pain, a strong uppercut set his teeth rattling while he lost his balance and fell onto his side.

Joshua wasn't finished. His eyes were wide and furious, his face pale under the splattering of his own blood. He seized his brother's tunic and punched him again, kneed his groin, then clambered on top of him and hit him over and over. His hits were not as strong as Harriod's had been, but the speed with which they were dealt dazed the nobleman too much to leave him time to react.

The flurry of motion was so fast, in fact, that it took everyone a moment to realize that Harriod was knocked unconscious.

"Mr. Ball!" the king called out.

Panting, Joshua stopped hitting his brother, but he still stared down at his bloodied face; Harriod's fine green tunic was still clutched in a death grip in his hand. His own eye was swollen, and his nose most likely broken, but as Josh looked down at Harriod . . . the man who had hated him, tormented him and his mother . . . His hands shook. He leaned down and screamed into Harriod's still face.

It rang out around the courtyard.

His pain, his grief, his desperation . . . It was a shout that ripped through a lifetime of suffering.

Joshua grew limp as he sat gasping atop his brother.

Then, Faucher's gentle hand appeared on his shoulder.

"You've won."

His lips quivering, Joshua rose to his feet, tears gleaming in his eyes as he glared at the men on the marquess's side, but they all either sneered or looked away in boredom.

Save for one knight . . .

"The witch! She cheated! She isn't supposed to shout during a spar!" He pointed at Kat accusatorily.

"I'm a woman! I get emotional!" Kat hollered back indignantly.

"Oh sure, that's helpful to your gender." Piers guffawed beside her.

"I'll take a hit for women if it means I don't have to apologize to that donkey-face."

"Fair enough."

The king stood from his chair, drawing everyone's eyes to him and calming the argument.

"There was no magical aura around Mr. Joshua Ball. His strength was not unnatural. I see no signs of magic use."

"Even if there were, *I'm* the one who challenged Lord Balls to a duel; it's only fair!"

"It's Lord *Ball*, Lady Katarina," Brendan addressed his sister-in-law sharply.

"What if I were talking about the two of them?!" Kat argued.

"That was an incorrect sentence structure then, and you should have specified for clarification," Mage Sebastian called from behind Kat.

Looking up to the sky and then over her shoulder, the redhead dropped her voice. "Will. You. Just. Be. Quiet?!"

The exchange was interrupted, however, when Joshua Ball stepped forward and faced the nobles who had sided with his brother, many of whom had tormented him countless times before. Then he looked to those who had come to stand in silent support. Then he bowed to the king.

"Your Majesty . . . I don't ask for much . . . *We* never ask for much." He gestured to his fellow illegitimate men. "We didn't even ask to be born to our parents, but our birthright or lack thereof doesn't mean we aren't going to create something honorable of our own. We should demand what is fair for our efforts!" Joshua's voice rose, the sheen in his eyes growing even brighter. "We have done nothing that should place the responsibility of our births on our heads. I'm going to fight, Your Majesty. For a proper place. A place of my own. Not my father's, not my brother's, mine. Can . . . Your Majesty . . . Can you respect that and acknowledge those efforts?"

Brendan stared down at the young man, who had a lone tear that had escaped his one good eye.

The king then proceeded to turn and peer at the noblemen on his left that were already laughing while glancing at one another. Then he looked to the right where the men supporting Joshua and Katarina stood stoically quiet, an air of pride and hopefulness emanating around them.

"It is a Troivackian ambition to declare you are going to fight for your power and your life. What's not to respect about that? I look forward to seeing who will turn the tide and who will remain as they are."

The vagueness with which the king spoke both confused and infuriated a number of people present since they couldn't be certain about what he meant, especially as the king then stood and unceremoniously took his leave.

It was over.

Joshua had won.

"DRINKS ON ME, LADS!" Piers hollered, shoving his fist in the air, and all at once, the men and Katarina broke out in a cheering ruckus before they poured into the sparring ring. Sir Cas and Conrad hoisted Joshua up on their shoulders.

"How are you feeling up there, Josh?" Kat shouted over the excitement as she skipped alongside her peer.

Joshua smiled and lifted his face toward the heavens. The look of peace and contentment he bore was a sight many of them would remember for the rest of their lives.

"I feel like . . . I can face every eighth, ninth, eighteenth, and nineteenth day of every new moon . . . and everything will be alright."

CHAPTER 17

PEACE OVER POTATOES

W hy am I carrying you again?"

"Because I'm tired."

"*You* were asleep when I got to our chamber. I haven't even *been* to bed yet."

"I'm still waking up," Kat mumbled into Eric's shoulder as she allowed her forehead to rest there as he carried her on his back to their destination.

The prince sighed while shaking his head wearily and hefting his hold behind the redhead's knees.

"I thought it was the wives who were supposed to take care of their husband's meals when they got home late at night."

"That was not my experience," Kat yawned back.

Chuckling dryly, Eric nodded to himself. "I suppose it wouldn't have been."

At last, the couple had reached the kitchens where Kat had persuaded her husband that they should go to have him cook his own late dinner/early breakfast of pancakes.

It was still cold and dark outside; the rest of the castle occupants were sound asleep in their beds, and so the pair got to experience the rare pleasure of solitude.

"If this keeps up, I'm asking Mr. Kraft about why you're so tired," Eric called back on a more serious note.

"It's 'cause I only went to bed an hour before you got back . . . an' . . ." Kat yawned again. "Because I'm still recovering after not sleeping for a month. I live like a normal person for a fortnight or so after."

Eric let out a sigh. That *did* make sense, but he couldn't help the paranoia brewing in his mind that she was pregnant with his offspring. Even

though it was still far too early to know such a thing yet, it occasionally
sauntered into his forethoughts.

Luckily for him, they had reached the kitchens, and surprisingly, there
wasn't a guard in sight.

It should've been their first clue that not all was as it seemed . . .

However, when Eric opened the door to the kitchen and found Finlay
Ashowan with a mixing bowl in hand, wearing a brown robe hanging open
while in relaxed trousers and a tunic, he was completely taken aback.

Fin blinked in bewilderment at Eric.

Eric gaped right back at him.

Kat let out a soft, sleepy moan into Eric's shoulder. "Are we there yet?"

The prince cleared his throat, prompting Kat to lift her head to see what
had stopped their progress, and upon seeing her father, regained a mite of
her strength to slowly slide off her husband's back onto her own two feet.

"Hello, Da," Kat greeted her father while putting her hands on her hips
and smiling wryly.

Fin casually noted his daughter wearing a similar sleep set to her husband, and that they both were in dark blue robes, then met Kat's gaze. Perhaps it'd been a gift from one of her fellow handmaidens . . .

"What're you two doing up?" the duke asked mildly.

"Eric didn't get back until now, so we were coming down for him to
cook," Kat explained briefly.

Fin's attention moved to the prince, whose expression had turned stony.
"What were you up to away from the castle?"

"That isn't . . ." Eric started to say, but his eyes fell to the house witch's
hands that were resuming mixing the food in the bowl he held, displaying
his usual habit of cooking while listening.

A small hitch climbed its way up the prince's throat. "The witness I
brought back from the duke's estate is a friend of mine."

"You didn't tell me about that." Kat looked at her husband interestedly.

Meanwhile, Fin had just dropped a dollop of butter into a frying pan,
and like magic . . . the smell had the couple's mouths watering in an instant.

"We've been a little busy," Eric reminded her while they proceeded to
make their way over to the kitchen table.

"That's true. So who is this person?" Kat and Eric slid into two of the
three kitchen chairs in front of the cooking table.

Had they always been there?

"Eli . . . Well, even I didn't know everything about him—nor do I know
everything now. Lad has a past he is rather adamant about staying the hell

away from. I first met Eli the second . . . or third? The third time I think that I was taken hostage to be ransomed. I had boarded with some Zinferan merchants, and we were heading back to their homeland, when the boat was taken by slave traders. Most of the men I was traveling with were killed, and I was taken onto the trader ship where they were already moving about fifteen people they had captured . . . Eli was one of them. He was the youngest one there, and I was given to understand he had been moved around a lot. To be honest, the slavers didn't seem all that inclined to sell Eli, and he never said why until more recently." Eric let out a long, weary breath. "Eli's a witch, *and* one of the Zinferan emperor's adopted children. If the rumors I've heard from the Zinferan court are any indication, I think it was one of the concubines who had him sold."

Fin had been looking at Eric with a mixture of alarm and shock as he shared the tale. "Gods. That poor boy."

"How old is he?" Kat asked while reaching out and casually gripping Eric's forearm.

A move that drew Fin's attention, but he didn't comment on.

"I was guessing around fifteen when we first met, so around sixteen or seventeen now."

"If the traders weren't interested in selling him, how did he fall into Duke Icarus's hands?" Fin asked with a furrowed brow.

Eric's mouth pursed thoughtfully. "When I left Eli . . . I'd put him on a boat headed back to Zinfera. I'd hoped that he'd maybe be able to return to his family and live his life freely again—I didn't know anything about him being a prince until I found him here in Troivack—however, I watched the boat explode. I didn't know they were carrying illegal moonshine, and I'm not sure what caused the fire, but I thought he died. Turns out the duke is the one responsible for the whole thing . . . He did it all to get his hands on Eli."

Fin straightened. "What is it about this boy that makes him so important?"

"Something about his magic . . . but he's like Tam. Doesn't want to talk about what his abilities are. He says it's because it's always brought him trouble. I've promised him that in exchange for helping us, we will give him a brand-new life. When we spoke today, it sounded like he wanted to go to Daxaria as soon as possible.

Fin let out a long breath as he molded in his hands what appeared to be shredded potatoes, which he then set into the frying pan and sprinkled with seasoning.

Kat's stomach rumbled loudly, making Eric shoot her a grin that she pretended to ignore.

"There is a lot of uncertainty around this Eli from the sounds of it. I'd be cautious about him," Fin mused aloud.

At first it looked like Eric wanted to argue the point, but he stopped himself as he rested his forearms on the table to look more directly at the duke.

"I agree there is a lot to be skeptical about, but . . . I still feel like I know his character. He and I survived some nasty scrapes, and he's saved my neck a time or two. Though there is one detail I haven't had a chance to talk about with His Majesty." Eric paused, and it was during this lull that Kat could see how tired her husband was. After all, he hadn't slept in nearly a full day . . . "Eli says the duke had arranged for him to kill me, and then he was supposed to be given to the devil. Of course that was before Eli knew it was *me* that he was supposed to murder."

Fin didn't say anything but listened intently as he flipped the potato pancakes, and the pan sizzled seductively as the faint scent of onions that must've been mixed in with the fare wafted over the small group.

"So Eli can testify against the duke." Kat sat up straighter, her eyes widening excitedly.

Eric winced and shook his head slowly. "The word of someone who's been enslaved against that of a duke won't go far in this court. It'd be better if Eli would let us announce he is technically royalty, but he refuses no matter what protection we promise. At the very least, he was able to let us know about the mercenaries and where a couple of the groups that were hired to add momentum to the rebellion were hidden. Because he received a higher education, he can point us in the right direction to gain more information about the duke."

Kat's shoulders slumped back down.

"His Majesty already sent a group to the enslaved people at the duke's estate. These are the people I wasn't able to properly free because we were being hunted the entire way back." Eric rubbed his eyes before a yawn escaped his mouth.

"Do you want me to give you a piggyback ride upstairs after food?" Kat asked sincerely while reaching out to rub her husband's back.

"Maybe. Or I might just fall asleep on this table," he managed, his eyes watering from the intense stretch of the yawn.

"It sounds like you've been working a lot." Fin's voice was quiet, and his gaze soft on the prince, a great deal of emotion brewing in his chest.

Eric met Fin's eyes, but the prince's feelings could not be gleaned by the house witch in that instant.

Instead of commenting on the tension, Fin turned around and procured three plates already filled with the potato pancakes topped with sour cream and chives. Thick sausages that neither Kat nor Eric had seen him cook were packed on the side of each plate with a healthy spoonful of sauerkraut.

The couple stared at the meal dazedly.

While his food was openly marveled, Fin set two forks beside their plates.

"What about you, Kat? What've you been up to today since I last saw you?"

"You mean when I had to remove my teacher from your arms so he could sleep off his drink?"

Fin cleared his throat with a vague smile before he rounded the table to pick up the third chair and bring it around so that he could eat his own meal facing the couple.

"Today I— Oh Gods. I've missed this," Kat burst out with her cheek stuffed with food. Her eyes fluttered closed as she savored the otherworldly tastiness of her father's cooking. "Mm . . ."

She didn't speak for a long while as she chewed her food. Fin smiled into his own plate as he took a couple bites.

Eric said nothing, but he was eating with great enthusiasm.

"Well . . . I registered most of the women who want to start learning self-defense, though it is a terrible idea for me to teach them. I have no gauge of what is normal for a person or not, but I guess I understand that His Majesty is thinking about what would make the women most comfortable . . ." Kat waved her fork and continued, "Honestly, the corridor was packed, so I'll have to finish taking their names later today. Though I wish there was more I could do about Harriod Ball's wife wanting to learn. She was there yesterday, and she seemed so earnest about it . . . then he had to come and be donkey dung about the whole thing."

"Oh! How did the match between him and Joshua go?" Eric asked, sitting up straighter in his seat and having swallowed enough of his food to have been able to speak.

"I still can't believe it completely . . . He won! Honestly, when Lord Ball had him on the ground, I thought he was done for, and I would've felt absolutely awful that I was the one who challenged him to the spar in the first place—

"Why did you challenge someone to a duel?" Fin interrupted seriously.

Kat hesitated answering, but Eric leaned a little closer to her in silent support. The two shared a brief look.

"Ah, well . . . he was bullying two of my peers, and then he was openly rude to me. So I had the grounds to slap him with my glove, which I'm itching to do again just for his wife. Joshua asked that he get to be the one to fight in my stead though."

A funny look filled Fin's face then, as his eyes drifted back to his plate and he gave a small laugh to his food.

"What?" Kat questioned while feeling tenuously relieved that he wasn't lecturing her for putting herself in danger.

Her father leaned back in his seat and, after a breath, moved his warm blue eyes up to hers.

"I'm just . . . seeing a bit of myself in you right now."

Kat flushed and twisted her mouth in the sudden awkwardness that came in the wake of such a comment.

"Kat's incredible. Anything she's taken on, she's handled," Eric added proudly.

His wife blushed scarlet, then hunched over her food. "That's not true. Most of the nobility still think women are useless and witches are demons."

"Some are starting to question it though. Remember, you aren't finished here yet," her husband reminded with a smile, his eyes crinkling.

Kat refused to look at Eric. Her face was already on fire, and she knew if she were any better rested, her aura would be flaring to life.

Fin watched the exchange between them and felt his heart ache in his chest . . .

He saw it.

The second they had come in and he had seen them acting freely with each other . . . He understood how easy and natural it was between them. He saw how madly they loved each other, but he also witnessed the way they leaned on each other, both literally and figuratively. Then to hear the work they were doing . . . and how encouraging they were . . .

The house witch felt himself start to accept it then. The fact that for both his daughter and old friend, it was indeed, the perfect match.

CHAPTER 18

WOEFUL WORKLOADS

Kat stood in front of the crowd of women she had lined up in rows that reached all the way down to the other side of the courtyard, her hands clasped behind her back as she eyed them shifting uncomfortably.

She had insisted they wore trousers and tunics for the occasion, and they all looked completely ill at ease in the clothes.

Kat resisted smiling.

Soon. Soon you will all see how wonderful pants are. I will convert you all . . . to the way of pants . . .

"I think this is everyone. Do you know what you would like to start with?" Sir Cas strode up to join Kat's side and peered at the young women.

Half the courtyard was designated to the women's training, and there had even been screens erected to stop the men from leering at them indecently, which Kat admitted was most likely for the better as she stared at the sea of nervous faces, save for one.

Dana stood in the front row and smiled shyly at Sir Cas.

The knight cleared his throat and nodded back.

"Thank you."

Sir Cas turned to look at the redhead in confusion.

"When Faucher finds out his daughter signed up to learn self-defense, I'll need something to distract him from killing me. Bringing up how Dana is still *very* much so interested in you is perfect for that."

Sir Cas raised an eyebrow, his expression tensing.

His reaction made Kat hesitate. "Wait . . . Do you like her back?"

The knight dropped his chin wearily. "I'm trying to avoid hurting her."

Kat cringed. "Oh . . . Poor girl. That's even worse. Pull the arrow out before it gets worse. Sir Cas, the longer you avoid dealing with it, the worse it will get."

Sir Cas slowly turned to face her directly. "I sincerely hope you know how ridiculous a statement that is coming from you of all people."

"Oyy. I'm happily married now. You can't say crap about me anymore!"

The blond knight smiled and shook his head before looking back to the young women, who still were waiting on them expectantly in the wintry chill.

"What are we going to teach them first?"

"Maybe start working on their endurance? Young noblewomen like them probably don't have much strength. What do you think? Have them run laps, then maybe attempt a push-up or two?"

Sir Cas shook his head. "Remember, they are learning self-defense, not training to become soldiers."

Kat let out a soft grumble. "Well, some of them I think want to learn swordsmanship . . . How about this? We split them into groups. We'll just see who wants to try the harder stuff, and that group we'll assume intends to try training and learning more seriously."

Sir Cas thought about the idea, tilting his head back and forth as he did so. "Sounds good. Which group would you like to take?"

"I want the ones who'll try the hardest of course."

Sir Cas chuckled. "I suppose that makes the most sense . . . You haven't ever gone easy with your training."

Kat grinned, then turned to face the women while placing her hands on her hips.

"Alright, everyone! Those of you who don't know, this here is Sir Cas! He will be helping me teach you all today with the blessing of His Majesty the king! We would like to split you into two groups! Those of you who wish to simply learn a few defensive moves, you will organize yourselves in front of Sir Cas, and those of you who wish to build your strength and endurance to eventually learn more advanced techniques, you will line up similar to how you are in front of me!"

The group of women broke out in demure whispers.

Kat leaned back over to Sir Cas. "In Daxaria, this courtyard would be in absolute chaos by this point with all the women."

The knight nodded with a smile. "My sisters would be climbing the walls."

It took a bit of time, but eventually there were two distinct groups that had formed.

Surprisingly, while Kat's group was smaller than Sir Cas's, it wasn't by as large a margin as they had predicted.

Even *more* surprising yet, Lady Selene Icarus was in Kat's group.

Selene even stood in the front row beside Dana. However, Kat could tell from her haughty expression that she was there for the sake of being difficult.

Kat did her best to not get too excited over all the things she was going to make the noblewoman do . . .

"Alright, everyone, first thing's first, you're all weak as kittens, so I want you to do thirty laps around the courtyard."

"*Thirty?*" Dana exclaimed before pressing her lips shut again after she realized she'd accidentally spoken aloud.

"Ah . . . too much? Apologies. Not sure what's normal for other people . . . Fifteen it is!" Kat cheered happily and pointed to the edge of the courtyard.

Most of the women exchanged apprehensive glances but began to gradually sidle over to the edge of their designated space to start running.

Dana was the only one who darted there excitedly and instantly began jogging around the yard. Seeing her enthusiasm, a few of the noblewomen started to abandon their hesitations about the task and instead focused on the fifteen laps.

Lady Selene, however, sauntered up to Kat, her arms crossed and her chin raised imperiously.

Say what she could about the woman's intelligence, Kat had to admit that the Troivackian noblewoman definitely knew how to wield her presence.

"*I'll* run the thirty laps. Once Prince Eric sees that you aren't that special, you should start counting your days as his wife."

Kat had to purse her mouth to stop herself from laughing.

Damn . . . the woman was funny.

Not that she was aware of the fact, but she was.

Here I was thinking that I would have to tease her a bit, but she just does it all to herself. I have complete faith that Dana was right that thirty laps is too much, so . . . let's see how this goes.

With her tongue poking the inside of her cheek, Kat nodded along to what the noblewoman said.

"Sure, sure. Sounds like a fantastic plan. Off you go!" she was able to say with what she hoped to be an encouraging smile.

"Just so you know, I could also easily do this while dressed looking *proper!*" Selene cast back coolly over her shoulder as she walked away.

Kat let out a soft whimper as she tried not to burst out laughing yet again.

At this rate, she was going to have bruised ribs just from trying to contain herself when conversing with Duke Icarus's daughter.

After a moment, Kat let out a sigh, forcing herself to settle back down as she watched Lady Selene start to run, her long chocolate-colored hair only partially tied back and already becoming entangled in the wind.

"Aah, this is turning out to be a *good* day."

Fin sat in the king's office, his blue eyes glinting as he stared at none other than Mr. Kraft.

His villainous father's former assistant.

"It is good to see you again, Your Grace," the coven leader greeted with a bow.

"I hear things are rather dire for witches here in Troivack, Mr. Kraft," Fin responded frostily.

The coven leader bowed his head. "Yes, they are."

Fin leaned back in his seat. "I also hear you have been running tests on Witch's Brew to see if you can learn more about it."

"Yes, Your Grace."

"And you've been running these tests in a secret location with the mage, who is petitioning Troivack's court to become the first official Royal Mage in the last twenty some odd years since the Tri-War."

"That is also true."

"Where are these tests being run?" Fin asked while holding Mr. Kraft's gaze.

"In a private location that His Majesty has permitted to be kept a secret."

"I will be asking to meet with those who are running these tests," the duke informed Mr. Kraft tonelessly.

"That . . . I can understand why you may wish to, Your Grace, however —"

"My familiar, Kraken, has information regarding Witch's Brew that could be helpful. While I have yet to ask His Majesty about this matter, please prepare for me to join you come tomorrow morning."

Fin stood up as Mr. Kraft opened his mouth, presumably to object.

However, the look the redhead gave him had him clamping his mouth shut. In that moment, he looked a great deal like Aidan Helmer . . .

After saying his piece, Fin took leave of the office that the king had graciously allowed the two men to use for the sake of privacy, and he decided to make his way down to the training grounds to see his daughter.

The house witch knew he still owed Eric an apology, but the prince had slept in, and by the time he was up, Fin had already started working on a plan of action regarding the son of the Gods . . .

However, there was still the concerning matter of Likon.

After suggesting that the young man take time to come to terms with his feelings, Fin had not seen hide nor hair of him, and it was concerning the duke.

He let out a long breath while descending the last of the stairs to the first floor.

There were so many things he needed to do to keep everyone—his daughter in particular—safe. Ever since receiving the letter from the Troivackian king about Kat facing the devil and Eric's abduction, the words of the Gods rang in his ears . . .

A child of yours saves a being very dear to us.

Back then the hint had been perplexing, but now it was terrifying.

Just what could Kat do to save a being they cared about? Was that being the devil? Or was it someone else?

With his thoughts spiraling farther and farther down into the familiar abyss that was a parent's woes, Fin grew blind to his surroundings and consequently almost didn't see Eric, who stood in front of him, though the prince hadn't noticed him either.

Staring at the future king and halting in his tracks, Fin observed the way Eric had his head tilted and the way he was utterly captivated as he stared out the castle doorway. Without needing to look or ask, Fin already knew what the reason for such an expression was.

The duke's heart broke a little, but he smiled.

His daughter had found someone who loved her the way he'd wished someone would.

Swallowing the lump in his throat and blinking back tears, Fin stowed his hands in his pockets and finished his journey to the prince.

"Afternoon," the duke greeted before turning to look out at the courtyard that he discovered had been divided in half.

"Hi," Eric returned, snapping out of his trance.

Fin regarded the outdoor scene and noted that there were two groups of women: the ones who were running, and the ones who Sir Cas was instructing in the farthest corner of their designated space from the doorway to the castle.

He watched quietly as his daughter would occasionally shout at the group she was charged with, alternating between encouraging cheers or instructions on how to correct their running forms. Every single one of the women in her group was sweating and gasping for breath; some had already been forced to walk the remaining assigned laps, as their lungs protested too much against the activity.

"Looks like she has a good number of women here," Fin mused.

"Mm," the prince responded noncommittally.

The prince's response had Fin turning to face Eric more squarely as he let out a labored breath.

"Eric, I'm sorry."

Eric glanced at Fin emotionlessly before letting out a sigh of resignation.

"I know you are. I'm still not your biggest fan anymore, but . . ." He paused, molding the words in his mouth before releasing them. "We *are* family now."

Surprising the prince, Fin smiled. "That's more than I deserve at this time, but I'll take it."

"Look, I do understand you've had a lot of responsibilities on your plate since becoming ennobled, and really, it *is* well established that you only ever wanted to cook and just got this far to please your wife."

Fin nodded, still grinning as he watched his daughter.

"I see where you were coming from when you made your decision about me years ago back when you first found out my secret. It's just with more recent events that I— Why are you smiling?" Eric asked irritably.

Blinking and giving his head a shake, Fin closed his eyes and pinched the bridge of his nose.

"Right. Sorry . . . I just . . . It really did just dawn on me that you'll be returning to Daxaria and announcing to your court that we're officially related by marriage."

"And?"

"Between Mr. Howard and Lord Fuks, I can't help but wonder who'll have the better reaction."

Eric stared at Fin.

The prince tried to fight off the laughter that burbled up in his chest, but he couldn't help it. He succumbed to the humor and dropped his face to his hand.

"Alina has already offered me a substantial amount of gold to have his expression painted when he finds out. Truthfully? I'm convinced she only accepted our marriage because of Mr. Howard's pending reaction," Eric recounted between gasps.

Fin laughed harder.

While the prince kept trying to regain control, he found he simply couldn't help it. It felt too good to be able to laugh with Fin again . . .

"Oh Gods . . . I bet you three gold Mr. Howard quits on the spot," Fin gasped while wiping his eyes.

"I'll bet you five that he shouts a lot first."

"Mm . . . I don't know. I could see him more just stalking out of the room and straight to the wine cellars."

"Well, then I guess we have a bet." Eric offered his hand to Fin, and after giving it a meaningful glance, the house witch clasped it and gave it a firm shake.

While the duke still felt as though he were drowning in worries, at the very least, things were starting to look up when it came to his relationship with Eric Reyes, and that was no small matter.

So, the two men continued watching Katarina coach the young women who had unfortunately fallen under her command, both silently cheering her on, and both content with the company they shared.

That is until Fin leaned over and whispered, "Eric, you like a giiiiirl."

CHAPTER 19

TEACHABLE TIMES

K at let out a sigh of pleasure as she turned her face to the sky with a beaming smile and closed her eyes.

She relished in the moment.

Savored it just as much, if not more, than when she consumed her father's peach rum pie . . .

Though she had no fear that the moment would be over too soon.

Oh, absolutely not.

For it was only the beautiful beginning.

Clasping her hands behind her back, Kat skipped over to a particular corner of the sectioned off courtyard.

"Oh, Seleeeene," she called out in a singsong voice, her red ponytail bobbing as she pranced.

The Troivackian noblewoman clutched a corner of the barracks wall, her legs visibly trembling as her breaths rasped.

"Darling, what lap are you on?" Kat asked sweetly.

"T-Thirty."

"Now, now. I only counted twenty-three, and my trusty helper, Sir Cas, says the same."

"Y-You . . ." Selene gasped, her face flushed and her eyes tearing in the cold. "Wench."

"Hey now, that's hardly fair. *You* volunteered to come today, and then you *also* volunteered to join my group, and then you just outdid yourself *yet again* and insisted on running the thirty laps!" Kat smiled wolfishly at the woman whose hair had been perfect at the start of the training, but now frizzed and waved out from her head wildly.

"Y-You can't run this . . . either," Selene started to say as her knees buckled dangerously.

"Love, I ran throughout the night the very first day of training, and it felt like a splendid warm-up. I'm not human though, so you're comparing a chicken to a horse. You're the chicken in this analogy. Just making sure that's clear."

Selene tried to glare, but the stitch in her side had her pitching forward. Kat caught her and threw her arm over her shoulder to start leading her back to rejoin the others who had finished their laps and were cooling down with some stretches that Kat had assigned.

"I don't . . . need . . . your help . . ." Selene began coughing.

"Right. You may want to have a warm bath, but if you can handle it? Jump into a cold one and go back and forth. Honest to Gods, it will save you from more muscle pain than you can imagine. Oh, also drink some warm honey water and eat some chicken. For your throat and for your nutrition. Very important for training."

"I won't listen to you . . . demon."

Kat stopped and turned to stare at the woman who, as they had started to move, had passively allowed herself to be half hauled by the redhead.

"See, why do you feel the need to hate me? I personally would love to see what you could accomplish with that stubborn nature of yours. As someone with a tenacity that has been called 'outrageous but effective' herself, you have my regards."

Selene's perfectly sculpted brows twitched, and it was then Kat realized that the woman hadn't entirely understood everything she said, so she tried to speak more simply.

"You like a challenge and don't like losing. I respect that about you and want to see you become one hell of a fighter. It'd probably also help you feel calmer on the whole. Trust me, it's helped *me* a lot."

"You think I want to destroy my future to sweat and, and, and train with nothing but poverty awaiting me at the end of the day?"

"Train up, then come to Daxaria. I'll hire you. No poverty necessary. If it's what you want? Go for it."

"You think I need *your* help? Are you looking down on me?!" Selene seethed while rasping. Her throat was raw from her heavy breathing in the cold.

"Not at all. You strike me as the type who'd bite a man's ear off, and I'm given to understand that here in Troivack, that is high praise. I consider that high praise as well, but it isn't quite the same to most Daxarians."

The noblewoman looked torn between wanting to hold on to her haughty anger and believing Kat . . . so she opted to fall into silence.

When the two women reached the rest of the students, Kat unceremoniously dumped Selene in the back row, making her release a squawk of surprise. The redhead proceeded to stroll through the rows of panting and sweating young women, grinning without a second glance back. She hadn't *entirely* reformed into a mature woman . . .

"Everyone, I think that should be it for today. Tomorrow, I will have you all begin with push-ups, sit-ups, and *then* have you run your fifteen laps. Any questions?" Kat asked loudly while giving a small smile of respect to Dana, who stood looking energized. Most likely thanks to all her walks and playing with her dogs, she was significantly fitter than the rest of her peers.

"Can we see you fight again?" one of the women called out despite still being doubled over.

By this time, Sir Cas was making his way over to her with his own group following behind.

Kat raised an eyebrow with a grin.

"Lady Talia, was it? You get bonus points for enjoying violence."

The noblewoman shifted awkwardly as a few of the women around her avoided making eye contact, though there were several discreet shared glances from under long dark eyelashes.

Their reactions told Kat that they, too, wished to see it again.

"Alright, Sir Cas?"

"Yes, Lady Katarina?"

"Would you like to spar with me for our students?"

The knight smiled, and out of the corner of her eye, Kat spotted several noblewomen lean toward one another and share interested glances as a result.

"A bit more space if you don't mind." Kat put her hands up and tapped the air, prompting the group to back up a step, all of them looking excited for what was about to happen.

"Did you want to use your magic?" Sir Cas murmured quietly.

Kat pondered the request while cracking her neck. "How about I try without it first and then introduce it for a second round."

"It's nearly the dining hour. How many rounds do you want to go?" The knight looked wary.

"Why? You're getting tired already?"

"And a little hungry, yes."

"You're too young to be worn out already! But fine. Let's just do the two rounds."

Smiling again, Sir Cas gave a slight bow of appreciation before addressing their audience.

"We will spar for two rounds. The first round, Lady Katarina will not use her magic, and the second, she will show how, with it, she can easily overcome me."

By then the women had straightened up and were watching, perfectly captivated.

Both Kat and Sir Cas rounded toward each other and drew their swords.

They tapped their blades together twice and lifted them to take their starting positions.

Then, feeling a mite emboldened by the admiration directed at her, Kat lunged forward.

Sir Cas, she realized instantly, was not going to treat the match as he did their training. When she attacked, he cast off her blade and, faster than a blink, was already aiming for her throat on a backhand horizontal stroke. Kat barely leapt back out of the way.

He had never fought so efficiently with her before.

Kat regarded him in silent question as she backed up a step, but she saw no emotion in his blue eyes . . .

She didn't get the chance to think about this unnerving change in him either, because it was Sir Cas's turn to come after her. He kept knocking her blade out farther from her body, but he was able to recoil tightly so that he was backing her up while hitting closer and closer to her hand, bearing down on her, the sing of steel and wind whirling around them. But in a single breath, they stopped.

Sir Cas's blade rested against her throat.

Kat swallowed with difficulty as she stared at her friend's face and the courtyard remained in suspended silence.

Then . . . the cold mask cracked, and Sir Cas was himself again. He smiled at Kat, though she could see the sheepishness in his eyes as he stepped back and offered her his hand.

She shook it.

"Er . . . Right. As you can all see, Sir Cas won that match. He *is* after all considered the genius swordsman of Daxaria!" Kat informed their audience while giving what she hoped was an easygoing smile.

The women were eyeing the two uncertainly.

With a wince and a contrite smile to Kat, Sir Cas stepped forward.

"I offer you all my apologies for that display."

The women collectively gasped as the knight bowed to them.

Not only were Troivackian men notorious for not apologizing, but apologizing to their womenfolk was practically unheard of.

"I especially am sorry to Lady Katarina." Sir Cas bobbed his head to her. "The reason I fought that way was both to demonstrate to you all as well as Lady Katarina that there are times when you *will* be faced with someone more skilled than you. It will be uncomfortable, and they will try to corner you. I want you all to see that Lady Katarina still fought. She didn't cower, and she knows the risks. My hope is that you all saw that she held her ground. She will learn from this exchange especially, as I have never fully faced her as a true opponent before as I am still technically her teacher, and I thought this would motivate her to learn from her mistakes and think on how to improve for the next time we spar."

Kat gaped at the knight.

He *had* to be bullshitting them. Or maybe he really was trying to inspire them all in his own roundabout way . . . ?

Had she perhaps caught Sir Cas off guard, and he'd just fought her instinctively?

"Alright, now . . . I'd like you all to see how, regardless of my own skill set, when Lady Katarina uses her full abilities, I don't stand a chance."

"Yes, and . . . the reason *I'm* showing you that is . . . I want you all to get used to seeing magic. I'm not an arsehole who is here working for devils or demons. I want to protect people, and I am perfectly capable of it."

The women didn't look as convinced when she offered her explanation as they had with Sir Cas's.

However, Kat didn't care. She would wear them down. She would show them her magical prowess over and over until they didn't give it a second thought.

She sheathed her sword.

Sir Cas raised an eyebrow but seemed to understand what it was she had in mind, as he gave a slow nod of permission.

Kat closed her eyes.

Some of the noblewomen shuffled a little farther away from their teachers.

It was Sir Cas's turn to attack her first with a downward strike. Only Kat's aura flared to life, making a couple women shriek, and when her eyes opened, they were filled with golden light.

Kat seized Sir Cas's sword arm with her left hand, and his throat with her right. She hoisted him in the air and proceeded to chuck him to the ground like a child that had become bored with their toy.

Then, just as quickly as it all transpired, Kat's eyes returned to normal, and her aura shrank back down.

"Feeling alright there, Sir Cas?" she queried good-naturedly.

"I know I said I wanted to end things quickly . . . but I didn't realize I'd have to become acquainted with the cobblestones as a result," the knight grunted as he sat up.

If Kat were honest with herself, part of the reason she had been so openly brutal was because she was still more than a little put off by Sir Cas's display earlier.

Even so, she offered her hand to him and helped him stand.

"Right. I think that is all for today, everyone. Remember. Baths. Warm water, then cold, and warm honey water to drink. If you can eat a good serving of meat in the near future, that would also be in your best interest," Kat informed them seriously.

"What about moonshine for the pain?" one woman called out.

Kat craned her neck over the crowd to grin at the one who asked.

She couldn't remember the woman's name, as she had been in Sir Cas's group and not her own.

The redhead pointed at her. "You. What's your name?"

"Lady M-Miriam Shelby."

"Lady Miriam Shelby, you and I should be friends. Feel free to drink with me anytime you want."

The young woman smiled shyly.

Sir Cas chuckled at Kat's side as she proceeded to wave her arms theatrically toward the doorway.

"Oh! And spectacular work today, everyone!" she hollered as some of the women limped their way up the steps to the castle while others tried to gracefully lean on an arm of a friend.

It was as she was watching them disappear inside that Kat realized she had had another audience she hadn't noticed.

There stood her father and her husband side by side, wearing two vastly different expressions.

Her father was staring at her lost in thought, but there was an intensity in his gaze that told Kat there was something he needed to tell her . . . Eric, on the other hand, was grinning proudly at his wife.

She let out a breath and tried to take comfort in the prince's positive reaction to her teaching.

Sir Cas leaned in closer.

"Now, *that* is the actual reason why I did what I did. I wanted to show off how good of a student you've become in lasting against me for as long as you did."

Spinning around, Kat stared at Sir Cas in shock, but this time when she looked at him, she saw the sincerity in his eyes.

Momentarily speechless, Kat rounded on him, her hands finding her hips.

"Wait just a Godsdamn minute. You've been holding back this *entire* time I've been learning from you?! I demand a rematch!"

CHAPTER 20

LIKON'S LAMENT

Likon sat in the tavern, facing the door and tucked away in an inconspicuous corner with his hood drawn.

Thankfully, given that it was winter in Troivack and the tavern itself was quite drafty, no one thought him all that suspicious.

A half empty bottle of Troivackian moonshine sat on the table, its green glass gleaming in the pale light from the window near the door.

Even the fire in the hearth behind Likon struggled to stay lit in the chill.

This is like a Daxarian winter . . . Strange, he thought numbly.

It honestly reminded him of the winter his parents had passed away . . .

It had been horribly cold and dry. That year hadn't been kind to the crops either, and so they had gone to sleep most nights hungry and awakened the next day weak and dizzy.

It was amongst the faded days that the fever had quietly come.

First his father, who stayed in bed while his mother with stiff fingers tried to finish enough mending for the local tailor to earn coin for food. Meanwhile, Dena would brush her hair incessantly, as she was desperately trying to catch the eye of the butcher's son.

Likon had noticed his mother's glassy eyes the day before he listened to his father's death rattle.

His father was a man of few words, yet he'd always exuded a warm presence. His smile was forever burned in Likon's mind . . . open and infectious. While slow in his steps, always steady . . . and yet, for all he meant to Likon, he had slipped away in a single breath that night. It was as though he were as inconsequential as a snowflake in the thick banks outside their house.

That had made the hurt inside Likon even worse.

That someone so important could leave as though it were nothing.

His mother was next . . . but she had seemed to have had a sense of what was in store after having buried her husband in frozen ground, placing a pauper's grave marker above.

She had told her children the name of the tailor she worked for that very day. Explained to Dena that he should be able to take her on as an apprentice, and if they ever lost their home and needed a place to live, to speak to him. She insisted that the tailor would at the very least let them sleep in his shop foyer until the spring.

In the days following, with tears running down her flushed cheeks, she told them over and over how she loved them, held them close, whispered their favorite stories when she could force herself to remain awake . . . She even sobbed in her weakened state how she wished she could've done more for them.

A few days later, she had left in the same insultingly quiet way her husband had.

Likon cried endlessly. He raged endlessly too . . .

It was in the midst of their grief when Dena had grown too desperate and made a mistake with the butcher's boy.

One that had her shunned from the tailor's foyer and scorned by all their parents' friends. Likon's unquenchable anger didn't help matters either.

Despite this, Dena remained strong, rummaging through waste piles for scraps and huddling in the corner at night with Likon in their rundown, cold house. Perhaps in two moons they'd have made it to spring and could travel to a new town to start over.

However, when Likon then came down with the fever, she wasted no time in going to Madam Nonata's in Austice. She didn't try to hold out or hope for something better.

She refused to risk letting her final family member go so easily.

In a week she was hired, primed, and presented to the customers.

Likon had recovered from his sickness thanks to the doctor she was able to afford after her first night of work, but he was never the same. While his sister was accepted with open arms into the brothel, Likon, on the other hand, for all his outbursts and defiance, was not. Perhaps if it had only been his grief that reared its head, then the women would've been more understanding . . .

In a year's time, he decided he wanted a job. He would work and make his own way. He'd find a place where people wanted him around because he was useful, and where he could be as angry as he wanted all by himself.

But then . . .

A pair of stunning golden eyes had found him, and his life was filled with a warmth he hadn't known since a time long before that awful winter where death's carriage had come and gone two times too many.

"Kat . . ." he murmured presently, the lump in his throat returning yet again.

She was taking her warmth with her as she drifted toward her new life . . .

Fin had been right.

It was her choice, and one she had a right to make even if it *was* most likely a mistake.

But . . . even though Likon knew she loved him like a friend and the duke and duchess had been the parent figures he had desperately needed, he was starting to feel that same chill again. The comforting clamor that surrounded Kat was growing muffled, and it yet again brought forth that same rage he had felt all those years ago.

Rubbing his hand through his hair, Likon then pinched the bridge of his nose, forcing the tears to stay back.

"U-Unlce Likon?"

Looking up, Likon let out a small breath and managed a half smile. "Hey there, Tommy. How've you been?"

Thomas Julian, the prince's assistant, fidgeted nervously and glanced around the tavern once before sliding into the booth across from his uncle.

"I can't be long. I was only able to come out as His Highness had an errand for me."

Likon's grip on his cup's stem tightened at the mention of the Daxarian prince.

"How've you been doing?" he asked instead while successfully shoving his emotions to a locked space in his chest.

"I've been well. His Highness doesn't criticize me much and is relatively polite—sometimes a little terse, but nothing awful at all."

"Is he still a drunk who takes Witch's Brew?" Likon didn't quite succeed at keeping the bitterness out of his voice.

However, his nephew was too jumpy about deviating from whatever his previous errand was to properly register it.

"No," Thomas Julian whispered while looking around them warily. "After he was kidnapped, he hasn't taken any Witch's Brew, and he rarely drinks . . . Well, compared to how he used to anyway. At least two or three nights a week he imbibes, but nowhere near the same amount. He's always in possession of his faculties when he does too. But, Uncle, there is one thing you didn't know about."

Likon's eyes hardened and flit to his nephew, making the young man momentarily freeze under the unfamiliar expression on his family member's face.

"Y-you didn't know about the soldier's spells."

Likon blinked in surprise, then frowned, making him look significantly more like his usual self.

"No. I can't say I knew about that. Are you . . . Are you certain that's what it was?"

Thomas nodded enthusiastically. "I've no doubt about it. He kept talking about digging holes . . . He's had a few spells, actually . . . Sometimes he's screaming for someone named Eli. Other times he's talking about how he trusted someone . . . He's almost always violent during them."

Likon leaned in intently. "Tommy, has he hurt you?"

"N-No. He . . . I mean he's come close a few times, but Leader Faucher told me certain Daxarian songs work at calming him down."

Likon let his shoulders slump in momentary relief.

He really wouldn't have forgiven the royal bastard if he'd harmed a hair on Tommy's head.

Then the realization dawned on him.

"Would Ka— Lady Katarina be in danger?"

Thomas couldn't help but smile as he shook his head, further mystifying his uncle. "*Him* hurt *her*? She's all he really cares about. Plus, if you've ever seen her fight, you'd know she can handle herself. Her magic can be terrifying, but she has gotten a lot better at controlling it."

Likon settled back down.

It still wasn't exactly what he wanted to hear, but the most important thing was that it sounded like at the very least Tommy and Kat were safe. For the time being, anyway . . .

"Anything else you'd like to report?" Likon took a hearty drink from his cup.

"I don't think so, Uncle."

Likon grunted, the liquor pleasantly burning his tongue.

After swallowing, he nodded his head distractedly. "Well, thank you for making time to see me with your busy schedule. Your mother sends her love."

Tommy beamed and, with a bob of his head, set to sliding out of the booth and making his way to the door.

As Likon watched him go, weaving in and out of the gigantic clientele of the tavern, he found himself smiling. "Still hasn't hit his growth spurt. Poor kid . . ."

He was just beginning to reach into his pocket to pull out his coins to leave on the table, with the intention of consuming the rest of his drink up in his room—though seeing his nephew had perked up his mood considerably—when two other figures slipped into the seat across from him.

Looking up, Likon was startled into putting his hand on his dagger.

"Hello there," the man on the right spoke. He wore a ruby red velvet coat, and gold earrings dangled from multiple holes in his ears. While he appeared perfectly human, his colorful appearance and something in his mannerisms gave him an otherworldly air . . .

Then again, his oddities were diminished by the massive being that sat beside him with purple eyes containing three pupils in each one. The tall being had long, light purple hair tied back and wore a midnight-colored robe of sorts.

"My name is Ansar, and I was hoping you might be able to spare me some of your time to hear a proposition," the man in the red coat and earrings informed him.

Likon studied the pair carefully before giving a scoff. "Are you two working for the devil?"

It was when Likon's gaze casually drifted over to the door that he realized something even stranger was happening around him . . .

Everyone was frozen.

No one moved.

Everyone in the tavern had halted in their tasks and stared blindly ahead of themselves.

Likon's eyes darted to the window and found that even the first flakes of snow that had started to fall hung suspended in the air.

"We do not work for the devil. Rather, our own mistress is trying to bring about his banishment from this world," Ansar explained smoothly.

Likon did his best not to stare around in open wonder.

He had seen magic before . . . but nothing like this . . .

"What do you want?"

Ansar tilted his head gracefully. "We are looking to minimize the damage of accomplishing such a thing. As you can imagine, the origin of all evil will not be cast out of this world without a fight."

Likon's eyes narrowed. "That still doesn't explain what you want with me."

"Impudent, human," the creature with purple eyes muttered.

Likon stared icily at the being, who openly glowered back at him.

"No need for hostilities. It would be much better for us all to be on the same side. What my mistress wants is to see the house witch and his family out of Vessa. Perhaps even back in Daxaria."

Straightening his shoulders, his hand still casually resting on the hilt of the dagger at his side, Likon's lip curled.

"You know, you might be surprised at the number of times I've had people request this of me. If you want Duke Ashowan and his family uninvolved, it means you aren't up to anything good."

Ansar sighed with a note of weariness. "I already told you, we're trying to prevent casualties. Surely you know the devil's interest in the duke's daughter, and furthermore, he even has the prince working for him as an informant."

Likon felt a muscle in his cheek twitch. "If you think I can't see through your attempt to manipulate me, you'd be wrong. But you have my regards for figuring out that His Highness annoys me."

"His Highness met with the devil in his carriage a day or two ago. Try asking him directly about it. See what he says." Ansar shrugged while folding his arms.

He appeared completely at ease with no indication of lying . . .

"Are you a witch?" Likon wondered aloud while succumbing to the urge to look around at the tableau surrounding him.

"No, no. This is the work of our mistress." The note of reverence in Ansar's voice wasn't lost on Likon.

"She can stop the flow of life?"

The imp grinned menacingly. "So narrow-minded. This isn't even the true scope of her power. This is merely thanks to a creation of hers that—"

Ansar held up his hand, stopping his companion's speech.

"Our mistress is indeed powerful. However, the Ashowan family has no place in this battle. It has been planned for decades, and they just happened to stumble into the situation. We are merely trying to protect them."

Likon turned the words over in his mind. He fixed his gaze on the two beings before him and didn't so much as blink as he made his observations and conclusions.

"I'm not a witch myself. The connection to nature and the like is far beyond my humble, human scope, but there is one thing that is obvious to even someone as powerless as myself." Likon pulled his coins free from his pocket and leisurely flicked one copper down after the other. "The Ashowans are never involved in something 'by accident.' Particularly when it is a matter so closely tied to the Gods."

Likon stood and faced the stairs of the inn. "I am going to go up to my chamber and close the door, and after that, I never want to see you again."

"Would you say the Ashowans care about you?" Ansar's voice was a little louder than before.

Likon rolled his eyes to the ceiling and turned himself back around. He didn't bother hiding his irritation. "They do. I'm not of their blood, but I'm no less of their home, and I can't be convinced otherwise. Even if I am lonely, I do know beyond a shadow of a doubt I am not alone."

In that moment, his own words firmed something in Likon's heart . . . Something he had been forgetting in the face of the blinding pain and fury of seeing Kat with Eric.

Ansar rose to his feet with his companion following. "A very wonderful thing for you and quite useful given the corner you've now placed us in. I'd apologize, but quite honestly it is for your own good."

Likon drew his blade in a flash, but it didn't matter.

Everything around him was suddenly spinning in a whirl of colors, though he could still see Ansar before him, watching him calmly; a dosed rag appeared out of nowhere over Likon's nose and mouth.

With his consciousness fading, he managed to stab backward in his struggle. The creature with the purple eyes he had figured was the one behind him let out a yelp, but the cloth remained pressed to his face.

With one final, feeble attempt, Likon drew his other throwing blade, wanting to send it hurling into Ansar's chest . . . but his hands were already clumsy, and so it clattered to the floor as his world went dark.

CHAPTER 21

A MEETING OF MAGICAL MEN

F in eyed Mr. Kraft coolly as the carriage swayed back and forth.
Mage Sebastian sat on the opposite end of the bench and tried to not look at the fluffy black cat that watched him without blinking.

A dusting of snow lazily descended from the sky, its flakes occasionally made to glitter by the sun that was breaking through the rolling gray clouds above them.

"Mage Sebastian, how is your application to the court going?" the house witch asked calmly, though his gaze didn't move to the coven leader in any great hurry.

"Ah, it . . . It is going very slowly, Your Grace. In light of the magical beast sightings and the recent attack, paired with the Witch's Brew controversy, His Majesty thinks it'll be best if we wait until these things are dealt with before we push my official appointment, though I have been permitted to sit in on the general council meetings and some of the inner council meetings, as the noblemen are at least willing to listen to my input."

Fin raised an eyebrow and gave a slow smile. "Don't worry. I think of Her Majesty as a close family friend, and if she wants you as her Royal Mage, I'm sure we can make something work out with everything going on."

Both Mr. Kraft and Sebastian stiffened in alarm.

Was the duke aware he was insinuating that he had the power to move the entire Troivackian council to his will?

Seeing their reactions, Fin gave a mystifying smile, then glanced briefly at Kraken, who gave him a slow blink in response.

The carriage ride continued in silence for a little while longer, however, when the towers of Vessa gradually fell away and were replaced by frosted desert and snowcapped mountains, Fin observed the change of scenery curiously but didn't say anything.

Meanwhile, Sebastian was openly studying the duke.

"Is there something you'd like to say?" Fin's manner of speech turned casual, and it alarmed both the men into sitting up taller.

"It's just . . . Your Grace, you are a bit of an enigma. You are powerless here in Troivack, and yet you don't seem ill at ease. You are a hero and a noble who rose from a commoner status, and . . . and . . . you're Lady Katarina's father."

The last part of his musings made Fin blink rapidly before reaching up to rub the back of his neck. "What's strange about being her father?"

"I always assumed she'd just come into existence by an explosion of some kind, as she is now," Sebastian replied before he could stop himself.

Fin chuckled, and while still smiling and shaking his head as his thoughts turned to his daughter, responded to the mage's outburst, "I understand. Believe me, she has *always* made dramatic entrances. Even when we found out her mother was expecting, it was . . . quite the scene."

"I can imagine," Mr. Kraft added quietly.

Fin's easygoing attitude pulled to a swift stop as his attention returned to the Aguas coven leader.

"I've heard from Leader Faucher you've been instrumental in helping my daughter control her abilities, but there was something I'm surprised you didn't notice."

Mr. Kraft frowned. "I'm not sure I understand, Your Grace."

"You observed when you and I first met that my power feeds in an endless supply to the feelings and sentiments of those who share in my home. You say I theoretically had an endless power flow."

Mr. Kraft's eyes grew wide. "How did you . . . I said that to the former king! You weren't anywhere near us when that conversation took place!"

"Well, our own coven leader at the time figured it out, but some of the Troivackian knights nearby had overheard you and relayed it to me later on."

Mr. Kraft relaxed a little, as though he had been half expecting Fin to admit that while in his home, he was also omnipotent.

"What is it that I missed with Lady Katarina? I've already pointed out how she feeds on magic and the intentions of those around her and it makes her more powerful."

"Can she redistribute what she absorbs?" Fin queried with feigned lightness.

"Well, that would . . . No. She would've said if she felt that!"

Fin raised an eyebrow. "Oh? Have you watched her try to fight with a group as opposed to one-on-one?"

"W-What?"

"I just happened to find something interesting yesterday as she was training the noblewomen . . . By the end of their lesson, they were all exhausted as they should've been after working out for the first time in their lives. Yet none of them were coughing in the cold as one would expect. None of them demanded water. While they were tired, they should have been in significantly worse shape. So it made me wonder . . . What if when the power is too overwhelming for Kat, is it possible she can redistribute to those she considers allies?"

Mr. Kraft's jaw dropped.

"T-Then she'd be . . ."

"An irreplaceable asset in the military," Sebastian said breathily, his eyes wide.

Fin nodded, his smile turning sad. "This is just a theory, but it does make the one question I saw that you wrote numerous times in your notes all the more interesting, Mr. Kraft. If Kat absorbs all the magical ability of another witch, including a curse, is she able to hold on to it and redistribute it?"

"T-The implications of such a power . . . Gods."

"Yes. Then on the other side of this, as much as I refuse to accept this should it ever happen, if Kat should ever die while overusing her magic—which I'm given to understand with her ability to absorb magic endlessly, is highly unlikely—what kind of curse would she release?"

The two men sitting across from Fin sat in dumbstruck silence.

Given everything that had been going on in their kingdom, they had not given proper consideration to Katarina Ashowan's growing powers. Nor the importance of forming answers on the theoretical limits of her magic.

Mr. Kraft had known when he'd first met the duke's daughter that she was frighteningly powerful, but if she could absorb the entirety of someone's magic *and* the subsequent curse . . . ? Well . . . she'd be considered one of the strongest witches to have ever lived.

The carriage pulled to a stop then, and so nothing else was said as the carriage door opened.

Stepping down from the vehicle onto the cobbled courtyard of a keep that was within a stone's throw from Vessa, Fin peered at the three square towers and the large three-story wall that surrounded them.

"This is quite the well-protected place." Fin's eyes roved over the guards of the house patrolling the walls with loaded crossbows.

Sebastian and Mr. Kraft exchanged glances but didn't comment on the duke's observation.

Meanwhile, Kraken had leapt down from the carriage and began sniffing the air.

"This is an interesting place, witch."

Fin nodded. "Should I be worried?"

Kraken sat down beside Fin, his magnificent chest fur fluttering in the wind. *"Not yet. I'll tell you if that changes."*

Beside the duke, Mr. Kraft and Sebastian stared at the legendary familiar, both with a mixture of disbelief that the feline was capable of defeating a dragon, but also aware that he bore a regality that warranted hesitation from the men.

However, their thoughts were interrupted when a noblewoman in her early thirties wearing a mustard-colored dress and a black fur cloak around her shoulders descended the steps of her keep.

Her wide, hazel eyes were striking alongside her otherwise Troivackian features, but the way she flit her gaze over Fin, he could tell his presence was both a surprise and unwanted.

"Mr. Kraft, Mage Sebastian," she greeted with a quick curtsy, her breath coming out as vapor before her face.

She was a beautiful woman, though there were lines of stress around her mouth and eyes that suggested she had undergone trying times. Her dark hair with a few long strands of white was braided over her shoulder, and a small beauty mark flecked under her left eye.

"Lady Elena, our apologies for the impromptu visit and our guest, however . . . his presence was ordered by His Majesty."

The noblewoman turned a questioning eye to the tall redhead.

"This here is Duke Finlay Ashowan of Daxaria."

Lady Elena stumbled back a step.

"Your Grace, this is Baroness Elena Souros."

Fin gave a dignified bow while Lady Elena had yet to recover from the shock of finding herself in the presence of the legendary house witch.

"Ah, and here is Kraken, my familiar," Fin introduced while gesturing with his right hand to the cat, who let out a small chirp.

While Fin had generally grown accustomed to the various reactions he received throughout the years when people met him, he had to confess that Lady Elena was taking a lot longer than most to collect herself . . .

Mr. Kraft stepped forward. "Lady Elena, I understand this is a stressful time, and I know we have much to fear, but . . . the duke is here to help."

Swallowing, the Troivackian noblewoman at last reclaimed her composure and dipped into a dignified curtsy.

"Welcome to my home, Your Grace."

Fin bobbed his head in acknowledgment.

"Would you . . . like to come in?" Lady Elena bowed her head and moved to the side to make way for Fin to have a clear path to the entrance of her keep.

Smiling gently, the duke stepped over to the noblewoman. "I promise no harm will come to you, Lady Elena. I only mean to help discover more about Witch's Brew."

The woman stared up into Fin's electrifying blue eyes, and while her facial expression didn't change, she did let out a small breath that relaxed her shoulders.

She lowered her chin slowly, and Fin proceeded to offer her his arm.

The two started to make their way into her keep, leaving Mage Sebastian and Mr. Kraft to follow behind them.

Mage Sebastian leaned over to the coven leader. "I know you told me that the duke has a curse on him where he ages more slowly than others, but it's easy to forget he is nearly fifty years old."

Mr. Kraft looked at the mage out of the corner of his eye with an eyebrow raised. "At a time like this, *that* is what you are thinking about?"

"There is a lot to be curious about when it comes to the duke!" the mage fired back defensively.

Mr. Kraft let out a quiet breath. "The entire family is a lifetime supplier of fodder for magical studies, but . . . I'm curious to see what His Grace has to say about the Witch's Brew and . . . well . . . the *rest* of Lady Elena's keep."

Mage Sebastian hesitated in his journey to the keep's front doors. "We're showing the duke the tunnels?"

"I've thought about it, and while the duke and I do not see eye to eye, I believe he will be interested to know what the Coven of Aguas *has* managed to do to protect our remaining members."

Mage Sebastian's eyes narrowed. "You want him to offer the Coven of Wittica's aid to help rebuild your own power."

"I want to leave a proper legacy for the witches of Troivack, Mage Sebastian. It is a worthwhile endeavor. Regardless of my position, I only wish to see my kind live safely in their homeland, and if the duke has the power to persuade the inner council to accept you as the Royal Mage? Then he might be able to help the Coven of Aguas as well."

The two men had reached the steps to the entrance and ascended them while still whispering to each other.

Only they were forced to halt in their tracks when the fluffy familiar belonging to the house witch sat in their path and stared up at them in the same unnerving way he had all day.

"Ah, pardon us." Mr. Kraft gave a shallow bow and sidled around Kraken.

Sebastian cleared his throat and did the same.

Once the two men had left the cat behind, Kraken's tail fluttered across the fine slate of the entryway.

The two guards at the door stared at him with frowns.

Kraken paid them no mind before he stood back up and sauntered toward the grand staircase with its bright red carpet running up the center.

Fin, Lady Elena, Mr. Kraft, and Mage Sebastian had gone around the staircase to another room to talk, but something piqued Kraken's interest . . . a smell that was unlike most he had come across in his life.

He had a small hunch about what it could be, but he wanted to confirm the matter before telling his witch about it.

And so, unbeknownst to Lady Elena Souros, Kraken set to sleuthing out just what secrets lay within the extensively protected keep.

CHAPTER 22

FIN'S FINDINGS

Fin nodded as he read through the notes pertaining to Witch's Brew. The room he found himself in with Mr. Kraft, Lady Elena, and Mage Sebastian had, at one point, been the keep's solar, but had been transformed into a researcher's paradise with shelves of various herbs and tinctures. Three tables had been set up: one for note-taking, one for running tests, and another for holding particular findings.

Upon reading through the notes that Mr. Kraft had handed to Fin, the duke learned their contents to be both interesting and disappointing as far as it came to learning more about the devil.

"Those who take Witch's Brew can see imps and pixies from the Forest of the Afterlife and magic. You indicated that they can even take on some of the abilities of witches nearby—though typically when that happens, they are prone to death. Do the witches they borrow abilities from experience any drawbacks during this time?" Fin queried while addressing Mr. Kraft.

"As far as we can tell, no."

The duke let out an aggravated breath. "You've confirmed that there is nothing like Witch's Brew naturally occurring in this realm?"

"Not in Zinfera, Daxaria, or Troivack." Lady Elena stepped forward. "However, the blue spots? They are a type of mold that is equally unique. Whether the mushrooms are a regular specimen of our world, and the mold changes it into a magical drug? I'm not sure. We have tried transferring the mold to a handful of fungal varieties but to no avail. The mold, when intro-duced to other plants of our world, seems to be absorbed . . . but we have not moved on to testing what said infused vegetables do with this mold."

Setting down the notes in his hand, Fin peered around the room. "I have a unique constitution; I'll try it."

"Your Grace, we cannot condone that!" Mage Sebastian burst out while moving to block something from Fin's view.

The duke raised an eyebrow and moved around him. "If this thing manages to harm me, it can tell us a lot. Though I only will consume a small amount."

Everyone but Fin wore matching looks of disgust and concern.

The house witch soon found out the reason why when he laid eyes on what looked like an old tomato that had the occasional furry spot along with the telltale bright blue sprinklings he'd seen on Witch's Brew.

"Ah. Are those furry spots . . . part of the mold on Witch's Brew? It doesn't look as bright blue."

"No . . . That is just . . . regular mold," Lady Elena explained with a wince.

Fin swallowed with difficulty.

Every inch of culinary expertise that lived in his being wanted to retch.

He swallowed. "Please . . . have some moonshine on hand."

Mr. Kraft swept over to the door hurriedly to make the request of a steward.

Gingerly, Fin picked the vegetable up, then closed his eyes to regain some of his resolve.

Everyone else looked away as he bit into the vegetable.

Setting the tomato back down in a hurry, Fin turned around.

He had already turned pale with green tinging his forehead.

As everyone waited in tense silence, they couldn't bring themselves to move. They weren't sure what would happen.

Then Fin's knees buckled, and his eyes filled with white magical light.

Half falling, Fin gripped his chest where his mother's symbol had brutally burned his skin, and he seized the edge of the nearest table, making all the instruments and bottles rattle.

"Godsdamnit! What do we do?!" Mage Sebastian shouted, his uncertainty and panic freezing him in place.

Mr. Kraft stared around Fin, distracted by the magic that no one else could see whirling about the house witch.

Fin could not see or hear the people around him as his vision was flooded with nothing but an empty white space, then blackness, then . . . he found himself standing and staring at none other . . . than Tamlin Ashowan. His son.

Terror filled the house witch.

He had only ever projected his spirit when one of his loved ones had felt intense terror.

Tam was standing in his father's study, book in hand, his own eyes filled with white light as he stared at his father's pale-faced projection. Behind him, the doors to the balcony were shut as the snow fell in thick flakes outside. The fire crackled merrily behind Fin, who looked around in awe.

"D-Da . . . ?! What the . . . What is happening?!" The book fell from Tam's hands as he took an unsteady step closer to his father.

"I . . . I had a bite of a moldy tomato that—"

"*You* of all people are dying of food poisoning?!" Tam exclaimed frantically.

"I might not be dying! You know your grandmother's curse should stop that. We're trying to learn more about Witch's Brew and—"

"You did this voluntarily?!" Tam breathed, his magic-filled eyes wide.

"We needed to know more. They think there is a witch opening portals here in Troivack."

"So . . . you are only here because of a portal?" Tam's shoulders relaxed.

Fin faltered. "That . . . That might be what this is . . ."

"*Might be?*" Tam drew himself straight once more.

Fin held up his hand to settle his son down.

A portal for the soul . . . That *did* make sense. Especially given that his time with his son was unlike when he'd seen Annika before he'd temporarily died . . . or when Kat had been terrified the year before. During both of those occurrences in the past, he couldn't speak or be heard, and he hadn't been able to remain there for as long.

"Everything will be alright, Tam . . . This is a good thing. I think this answers a few questions. Though I don't know how long these effects will last."

Tam clumsily leaned on the desk. "Great. Not only does every single one of my family members abandon me to run *two* noble houses on my own, now I am partially blind!"

"I didn't know Likon had stowed away on the ship until we were halfway to Troivack."

Tam sighed and wearily reached up to rub the back of his neck. "As annoying as this is, I understand . . . I do. We're all worried about Kat. How is she, by the way?"

Fin hesitated and considered how much he should tell his son given his unknown length of time in this state of limbo. Then again, he wouldn't have a chance to tell him anything until they'd all returned home. Informing him as he was as opposed to a letter might be the better option.

"She's . . . well. However . . ."

Tam waited expectantly as he once again regained control of his emotions.

"She's married."

The brief spell of calm Tam experienced vanished. "*What?! To whom?!*"

Fin let out a sigh. "His Highness Prince Eric."

Tam's jaw dropped. "Da, that is *not* funny! You can't be serious! What did Mum say? Oh Gods, what about Likon?!"

Unfortunately, as Fin opened his mouth to offer his son more of an explanation, he felt a familiar tug in his being, and his study back in Daxaria began to fade from view, however, he could hear his son say one final thing before the office was gone from his sight.

"*Now* you disappear?!"

As Fin's vision gradually cleared of white magic, he found himself on the floor of the solar in Lady Elena's keep.

"How can we tell the king he died voluntarily?!" Mage Sebastian shouted frantically from somewhere above the house witch.

"His Majesty is familiar with the Ashowan family; he will understand that—"

"No need to carve my tombstone yet," Fin announced wearily from the floor.

His entire being felt as though it had been run over by a carriage, and all he wanted was to fall into a dreamless sleep.

"Good Gods! What happened to you?!" Mr. Kraft blustered while offering a hand to Fin and helping him to his feet.

The movement made the room momentarily spin before the duke.

Placing his hand on the table nearest him, Fin gratefully accepted the goblet of moonshine he had asked to be delivered beforehand from Mage Sebastian.

"Are you certain you should be drinking that? Technically you did just consume a component of a drug," Lady Elena asked while wringing her hands.

She looked terribly pale.

Fin took a large gulp of the burning liquor before responding. "As I said, I have a unique constitution."

Despite his confident response, Fin had to admit he was feeling significantly more unsteady on his feet than he would've liked.

"I appeared in the study of my home. I spoke with my son in Daxaria."

The room fell into stunned silence.

"I think," Fin continued slowly, "I think the mold has the ability to portal away a person's soul."

"Then where is it the people who take Witch's Brew are being transported to?" Mr. Kraft insisted, his mind racing through the implications of Fin's discovery.

"You said they see creatures from the Forest of the Afterlife. Is it possible . . . their souls are wandering between the realms?" Fin continued while noticing his legs were starting to tremble less.

Mr. Kraft nodded thoughtfully. "I've never heard of such a thing done before, but . . . given that there is the involvement of the devil and ancient beasts, that could be the case."

"Why were you transported to your home and not the Forest of the Afterlife?" Lady Elena wondered wisely.

Fin wasn't able to form any sound reasoning for that question, so he furrowed his brows and lowered his gaze as he tried to piece it together.

Just then, a repetitive pawing at the door interrupted the small group. Fin gave a wry half grin.

"Right on time. He always has to make an entrance before giving all the answers . . . I swear that's where Kat learned it . . ." the duke muttered half to himself while crossing the room. He proceeded to open the door to find Kraken sitting and waiting regally while the two guards stared down at the feline at a complete loss as to what they should do about his presence.

The fluffy familiar sauntered into the room, leaving Fin to close the door behind him.

"This is a most interesting keep, witch. Are you aware there is a labyrinth of tunnels that range farther than I can smell underneath us?" Kraken meowed.

Fin froze and looked at Lady Elena with wide eyes.

The noblewoman, taken aback by his reaction, unconsciously shuffled backward.

"Lady Elena, would all the extra security around your keep have something to do with a large amount of hidden passageways underneath us?" the duke asked lightly.

The noblewoman looked like she was about to throw herself onto her knees and beg for her life when Mr. Kraft stepped forward.

"Lady Elena has been instrumental in keeping the witches that remain here in Troivack safe. They have been forced underground to avoid being slaughtered in the streets."

"I was only asking out of curiosity for the time being. Now, Kraken . . . before I hear more about these tunnels . . . we've learned something interesting." Fin breezily glossed over the matter of the tunnels, knowing that it was a far graver matter than he was letting on but wanted to tackle one dilemma at a time.

After relaying to his familiar the details of what the group had started to deduce in light of Finlay's experience with the moldy tomato, Kraken gave a laughing chirp.

"*Goodness . . . I thought you knew more about Witch's Brew than that! I asked you if you needed me to tell you more about it, and you said you and your mate had run all the necessary tests!*"

"Wait . . . you *knew* it was transporting people's souls?!" Fin exclaimed in alarm while rounding to face his cat directly.

Mr. Kraft, Mage Sebastian, and Lady Elena watched, perplexed as they were unable to hear Kraken's side of the conversation.

"*Yes. The imps and pixies have been trying to lure the broken souls that consume Witch's Brew to the Forest of the Afterlife for years now. The only reason there weren't more taken in exchange for the beasts in Daxaria was because I showed them the true might of the empurror!*" Kraken meowed imperially.

Fin's jaw dropped.

His mind was still sluggish from the effects of the mold, but as he pinched the bridge of his nose and pieced through the information, he stared down at his familiar eagerly.

"What do you mean in exchange for the beasts?"

Kraken blinked up at him. "*Witch, have you gone senile? You should know better than anyone that creatures crossing the boundaries of the realms must pay the price. A soul or more from our realm could bring over the ancient ones. Though most are not clever enough to do so without direction. A single soul could most likely bring a pixie or two.*"

Fin wanted to sit down as the realization settled heavily on him.

"Kraken . . . what did I say . . . about telling me everything you learn . . . ?"

"*There was nothing to tell you. No one in Daxaria was in harm's way . . . though if I am to successfully take over Troivack, I will need to take the beastly brutes in paw.*"

"W-What is he saying?" Lady Elena leaned forward, dropping her voice to a whisper.

"He says that the Witch's Brew is a means of exchanging human souls to the Forest of the Afterlife in order for the ancient beasts to come here."

Lady Elena covered her mouth, horrified. Mage Sebastian stood straight. And Mr. Kraft looked grim.

"Kraken, why was my soul transported to our home in Daxaria when I consumed the mold?"

"*You ate such a thing?*" Kraken's note of disgust was not lost on Fin. The feline huffed before continuing. "*I do not completely understand how it works. I only know that is what is being used as a ticket of sorts.*"

Fin turned to face the trio of Troivackians that awaited to hear what else was said.

"Kraken doesn't know why I wasn't transported to the Forest of the Afterlife, but . . . this is already more information than I thought we could obtain. Is there anything *else* you'd like to share with me?" The house witch addressed Kraken again.

The familiar didn't respond straight away and instead tilted his head as he stared up at Fin pensively.

"*Would you like me to go to the Forest of the Afterlife to learn more about the mushrooms? It's been a while since I put the fear of my claws in some of those ethereal fools.*"

Silence followed.

Fin knew at that point in his life, he shouldn't be surprised to learn that his cat was capable of crossing realms . . . and yet . . . Amazingly, he was. . . .

CHAPTER 23

QUESTIONS AND QUEENS

Sir Cas, are you ready yet?"

"Lady Katarina, I'm only halfway through my sandwich."

"But you keep talking with Conrad! You're taking forever!"

"Why don't you fight Sir Marin again?"

"He says he's too tired!"

Sir Cas sighed.

He was regretting revealing to the redheaded noblewoman that he had been holding back his skills with the sword.

The woman had always been driven to learn about sword fighting and improving beyond human bounds, but the voraciousness with which she desired to be as good as, if not better than, Sir Cas had her nagging him constantly to spar with her and teach her more.

Meanwhile, the Troivackian knights had slowly been acquiescing to sparring with her, realizing that there was no shame in doing so, as she had technically beaten one of their elite knights.

Though some discovered this was a poor judgment call on their part because they left sparring with Katarina Ashowan more tired, sweaty, and bruised than they had after actual skirmishes . . .

"Lady Katarina?"

Kat turned toward the voice calling out to her from the courtyard entrance.

Sir Cas, who had been seated on the stairs and enjoying his lunch with Conrad, turned around to look at the king's assistant as well.

"Our king and queen have asked that you attend an inner council meeting today," Mr. Levin called out, his gaze resting stonily on the redhead.

Kat had never really understood why she always had the impression that Brendan Devark's assistant hated her . . . At first, she had assumed he felt antagonistic toward her because of her being a witch or because she was Daxarian.

However, he was perfectly fine with Mr. Kraft and Alina . . .

Sheathing her sword, Kat made her way up the stairs to the assistant who waited for her, and she gave a brief wave of farewell to Sir Cas and Conrad.

"What is the meeting about?" she asked while Mr. Levin fell into step beside her.

Kat observed that his escorting her at her side was meant to be a slight, as it was common practice in both Daxaria and Troivack that he would be expected to follow behind her unless given permission otherwise.

"The meeting is pertaining to Sir Herra's alleged attack on you and a few other matters I'm not at liberty to share at this time."

Kat's gaze cut to the assistant, her golden eyes gleaming a little brighter. "I thought the hearing of Sir Herra was to be discussed with my father present. He left this morning to attend to matters elsewhere, and I find it especially interesting that you call it an 'alleged' attack."

"That is what the council is deciding today, Lady Katarina. A man is not made guilty before the council meeting."

"Then do you keep innocent men locked up in the dungeon just for fun?" Kat wondered frostily.

The assistant fell quiet, though from the way his jaw shifted, Kat could see he was trying to control a larger emotion.

"We needed to observe him, and given that it *might* have been an attack on you, the future queen of Daxaria and the daughter of a duke, we took extra precautions."

Kat raised an eyebrow and kept staring at the man.

"We didn't get the chance to chat much last time we met in Daxaria, but have I done something in particular to offend you?"

Mr. Levin stopped in his tracks and gave a shallow bow. "Not at all, Lady Katarina. I did not realize I seemed hostile."

Kat's eyes narrowed as she stared at his bowed head.

He was full of shit.

Then again, considering Kat had just *barely* started getting the knights to train with her, acknowledged that, yet again, Mr. Levin may just be someone that took a while to win over.

That is unless Kat fought dirty . . .

"Mr. Levin, have you met my familiar, by chance?"

The assistant straightened in a hurry. "I do not need to meet Pina Colada."

A slow grin started to climb her face.

"Lady Katarina, I am allergic to cats."

The redhead continued smiling devilishly at the assistant until she turned and resumed her journey to the council room.

The assistant let out a grumbling huff before mastering his expression again.

However, his control was tested when they arrived at the council room doors and found Pina sniffing the nose of one of the guards who was lying on his stomach and smiling at the little kitten as she inspected his face while the other guard (also lying on his belly) watched her with his chin propped up in his hands.

Mr. Levin cleared his throat angrily.

The two men jumped to attention in a hurry.

Kat hid her smile from the men as she bent down and scratched Pina's cheek.

"I've been summoned by Their Majesties?" she greeted the guards while barely keeping the smugness from her face.

The men, avoiding Mr. Levin's furious stare, bowed in response and proceeded to open the doors for Kat.

Feeling in too good of a mood to be sitting in on such a somber meeting, Kat did her best to dampen her perkiness as she regarded the long table of serious noblemen, then the king and queen with a bow.

However, there was another figure out of the corner of her eye that she turned to look at and discovered none other than . . . Rebecca Devark.

"W-Wh—"

"Lady Katarina, Lady Rebecca Devark has been asked to return to court in order to help receive your mother, Duchess Ashowan," Brendan Devark announced loudly over everyone's heads.

Kat had gone rigid, her entire body flooded with tingling shock.

She glanced over to Alina, but the queen betrayed none of her true thoughts.

So Katarina took it upon herself to hide her own feelings on the matter as she faced Rebecca Devark and issued a shallow bow.

"Ma'am, you seem to be in good health."

Rebecca Devark's dark eyes roved over Katarina's uniform before she curtsied back.

"Congratulations on your marriage, Lady Katarina. I had just issued my sentiments to His Highness." The former queen nodded regally toward Eric, whose gaze was sharp on the former monarch from his seat at the table.

Kat's gaze lingered on Rebecca Devark's face. The square jaw, the thick, sculpted eyebrows, and her bold mouth. Her hair still wrapped in a dark cloth, and her winter garb of a long sleeve black dress still the epitome of modesty and regality.

She looked well rested despite her severe clothing choices. The time away from court had done good things for her . . .

If only she had succeeded at pulling the stick out of her—

"Lady Katarina, Lady Rebecca, once you are seated, we can proceed with the meeting," Brendan Devark called out.

The room erupted in more whispers, and even Rebecca Devark wasn't able to hide her shock.

"T-The former queen will also be joining in on the meeting?" one of the noblemen spluttered from his seat while leaning forward to stare down the table at Brendan.

Kat noticed that there was an air of hesitancy.

Apparently, removing Lord Ball as the voice of outrage had succeeded in subduing the council.

"My mother will need to be apprised of the situation pertaining to the attack against Lady Katarina in the event that Duchess Annika Ashowan wishes to know more, and we need someone who understands the current status of the castle while my queen attends our meetings and the trial." Brendan answered the bald-headed nobleman, making him visibly struggle not to hunch his shoulders under the king's indomitable eyes.

When no one else attempted to argue, Katarina made her way over to the empty seat beside Eric, who stood and pulled out the chair for her.

From her place at Brendan's side, Alina Devark watched her mother-in-law and noticed with no small amount of satisfaction the utter bafflement on the woman's face as she realized that no one dared to question Katarina's presence or think it to be strange.

While Rebecca gradually regained her composure, she made her way over to the chair at the far side of the table that was placed at the very end, opposite to her son and his wife.

Alina took the opportunity to glance at Duke Icarus and noticed that the man was, as he often was, completely nonplussed. It unnerved her somewhat, as the queen started to suspect that the vile man was plotting something else . . .

However, there was nothing more they could do until they dealt with Sir Herra. Especially as gathering incriminating evidence against Duke Icarus for illegally trafficking people and enslaving them was taking more time than they had hoped . . .

Alina worried they'd have to try to bring Zinfera into the entire matter, which given their own unstable state, made things even trickier and could prove to bring more troubles than solutions.

Alina turned to look at her husband.

Brendan shared one brief, gentle look with his wife before addressing his council again.

Alina closed her eyes and took a slow breath in.

One step at a time.

Things would work out one way or another . . . After all, the infamous house witch was on her shores, and she had no doubt that between Katarina and Fin, they would resolve things for the better.

Who knew? Maybe even Kraken would help somehow . . .

Fin leaned against the desk in Lady Elena's office, still recovering from the impromptu spiritual journey to his son. He and Kraken had been permitted to use the room in the name of privacy, and the house witch was rather grateful to have less people around him as he gradually finished processing the mold he'd eaten.

"I'm not sure why you always feel the need to make a ceremony of things. I could've done this back in the other room."

Fin's eyes narrowed momentarily as his familiar stared back at him from the floor, nonplussed.

Mr. Kraft, Mage Sebastian, and Lady Elena had gone to continue their discussion on the implications of their discovery of the magical properties the mold possessed.

"Can all cats traverse realms?"

"Yes."

"All the times I woke you up thinking you had stopped breathing . . . or asked if you were staring at anything in particular, you always said no . . . Were you in another world? Why did you not say something?!"

"It'd be wildly annoying and a waste of my precious time to have to explain it to you. I'm only telling you this now, as it seems if I do so, I can start my takeover of Troivack. Though your kitten's familiar, Pina, is a little bit of a problem on that front. She is quite the little seductress."

Ignoring the topics of taking over yet another kingdom and his daughter's familiar, Fin continued interrogating Kraken.

"*Why* is it cats can cross into other realms?"

"We're magnificent creatures."

"That doesn't answer the question."

Kraken yawned, already bored with the conversation. *"Do you want me to go to the Forest of the Afterlife or not?"*

"Yes, I do." Fin sighed wearily. "We need one of the mushrooms to run additional tests. If you spot anyone there that doesn't belong, can you let me know?"

Kraken blinked.

Fin knew that was as much of a confirmation as he was going to get.

"So how does it work?" Fin asked while folding his arms.

Kraken turned and sauntered toward the door. *"Let me out"* the familiar commanded with a chirp before reaching his tufted paw up to stroke the door repeatedly.

Taking a moment to calm back down, Fin pushed himself up off the desk that had at least an inch of dust on its surface, and he crossed the room to open the door for the fluffy feline.

Kraken darted out of the room with surprising nimbleness that he often didn't show. Alarmingly, when Fin poked his head out the door to ask Kraken where he needed to be in order to cross realms, he found that his familiar had already disappeared.

The Forest of the Afterlife was foggy as usual when Kraken first arrived . . . though he could tell this wasn't the same corner of the woods that he had entered when he'd given his warning to the imp several years ago . . .

As he sauntered over the mossy ground and peered at the peaceful trees with rays of sunlight streaming through the occasional gap in foliage, he took in a small breath.

It was a little unnerving coming to the Forest of the Afterlife, but Kraken would never outwardly admit it. Especially because the reason he became a little less assured was because he could no longer feel the connection to his witch anywhere near as strongly as before.

As he trotted on, he listened to the peaceful birds singing and noted the clean, fresh scent of grass and new growth and tried to find peace in it.

He sniffed the air again.

Hm, the gateway I need is farther away than I realized . . . Perhaps I should try and hunt down a pixie and force them to take me there to save time . . .

Kraken had just finished darting under some ferns when the quiet murmur of voices reached his ears.

Turning his head sharply, his pupils widening, he peered amongst the shadowy underbrush toward where the voices were coming from.

Then, after a moment of quiet stillness . . . he identified who the voices belonged to and began to bound in that direction.

Breaking free of a white, flowery shrub, sending tiny petals fluttering all around him, Kraken peered up at the humans who had long ago left his own realm to join the Forest of the Afterlife.

"Kraken?! Oh, dear, did you board death's carriage? Fin must be heartbroken . . ."

Resisting the urge to become irritable over having to reiterate that these particular souls had seen him many times before and had already learned that cats could traipse realms, Kraken silently reminded himself that those in the Forest of the Afterlife did not always have cohesive memories . . .

"Greetings, I am only here to find some items that might help my conquering of Troivack . . . and to help my witch sort out a problem that might concern one of his kittens."

Standing up from the tree-woven chairs and table from where they sat, the two people stepped over to Kraken and smiled down at him.

Kraken peered back up into the kind, smiling faces of Katelyn Ashowan . . .

And Ainsley Reyes.

The former queen of Daxaria.

CHAPTER 24

TAKING A CATWALK

In the Forest of the Afterlife, there were many interesting spots and clearings.

In some places, castles rose out of stone, some had hammocks made of flowers and vines that awaited any idle soul who wished to rest. Then there were the cliffs that gave way to magnificent starry skies; the souls that wandered its realm could drift through and peer out over the expanse of heavenly stars. Some of the beings that lived in the forest liked to marvel that they once lived in a world that was far larger than they had ever realized while alive.

Sometimes a clearing with tables and tasty treats and teas would appear for those who wished to have company. In a grove of birch trees, someone could stumble upon a rousing game of cards amongst beings both ethereal and those that once lived.

However, it was also a common sight for there to be the casual meandering of felines that would traipse through the world, curiously observing everyone and everything for snippets of time before returning to the land of the living.

No one really thought much about such a thing . . .

Especially as none of the cats were known to talk.

That is until Kraken, familiar to the house witch, came to be.

In the world of the living, only his witch could converse with him, but there in the Forest of the Afterlife, Kraken was free to talk with whomever he pleased. It was something of a mystery that the Gods should bless an animal with such a gift.

Kraken thought it made perfect sense. After all, they had made him divinely fluffy with superior intelligence. Why wouldn't he be given such a useful ability?

Because he was unique, however, Kraken had become something of a celebrity in the Forest of the Afterlife, and, delighted that they could converse with a creature as enigmatic as a cat, he found that he would be chatted up far more often than he would have liked.

It was one of the reasons he didn't frequent the afterlife . . . He didn't like being hounded as a beast of entertainment.

Though, he had made a point to visit a few times a year to update the mother of his witch on how everyone was doing. Sadly, she didn't always remember the details, but Kraken did his best not to mind. It wasn't Katelyn Ashowan's fault after all.

The Daxarian queen had been a newer addition to the forest . . . and she often asked about her husband and children.

Kraken had begun visiting less often as a result . . . He'd always liked the queen and didn't have the heart to tell her the truth about how her loved ones were doing in recent years, what with the prince kitten disappearing.

Though she did always laugh magnificently anytime Kraken told her some new small assertion of dominance he'd bestowed upon her husband. Relieving himself on the rug right by King Norman Reyes's bedside so that he had to step in poop the very first thing in the morning . . . The occasions he had casually drunk out of the king's goblet when he wasn't looking and left tufts of fluff behind . . .

All good times.

"After we find these mushrooms, you'll go back and tell Fin, and that will help?" Kate asked airily as they wandered through the forest, occasionally greeting people as they walked.

"Yes. There is someone who is using the mushrooms to forcefully exchange human souls for ancient beasts—and the type of people who consume these mushrooms are the ones who are almost instantly transported to the Grove of Sorrows."

"Whoever planned this is quite cunning," Ainsley noted as she walked beside Katelyn.

"One thing in particular that rubs my fur the wrong way is that I've heard this person is nearby in the castle. I should be able to smell someone who is around Witch's Brew regularly, but I cannot. They are hidden from me," Kraken confirmed as they moved through the trees that began to thin.

"Is there anything you know of that could block the scent?" Katelyn wondered seriously.

The familiar didn't respond immediately. "A few things. Stronger smelling things . . . or perhaps they haven't been around the Witch's Brew in a while and only rely on other people to handle its creation . . ."

"Why can't we just tell the Gods? Or what about the ancient beasts still lurking on the outskirts? Couldn't we ask them?" Ainsley frowned as she sifted through the possibilities.

"The ancient beasts are loyal to whoever they believe will bring them back to the other realm or who will help the devil. As for the Gods . . . they are being exceptionally quiet about this entire thing. Most likely because of their son being involved." Kraken sighed, for once his haughtiness tinged with his age.

Hearing this, Katelyn Ashowan leaned down and scooped up the fluffy feline in her arms.

Giving him an expert scritch around his head and ears, she saw Kraken allow himself to grow limp in her arms.

"I must say, you are a rather delightful selling point to succumbing to death's carriage," Kraken purred happily.

Kate smiled sunnily down at the feline. Her warm brown eyes were as bright as they had been in her youth, and her wavy brown hair thick and healthy. She looked like she was back in her prime again, as did Ainsley Reyes.

"Ah, I can't believe I forgot to ask! How are my grandchildren?" Katelyn mused happily. The weight of earthly situations never fully rested on her.

Kraken's eyes had been in the process of rolling back and his mouth falling open as Kate found an exceptionally delicious spot to scratch along his cheek. Mention of Finlay's kittens, however, had him begrudgingly coming back to his senses—at least until Ainsley reached over and gently massaged the silky fur of his paw while lingering along his imperial toe beans.

"Aaaauuurrrgh . . ." Kraken tried to talk but drooled a little instead. "The queen kitten . . ."

"Oh, you mean Alina?" Ainsley asked helpfully.

"Yes. She is having her own litter now."

"How wonderful!" The former Daxarian queen beamed, tears rising in her eyes.

"Ah . . . and . . . the fiery kitten and prince kitten are married . . ."

Both Kate and Ainsley stopped their adoring pets to stare at the feline in astonishment.

"Do you mean to say that Katarina is married?"

"To my son?!"

Both Ainsley and Kate stared at the fluffy feline, who was wondering why in the world the scritches and massage were not resuming.

The two women then looked to each other and burst out laughing.

"Gods . . . Mr. Howard must be having a conniption. I should ensure when he arrives here in the forest that his favorite wine is on hand," Ainsley gasped.

"I'm not sure I remember your son . . . but I just cannot believe that my little Katarina is married!" Kate sighed, her eyes growing distant and starry as they often did.

Kraken squirmed out of Kate's arms. If there weren't going to be any proper pets, then they needed to continue on their journey.

The two women shared a knowing look before they followed after the cat. Kraken was always a persnickety beastie.

As the trio walked, however, their former good mood faded and a funny somberness settled over them as the forest continued to darken and mist rose around them. At first it could have been played off as a trick of the eyes, but soon it grew thicker . . . and thicker . . . The flowers of the forest disappeared, and they found that no matter how far they walked, every tree and stone looked the same.

"Kraken, I'm . . . I'm not sure I like this part of the forest . . ." Kate announced warily while blinking with a frown. She was feeling . . . strange. As though . . . As though something were happening to her . . .

"I feel it too," Ainsley whispered, suddenly stopping.

Kraken looked back at the two women that had decided to join him on his journey into the woods and chirped.

He had been to that part of the forest many times before . . . yet he had never felt peculiar. Why was it those who had passed away felt strange there? The entire forest should have felt natural to them.

When he turned back around, however, he perked up.

There.

The smell of the mushrooms!

Unlike Witch's Brew, however, the scent didn't have the sickening sweet, decaying odor . . .

Kraken trotted faster toward it, following his nose.

Hesitantly, Kate and Ainsley followed him.

They were feeling heavy and as they stared around themselves, everything seemed to feel a lot clearer to them . . .

"Ah! Finally!" Kraken announced as he made a sharp right.

As if by some trick of the trees, a ring of stones appeared, standing at least fifteen feet tall with nothing but grass within its circle . . . though surrounding the inside of the circle of stones . . . were the mushrooms.

Kraken entered the ring easily and sniffed the nearest mushroom without hesitation.

"Something is wrong . . ." Ainsley announced weakly.

"I haven't felt like this in . . . in . . . Gods!" The realization and alarm in Kate's voice drew Kraken's attention once more.

"I feel like I'm . . . I'm alive again. My mind feels sharper . . . I . . . I can remember things . . . Gods! I kept forgetting everything you told me, Kraken! I kept forgetting how old Fin was . . . How old my grandchildren were . . . Kraken, what in the world is happening?!" Kate demanded, her hands flying to her hips, her eyes sharper than they had ever been in the thick of the forest. She stood just outside the ring of stones with Ainsley gradually moving to join her side.

The familiar stilled as he stared in awe at the two women who not only seemed more clearheaded . . . but had also no longer looked as they had in their primes . . . Instead, they looked the ages they had been when they had died . . .

Sniffing the mushrooms again, Kraken bit off a stem and made his way back over to Kate and Ainsley. Setting down the item he intended to take back to the earthly realm for Fin, Kraken regarded his two impromptu companions seriously.

"You've come to an unnatural portal. It could be that if you passed through it, you could resurrect yourselves . . . Though I cannot say what the price for such a thing would be. Most likely the deaths of thousands of people . . . perhaps even an entire kingdom."

Kate and Ainsley stared at each other, then back at Kraken.

"What if that is the purpose of the portal? Of all the exchanges? Someone keeps increasing the value of beings passing through until someone, or something even bigger can enter the other realm?" Kate asked as she began pacing amongst the ferns.

Looking around at the misty trees, Kraken could sense beings growing closer to them.

"What makes you pounce to such a conclusion?" the familiar asked while keeping an ear out for the mysterious creatures lingering nearby.

"Well . . . I'm thinking what powerful person could want with such a thing? If I were the devil, or someone who wanted to be rid of the devil, I would try to find a way to send them into another realm entirely. *If* I knew it was possible and a way to do it," Kate reasoned while reaching up and rubbing the back of her neck thoughtfully.

Kraken sat quietly with his thoughts for a few moments before answering.

"That would make sense. But from what I hear, the devil believes there is a woman after him, so that means she has created this portal and intends to shove him through."

"A witch is doing this?" Ainsley interjected while moving forward. Her regal bearing had returned alongside her clarity of mind.

"No one knows who is doing this. Which is why I came here for the mushroom," Kraken explained patiently. He normally wouldn't bother, but the two women seemed to be eager to figure the situation out. And if they could? Well, it was no fur off his nose.

"Someone with a grudge against the devil certainly doesn't narrow it down," Kate muttered half to herself.

"And the Gods have tied my witch into the whole endeavor," Kraken reminded while resisting the urge to yawn.

Kate blinked, then halted her movements. "Where is the first witch?"

At this, Kraken tilted his head. "Dead. Ages ago. The devil defeated her."

"But then she would've been here in the Forest of the Afterlife," Kate pointed out, her right hand vibrating as her mind whirred through her thoughts at lightning speed—it was precisely the way she had been when she was forced to think through her medical diagnoses back when she had been alive.

"You think the first witch is alive?" Ainsley queried with open astonishment.

"Well think about it! This drug is called Witch's Brew . . . She has a vendetta against the devil, and she has connections to the afterlife! What if . . . What if she wasn't killed, but instead weakened? What if this is her way of one last fight against her brother?"

Kraken sat perfectly still.

He had forgotten Finlay had come from such a brilliant mother cat.

"That could be. For now, you two should return to the depths of the forest where it is safe. If it is the first witch? That means she would have eyes and ears everywhere . . . Though, how she would have convinced the ancient beasts to join her side still makes no sense to me," Kraken mused aloud.

"Perhaps she promised them something in exchange . . . Oh, I wish we could talk to them!" Kate lamented irritably while her right fist pounded the air in frustration.

Ainsley folded her arms over her middle. "We need to figure out who the first witch is and what her motive is . . . then it'll be easier to figure out what we should do."

"Assuming it *is* the first witch. That is still a mere guess," Kraken reminded.

"While it does seem like the obvious answer . . . perhaps it isn't the first witch. Maybe the devil simply found his match in a human woman who is determined to see him vanquished." Ainsley shrugged, though her eyes were lost in thought as she, too, pondered the puzzle before them.

Without bothering to say another word, Kraken bent down and picked the mushroom back up.

The creatures in the mist were already disappearing, and he could take a guess where they were going . . .

They were going to warn their mistress that a certain plan had been figured out. Or perhaps they hadn't guessed correctly at all, and there was simply no reason to show themselves . . .

Kraken turned back to the stones and made his way toward a particular opening he recalled without another word to his witch's mother or the former queen. He would see them again, but his instincts were starting to make his fur stand on end . . . Kraken needed to tell his witch everything he had learned.

I suppose it'll be a little more annoying to take over Troivack than I origi-
nally thought . . . Ah well . . . How many ancient beasts could they have
brought into our realm anyway?

CHAPTER 25

A DAUNTING DEBRIEFING

Sitting in the king's office, feeling rather cramped were Finlay, Katarina, Brendan, Faucher, Alina, Eric, Mr. Kraft, Mage Sebastian, and last but far from least . . . Kraken.

The fluffy feline perched in the middle of the circle of people, blinking slowly as he fought off the urge to sleep. He knew he had to share the important information he had gathered from the Forest of the Afterlife, but he also needed his royal nap.

"We left the mushroom Kraken retrieved with Lady Elena to run tests, but that isn't all. Kraken says the first witch has never been seen in the Forest of the Afterlife any of the times he has been there, and he is wondering if perhaps she may be the woman that the devil is searching for," Fin explained, breaking the silence once everyone had situated themselves.

Kraken's tail swished. He had conveniently left out the detail that Finlay's mother and the former queen of Daxaria were the ones to help him form such a theory. He had long ago been warned by his old mentor, James Paws, to never mention that he was capable of speaking with the deceased souls who roamed the next realm. Apparently, it would be distressing to the humans . . .

"The first witch opening portals?!" Mr. Kraft spluttered. Kraken hadn't relayed any of what he had learned until that very moment, and so everyone found themselves in similar states of astonishment.

"Possibly . . . Kraken doesn't seem fully convinced of this. He's saying he just found it strange that no one had ever seen or heard anything of the first witch in the other realm," Fin clarified, though he was frowning as he, too, tried to wade through the heft of information they had received from his familiar.

"Couldn't it simply be a woman who has a familiar like Kraken that is retrieving the mushrooms, and the mushrooms themselves are responsible for the portals?" Mage Sebastian countered reasonably.

Everyone looked to Fin, who tilted his head, his eyes fixed on the floor as he rubbed the back of his neck. "It's entirely possible. At the very least, I'm hoping that we get more information after we test the mushroom we acquired."

"If it *is* the first witch, then it is possible that the devil asked me whether Kat could kill a deity because he wants Kat to kill her, and he isn't worried about himself at all," Eric speculated, his hazel eyes filled with ominous shadows.

"Wouldn't it make sense if it was the first witch to approach Kat and offer to team up? They are both witches, and technically wouldn't Lady Katarina be a distant relative?" Mage Sebastian mused while glancing at Mr. Kraft and then the Troivackian king.

"The devil *did*, however, also hint that the woman he is searching for is not a witch. Though it could be he is just trying to persuade us to join him, as the first witch would be the more obvious choice to help . . ." Alina added.

"*Is* it obvious?" Eric interrupted. "She has killed people, been drugging people, attempted to bind Kat's magic, destroyed Faucher's keep, and those are only the things we know about."

"Didn't the devil say he'd be in touch with you so that you could give him information?" Kat turned to her husband.

"That's true, but I have no way to contact him myself," the prince confirmed, his gaze moving to Brendan. "Will I have your permission, Your Majesty, to share all this information with him?"

The king's dark eyes didn't betray his thoughts as he listened to the conversation without questioning or adding anything.

Everyone waited in silence for his input.

"The devil says the woman is in my castle. I want to know what will happen if they meet," Brendan responded slowly. "Furthermore, how can we best keep my people safe? Thus far, there has been little interaction between the beasts and the Troivackian civilians, however, with Lady Katarina's presence, things have been escalating. If keeping the peace means sending her back to Daxaria, I will." Brendan locked eyes with Eric and stared levelly.

The prince didn't react and instead turned to Kat, who was already gripping her hand into a fist at her side.

"We don't know that they will stay harmless if I leave. Couldn't it just be that I'm the biggest threat . . . ?" Kat trailed off, her golden eyes falling to her father's familiar. "Besides, they acted significantly more afraid of Kraken than me. I seemed more like an annoyance to the two beings that came to bind my magic at Faucher's keep."

Kraken had crouched closer to the floor, his eyes barely open, though he did let out a short chirp.

"They have excellent reason to fear me."

No one but Fin understood him, and the house witch didn't see a need to translate that particular declaration.

"I understand it is remarkable that Kraken can walk across ethereal borders and has superior intelligence," Mage Sebastian started to say.

"For a mage you aren't all bad." Kraken purred quietly.

"Though is there something other than crossing borders and communicating with different beasts and people that would make him fearsome?"

"You should get your spectacles adjusted. Your nearsightedness is making you seem foolish."

"You speak as though that isn't something to be terrified of. Information is valuable, and Kraken has an endless source of it. In a day, he has discovered things that we never would have been able to in decades without his help," Mr. Kraft pointed out, a note of awe mixed with severity. Both men were unaware that the familiar was getting annoyed with the mage.

Brendan nodded in agreement with the coven leader's input.

He agreed wholeheartedly.

"Are we not going to discuss the matter of the tunnels beneath Lady Elena's keep?" Kraken sniffed tiredly.

"Right . . . Mr. Kraft, I did not have a chance to ask further about this, but . . . What are the tunnels underneath Lady Elena's estate being used for? Kraken says they run far enough to sprawl well into Vessa."

The coven leader stiffened and straightened his shoulders as the Troivackian king's gaze snapped to him and hardened.

"What is the duke referring to?" Brendan growled and stood.

The air in the study became uneasy. Brendan had become significantly less threatening on a daily basis since his marriage to Alina, however, that didn't mean he couldn't be extraordinarily terrifying should he need to be.

"Y-Your Majesty, I did say that taking Mage Sebastian to Lady Elena's keep needed to be kept secret and as few questions as possible should be asked."

"Tunnels beneath Vessa isn't a small matter." Brendan drew closer to Mr. Kraft, who grew pale as he bowed instinctively before the king.

"Your Majesty, I vow to you, on my honor, we have never used the tunnels for anything that would be deemed harmful or duplicitous to your rule and the law. It was only a means of protecting the surviving coven members."

"You reported to me that only five members still lived." Brendan bore down on Mr. Kraft, who, despite being more than two decades the king's senior, slipped off his chair onto his knees as though he were about to be sick.

"I-I only lied to protect them."

"Mr. Kraft, for deceiving me, I may have you charged, and I will be negotiating your removal as the leader of the Coven of Aguas in the near future," Brendan's voice rumbled. "Consider yourself lucky that I am not removing your head from your neck this instant."

Mr. Kraft trembled, and most people in the room couldn't help but pity the normally proud man.

"Your Majesty," Mage Sebastian's voice rasped, and when the king's eyes moved to him, the mage realized he had made a grave error in speaking at all.

"You were an accomplice to his deceit. Your petition to join the court as Royal Mage is hereby terminated. I will be nominating Lady Kezia in your place."

Sebastian turned pale.

Finlay interrupted somberly, rising and stepping forward which summoned Brendan's attention to him. "Your Majesty, while this is not my kingdom, it's notorious that the courtiers closest to you brutally slaughtered countless witches in the past few decades. You yourself have avoided contact with the coven and offered no support. Mr. Kraft, like yourself, was charged with protecting his people."

"Is this the Coven of Wittica officially intervening on Mr. Kraft's behalf?" Brendan's tone was dangerous, and his eyes sharpened.

Fin sighed but straightened himself with visible effort. It was times like this that it really was obvious how much he hated political work . . .

"Erm, pardon me saying this, but in the words of Faucher . . . an enemy can exploit any crack in our ranks if given the opportunity," Kat interjected while she, too, came to her feet and sidled closer to the king. "This may not be the time to start dropping heavy-handed sentences amongst the few of us who know everything that is going on."

Brendan looked at her, then he looked at Eric, who stared back in silent support of his wife.

Faucher was watching the king stoically, though there was a faint twitch at the corner of his mouth that hinted at a smile he may or may not have been hiding.

The king raised an eyebrow, then once again addressed the coven leader. "You will be punished. However, Lady Katarina, or rather . . . Leader Faucher's wisdom is not out of place." Brendan let out an agitated huff and stepped back beside Alina, who looked a mite fearsome herself as she regarded the coven leader and mage.

"You had months to realize His Majesty was trustworthy. While I can respect your desire to protect the witches of Troivack, we would have had no choice but to condemn you should anyone else have discovered the existence of these tunnels," Alina chastised seriously.

Mage Sebastian joined Mr. Kraft on his knees.

"We apologize for this deception, Your Majesties," the two men spoke in perfect unison.

Brendan regarded the mage and witch unemotionally and allowed the only sound in the room to be the crackle of the fire that warmed the space behind him. It was clear he wanted to ensure the gravity of their choices weighed appropriately on both Mr. Kraft and Mage Sebastian.

"I will be interrogating Lady Elena. You do realize that it is possible this witch who is threatening my kingdom could be in these tunnels, and perhaps the reason she is so close is because she has been hidden underneath my city?" Brendan rumbled, though he didn't appear as close to instigating violence as he had been moments before.

"I know every witch in those tunnels. None of them has the ability to open a portal." Mr. Kraft's voice turned steady when discussion of exposing the members of his coven surfaced.

"How many of them have familiars?" Kat asked while crossing her arms.

Her gently implied point gradually sank in for everyone present.

If all cats could cross realms, that meant that a regular witch could've gotten their hands on the mystical mushroom from the Forest of the Afterlife.

Mr. Kraft opened his mouth to defend his coven yet again but found he couldn't think of one reason that would guarantee everyone's innocence.

He closed his mouth, the dark lines under his eyes suddenly appearing darker than they had before in the dancing shadows of the room.

"I will take Your Majesty down into the tunnels at your earliest convenience."

Brendan raised an eyebrow. "If it weren't so late and the state of Sir Herra's unresolved trail, I would demand to be taken there this evening.

However, I believe most of us must return to the council room. I only issued a rest for the dining hour."

Mr. Kraft and Mage Sebastian remained kneeling on the floor.

"The trial started without my presence?" Fin rounded on the king angrily.

"It was only the character witnesses you missed," Kat informed her father glumly. "Gods, his friends can prattle on . . ."

"While Sir Herra has committed a grave crime, he has saved many lives during his career as a knight, and prior to this incident has served his kingdom well," Brendan countered at Katarina seriously before addressing her father.

The duke didn't look away from the king, but Brendan remained guiltless in his response. "I held the trial off for as long as possible, but my court has been in chaos, as they are frightened of poisonings, and many of them are of the belief that Sir Herra was possessed by a witch. We will need to have an overwhelming amount of evidence to reaffirm that witches are incapable of controlling others."

Fin closed his eyes and rubbed his face. The old misunderstanding was terribly annoying . . . He hadn't missed having to battle others about it back in Daxaria.

"Shall we all return to the council room?" Alina volunteered imperially, hoping to move things along.

Brendan's exhausted gaze rested on his wife for a moment before he gave a small bow to his queen and offered her his arm to escort her back to the council room.

"By the way, Da, you'll get to meet His Majesty's mother today," Kat informed her father. The king and queen swept past the group toward the door while Mr. Kraft and Sebastian remained on their knees, waiting until everyone had left.

Fin looked at his daughter with a frown. "The woman who bullied you in the castle is back?"

Kat nodded while stretching her mouth to one side and raising her eyebrows.

The duke let out an irritable breath.

"They brought her back to help Mum be comfortable. Lady Rebecca Devark apparently knew Mum back when she lived here in Troivack."

Fin stilled, and Kat found herself taken aback by the abrupt hesitancy.

However, she didn't get the chance to ask about the odd reaction, as the house witch overcame the brief spell of surprise and strode from the room purposefully as though he intended to speak with Brendan Devark about the matter . . .

Puzzled, Kat stared after him as her husband rejoined her side, though the prince was eyeing Kraken, who had at last dozed off peacefully, still in the center of the room.

"I'm starting to see what you mean about my da not being forthcoming."

Eric cast an apologetic side-glance at his wife. "We'll confront him another time. Are you certain you're alright being around the former queen again?"

Kat cracked her neck and permitted herself to grin, as no one but the mage and coven leader remained behind with them.

"I'm not worried . . . especially now that Kraken is here. You see, I imagine he might be able to *charm* Lady Rebecca in the same way he did your father."

Eric's face turned blank, and Mr. Kraft and Mage Sebastian looked at each other in equal bafflement.

Then . . . the Daxarian prince broke out in laughter, further perplexing the Troivackian men.

However, as he chortled, and even Kat gave the occasional cackle, a quiet purr began to rumble from the fluffy familiar on the floor who had heard the entire thing.

Lady Rebecca Devark, former queen of Troivack, had no idea the vengeance that was about to descend upon her life . . . Her shoes were already looking mighty appealing in Kraken's mind as the *best* spot to relieve his late-night bowel movements.

Ah, the things he did for his dear witch's kitten.

CHAPTER 26

JARGON OF JUSTICE

T hank you, Lord Adam, for your testimony," Mr. Levin called out, though even the stern assistant couldn't fully keep the boredom from his voice.

The young man nodded respectfully and once again took his seat.

Meanwhile, Kat had her head propped in her hand, and her eyes were half closed.

Even Alina looked as though she might let loose a yawn at any moment.

Sir Herra's father, in an effort to keep his son alive, had opted for the Tire Everyone Out approach before making his concluding arguments and appeal.

Surprisingly, Brendan Devark didn't try to interfere with his vassal's methods.

At first Katarina, Eric, and Alina had assumed it was because he was buying time for Finlay Ashowan to join the meeting, but even with the inclusion of the house witch, the king had sat silent as character witnesses paraded in and out. Everyone participated, from the lowliest servants, to the squires, to the knights, and now to his friends and acquaintances.

It was at the point where no one would be surprised if they brought in the family horses as evidence of his upstanding character.

Kat looked at Brendan wearily, wondering just how much longer he was really going to let things go on.

However, it was her father who wound up deciding he would be the one to put an end to the superfluous display.

"Pardon me, Lord Herra, while I recognize that you are doing your best to protect your son, you must understand that I am also trying to protect my daughter. Sir Seth Herra threw at Katarina what we have discovered to be a potent form of powdered Witch's Brew. Which not only is an illegal drug but can also be deadly. This trial should be proceeding on the charges of attempted murder." Fin's voice rang sharply in the chilly council room that was already growing dim as the day wore on.

Lord Herra frowned angrily and opened his mouth to retort when Brendan Devark at last raised his hand and resumed control.

"Lord Ashowan is correct. This attack of your son's could lead to a war between Daxaria and Troivack. As noble and hardworking as Sir Herra has been thus far, he made a grave error in judgment and has risked the lives of an entire kingdom. However," Brendan added before shifting his gaze to the elite knight, who stood looking unkempt in shackles on the left side of the council table with guards surrounding him, "I will be open to lessening his sentence should Sir Herra implicate the men who put him up to the assault."

"He has not said anyone helped him," Captain Orion interrupted, his voice a little too loud.

The king regarded the military man without saying a word.

Instead, he let silence stretch in the time after the outburst. Everyone's attention moved to Captain Orion, who, despite the biting cold surrounding them, had a thin sheen of sweat near his hairline.

"I never said 'helped.' I was implying that someone had ordered him to attack Lady Katarina. Though if there *was* someone helping him, I'd like to know that as well," Brendan continued, his unblinking stare unnerving almost everyone. "What I had asked for was to know *who* ordered Sir Herra to attempt such a thing."

"Your Majesty, why would you assume our elite knight did not orchestrate this attack on his own? He may have simply been seeking vengeance on Lady Katarina after she made him apologize," Lord Miller pointed out reasonably.

It was Milo Miller's turn to be subjected to the king's weighty stare.

Again, the monarch did not hurry to speak.

It took a few tense moments, but eventually Brendan got around to letting everyone know his thoughts.

"Before answering that, I would like to turn my previous question to Sir Herra." The king adjusted his attention to the elite knight, who showed no signs of having heard the monarch.

"Sir Herra, why did you attempt to drug Lady Katarina?" Brendan's voice was quiet, but firm.

The elite knight's lifeless gaze didn't move from the floor.

Kat sat up straighter.

"Sir Herra, I will again remind you that whoever may have put you up to this task may be threatening countless lives, and as an elite knight who swore to protect the kingdom and crown, on your honor, you should answer."

The knight still did not respond.

Kat leaned toward the king and whispered, "Can I try bringing in my familiar? She's remarkably persuasive."

Brendan didn't shift his attention from the knight, but Alina leaned over instead and, matching her friend's volume, responded, "Remember back in the king's office that Troivackians have the old prejudice that witch's possess magic that alters people minds? That wouldn't help matters right now."

Kat slumped her shoulders. "Damn . . . What if *I* just want to see her?"

Alina gave her friend a *you know why that's a bad idea* look, then she, too, regarded the knight on trial.

However, the two women needn't have hurried to end their whispering, as Sir Herra still did not speak or even lift his eyes.

"Sir Herra," Brendan started again. "If you continue to bear this trial in silence, I will have no choice but to have you executed."

Lord Herra shifted forward and opened his mouth to object, but when he saw the hint of pain in Brendan's eyes, closed his mouth again.

He could sense that the monarch truly did want to find a means of saving his son . . .

"Seth . . . Seth please, please respond to His Majesty. I know you would not have done this on your own," the man begged his son while emotions choked his voice. "You would've only done this if you thought you were helping our king."

Despite his best efforts, Lord Herra's eyes welled with tears as he stared at Seth.

"Pardon me, Your Majesty," Eric addressed Brendan, his expression icy and formal.

Regardless of the gut-wrenching emotions being displayed, he appeared unaffected.

"I'm surprised we have not heard the testimony of one particular individual."

Kat rounded on her husband, her golden eyes wide and shooting daggers. Eric did not need to look at his wife to know the words she was thinking.

For the love of the Gods, stop. If I hear one more testimony, I'll jump out the window.

Brendan blinked in confusion over who the Daxarian prince could possibly be talking about.

"Why have we not heard from Caleb Herra, Sir Seth Herra's younger brother?"

A fresh wave of unease rocked the noblemen.

Everyone had known but never acknowledged the fact that Sir Seth Herra had tried to have his younger brother murdered to stop Caleb from outshining him.

"Caleb Herra has not only trained with Lady Katarina, but he is a member of Lord Herra's household. He may have insights or have heard something from mutual acquaintances," Eric continued seriously.

Brendan's expression, while not threatening per se, was without a doubt ominous.

He did not like that the Daxarian prince was seeking to make the experience even more painful for the Herra household.

However, given that Seth *had* attempted to harm Lady Katarina, the king could understand Eric's reaction.

"His Highness makes a fair point. Leader Faucher?" The king looked to the military leader.

"Yes, Your Majesty?"

"Please summon your student Mr. Caleb Herra here for questioning."

"Yes, Your Majesty."

Faucher was on his feet and stalking from the throne room without a moment's hesitation.

Kat stared longingly at the doors.

"Given that it's you he tried to drug, you're awfully casual about this," Eric murmured under his breath to his wife.

"I'm saving my emotional outbursts for the sentencing. If I were raging through this entire meeting, I'd turn this room into a sauna."

"You know what a sauna is?"

Kat raised an eyebrow at Eric. "My father's best friend is Lord Jiho Ryu. Of course I know what a sauna is. He goes on and on about missing Zinfera solely because of the saunas."

Eric closed his eyes and nodded in understanding. "Right. I forgot. Have you ever been to one?"

"A sauna? Me? Why would I do that to myself?"

"I hate to interrupt your private conversation, but talking about saunas in the midst of a murder trial is far from appropriate," Alina uttered, her hazel eyes flashing.

Both Eric and Kat looked at each other in wordless communication before addressing the queen.

"Sorry. It does get tiring being dire and serious *all* the time though," Kat returned carefully.

Alina's lips pursed as she leaned back into her throne, her annoyance at her brother and sister-in-law not at all improved.

Meanwhile, Finlay Ashowan, who sat across from Prince Eric, was staring at the table deep in thought.

Turning his chair the rest of the way around Fin squared himself properly to study the elite knight on trial.

He eyed Sir Herra's hands that were clasped in front, the militaristic bracing of his feet, the vacant stare . . .

He didn't seem nervous despite the fact that his life was on the line, nor did he seem angry or smug.

Was he terrified? Or was something else wrong with him?

The longer Fin kept staring at him, the more perplexed and eventually disturbed he grew.

"Your Majesty, can I have a private word with you?"

Brendan had noticed Fin's shifting reactions and had become curious, and so with a slow nod, he and Fin rose and stepped a few feet away from the council table while everyone else whispered amongst themselves.

"Your Majesty, while you know I do not have my regular magical abilities while away from my home, there are little things I am still able to do regardless. Cook amazing meals, fold any household linen perfectly, and . . . sense what someone is craving."

Brendan raised an eyebrow but did not bother prompting the house witch to continue.

"A privileged man who has been underfed in a cell for days should be craving *something. He* isn't. He isn't craving meat, or bread, or moonshine . . . absolutely nothing. And yet he feels somewhat balanced. Something is not right with Sir Herra."

The king's eyes darted briefly to the knight and then back to Fin, his features still. "What could be the reason for it?"

"I've never felt it before, so I can't say. Who would have had access to him in his cell?"

"Guards and knights, all who are standing here today."

"What about any of the nobles?"

"None of the nobility were permitted to speak with him."

"Would any of those knights or guards be in the pocket of the nobility who are part of the rebellions?" Fin questioned next, knowing it was a sensitive topic that could cause a significant stir amongst the Troivackian courtiers should he be overheard.

Brendan pondered the question seriously. "Anything is possible."

Fin sighed agitatedly. "What if he has taken the powdered form of Witch's Brew? We've not tested what it will do to a person yet. It could potentially reduce mental faculties."

"How long would it take to discover what it does?"

"I can ask Lady Elena tomorrow when the investigation takes place. I don't know if they've had a witch who has been able to take it or if they have found another means of testing."

Brendan cleared his throat and shifted awkwardly. A sure sign he was about to say something he was uncertain about.

"Lord Ashowan . . . your daughter has . . . a unique constitution, as I know you are aware of. It could be that—"

"I am not allowing Kat to test the drug." Fin's light blue eyes flashed. "*Especially*, Your Majesty, when someone was trying to dose her with it. There might be something to the drug that is meant to affect Kat specifically."

Brendan paused then. "Lord Ashowan, what *does* Witch's Brew do to witches?"

"It . . ." Fin trailed off then faltered. "Well, we are made of flesh and blood just like everyone else. It should affect us the same."

"However, wasn't it reported that people who ingested it took on the abilities of witches nearby?"

Fin paused before responding. "At times. Not always though."

"It's all tied together somehow, Lord Ashowan. I want to know exactly what it does to witches and its effects are in this powdered form. After Mr. Caleb Herra's testimony today, I am recessing this trial until we have those answers."

While not thrilled at the notion that his daughter's attacker was not experiencing imminent justice, the lack of craving in Sir Herra was off-putting enough to subdue Fin's protests.

The Troivackian king was right.

There were too many unanswered questions . . .

His hands finding his hips, Fin stared at the king's back as the monarch returned to his seat before then examining the rest of the nobility present.

Despite having struggled for weeks on end to make it to Troivack, dealing with delayed and changed messages when his travel plans kept being altered, Fin had known all along that he was in for a far greater world of difficulty once he'd arrived.

It wasn't hard to predict; he was in a court where he had no power, literally and figuratively, and had few if any connections . . .

Sighing, Fin found himself missing his wife more than ever.

She would have a foothold in the group in no time, but until his beloved reached them . . .

Maybe I'll try making ribs and fried potato wedges to see if that'll soften some of the nobles toward me . . .

CHAPTER 27

PINA'S PLIGHT

K at trudged through the castle corridor.

As it turned out, her peer and fellow student, Mr. Caleb Herra, had not been on the grounds and had in fact returned home to console his mother, who had been devastated ever since Seth Herra had been imprisoned. As a result, the council decided to conclude the meeting for the day. Many of them were too exhausted or hungry to bother trying to force a decision right then and there, and even if they had, Lord Herra looked more than ready to battle them on that suggestion.

"Fin says he's going into town to talk to Likon about the powdered Witch's Brew testing," Eric announced to his wife as he caught up and fell into step beside her.

Kat's tired eyes sharpened instantly at hearing her childhood friend's name, then dimmed sadly.

"I hope he's come around a bit since being away . . . I know a lot of his initial reaction was because of what happened to his sister . . ."

Moving his hand into his right pocket, Eric began opening his mouth to find out what had happened to Likon's sister when Broghan Miller barreled up to the redhead.

"Ashowan! Problem! You need to come! *Now!* Please, before my brother finds out!"

"Isn't your last name Reyes now?" Eric asked with a wry eyebrow arch.

Halting in her tracks and staring in alarm at her peer, Kat ignored Eric's observation as her mind raced with whatever could have happened.

"It's . . . It's Pina," Broghan gasped while hastily stepping aside for one of the noblemen who passed by the trio.

"What happened to Pina?!" Kat demanded, her hand automatically moving to the hilt of her sword.

Broghan Miller's eyes darted to the noblemen that continued to stream by them nervously before he leaned closer and dropped his voice so that only Kat and Eric might hear his next words.

"She's . . . She's been arrested."

Kat's hand fell from her sword hilt. "Come again?"

"I'm not sure I understand either," Eric joined in with a bewildered tilt of his head.

"Your kitten has been arrested!" Broghan hissed frantically. "If my brother finds out, he might slaughter half the king's army!"

It was Broghan's genuine terror over whatever violent vengeance Sir Cleophus Miller might invoke in light of the familiar's arrest that made the news finally sink in for Kat.

"W-Wait . . . They arrested my cat?! Those bastards!" she burst out furiously, then took off in a sprint, leaving Eric and Broghan behind as she headed toward the dungeons.

Eric, however, was still struggling with the concept as he opened and closed his mouth twice more before looking to Broghan Miller.

"Is this a prank?"

Broghan shook his head vehemently. "Gods, I wish it was. She was arrested on grounds of magical mind tampering."

Eric's jaw dropped and his eyes squinted at the younger man, at a complete loss about what to say or do . . .

However, Broghan didn't plan on waiting around when so many lives were at stake, and so he turned and ran after Kat.

Sensing that there was something outrageous afoot, Eric followed suit.

Well . . . Kat did warn me she wasn't going to be the typical wife. It'd make sense if her cat wasn't a typical cat either . . .

"What if they have her in shackles!" Kat fretted while rushing down the winding stone steps with Eric and Broghan on her heels.

"Oh Gods! They'd be too heavy for her to move!" Broghan gasped in response.

"Right . . . I don't actually think they have shackles that are small enough for Pina . . . Plus I've never heard of anyone shackling or arresting a cat . . ." Eric contributed while trying to remain the voice of reason.

Unfortunately, there wasn't time for his perfectly logical point to be properly processed before they touched down on the dungeon floor where there was a crowd gathered.

Men were standing packed shoulder to shoulder, and many of them were shouting.

Some of the snippets that Broghan, Eric, and Kat overheard were: "Injustice!" "Satan's work!" "You sicken me!"

Kat glanced back fearfully at Eric before wedging her shoulder between two of the men at the back.

As she moved farther into the surprisingly well-lit dungeon, the dull roar of men around her increased to a din.

She was surprised no one tried to stop her as she continued to muscle her way through. Miraculously, her aura wasn't even showing yet . . .

Kat tried to peer into the many cells to see if she might find her familiar chained up somewhere, but alas, she couldn't see over the many heads of the Troivackian men that surrounded her.

Adjusting her search to locate anyone who looked to be in charge, she spotted the gleam of a chest plate three rows down. A man holding a piece of parchment taped to a board and a quill in hand was scowling at the crowd before him. Just as Kat was about to make her way through to go speak to him, he let out a bellow of his own.

"EVERYONE! SILENT!"

Incredibly, the unruly crowd did settle down . . . for a moment.

"I was here before him!"

"No, you weren't! We got here together, an' I bought the last round at the pub the other night, so I should go first!"

Another scathing look from the knight with the board and chest plate had the pair of men that had been arguing fall silent.

Kat took this opportunity while everyone was distracted by the argument to slip through the final rows of people and step before the man whom she was presuming to be in charge. Behind him were two other burly soldiers that were appropriately frightening for men who were tasked with guarding a dungeon.

"Hi, I'm not sure what is going on, but I'm here for my familiar, Pina."

The men behind Kat shuffled backward away from her.

She didn't bother looking at them.

Instead, the knight she faced, with his square jaw and dimpled chin, raised an eyebrow at her.

"I see. Then perhaps you are the person who should be handling this matter."

"Handling what matter?! What is going on?! She's a cat! Why in the world was my *cat* arrested?!"

The man held up his hand as though trying to calm Katarina down, and she had to fight the urge to snap his wrist.

"Now, now. I am Sir Beloff. I am the knight who is in charge of the castle dungeons, and I am handling the arrest of Pina Colada. However, I am not as familiar with the procedures concerning this unique case."

"You mean the idiocy of some nobleman who ordered the arrest of a cat?" This new question came from Eric, who had managed to join his wife's side, though it had been a troublesome endeavor.

Sir Beloff raised his chin before bowing to the prince.

"She was arrested on suspicion of mind tampering. I admit . . . I . . . I can understand how such a conclusion was reached now having met her." The knight had a faint blush rise in his cheeks as he cleared his throat.

"Where. Is. My. Cat?" Katarina growled while leaning forward threateningly, her eyes glinting with sparks of magic.

The knight recoiled slightly, gripping the board in his hands closer to his chest.

When he composed himself again, he gave a cough before speaking while also attempting to appear aloof.

"Lady Katarina, I assure you she is perfectly comfortable." Sir Beloff leaned aside then and revealed what the two imposing men at his sides were actually guarding . . .

There, on a purple plush velvet cushion, lay Pina. Her paws curled under her body, and her eyes were large in the low light of the dungeon.

A chorus of warm *awes* came from the men behind Kat and Eric in perfect unison.

Eric was beginning to wonder if he was trapped in one of the most realistic and possibly strangest dreams of his life.

"Is this . . . Is this truly not a prank?" he found himself asking while Kat attempted to move forward only to have Sir Beloff stand in her way.

"I assure you, Your Highness, this is of the utmost seriousness. Look at what she has done to all these respectable Troivackian men."

"Who ordered this?" Eric queried next, his tone turning imperial.

"That would be Lord Ball."

"LORD BALLSACK GOT MY CAT ARRESTED?!" Kat exploded crassly while seizing the collar of Sir Beloff's tunic and wrenching him down to be eye level with her.

The knight's throat bobbed as Kat's aura flickered around her.

The group made a collective unspoken decision not to chastise the red-head in that moment for her insult of the nobleman.

Eric gently touched his wife's shoulder. "Kat . . . they can't arrest an animal, and furthermore, she's Daxarian. I'm relatively certain there would have to be a whole investigation conducted prior to her arrest, and she would be permitted to stay with you during that time. If they were to treat the complaint as though she were a person, that is . . . This is absolute lunacy, by the way."

"Hang on! I was on the ship with Your Highness! Lady Katarina found her on board a Troivackian vessel — that makes her Troivackian!" a man called out from somewhere near the middle of the dungeon.

Kat's head turned slowly to stare over her shoulder, and she succeeded in making the men shift backward into one another as they tried to retreat from her wrath.

"We were on Daxarian waters," Eric hollered back.

"She may have been born on the ship, making her Troivackian," one of the guards who stood behind Sir Beloff and beside Pina contributed sternly with a nod.

"That was never confirmed. She was old enough to be weaned from her mother, meaning she could have been born on Daxarian soil and moved to the boat— Why the hell am I arguing citizenship of a cat?" Eric asked more to himself then anyone present as he lowered his face to his hand.

"If she is bonded to a witch, then she belongs to the witch." Kat continued the discussion through gritted teeth, completely ignoring her husband's exasperation. "Watch."

Releasing Sir Beloff, Katarina straightened.

"Pina, come."

At first, nothing happened, though everyone waited silently regardless.

A feat they were most happy that they did, as Pina then pounced onto Sir Beloff's shoulder, and from there, straight into Katarina's arms.

The men behind Kat went ballistic.

Turning around to face the adoring crowd, the redhead frowned while Pina nuzzled her ear lovingly.

"I . . . I thought you were all here to demand her death."

The men gasped.

"Of course not!" One of the knights approached Kat, separating himself from the crowd as though he were their spokesman.

"Lady Katarina, I was trying to tell you." Sir Beloff sighed behind the redhead, making her round back to face him. "These men are here to petition for her release."

"That isn't terribly strange, I suppose. People petition for the release of prisoners all the time—"

Eric was interrupted by the man who had spoken on behalf of the crowd moments before.

"And we want to pet her! Maybe hold her. If she's fine with it of course!"

At long last, Kat looked as astounded and exasperated as her husband.

The couple looked at each other and then back to Sir Beloff. "Is this true?"

"I was taking names for the petition, but they were also intending to go down the list for who would be first to . . . pet . . . or scritch— Have you noticed she likes cheek scritches?"

"Of course I know she likes cheek scritches!" Kat snapped while she proceeded to do that very thing while holding Pina firmly against her shoulder as though one of the adoring knights might try to snatch the kitten from her arms.

"Wait . . . So why were you arguing so intensely about her being Daxarian or Troivackian?" Eric was barely following along, but he was doing the best he could.

"Our petition for her release will carry more weight if she is Troivackian," the other man who had been guarding Pina explained.

"Right . . . right . . . I . . . I really don't think I can take much more of this . . . Kat, you didn't happen to put something strange in my coffee this morning, did you?" The prince once again addressed his wife before covering his mouth and rubbing it.

"I promise I didn't this time."

"What do you mean 'this time'?"

"Well, sometimes you complain about being sore, and you refuse to take any painkillers because you're stubborn and don't want to admit you're old, so—"

"Kat! Honestly? You're dosing my morning coffee?!"

"Just with a bit of willow bark! Nothing that bad!"

"You said I was imagining things when I said it tasted earthy! And yet you've been slipping in a painkiller. You know that could be harmful if used for too long!" Eric rounded on Kat in exasperation.

"It's not all the time! Just this morning, really!"

As the situation continued to descend into the darkest depths of absurdity, things were about to reach entirely new levels when a roar that could've rivaled a dragon's shook the dungeon walls.

"Oh Gods . . . he found out," Broghan all but whimpered, his eyes fixed in expectant horror on the arched dungeon doorway.

"Right . . ." Eric rounded on Sir Beloff. "We are going to tell Sir Cleophus Miller that Pina was down here hunting rats and everyone just wanted to watch her, got it? We are going to treat her as a Daxarian for the sake of these charges so that we can walk out of here, and therefore you will not be punished by Lord Balls— Pardon. Lord Ball."

Sir Beloff looked momentarily torn by the prince's forceful instruction, however, when Sir Cleophus Miller appeared in the doorway holding his unsheathed great sword and his eyes thirsting for blood, he nodded hastily.

"Smart decision," Eric whispered while turning around and waving to the gigantic knight that could and *would* most likely crush an average man's head in his hand should they attempt to harm Pina in any way.

"Ah, Sir Miller! Sorry to say you missed the show! Pina just caught a mouse! It was adorable!" Eric cheered.

"I thought you said it'd be a rat," Sir Beloff whispered urgently.

"I changed my mind. I was forgetting how big your rats are. It's a lot more believable this way," Eric retorted while doing his best to smile and look casual while holding Sir Cleophus's gaze.

Kat watched the scene unfold and decided her husband's course of action was indeed the smartest one and that she may as well help things along.

"Alright, baby girl, your most devoted worshiper has come. Please do your best to calm him down, hm? I really don't want to have to stay up late explaining why there was a mass slaughter in the king's basement. Alina would be livid," the redhead whispered in between peppering Pina's cheek with kisses.

The kitten gave a small mew.

Meanwhile, the men had practically climbed atop one another to clear an aisle for Sir Miller, who still hadn't put his sword away.

Upon reaching Eric, Broghan, Kat, and Pina, Cleophus halted, his boots thudding against the stones beneath his feet.

Even Sir Beloff and his guards shrank back fearfully.

"Sir Cleophus, how are you this evening?" Kat asked brightly.

The knight didn't answer. His beady eyes instead fixed themselves on Sir Beloff.

"I heard Pina was arrested."

"O-Oh, it . . . It is a matter to be investigated. These men here are all willing to sign a—"

"Who?"

No one needed Cleophus to expand on what he meant.

"L-Lord Ball." Sir Beloff looked as though he were on the verge of wetting himself.

A rumbling snarl clawed at Sir Cleophus's chest before he turned back around and headed toward the stairway he had just descended from.

"Oh Gods, he might kill Lord Ball!" Broghan made to follow his brother when Kat reached out and seized the back of his tunic, stopping him.

"I'm not *that* merciful of a person. Let the crumbs fall where they may."

Broghan stared wide-eyed at the redhead despite her breezy tone.

"Besides, if he *does* kill Lord Ball, that means his wife, Elyse, can join my next class! All's well that ends well. Now, come along. I think it's about dinnertime and I'm about ready to eat twice my normal amount after all the suffering we endured today."

"I think I might go to bed," Eric informed his wife dazedly.

Pina let out another mew and stretched her neck toward the Daxarian prince.

Taking her from Kat's arms as the kitten indicated she wished, Eric grasped Kat's hand with his free one and gradually set the pace as they headed down the aisle of bodies for the dungeon exit. Broghan Miller trailed behind, still tormented with his anxieties.

As they made their way back up the stairs, the prince managed to spare one final thought on the whole endeavor . . .

"Remind me to ask Mr. Julian to look into laws governing the citizenship of animals tomorrow morning just to be on the safe side."

Kat grinned.

She knew she'd married the right man.

CHAPTER 28

A MORNING ALARM

Eric and Kat lay peacefully asleep. The warmth under the blankets were a stark contrast to the frosty morning outside.

The fireplace was still warming the room with its glowing coals, letting out the occasional pop or crackle.

Servants were only just starting to begin their days, as the sun had yet to crest the horizon, and the quiet brought a calm that even the most troubled of minds would find soothing.

That is until Katarina sat up in her bed with a jolt and jumped out in a hurry.

Due to his years making his living as a mercenary and surviving in dangerous situations, Eric was wide awake in an instant after her, his hand already reaching for the dagger on their bedside table, his gaze flying about the room.

"What is it?" he asked when he didn't see any imminent threat.

Kat gnawed on her cheek, her hand flying to her middle.

"Pardon me a moment." She then turned and fled the room.

Eric opened his mouth to ask another question, but after a moment, his tired mind caught up and he lowered his gaze to Pina, who was curled up comfortably by the fireplace on a royal blue folded blanket Kat had set down for her.

"I told her not to try the marinated hot peppers before bed," he informed the familiar with a shake of his head before a yawn claimed him.

The prince had just about fallen asleep once more when their chamber door opened again and Kat returned. After closing the door behind her, she crawled back into bed.

"What did I tell you? Spicy food before bed is a bad—"

"I'm not pregnant."

Eric's eyes flew open, and he rolled over on his side to stare at his wife. "Pardon?"

"My courses just started. I'm not pregnant," Kat explained as she snuggled back down under the coverlet.

"Ah." The prince nodded and eased onto his back. However, after spending a bit of time absorbing this information, he rotated back to his side to face Kat, whose eyes were already closed.

"What are your thoughts on this . . . ?"

"That now I have the perfect reason to drink a lot of moonshine all day."

"Then you aren't upset we got married when we could've pretended our encounter never happened?"

Kat opened her eyes again and raised an eyebrow. "I was relatively certain I wasn't pregnant even before getting married. The timing wasn't right."

Eric failed to give any outward reaction.

"Are *you* upset?" she questioned with a chuckle lurking in the back of her throat.

"A bit disappointed."

Kat blinked and shifted back to better stare at her husband and show him her astonished expression.

"It would've been a lot easier to make you go home and stay away from the conflict that's brewing if you were," he explained hastily when he realized belatedly how his words could have been misconstrued.

Kat relaxed a little, but instead of being angry, she found herself annoyed. "Even if I were expecting I wouldn't leave. I told my da the same thing, and nothing either of you say would've changed that."

Eric paused.

Admittedly he had become distracted with how beautiful his wife looked thanks to not quite being free of his groggy mind.

He marveled over her magnificent eye color and the way her loose sleep shirt exposed her narrow collarbone . . .

Rather than responding to his wife's bold declaration, he leaned forward and planted a kiss on her forehead.

"There's no point in being mad about it now. I'm sure we'll find new things to fight about in the future."

Kat let out an irritated grunt.

Eric simply pulled her closer to him and closed his eyes. "Shh . . . You can be mad at me after the sun rises."

Kat didn't immediately relax into his embrace, as she was still sorely tempted to pursue a fight right then and there . . . but then Eric started gently combing his fingers through her hair and occasionally giving a small scratch on her head, and before she knew it, she was lulled back into a restful doze once more.

That is, until loud, repetitive pounding on the chamber door roused the couple yet again.

"Godsdamnit," Eric mumbled before rolling away from Kat so that she might be able to see who their impromptu visitor was while he rubbed his eyes.

Rising to her feet and hastily throwing on a robe, Kat crossed the small room that she and Eric still didn't feel the need to vacate in favor of a bigger one, and she opened the door.

Her father stood there with Kraken at his side, bags under his eyes and an indescribable amount of fear and pain in his face.

"Kat, is Eric with you right now?"

Alarmed at her father's state, Kat frowned and was about to ask what was wrong when her husband interrupted her.

"I'm here, Fin. What's wrong?" Grasping the door and pulling it wider, Eric stepped beside his wife.

"It's . . . It's Likon. I went into town yesterday to try to talk with him about the powdered Witch's Brew, but the innkeeper said he disappeared days ago. He left all his belongings in his room, so he didn't just bolt . . . Something's wrong."

"Was there any sign of a fight?" Kat insisted as her hand holding her robe closed tightened into a fist.

"No. Nothing like that. Kraken says there is an inordinate number of pixies in the tavern, and some are talking about an imp that was there not that long ago with a strange man . . ."

"It's the devil."

"Ansar."

Both Kat and Eric said at the same time.

The couple looked at each other, both surprised at the other's response.

However, Kat was far more concerned than her husband was by that point.

"If it was a man and an imp, it sounds like the one who tried to bind my magic more than a month ago . . . The man's name was Ansar, and when he attacked, he had both the imp and the stone golem with him."

Kraken let out a long meow.

Fin looked down at his familiar before translating. "He wants to know if you caught the name of the imp?"

Kat shook her head, then looked down to answer Kraken directly "No. I didn't hear one . . . Gods. The stone golem disappeared into thin air after attacking the keep . . . What if they took Likon to another realm?"

Another shorter meow was Kraken's response.

"He says that it doesn't make sense that the golem disappeared before. Once an exchange has been made between realms, they shouldn't be going back and forth." Fin shook his head wearily.

"What if it's because the rock golem was a lot bigger? What if it's harder to keep in our realm with just a lone soul?" Eric questioned while glancing to his wife, then back to Kraken.

The familiar chirped.

Fin tilted his head side to side. "That might be why. Either way, I have no idea where Likon is. I spent the night visiting every business in Vessa we have ties to, but no one has heard a thing. Or if they have, they are keeping their mouths shut."

"Da, have you not had any visions? If not, then Likon isn't afraid!" Kat pointed out earnestly as her father began to rake a hand through his unkempt hair.

"That's true, but I didn't see anything when you were kidnapped either. It's also possible they are keeping Likon dosed."

"Shit . . ." Kat cursed, her throat growing tight.

"I'll throw on some clothes and come with you to the king. We can speak with Mr. Kraft about joining me in Vessa. I know a few well-hidden haunts in this city, and with his magic of sight, I might be able to find something."

"I'm coming with you," Kat announced.

"Unfortunately, that's not possible," Fin admonished, his gaze meeting his daughter's. "The matter of your familiar being arrested has not been entirely settled. Lord Ball is kicking up a fuss, though he still remains bed-ridden after his fight with Joshua and now Lord Herra is supporting him. Both are claiming everything that's going wrong is your fault and Pina's."

Kat's eyes narrowed. "Cleophus didn't finish the job and deal with Ball?"

Fin blinked. "Did you . . . pay a knight to kill a nobleman?"

"Of course not. He wanted to do it all on his own. I just didn't stop him."

The duke looked at Eric, who gave a shrug and a nod of confirmation.

Close enough of a recounting.

Letting out a long, burdened breath, Fin looked down at Kraken. "Of all the bloody ridiculous things people have done to oppose me in my life, getting a cat arrested to oppose *you* my dear, Kitty Kat, has me soundly beat."

Kat gave a brief half smile before her worry for Likon quashed the momentary reprieve of seriousness.

"I'll let you know the second I learn anything," Eric assured his wife.

Kat faced him, terror and concern bright in her eyes.

"Eric, I'll wait for you to get dressed out here. Kat, you're to go to the council room after breakfast. I'll be present for all the meetings here on out. At least until every finger stops pointing in your direction."

A hiss near the trio's feet had everyone looking down to see that Pina had poked her nose outside the door curiously. Kraken was backing away from her, his fur already rising.

"Kraken, just what on earth is so terrible about my familiar?!" Kat demanded feeling far from patient given the progression of her morning.

The emperor let out a threatening grumble that had Pina freezing in place, her eyes already wide in the dim lighting of the day.

"He's still bent out of shape because he doesn't understand what language she's speaking and he thinks now she's doing it just to irk him," Fin clarified.

Kat looked down at her adorable familiar and scooped her up into her arms while sliding outside her chamber so that Eric could dress himself.

"Pina, you can trust Kraken. He's like . . . He's like an uncle to me. Or a stepfather to you!"

The feline didn't respond, only purred.

Kraken wasn't having any of it, however, and so he proceeded to turn and saunter down the corridor.

Fin watched the fluffy haunches retreat while shaking his head, closing his eyes, and rubbing the back of his neck.

"You should go sleep for a few hours, Da." Kat suggested quietly. "I'm worried about Likon too, but if you're too tired to think clearly, you won't be much help to anyone."

The tip of Fin's nose was pink from having spent his night outside in the cold, and his brilliant blue eyes were dull with exhaustion, but when he smiled at his daughter . . . he seemed the untouchable hero she had always seen him as when she'd been a child.

"I will. I'm really hoping your mother gets here soon."

"Well . . . I . . . I guess." Kat briefly grimaced.

For a moment, Fin was taken aback by his daughter's lackluster reaction to hearing that she'd get to see her mother again so soon, but then his eyebrows shot up. "Holy antlers . . . I completely forgot about *your* alarming amount of news with everything going on."

A slow smile climbed Kat's face. "Oh-ho. Now do you see what I mean? It's easy to forget things!"

Fin's unimpressed look did not convey a shared sentiment. "Your mother will be able to help us manage these Troivackians . . . She's always been a lot better at this politics business."

"I know, but I only just got used to the idea of being married, and I'd hate to die right when we're all getting along."

Fin looked at the ceiling. "Whatever your mother does in reaction to your news we'll handle it then. One thing at a time. First, we need to find Likon, then we need to figure out just what in the hell is going on with the devil, the mystery woman, and this rebellion in Troivack."

Kat scratched Pina's cheeks and tilted her head in agreement with her father, and by the next breath, the chamber door was opening and Eric stepped out in a fresh set of all-black clothes.

"Ready to go?" the prince asked Fin while pulling on his coat.

Fin gestured toward the corridor before them in answer, and so Eric hastily dropped a kiss on Kat's cheek and set off ahead of his father-in-law.

"Oh, by the way . . ." Kat cleared her throat and summoned her father's attention back to her. "You . . . You aren't going to be a grandfather in the imminent future."

Fin stared dumbly at his daughter for a long while before he closed his eyes, pursed his lips, and turned away.

"Great . . . Great news . . ."

"Are you still uncomfortable hearing about my courses?"

"It's uncomfortable when you scream about it during a bout of food poisoning and when it now has . . . *implications* . . ." Fin cleared his throat. "I'll see you later."

Kat waved off her father, who was already falling far behind her husband who had decided not to give any sign of having heard the interaction between his wife and father-in-law.

Turning to stare at her familiar in her arms, Kat pressed a long kiss on Pina's forehead.

"I really hope they find Likon soon . . . We never even got to make up after our fight."

As she retired back into her chamber, already feeling awful about the day ahead, Kat hoped with no small amount of optimism that maybe, by dinner, they would have at least found Likon and brought him back safely.

Amazingly, if all that was worrying Kat was the thought of having to confess everything that had happened in Troivack to her mother, she felt like things wouldn't seem quite so grim . . .

CHAPTER 29

A CLEAN KILL

Katarina and Fin were speaking in hushed tones on their way to the council meeting. Both were brainstorming furiously about Likon's absence when they simultaneously realized someone was standing in their path . . .

The father and daughter halted and looked up to see Rebecca Devark staring at Finlay Ashowan as if he were a ghost.

Fin's tired face grew taut. He'd seen that look many times before. He knew it was when someone who had known his father laid eyes on him . . .

"Good morning, ma'am," Kat greeted sternly before bowing.

Fin bowed next, and Lady Rebecca curtsied after him.

"If you will excuse us, we need to attend today's council meeting as well." Kat started to resume her trajectory toward the council room.

"Lady Katarina, I was wondering if I may have a brief word with you," Lady Rebecca called out while regaining her composure and lowering her eyes dutifully.

"You've had several just now," Kat retorted childishly.

The twitch of annoyance in Rebecca's thick black eyebrow was not lost on either Fin or his daughter.

"It will not take long."

Staring at the woman with open irritation, Kat let out a grumbling breath. "Very well."

Fin eyed his daughter, caught between wanting to be disapproving of her rudeness while also remembering that the former queen had been the one to ostracize his daughter ruthlessly.

So instead of commenting on either fact, he said, "Kat, I'll save a seat for you in the meeting."

Kat didn't take her eyes off the former queen's face but gave her father a brief wave.

Once the two women were alone, Rebecca's eyes roved over Kat in her uniform much as they had the previous day.

"Are you here to judge or talk to me?" Kat questioned, her gaze boring into Rebecca Devark's face.

"I've never seen a woman wear trousers before. It takes time to get used to," Rebecca countered evenly.

"Right, well if you've gotten your eyeful, I better get to the council meeting. And don't bother me again over something so pointless." Kat turned her toes to leave.

Taking in a sharp breath and lowering her chin, Rebecca tried again.

"Lady Katarina, I wanted to hear precisely what has been happening in my absence. My daughter-in-law refuses to take a meeting with me, though I hear I am to be grandmother to a future heir. His Majesty is too busy to speak with me, Lady Kezia refuses my requests, claiming she needs to tend to her son, and—"

"Am I supposed to feel bad for you? You did this all to yourself." Kat scoffed, a pulse of magic running round her eyes. She had noticed that the former queen was speaking as though Alina and Brendan's child would be her first grandchild and had completely jilted Kezia and Henry's son, Elio.

Rebecca's eyes darted to a pair of noblemen that passed by and bowed their heads quickly to both her and Kat, who folded her arms and bobbed her head in return.

Once they were out of earshot, the former queen continued, "I am not trying to garner sympathy. I am trying to learn what has been happening in this castle so that I might be useful."

Kat did her best to keep her tone level. "You'll have to earn back everyone's trust then. Do what you tried to make me do. Be quiet and dignified. Maybe by the time Alina gives birth, she'll let you hold her child . . . Though I *am* curious, how did you manage to return to court after only a few months?"

"I could ask the same of you," Rebecca returned with an edge in her voice.

Kat smirked. She could tell being utterly powerless and ignored was driving the former queen a mite mad, and given the morning the redhead had been having, she was not in a particularly generous or kind mood either.

From the sounds of it, Rebecca hadn't even heard about her sparring match in light of the more pressing news about a possible heir to the

Troivackian throne and the marriage of the prince of Daxaria to the daughter of the house witch.

"Did you really only come to greet my mother? If that's the case, I don't recommend unpacking," Kat informed the former queen harshly.

Rebecca stared at Kat for a long while without speaking.

At last, she said, "You seem angrier with me now than you did last time we spoke. Is there a reason for this?"

It was Kat's turn to take her time responding, as another throng of nobility and servants passed by, and more than a few heads turned curiously in their direction.

"Last time we spoke, I was barely recovered from having faced the creator of evil, and I was in a good mood. Now, was that everything, ma'am?"

The corners of Rebecca's dark eyes tightened. "Given your uniform and some of the whisperings I've heard, you have learned swordsmanship. Why?"

Amazingly, the tone behind the question wasn't hostile or condescending, but rather, curious.

Despite wanting to call the woman an old bat and be on her way, Kat was able to rummage up the recollection that she *did* want to encourage women to be open to learning how to fight . . . So with great struggle, she set aside her animosity in an attempt not to color the former queen's thoughts on the endeavor.

"I did it because I knew it was something I was meant to do, and it suits me better than any ladylike lifestyle." Breaking free from the conversation at last, Kat gave a shallow bow. "Good day, ma'am."

Taking her leave, Rebecca Devark stared at Katarina's erect back as she marched down the corridor in the direction of the council room.

The young woman, while still wildly inappropriate in much of her conduct, *did* seem to fit the role of rough soldier outrageously well . . .

It seems like my daughter-in-law is succeeding in changing a lot more than I anticipated. Whether these changes will last, however, remains to be seen.

Kat scowled.

Pina napped.

Cleophus Miller stared.

He didn't need to express anything in his statuesque face.

Everyone knew the man was one casual insult away from a bloodbath.

Alina gaped at the knight, and Brendan looked remarkably . . . humored.

"We shall now commence our meeting with regards to . . . Miss . . . Pina Colada . . . and whether the . . . *kitten* is responsible for magically tampering with the minds of Troivackian vassals." Even Mr. Levin, the man who wasn't exactly subtle about his disdain for Katarina, was struggling to take the subject of that day's meeting seriously.

"Of course! It must have been the beast that made my son lose his senses and attack Lady Katarina!" Lord Herra burst out while jumping to his feet.

Brendan Devark raised his eyebrows, his expression candidly conveying that he found the entire thing ridiculous.

"What purpose would it serve the kitten if her own mistress were attacked?" he questioned bluntly.

"Why to . . . to implicate my son! Lady Katarina had a vendetta against him and knew she wasn't in any immediate danger!"

"Are you forgetting, Lord Herra, that the men who were to spar with Lady Katarina were not permitted to be around the familiar?"

"Why was that though?" Duke Icarus questioned loudly, a pleased shine in his eyes that darkened Brendan's mood instantly.

"Everyone finds Lady Katarina's familiar adorable, and so they did not want to upset either of them as a result. It's much the same as when someone adores a child and, therefore, wishes the mother well as a result," Alina returned while keeping her voice light and breezy and resting her hand on her growing belly.

Duke Icarus gave an almost imperceptible eye roll as he turned back to the council.

"Our men-at-arms are battle hardened; they do not turn weak in the face of an animal that is merely cute. It must be magic."

"You think Sir Cleophus Miller is weak?" Kat asked with a derisive laugh.

Duke Icarus risked a glance at the beastly knight, who was staring at him in a way that made even *him* recoil.

"If I may interject," Fin called out, making everyone's head swivel toward him. "We've had these accusations discussed . . . at length . . . in Daxaria as well." The house witch didn't bother hiding his weary exasperation. "Altering the minds and wills of people is against the wishes of the Gods. They never have and never will give such magical power to anyone. Including witches. While you may wish to question my words on this, I have brought with me all accounts and reports submitted to the Coven of Wittica since its creation as well as all ancient texts referring to this."

Kat blinked at her father in amazement.

He noticed this and was unable to resist adding, "The number of times this misconception has been spread has made it so that I travel with these records every time I visit somewhere new. I also have the accounts from the Zinferan and Lobahlan covens . . . Do I need to dig up some from the Coven of Aguas as well?" Fin drawled while fixing Duke Icarus with a caustic stare.

There was a lot of throat clearing after Fin's announcement.

"What about familiars? Your own familiar has become a legend in his time for his prowess," Duke Icarus continued, though even he could sense he was losing his foothold.

"My familiar is infamous because I can understand him and he has superior intelligence, not because he can alter minds," Fin returned effortlessly.

"Then what reason could there possibly be for what must be at least a hundred nobility, knights, and serving staff combined being so wildly enamored with a mere *cat*?" the duke demanded while leaning forward in his chair, his fingers laced together.

"She's a cute cat. Animals don't ask anything, demand anything, or judge us the way humans do. It's easy to find solace in a creature that not only is endearing in appearance but is also content just to be in your presence," the house witch explained, his eyes thoughtful and his voice softening.

There was a soothing quality to his tone that created a relaxed air about everyone as they all began to concede that they, too, had a favored horse or pup at home that earned a good amount of adoration . . . And a well-behaved cat that let anyone pet or hold her? Why wouldn't people be a little kinder toward her?

"I think Lord Herra is simply desperate to have his son pardoned," the first whisper started.

"Lord Ball *is* concussed right now . . . he wasn't even in his right mind when he gave the order."

"I wouldn't be surprised if it was Duke Icarus who told him to have a kitten arrested."

Duke Icarus's head snapped around to look down the table, but when he did so he was not able to catch the culprits who were speaking against him, as everyone stopped talking and stared back; they were all regarding him pityingly.

He gritted his teeth, then redirected his attention to Finlay.

"I move to dismiss these charges against the kitten, Pina Colada. Lords, do I have the majority vote on this?" the king called out ceremoniously before the duke could find another point to argue.

Everyone save for two or three hands went in the air.

"Excellent." Brendan nodded and did well at hiding how pleased he was by how effortlessly the matter was wrapped up. "Currently, we are still awaiting results on the Witch's Brew testing, so we will not be continuing Sir Seth Herra's trial today."

A faint sigh of relief could be heard from Lord Aaron Herra.

"Instead, we are going to be discussing the discovery that Duke Sebastian Icarus has been illegally participating in human trafficking in order to enslave people to work his vineyards."

The room fell into stunned silence.

"I had intended to bring this matter to light after Lady Katarina's sparring match, however, the attack took precedent."

"Your Majesty, this is hardly—" Duke Icarus blustered, but one smoldering look from Brendan had him closing his mouth.

"You have in your possession nine hundred and thirty-six enslaved people across your various estates."

The room erupted in grunts and exclamations of surprise.

"I obtained this information after His Highness Prince Eric Reyes—who, unfortunately, could not attend today's meeting—had mercenaries under your employ, Duke Icarus, attack him. I also have a witness who has given testimony that they were blackmailed into attempting an assassination of the Daxarian prince."

The room exploded.

Duke Icarus's eyes went wide.

Kat smiled coldly at him though he didn't turn to look at her, and Alina stared unflinchingly at the duke, hungry for his demise.

"That is slander! I have no—"

"*Two* mercenary groups that had been in pursuit of His Highness after he fled your northern estate have been apprehended and interrogated. We have since received their confessions, *and* they admitted they had been instructed by not only you but also your brother. Mr. Levin has compiled the evidence for everyone here. In addition to these grave offenses . . ."

Duke Icarus looked as though he were about to faint, but Brendan had always been one to enjoy a clean kill.

"I was told *you* were the one who had a private audience with Sir Herra prior to the match and that Captain Orion colluded with you in order to place Sir Herra in one of the matches with Lady Katarina. Captain Orion signed his confession to Leader Faucher this morning. After yesterday's meeting, Leader Faucher suspected who was responsible behind the scenes given the events of the day of the sparring, and it would seem he was correct."

Lord Herra's hand slammed on the table, and he rose from his seat furiously. He looked ready to execute the duke himself.

"Duke Icarus, you are hereby under arrest for your many crimes, and your brother will be summoned for a trial in the coming days. Given that you were using your ships to take part in the illegal act of human trafficking, they have all been commandeered and are now under the crown's property as the investigation continues. I have additional proof on this, however, it will be saved for your brother's trial," Brendan finished while Duke Icarus leaned back as though foolishly debating whether to run.

His inspiration died quickly when his eyes shifted to the right and he startled at the sight of Sir Cleophus Miller looming over him with Pina purring on his shoulder.

"Duke Icarus, you will be escorted to the front steps for the first stage of your execution. May you reflect upon your sins in the Grove of Sorrows."

Sir Cleophus Miller's hand seized the duke's shoulder and hauled him to his feet.

"I-I-I was framed by my brother! By the mercenaries! Your Majesty! You must believe I would never—" A sharp jolt from Sir Cleophus silenced the man as he stumbled out of the council room.

The council that remained sat in stunned silence.

It seemed as though the powerful Icarus dukedom was on the precipice of utter ruin.

Kat slumped back in her seat and smiled at Alina over Duke Icarus's empty seat and lowered her voice so that no one else could hear.

"Now *that* is what I call a council meeting."

CHAPTER 30

THE TOLL OF TORTURE

Duke Sebastian Icarus knelt on the stones in front of the castle steps, his normally cool disposition a thing of the past. Clouds rolled overhead of the bleak scene below. Though at the very least, the wind that made the duke's hair flutter had a touch of warmth to it . . .

Brendan bore down on the man, his official great sword sharpened and ready at his side.

"Duke Sebastian Icarus, I will give you one chance to rise from your knees and prolong your life in order to get your estate in order."

Sebastian's eyes jumped up to the monarch. "Oh . . . Gods . . . Thank you, Your Majesty. I knew you were a wise and gracious—"

"You have my wife to thank," Brendan informed the duke, his dark gaze boring into the nobleman.

Sebastian Icarus paled as his gaze shifted to Alina, who approached and stood at her husband's side while the rest of the inner council members looked on from the top of the great steps to the castle.

The queen stared down at the duke, the red and black gown she wore striking against the bleak surroundings as she then raised a dispassionate eyebrow.

He would've thought she'd look triumphant . . . but the Troivackian queen looked more stressed than anything.

Alas. The notion of being disgusted by violence was foreign to the duke.

"Duke Icarus, I would like to discuss several grave matters at length while you are in your prison cell. Matters such as where you obtained the powdered Witch's Brew, who else oversees your hired mercenaries, and what the rebellion's long-term plans are. If you cooperate and answer these questions honestly, you might even get another year to live." Alina tilted her head, her tone emotionless.

Hatred flamed in the duke's eyes as his hands clenched into fists behind his back.

"You cursed wench. I'll never tell you a damn thing. May you rot in hell." He spat on the hem of Alina's dress.

Then his right arm was gone with a swift, silent swing of the king's sword. Duke Icarus howled.

Alina swallowed with difficulty but did everything she could to force herself to watch . . . She knew she couldn't be seen cowering now in front of everyone . . .

"Apologize," Brendan seethed. "As you know, Duke Icarus, this is only the beginning of the Troivackian Jigsaw method. You will apologize and divulge everything you know, or your remaining days will be spent in what feels like an eternity of agony."

Duke Icarus sobbed on the ground.

Meanwhile, Finlay Ashowan, who stood by the castle doors with the council and his daughter, turned his back on the gory scene.

"Come, Kat. We don't need to see this," he murmured, his voice tight.

Grimacing, Kat didn't object or resist as her father guided her away from the spectacle.

Once they had returned to the entryway of the castle, where there was a throng of nobility and servants alike all waiting to hear about what was taking place, Fin wasted no time in pushing through the crowd and steering his daughter toward the nearest empty room—which happened to be a drawing room for guests to meet in the mornings.

"Have you had to see a lot of things like that?" Fin asked his daughter gravely once the two of them were alone.

Kat stared at the floor, her complexion far paler than usual. "Only when they had to behead the assassins at the coronation."

While she had been pleased with finally seeing some form of justice befalling Duke Icarus, torture was an entirely different matter.

Fin took in a sharp breath and shook his head while staring around the room, at a loss for a moment as to what to say.

"I won't lie . . . I am shocked that Alina is able to handle this."

"She has her moments where she struggles. She's doing her best," Kat explained while battling down her own nausea.

Fin sighed. "I sincerely hope she is able to gentle some of Troivack's harsh ways, but I don't envy the amount of work she will have to put in."

Kat's mouth twisted. "I feel even worse because I'll have to leave her in a few months."

Nodding, Fin squared himself in front of his daughter. "I was going to return to Lady Elena's keep today to see the tunnels and perhaps find out what is happening with the investigation of the Witch's Brew powder. Would you like to join me?"

Kat shook her head. "I want to wait to see if Eric is able to find out any information about where Likon is."

Fin gave a sad smile as he reached up to touch his daughter's arm comfortingly.

"We're all praying that he comes back safe soon . . . When I return from Lady Elena's keep, I'll take a short rest and resume my search in Vessa for him. Maybe you can join me then."

Kat bobbed her head and crossed her arms over her middle. She had a horrible uneasy knot in her stomach about Likon's disappearance, and it wasn't getting any better . . .

"Come on . . . It helps to stay busy. What will you do while you wait for Eric?"

The father and daughter started to make their way back to the door of the drawing room as they both collected themselves to face the castle occupants.

"I have to train the women again today . . . Then I have to practice with Faucher . . ." Kat replied though her gaze remained lost.

Fin closed the door behind them. "I suppose I'll see you at the dinner hour then."

Kat gave a tight-lipped smile of confirmation as they faced each other in the corridor.

Leaning over, Fin kissed his daughter's forehead, then proceeded to give her one final pat on the arm as he set off to order a carriage for his trip to Lady Elena's keep.

Standing alone in the hall, Kat closed her eyes and let out a long, slow breath.

Well . . . at the very least, Duke Icarus has been dealt with . . .

Upon opening her eyes again, Kat gave herself a stern nod.

Her father was right. She couldn't let her worries cloud her mind.

There were still more threats and dangers that hovered over them, and if they were going to come out unscathed from whatever chaos was brewing, then she needed to be prepared for anything.

"Good morning, Likon."

He remained silent.

"I thought you might like to know your adoptive father has finally figured out you're missing. It only took him . . . What has it been . . . a week?"

The sound of a wet rag being wrung out and water trickling into a full basin reached his ears.

"I even heard Prince Eric Reyes is poking around Vessa as we speak. His wife must be terribly worried about you."

Likon tried to open his mouth, but his tongue felt thick and heavy . . .

"Don't worry, you'll see your beloved Ashowan family again . . . eventually. It'd be nice if you also happened to share a bit of information while we wait."

Likon forced his eyes open and nearly retched. He saw the fibers of a black bag . . . and that was it.

So he closed his eyes again, that is, until the bag was yanked off and the blinding light of day seeped through his closed lids, making his head pound.

"I really don't like having to do this either. I'm just trying to improve the world. Maybe carve a little place of my own here as well . . . Though I still have to take care of some loose ends, and unfortunately, Lady Katarina is starting to make that difficult. I don't have anything dreadful against her . . . I'm just trying to protect myself and the world from the devil. Who wouldn't understand that?" the woman asked mildly.

A cool, refreshing cloth pressed itself to Likon's forehead, and he bit back a moan of relief.

"I'll release you once I'm a little better prepared, or once everything is dealt with. In the meantime, all I ask is to know which of the brothels the Ashowans have invested in, and how many of those could another investor still become the majority shareholder of? I don't even want to muscle the family out . . . There isn't a need to right now anyway. Especially, as from what I hear, Tamlin Ashowan isn't the visionary his mother is."

At the mention of Tam, the man Likon had grown up with and considered a brother, he forced himself to gaze upon his kidnapper . . .

Only she stood behind him.

"W-Why . . . is Lady Katarina . . . a problem . . . ?" Likon hunched over his middle. The need to be sick increased drastically after speaking.

The woman sighed.

"She has the ability to restore power to the Coven of Aguas, which would be troublesome. I think it's wonderful that the queen wants to expand women's rights in Troivack, however, when the council realizes that they can barter to reinstate the coven instead of going along with the proposed agenda for improving women's rights? It isn't hard to guess what they'd opt for to keep her in check."

"W-Why—" Likon vomited on the floor, narrowly missing his trousers. "What if . . . Her Majesty . . . can do both?" he rasped once finished.

"After years of grueling away, she might, but I don't particularly want the coven to have power again."

"You . . . You seem to be fine with answering questions . . . Why . . . are you hiding?"

"I don't mind you knowing about my motivations. It's a nice conversation, and I'm hoping that if you understand me better you may become sympathetic to my plights."

"How come you don't . . . reveal yourself to other people if . . . you think you're in the right?" Likon could feel his weak grasp on consciousness slipping away . . .

"Oh, because I have a few methods that may not be well received by the general populace."

Likon tried to turn to look over his shoulder at his captor, but the woman seized his head, stopping him. Colored spots danced in front of his vision, threatening him with imminent blackness.

"W-Why don't you want witches . . . in power?" he asked next, though it continued to be torture getting the words out.

"They're powers are volatile, and yet they are starting to assume positions of power. That is not what they were originally meant to do. The Gods have already begun tampering with the original laws of their magic by creating mutated witches. If this continues, the balance of the world will become even more skewed. Witches need to return to their roots and allow humans to try to survive with an understanding of working cohesively with nature under their guidance. Humans should not be making business deals and allowing witches to manage nature *for* humans to dominate the world."

"Why aren't you working with the devil if you . . . both don't like witches?"

The woman laughed.

"The devil loves witches! You think he wants them gone? He adores playing with them. Why do you think he always has a witch subordinate close to him in every one of his lifetimes?"

"But then—"

"That's enough for today. I'm afraid I have to go before anyone comes to find me. Don't worry though, Likon. We'll talk again soon. After all, I could see us working amazingly well together. What with your brilliant, cunning mind, your connections . . . and unlike Tamlin Ashowan, I think you are far more innovative."

Likon fluttered his fingers and felt them tingle, but his wrists were too tightly bound for him to do anything else.

Before leaving, the woman's hand gently raked through his sandy brown hair in an almost affectionate way . . . Shortly after, Likon could hear her footsteps falling away and the sound of a heavy door closing.

At the very least, they hadn't dosed him again.

Likon had never had the misfortune of trying Witch's Brew before, and he couldn't say he understood the appeal.

He had been in and out of a daze ever since he had been taken, though he'd mostly been unconscious save for the occasional broth he'd been force-fed.

Looking around the room, Likon tried to find any discerning details that could give him a hint about where he was being kept.

It was a cave-like dirt room with a lone circular hole high above him in the carved out ceiling that looked at the sky. However, despite it being open to the elements, the room was warmed by the two torches that remained lit.

Of course, the fact that the hole overhead wasn't even big enough for Likon to climb out helped keep the cold air at a minimum. Plus, it was at least fifteen feet away from where he sat . . .

Next, Likon then tried to listen for any noises . . . Perhaps there were people nearby . . .

But he heard nothing.

He sighed.

His feet were shackled to the ground of the cave, so he couldn't even turn around properly to see what the door looked like behind him. Peering back to the hole, he hoped it at least wouldn't start raining on him anytime soon . . .

However, when he lifted his chin, instead of seeing the sky, he found an otherworldly face staring down at him with dark, ruby red eyes. The creature smiled down at him, revealing tiny, sharp pearly teeth.

Likon's eyes rounded in terror.

He had never seen a beast like that before. The face was made of sharp angles, its eyebrows and eyelashes feathery, its skin chalk white, as was its hair . . . But perhaps it could help him.

"H-Hello?" he called up.

The creature smiled even wider, opened its mouth . . . and let out an ear-piercing scream that shot an unholy amount of pain coursing through Likon's already aching head. He closed his eyes, and a shout of his own escaped his mouth, but the shrill shriek drowned him out. It sounded like thousands of steel nails being dragged down glass, and it grew louder and echoed around him, warbling . . . The sound was making his entire body ache . . . Waves of intense pain that made him feel like his muscles were reverberating and tearing apart kept overcoming his senses.

And that was the last thing he could remember as the agony engulfed him until his mortal body was forced back into the safety of unconsciousness.

CHAPTER 31

BARKING UP THE WRONG TREE

You've been walking long enough! Come on, let's move!" Kat hollered from the middle of the training space that had been set up for the young women who had committed themselves to learning self defense under her tutelage.

A series of groans echoed as everyone, once again, forced their throbbing, weary legs to resume a halfhearted jog.

Surprisingly, every noblewoman that had originally signed up had returned.

Everyone except for Selene Icarus, whose father happened to be getting tortured and shunned in front of the castle doors that very moment.

Kat's stomach lurched unpleasantly at the reminder, and she struggled to push her thoughts free of the fact . . . A new, urgent desire to return home to Daxaria where everything was overall much happier, kinder, and more comfortable reared its head.

A gentle nudge under her right hand drew Kat's gaze downward to see Boots, one of Dana's dogs, panting contentedly at her side as his mistress continued to run laps around the yard.

The redhead smiled at Boots's warm, beautiful brown eyes. "Ah, you're a good pup, aren't you?" she cooed while giving the beastie an affectionate scratch behind the ears, sending his nubbed tail into a furious wag.

The pleasant distraction from her troubles didn't last long, however, as one of the young women under Kat's tutelage halted in her tracks, doubled over, and vomited on the courtyard stones.

"Aah . . . that's probably not a good thing . . ." Kat made her way over to her pupil.

Dana had already reached the girl's side and was speaking quietly to her, her hand on her back as she waved to a steward who stood nearby on the steps, ready and waiting with flagons of water for Kat's students.

Kat stood back while the man handed off the beverage to the young woman. She waited for her to take a mouthful of water before speaking.

"You're welcome to take the rest of the training time off. I'm sorry if I've been pushing you too hard today," Kat apologized while reaching out and patting the young woman on the shoulder.

The girl couldn't have been older than fifteen years old. She had lovely long, wavy black hair, clear skin, a soft jaw, and big round eyes. Her innocent appearance made it all the more surprising that she had chosen to join Kat's more difficult class.

"It's my fault for eating such a big breakfast . . . I want to keep training."

"Resting is part of training" — Kat grinned — "but I like your enthusiasm. Go sit on the stairs, and when we start learning stances, I'll let you join in again, alright?"

The young woman nodded with a relieved smile and stepped around her splatter of sick that her fellow young women had already redirected themselves around.

Kat turned to Dana, still smiling. "By the way . . . you wouldn't have happened to mention that you're taking my lessons to your father, hm?"

Dana flinched, cleared her throat, and then rejoined the rest of the women running without bothering to even try to lie her way out of the question.

Kat sighed and looked down again at Boots. "I tell you, that girl is far bolder than anyone in her family realizes . . ."

The redhead made her way back up the stairs to where Sir Cas was speaking to his group of adoring female protégés, however, when he saw her approaching, he excused himself and slid over to her.

"Everything alright with Lady Gwyn?"

Kat nodded idly. "Poor girl is just pushing herself too hard today."

Sir Cas's expression was uncharacteristically grave. "She's probably worried and not thinking clearly. Lady Selene Icarus is the noblewoman she waits on . . . She might be cast into shame from mere association, given the duke's scandal."

Kat's brow crashed down.

She really didn't want to have to think about more depressing news . . .

"Excuse me!"

The Daxarian duo turned toward a knight who had approached them both. Kat instantly recognized the man as one of the knights she had sparred with during her official duel.

"Sir Marin! Great to see you!"

The Troivackian bowed in greeting. "I'm afraid Leader Faucher has asked that you conclude your training with the young ladies today. He wishes to train our distance archers, and we require the full use of the courtyard once he returns from his . . . *meeting* with Duke Icarus . . ."

Kat bobbed her head in understanding. She recalled Faucher mentioning that after facing the stone golem, he wanted their men to improve their accuracy in the hopes that they could maybe strike the golem's eyes.

Once she and Sir Cas had successfully sent their pupils back indoors and helped to clear away the partitions in the courtyard, the redhead was surprised to see Lady Dana sitting and waiting for them on the steps to the castle.

Kat thought she would've tried to avoid being caught by her father.

Then again . . . Kat glanced at Sir Cas, who was in a rare state of disrobement, as he had removed his formal vest and rolled up his sleeves as he worked despite the cold. The blond knight even had a streak of dark grime across his forehead from where he'd absentmindedly wiped his sweaty brow.

A slow grin climbed Kat's face as she stared at Dana's starry eyes and slackened jaw. And she kept staring until the young woman realized she was being observed and blushed scarlet as a result.

Luckily, Sir Cas was oblivious as he fell into a conversation with one of the Troivackian knights.

Making her way over to Dana, Kat's mischievous smile broadened.

"Well, well, well. Aren't you becoming quite audacious," Kat teased in a singsong voice.

Dana buried her face in her hands while Kat lowered herself down to sit beside the youngest Faucher family member.

"So . . . are you hanging around here to . . . watch the knights train, Lady Dana?"

"I-I might be interested in archery . . ." Dana managed to respond, though she couldn't bring herself to look at her friend.

"Mm-hmm . . ." Kat drawled while she looked at Boots, who, while seated beside his mistress, still shared a look with Kat as though he, too, knew what was afoot.

Dana sighed and dropped her chin to her chest, then risked looking up at the group of knights where Sir Cas had situated himself.

"I keep wanting to believe it's just a crush, but I can't get over him . . ." she lamented wearily. "I've never liked any man as much as I've liked him . . . He's considerate and sweet . . . He listens to what I say, and I just feel better when he's around."

Kat listened seriously. It was rare for Dana to confide so openly, and it was breaking the redhead's heart to know that the knight responsible for the kindhearted young woman's feelings did not share them.

"Give it time," Kat responded while stretching her legs out and crossing them at the ankles. "One day, you might find yourself feeling a little less toward him, or perhaps someone else will catch your eye. Or better yet . . . a new puppy!"

Dana gave a faint laugh at Kat's words. "I guess he told you he doesn't think of me in the same way I think of him."

Kat pressed her lips together and filled her cheeks with breath as she struggled to find any comforting words for her mouth to form in that moment.

"It's alright. Maybe one day it'll be different. Either for him or for me . . ." Dana pulled her knees closer to her chest and rested her chin on top of them as she stared at the knights more passively than before.

"Dana, why are you participating in my class?" Kat questioned, hoping her younger friend's bout of honesty would continue into this new topic.

Dana smiled. "Because I've always felt like I didn't fit in with my family . . . And . . . getting to learn how to train and handle a sword? It makes me feel closer to my father and brothers . . . even if they don't know about it yet."

Kat reached an arm out, and after wrapping it around Dana's shoulders, tugged the young woman closer to herself. "They . . . are going to kill you when they find out. I mean, they'll start by killing me as a warm-up, but you'll be next. They might even lob off Sir Cas's head next time he sleeps for good measure."

Shockingly, Dana didn't become fearful over the reminder. "I know, but . . . I'm a Faucher, and you've already started proving that women aren't just property to protect. Even if you are a witch."

Kat gripped Dana tighter and stared out over the courtyard.

Oddly enough, Boots perked up energetically in their quiet and began to wander over to the men as though curious about something . . .

The two women watched, both puzzled by his behavior, and so they rose and decided to follow Boots to see what was happening.

As they proceeded into the courtyard, there were several Troivackian knights who did a double take as they registered that Lady Dana was at Kat's side, but the two women pretended not to notice as they tried to find where Boots had disappeared to.

At last, they found that the loyal mutt had sought out none other than Sir Cleophus Miller, who had Pina on his shoulders.

The kitten had her back arched, and a weak, adorable hiss came out as she stared down at the dog who whined hopefully up at her.

Cleophus grunted threateningly down at Boots.

Kat started to laugh. "Jeez, I guess Pina's cuteness translates across all species."

However, just then, when Boots inched closer to Cleophus, his stubby tail wagging curiously, the knight gripped the handle of his sheathed sword at his side and started to pull it from his belt. Kat opened her mouth to stop him—regardless of the fact that he had kept the weapon sheathed—but didn't get the chance.

"*What do you think you are doing?*" Dana stepped forward and glared up at the knight as Pina continued inching back behind Cleophus's head to put even more distance between her and the dog. "Boots, come!"

Boots rounded back to his mistress, his ears drooping as he was forced to give up on a formal introduction to Kat's familiar.

"Dana—" Kat was about to try ushering the young woman away and apologize on the knight's behalf, but Dana was deaf to her.

"Who do you think you are? Pulling a sword on a dog?! You didn't even try to tell him to sit or stay!" Dana hollered up at the terror that called himself a man.

The knights all shrank away from the scene. They were either mortified of or nervous for Cleophus's reaction.

The knight let out a growl toward Dana that had several knights flinching.

"What? Are you no better than a mutt yourself? *Speak!*" Dana roared up at Cleophus while moving closer, her hands clenched at her sides.

She was easily a third of the knight's size, and yet the shout from her filled the courtyard.

Cleophus released his weapon and instead folded his arms over his chest to scowl down at Dana.

"You know, Cleophus, given that Pina is *my* familiar, I do have to agree with Lady Dana here. I appreciate you want to protect Pina, but you don't always have to go for the violent solution. Besides, if you were going to use violence on anyone, why the hell is Lord Ball still alive?!"

Cleophus's eyes darted to Kat, who had moved to stand behind Dana. "His wife wouldn't let me in the room."

"Godsdamnit, Elyse, you should've just stepped out for tea . . ." Kat lamented under her breath.

"Hey! You!" Dana shouted again, making Cleophus's attention shift back to her. "Stay away from my dogs and don't *ever* threaten them again!"

The knight towered over the slip of a woman, his expression blood curdling.

No one could think of how best to intervene . . . Even Kat was grimacing behind Dana.

"Keep your mutts away from Ms. Pina Colada," he warned ominously in return, black foreboding filling his tone.

Amazingly, Dana leaned even closer, her round face every bit as fierce. "Threaten or hurt my dogs, and I'll see to it that you're the one helping me walk them every day! You'll have to leave Pina alone all morning."

Sir Cleophus was starting to bare his teeth in such a way that everyone could tell would lead to a roar, when lo and behold . . . a new interruption graced them all.

"Oyy! Why in the world does it sound like Dana is here . . . ?"

The unmistakable voice of Piers echoed over the many knights' heads.

"Don't be preposterous," came the incensed retort from Dante.

Sir Cleophus cast a cold smile down at Dana. "I think it's time for you to leave."

Unwilling to be chased out and not have the last word, Dana looked down at her dog.

"Boots. Relieve."

"Dana, what are you doi—" Kat's incredulous, breathy question was cut short as the ever obedient Boots stood, turned, and proceeded to piss all over Sir Cleophus Miller's shoes.

The only sound in the courtyard was the steady stream from the canine landing on its mark.

During which time, Dante and Piers broke through the crowd to the scene, and upon laying eyes on their very own sister scowling up fearlessly at Sir Cleophus Miller while her dog issued a special kind of insult, both found themselves at a complete and utter loss for words.

That affliction, unfortunately, did not last long.

CHAPTER 32

GROWTH AND DECAY

Faucher stared down at Dana.

Piers, Dante, and Conrad stood behind him, while Lady Nathalie waited behind her daughter . . .

Kat lingered inconspicuously near the door of Faucher's bedchamber.

She had greatly wished her presence for the family matter wouldn't be necessary. Unfortunately, her silent pleas were ignored.

"Dana. Explain yourself." Faucher was unable to growl; his emotions were too heady.

While Dana was looking uncharacteristically bold in her father's presence, his question made her cheeks flush despite the chilly air.

"I joined Lady Katarina's group to learn how to fight and defend myself."

Faucher's face drained of what little color it had. "Why?"

Dana looked at Kat, to which the redhead gave a tight-lipped smile and tilt of her head as if to say *You should probably tell him.*

"Because . . . Because I'm a Faucher too, and I've always wanted to learn. I-I just always knew you'd say no."

Faucher turned away, unable to swallow the lump in his throat to make way for the words he wished to say.

"Why in the world was your dog pissing on Cleophus Miller's boots?" Piers barked.

His mother straightened and cast her son a warning look for his uncouth language.

Dana's eyes narrowed when she looked at her brother, which instantly had the man flinching in a mixture of surprise and uncertainty. "He was going to hurt Boots, and he was being rude."

Piers considered her response—and his mother's look. "Fair enough." He then leaned over to look at Conrad, who stood on the other side of Dante. "You should have seen her. Everyone else was terrified of Sir Miller, but our little mouse over there stared him down."

Conrad raised his eyebrows, impressed.

This interruption from his other children helped Faucher overcome his speechlessness as he rounded back on his daughter.

"You will have to apologize to Sir Miller."

"I won't."

Faucher reared back at Dana's quiet words as though she had struck him.

"He wronged me first and refused to promise not to hurt my dogs."

Faucher's eyes bulged from his head as he regarded his youngest child.

Kat began to sincerely worry that the poor man was about to have a heart attack.

"Dana. You are to go to your room and stay there until I decide on your punishment. And you are to cease attending Lady Katarina's lessons instantly."

"How is that fair?!" Dana exploded, further shocking her family. "Lady Katarina can learn, but I, your own daughter, can't?"

"She is different! She's a witch with strength that surpasses most men, and—"

"All the more reason for me to learn! What if something happens because I'm weaker and I need to defend myself?" Dana continued, though her hands that gestured in the air were trembling.

"Dana, you know that suggesting your father is incapable of protecting you is an insult," Lady Nathalie reminded softly.

The young woman looked at her brothers, fury and pain bright in her eyes. "Then why do you all need to learn how to fight? Shouldn't Father defend you too?"

"It's different," Faucher started to say, though his voice was thick.

"No! It isn't! In fact . . . it's even more important for me! What if after I get married, I'm widowed with no one to protect me? Or, or what if my husband is a beast who hurts me?!"

At mention of a man laying a hand on his daughter, Faucher regained some of his former ferocity and leaned closer to Dana, his dark eyes intent. "If a husband harms you, I will take every limb from his body."

"What if it's after you die?!" Dana persisted desperately. "Or what if he bars me in my own home? I can't be protected from everything in the world, but I can at least know how to fight back for myself!"

Kat felt emotion flicker in her chest.

She had made such arguments time and time again with her own parents back when she wanted to learn swordsmanship . . . However, unlike herself . . . Dana had even better reasons than her own. Troivackian men expected subservient wives, and Dana didn't have the magical power behind her, or in Alina's case, a king for a father.

"Faucher," Kat started, but the man snapped to her so quickly, it startled her into silence.

"I will get to you when I'm finished here." The seething fury in his eyes was potent enough to make Kat recoil.

She had never seen him so livid with her.

"Kat didn't do anything wrong! If anything, she . . . She's helped! I know . . . I know now that I can feel a part of the Faucher family if I want! I can learn how to fight if I try hard enough. And . . . And . . ." Tears were already running down Dana's face as she hollered at her father's back. "And thanks to Kat, I know now that you do actually love me!"

Silence hung in the air as Faucher slowly looked back at his daughter.

His own eyes were becoming suspiciously wet in the wake of Dana's words.

"Dana, are you mad?" Piers asked in awe. "Da loves you more than any of us."

"I n-never knew that until recently though! I-I thought because I was a girl, I would never be enough!"

"Oh, Dana—" Lady Nathalie's heartbreak over her daughter's confession made her reach for her, but Faucher held up his hand, stopping his wife.

He stepped closer to Dana, staring down at her, a subtle quiver in his cheek.

"You . . . are . . . and always have been . . . the most important person in the world to me."

Dana wiped her overflowing nose and eyes on her sleeve. "Then why—"

"I can't lose you or see you hurt." Faucher's simple answer drew out a lone tear from his eye. "You're the . . . the most precious part of this family."

Unable to hold back her emotions to say any more, Dana broke down in a sob as her father pulled her into his arms.

The two stood embracing each other while the sons behind Faucher shifted uncomfortably.

While the emotional exchange between father and daughter was touching, Kat wondered how Faucher's sons felt after hearing confirmation that their father favored their sister.

Were they jealous? Hurt? Or angry?

When she regarded them, Kat saw there was a sad acceptance in their features. They had always known, but it did still sting.

Though unlike his brothers, Dante had a knowing glint in his eyes that reminded the redhead he had two daughters of his own . . .

With things having resolved the way they had, Kat stealthily turned to the door while giving a nod toward Lady Nathalie before taking her leave.

Faucher could ream her out later.

For the time being though, the scene needed to belong only to Faucher family members.

Fin sat looking grim across from Lady Elena, his hands loosely clasped over his clean white tunic and navy coat.

The noblewoman wore a dark purple dress that day, her fine black fur cloak around her shoulders.

She stared at the Daxarian duke with increasing nausea and terror.

"T-The king is going to come and investigate the tunnels?"

Fin gave a single nod.

"When?"

"Most likely tomorrow. Guards are outside right now, however, and will enter once we finish speaking. I'm sorry, Lady Elena . . . but everything needs to be communicated if we are to have any chance at stopping what is coming."

The noblewoman looked to the ceiling of the experiment room.

"I'm going to be arrested, aren't I?"

Fin took his time answering. "Not necessarily. His Majesty is fair and acknowledges that witches had great reason to hide themselves. If you are compliant, he will look upon you favorably."

"Will the Coven of Wittica help me?"

Fin sighed and leaned his elbows on his knees. "They might, but given that you aren't a witch, it—"

"But I *am* a witch!" Elena burst out desperately.

Fin sat up in surprise. "You are? But why did you not—"

The two were interrupted by a mass of fluff streaking through the open door to the room.

"*Fin! Fin! This woman is a witch! A mutated witch!*" Kraken meowed excitedly.

"Uh, er, yes, she was just telling me about that . . . What about it?"

"*Her familiar! I've been speaking to him. You must meet him!*"

The house witch raised an eyebrow and glanced briefly at the noble-woman, who was frozen in place, as she had no idea what was being discussed between Fin and Kraken.

"What about her familiar?"

"Oh Gods. No," Lady Elena uttered instantly, her eyes growing round.

Fin frowned at her alarmed tone.

However, before he could ask another question, he was distracted by movement near the doorway, and when he discerned what it was that had caught his eye, Fin's mouth opened in wordless confusion.

He then glanced at Lady Elena to see if it was normal for such a creature to be in her home . . .

Her head was in her hand, making it difficult to discern.

"Lady Elena . . . given that you have just told me you are a witch . . . am I right in guessing that *that* is your familiar? I'm admittedly pretty tired today . . . so pardon me if I am wildly off my mark."

Fin stared at the animal as it waddled closer.

"*He's even bigger than Fat Tony ever was . . .*" Kraken marveled aloud.

When Lady Elena still hadn't answered Fin, the house witch took it upon himself to shamelessly gape at the ginormous animal that had finally reached them and plunked itself down.

A tenuous laugh left Fin's lips, though he tried to cover it by clearing his throat.

"L-Lady Elena . . ." he rasped. "Forgive me. I've never met a familiar quite like yours before . . ."

"You can laugh," the woman responded at last, albeit with a slight groan.

Her reticent attitude made Fin bite the side of his tongue.

The familiar scratched its protruding gut.

The duke's shoulders trembled helplessly.

He looked at Lady Elena, silently begging her forgiveness.

The noblewoman, with her cheeks flaming red, rolled her eyes to the ceiling.

"Yes . . . Your Grace . . . my . . . my familiar is indeed . . . a raccoon. His name is Reggie."

The raccoon, wider than some dogs were tall, peered up at Fin, its black eyes studious and intelligent.

It chirped and held out a paw to the house witch.

Blinking, Fin reached out and gingerly shook the racoon's offered paw before leaning back in his seat, crossing his arms, and pursing his mouth.

"My ability," Lady Elena started with a sigh. "Is garbage and decay. As a mutated witch, I am able to make mold grow on any organic plant matter, or have it decay instantly, and I am able to naturally identify what is valuable and what is naturally garbage."

Fin nodded along, still struggling with the fact that he had just given a handshake to a raccoon.

With great effort, he tried to think of another possible implication for Elena's abilities.

"Are you able to kill humans and animals with your ability?"

"I've never tried." Elena shook her head adamantly.

Fin wasn't entirely sure he believed her as she shifted uncomfortably, but he figured Brendan Devark would be asking her the very same question soon regardless.

"So that is one of the reasons Mr. Kraft revealed to you the details of the study of Witch's Brew?"

"Yes. The moldy blue spots on the mushrooms? He wondered if I would be able to re-create it."

"And? Can you?"

"No. I can keep it alive once it is removed from the mushrooms, which is how we managed to transfer it to the tomato you ate, but I cannot re-create it. The mold itself, from what I understand, is even more mystifying in nature. It's a different kind of decay . . . After a while, when it completely consumes whatever it has been growing on, the item dissolves to nothing. Most mold is a part of decomposition, but the whole fruit or vegetable doesn't just disappear."

Fin rubbed the back of his neck. "And it's the mold that is responsible for the transportation of the soul . . . Now I guess we need to know what the mushroom does."

"Oh, I can answer that. Thanks to Kraken, I was able to study it using my abilities, and I learned that it kills your body slowly and creatively." Elena perked up with renewed energy as she recalled the details of her recent discovery.

Fin balked. "Creatively killing them? How do you mean?"

"I think the mold forces the soul through a particular portal in the Forest of the Afterlife, one that maybe is linked to where the mushroom itself grows. It could be that the mushroom forces the body to shut down so that the soul is able to pull free more easily to be transported. However, because some people have a higher tolerance for drugs, and their doses vary, not everyone who ingests Witch's Brew dies."

"How is it that the people who consume it are able to absorb a small amount of a nearby witch's power?"

"I'm not completely clear on that one . . . It could be that anything magical nearby simply gets drawn toward the person responsible for creating a portal to the Forest of the Afterlife as a result of their drug use," Lady Elena theorized, but from the look on her face, she wasn't confident.

Fin shook his head in awe. "Gods. The more we learn of this drug, the more terrifying it is. Kraken? What was it about Lady Elena's familiar you wanted to discuss?"

The fluffy feline purred. "*About time you remembered I was here. Reggie was just telling me that the familiars in the tunnels are all talking about how they can sense sirins close by.*"

Fin stood up in alarm.

Sirins.

The final mystical elemental beast from the Forest of the Afterlife aligned with air . . .

"Lady Elena, you need to take me down into these tunnels straight away."

The noblewoman rose to her feet, uncertain of what was happening, when a knock on the open door drew their attention.

"Duke Ashowan?" A steward serving the baroness bowed. "I have received word from a messenger from the castle that your wife, the duchess, has arrived in Vessa."

Fin's heart dropped to his stomach.

For a moment, he found himself utterly frozen in place, unable to move.

Luckily, Kraken was there to help snap his poor witch out of his trance.

"*Come along, you overgrown kitten. Time to go meet your mate and tell her everything. I promise to keep your side of the bed warm the next few nights after she kicks you out, so don't fret too much. Though sadly, I think these tunnels will have to wait.*"

CHAPTER 33

THE DESCENT
OF THE DUCHESS

Kat paced the castle entrance hall while wringing her hands.
She sincerely hoped her da would make it to the castle before
her mother as he would hopefully be able to help stave off any immediate
murder attempts . . .

"Kat!"

The redhead turned hopefully, but instead of her father was greeted with
the sight of Alina and Eric speedily making their way over to her as servants
bustled around in preparation for Duchess Annika Ashowan. Unlike Fin's
arrival, they at least had a chance to get themselves organized before she
crossed the threshold.

"Eric, did you and Mr. Kraft find out anything in Vessa?" Kat implored
while seizing her husband's arm.

The prince shook his head. "I'm sorry, Kat, it really is like he vanished
into thin air. Mr. Kraft tried to talk to the pixies that he saw, but none of
them were very helpful."

Kat let out an agitated huff, her anxiety only increasing.

"Hopefully, your mother can find out something from her own contacts
here in Troivack." Alina reached out and grasped Kat's free hand.

"Ideally . . . though it might be after she kills me," Kat lamented, her
gaze turning back toward the enormous front doors.

A steward rushed up to the trio. "Pardon me, Your Majesty, Your Highness, Lady Katarina," he uttered hastily before righting himself. "His Grace
Lord Finlay Ashowan has just arrived at the knight's courtyard."

"Oh, thank the Gods." Kat wasted no time in sprinting down the nearest
corridor.

The brother and sister shared a worried look.

"Eric . . . Do you have any idea how terrifying Lady Annika can be?" the queen murmured.

The prince raised an eyebrow. "Do you?"

"I've discovered quite a bit since I've been crowned . . ."

"Is that why you insisted on bringing Rebecca Devark back?" Eric asked lightly.

Alina's eyes went wide. "How did you find out?"

Eric tilted his head. "I was guessing, but it turns out I'm right. Alina, you know it could be Rebecca Devark who is behind everything going on. Why did you bring her here?"

Alina looked away, frustrated with herself for revealing her secret so thoughtlessly.

"It's easier to keep an eye on her here, and who better to observe her than Lady Annika? We both know that, while a little bit of a wild card, the duchess is going to protect Kat, and she will do everything in her power to figure out who is trying to get Katarina out of the way."

"That might be true, but it also gives Rebecca the chance to find out what we've learned. You could've kept her in an estate off the castle grounds."

Alina opened her mouth to argue that it wasn't her brother's call to make, when a knight interrupted them for a second time.

"Pardon me, Your Majesty, Your Highness. Her Grace Lady Annika Ashowan has arrived."

"Where is His Majesty?" Alina questioned the knight, who stood at attention sharply.

The man was saved having to answer.

"My queen," Brendan's booming voice called out from the stairway.

Alina propelled herself away from her brother and waited for her husband, who rushed down the stairs while handing the notes he was holding to Mr. Levin.

"Has the duke returned?" Brendan asked his wife the moment he touched down on the main floor.

"Kat just ran off to get him. If they hurry, they might make it back to—"

"We're here!" Kat gasped as she and her father skidded to a halt before the king and then issued sloppy bows.

The timeliness of Kat's return meant her father had already been bolting to the front doors when she'd found him and poor Kraken was only just catching up to them.

"Wonderful. Duke Ashowan, would you like to be the one to receive your wife?" The Troivackian king took Alina's hand and rested it on his forearm as the group started to make their way to the doors.

"Of course," Fin panted, still catching his breath. But when he looked at Kat again, he registered her appearance as she held her husband's hand.

"Kat, you're wearing your uniform. Get changed into a dress and meet us in the solar. Your mother will follow protocol anyway; it'll buy us a bit of time to not make a scene," Fin planned out while eyeing the prince and his daughter.

Eric and Kat shared a look, and both nodded before the redhead took off up the stairs.

"I don't think we were this panicked when King Norman Reyes or the Zinferan emperor visited us in the past . . ." Brendan rumbled to his wife.

Alina didn't bother commenting as they strode toward the doors. They both knew why the situation they were presently in was entirely different.

Eric fell into step behind his sister, Fin at his side until they reached the front doors that were then opened.

The house witch proceeded to make his way around the king and queen and down the first two steps as tradition dictated.

Amazingly, all evidence of the earlier gruesome brutality toward Duke Icarus had been washed away from the stones in front of the castle. Instead, in the center of the courtyard at the end of the aisle of servants sat an inconspicuous black carriage.

The footman that stood by at the end of the aisle waited until Brendan gave his nod of assent.

The man then stepped forward in the quiet and opened the door.

The first to step out was Clara, Annika's most senior handmaiden and closest friend.

Clara was renowned for always looking the same no matter the situation with her tight, white-blond bun and flawless, conservative black dresses. Some people thought of her as a frosty woman as a result, but she had never seemed to care.

Clara finished exiting the carriage while giving a nod of polite thanks to the footman, then moved aside and curtsied before the carriage door, her hands clasped against her skirts as the duchess appeared next.

Annika Ashowan wore a striking white dress with silver trim that matched the velvet cloak around her shoulders. Her white and black streaked hair was piled on top of her head with shaped tendrils floating around her face.

With the bearing of a queen, she regarded the courtyard scene before her regally and without an ounce of emotion.

As Annika walked toward the castle, the servants proceeded to bow and curtsy, while Fin, unable to fight off a half smile, descended the rest of the front stairs until he could meet his wife at the bottom.

Taking Annika's hands in his own, Fin leaned forward and brushed a kiss on her cheek. "I've missed you," he murmured warmly.

The duke leaned back, and while Annika's gaze was firm, he could see that she was just as relieved to see him.

"I've been hearing some interesting things on my journey here," she informed Fin with a deceptively calm tone.

"Things have been managed to a point, but you'll hear the details soon enough. Shall we go greet the king and queen?"

Annika lowered her chin gracefully, and so without further ado, the couple began to ascend the stairs to the Troivackian monarchs.

Upon reaching the top, Fin and Annika issued proper curtsies and bows, which Alina and Brendan acknowledged with arches of their necks.

"Duchess Ashowan, thank you for making the journey to Vessa," Brendan greeted.

"It is a pleasure to return to my homeland, Your Majesties," Annika responded demurely, her eyes cast down.

"Lady Jenoure, a bath has been prepared for you in your quarters. Afterward, would you do me the honor of sharing a meal in the solar?" Alina spoke next.

"The honor is entirely mine."

Alina looked to Fin, who gave her a quick, appreciative smile.

Eric then approached from the sidelines and bowed. "Duchess Ashowan, I have not had the chance to congratulate you on your new title."

The way Annika's gaze lingered on the prince told Fin that his wife had most *definitely* heard some of the rumors pertaining to Eric and their daughter . . .

He fought against the urge to nervously rub the back of his neck.

"Thank you, Your Highness. It is good to see you in fine health."

An appropriate, practiced, and docile response.

Eric did his best to smile politely before he returned to his spot near the wall.

Brendan and Alina didn't waste any more time making their way back into the castle, their demeanor confident and at ease, but their insides were storms of uncertainty.

However, a direct attack was rarely Annika Ashowan's method. So she played the part of the dutiful guest without a word, even though there were more than one or two servants who broke out into whispers as she passed by them on her journey to her and her husband's chamber.

Brendan parted from the group, excusing himself to return to work.

Upon reaching the duke and duchess's room, Alina stopped and turned to address Annika.

"I will part with you here, Lady Ashowan. I look forward to us sharing a meal together again and getting the chance to catch up with each other."

Annika smiled, then tilted her head. "Of course, Your Majesty. Congratulations on your coronation, and I hear you are expecting the future heir to the Troivackian throne as well. Your father will be thrilled to learn of this."

"Thank you for saying so. I look forward to writing to tell him the news. Unfortunately, things have been too busy around the castle since my coronation."

"Of course. I hope my daughter has been of help to you during this time of transition."

Alina's face turned to stone for a breath as she faltered for a response. "Of course, Your Grace."

"Where *is* my daughter presently, Your Majesty?"

Having overcome the initial question, Alina was better prepared for the next one. "Lady Katarina is in her chamber and should be joining you shortly. If you will excuse me, Your Grace, I must see to our meal."

Alina lowered her eyes briefly, and after waiting for Annika and Fin to curtsy and bow respectively, took her departure with her own two maids following behind.

Annika looked over her shoulder to where Clara had dutifully stopped behind her mistress and gave a small gesture with her chin before looking at her husband, who proceeded to open the door for her.

The pair crossed into their chamber, Kraken stealthily slipping in before the door closed behind them.

Once in their room, where there was indeed a bath drawn and fortunately no maids ordered to attend the duchess, Annika faced Fin, showing her true thoughts in her face.

"Just what the hell has our daughter gotten herself into this time?"

Fin grimaced. "Quite a bit."

Annika closed her eyes, rubbing circles at her temples. "There is a scandal of sorts with her and the prince? *And* she was arrested?"

The last bit of gossip threw Fin entirely off course, making him open his mouth and hesitate before responding until he realized where the confusion lay.

"Ah, no. She wasn't arrested."

Annika sighed with relief, her hands falling away and her weariness revealing itself. "Thank the Gods. I wasn't sure what madness she had—"

"It was her familiar who was arrested, not Kat."

It was Annika's turn to find herself at a loss for words.

"Though speaking of familiars, I met a raccoon familiar today, and I have to admit . . . that beast . . . *has* to have magic. It easily weighs the same of a medium-sized dog, and I have no idea how it can move!"

"I beg your pardon?"

"I'm serious! I was trying to be nice about it in front of Lady Elena, but I won't lie, I am almost certain I'm going to be losing sleep over trying to wrap my head around how that thing got so fat. Lady Elena insists she has tried everything to make it lose weight but claims he remains the same no matter what. I don't even know how long raccoons normally live, but—"

"Fin, I'm still stuck on the matter of a *cat* getting arrested?"

"Ah . . . right. Don't worry. That was cleared up relatively quickly, though there is still a pretty heated debate carrying on amongst the knights about whether Pina is Daxarian or Troivackian. I'd avoid that topic if I were you."

Annika held up her hand to stop her husband's rambling. "How much sleep have you gotten?"

Fin tried to remember the last time he slept, but the answer eluded him. "Not much. Listen, I know we had to limit communication as much as possible while we traveled, but I've been busy trying to find Likon and—"

"It hasn't escaped my notice that you've avoided the matter of whether or not there *was* a scandal between His Highness and Kat?"

At this, Fin held his breath and pulled his hands to his hips as he avoided his wife's gaze.

"Things are . . . more or less sorted out . . . but I think that's something that might best be heard from Kat."

Annika's eyes narrowed. "What in the world did she do? Was the devil not the only piece of shocking news? If it were anyone other than Kat, I'd doubt anything else could be more alarming."

Letting out a long, drawn out breath, Fin raised his hands and gently pressed his wife back toward the bath.

"Bathe. Then we'll go eat, and you'll hear everything. You look like you've lost weight since traveling. I'll go to the kitchen and make sure you get something delicious."

The duchess did not look to be in a patient mood, but her husband was darting over to the door before she could do much else.

"Fin?" she called out one final time, pulling her husband's attention back to her. "I'll leave tonight to see what I can find about Likon . . . assuming I don't have to save our daughter from anything horrific."

It was after receiving this last bit of news that Fin finally could see the well-guarded motherly worry in Annika's eyes, and so he made his way back to his beloved and pulled her into an embrace.

"Everything with Kat will be alright, and we're going to find Likon one way or another . . . I just also happen to think . . . that maybe having an extra bottle of moonshine on hand during our dinner isn't a terrible idea."

Annika grumbled into Fin's chest. "Very well. Though I swear, if I find out she punched another noblewoman, I'll have to think of a whole new class of punishments for her when we get home."

Fin was grateful that he was still holding Annika and therefore she couldn't see his face, as he winced and didn't bother to reply to his wife.

Sorry, love. I don't think you'll be able to punish Kat quite so easily anymore . . .

CHAPTER 34

MUM'S THE WORD

I want to start with the worst news."

"Why the worst news?"

"Because we tried going from the least of the bad news to the worst with my da, and that was a wreck. So start big, and then the rest won't seem so bad."

"Which of everything that has happened will be the worst news to your mother?"

Kat tapped Eric's nose with a fleeting grin.

"Ah. Still me?"

"Still you."

Eric took in a deep breath while dropping his head back. "Alright. Should I go in with you?"

"I mean . . . you *can* . . . I don't know that it'll help at all."

"What about moral support?"

"That would be lovely if I weren't soon to be a dead woman."

Eric tilted his head as he stared down at Kat, his hand finding his pocket.

The couple stood a short way from the solar door where they had received word the duke and duchess awaited their daughter's presence.

"Come on. We've survived lots of things so far. The devil, assassins, your father—"

"My cat getting arrested."

"I don't want to talk about that." Eric's encouraging expression dropped. "I'm still having a hell of time convincing the Troivackian knights that she's Daxarian, and I'm pretty sure they're all studying law in their spare time to better argue it . . ."

Kat smiled. "I think it's rather sweet of them."

Eric rolled his eyes at the ceiling. "Plus, we're still trying to get information out of Duke Icarus before we finish him off—the man is incredibly resilient."

"I get it . . . We've overcome quite a bit . . . but . . . my mother . . . well . . . even *you* said she's infamous and frightening to criminals."

The prince paused at this reminder. "I suppose I have also been warned how problematic some mothers-in-law can be."

"Was it Alina warning you?"

Eric sighed and stared at his wife with a small smile. "I know you're stalling now."

The redhead slouched guiltily.

"Alright, come on. Let's get this over with. And if it gets bad, just remember, after this we have no one frightening left to tell. In fact . . . just envision Mr. Howard's reaction. I'll have you know it took a lot of threats and bribes to try keeping news of our marriage from being sent off to my father."

At being reminded of Mr. Howard, the Daxarian king's dramatic and perpetually exasperated assistant that had been irritated by her father for decades, Kat perked up.

Eric was right! There was so much left to live for!

Turning toward the solar, Kat took long rejuvenated strides, though she stumbled a little as she approached the guards at the door.

She had forgotten to walk like a lady instead of like a soldier, and her dark yellow dress had gotten caught under her feet.

Eric's hand appeared at her back, steadying her as they both nodded to the guards, who bowed to the couple before knocking on the door behind them, announcing Kat and Eric's arrival.

Kat's hands curled momentarily into fists before she lifted her chin and entered the chamber.

Upon crossing the threshold, she was greeted by the sight of her mother, sitting with her back perfectly straight, a white teacup in hand and a table ladened with dinner. The duchess wore a pearl-colored gown and amethyst jewelry with her hair piled atop her head. On her right sat Fin, whose hands were lightly clasped and resting on the table, his shirtsleeves already pushed up informally.

Annika turned and looked over her daughter as Eric closed the door behind himself.

The duchess rose with a smile and crossed the room. Once she had reached Kat, Annika lifted a hand and cupped her daughter's face, her brown eyes warm . . .

Kat felt herself melt under her mother's touch, and before she could stop herself, she wrapped her in a strong embrace.

"I've really missed you, Mum," Kat croaked, surprised by how emotional she was becoming.

She hadn't realized how, with everything going on, she really had wanted her mum . . .

Annika Ashowan had always known how to take care of things and had always been there for Kat to the best of her ability. She was strong and steady, and it had just dawned on her daughter then how incredible she was.

Annika hugged Kat back, stroking her head and holding her daughter close.

"I've missed you too. Ah, let me see, my girl." Annika pulled away, though her hands clasped Kat's, not quite ready to relinquish her daughter.

Under the duchess's keen scrutiny, Kat could feel herself blush.

"You've put on some weight amazingly enough . . . though it appears to be muscle. I take it you are training quite often with the sword."

Kat winced. She could hear the beginning of a dreaded question cropping up, and it would mean that she would have to reveal something before sharing her worst news.

So she panicked, and during that panic blurted, "I got married."

Annika's studious expression dropped.

She stared blankly at Kat while also standing perfectly still.

"Gods, Kat . . . did you have to say it like that?" Fin half moaned while covering his eyes with his hand.

Annika still didn't react.

That is, until Eric cleared his throat uncomfortably and positioned himself beside Kat.

The duchess blinked, then stiffly turned toward him.

"Your Highness . . . Are you present to tell me you sanctioned her union with another man on our behalf? Or . . ."

Eric cleared his throat again and bowed.

"I see."

Annika returned her dumbfounded stare back to her daughter.

"I'm guessing there is a reason you two had to get married in a hurry?" Her voice was faint, but it was difficult to tell if it was due to barely restrained anger or shock.

"You're not going to be a grandmother," Kat assured hastily while straightening her shoulders as though under questioning from her superior.

Annika swallowed and allowed herself a breath of relief.

"Then why was this rushed?" she asked with a forced calm, her gaze moving briefly to Eric before returning to her daughter.

"Er . . . well . . . we weren't . . . *completely* certain for a time that you wouldn't be a grandmother . . ."

Annika once again turned into a living statue.

One that no one dared tried to move.

She then rounded back to the table and sat back down, her stare directed straight ahead.

"Fin. I would like you to open that spare bottle of moonshine for me now."

The house witch wasted no time in reaching beside the table, yanking the cork free from the bottle, and filling her empty teacup with the liquor.

When the task was completed, Annika reached forward and raised the cup gracefully to her mouth before draining it and setting it back down in its saucer.

"Another."

Fin topped up the cup without any argument.

After polishing off the second serving, she casually took the moonshine from her husband, and drank straight from the bottle for the span of two breaths, the liquor going down by an inch or two in the bottle.

When she had finished inspecting the Troivackian moonshine—moonshine that was infamous for its unholy strength and potency—and for its calming benefits—Annika set the bottle on the table and regarded her daughter.

"That isn't everything, is it?"

"Er. No. I've had people attempt to poison me, and I got stabbed again. Then I was exiled—but that was all a ruse for me to learn sword fighting in private. I learned sword fighting; got really good at it. I have an indentured peer because he attacked and almost killed me—it's fine, we're kind of friends now."

"Let's not get too excited about forgiving Broghan," Eric added darkly.

"Alright, alright . . . I also fought against a few knights in an official spar to prove that women should be allowed to fight—and that witches aren't all bad. I won those matches and now am training a bunch of noblewomen how to defend themselves until I leave to return to Daxaria—which I refuse to do until I help Alina and the king defeat the devil, or at least figure out who this woman who is plotting against him is. Oh right. I rescued Eric after he'd been abducted by the devil, and I almost gouged the devil's eyes out. The devil also goes by Sam, and I just think that name isn't at all suited for him."

Annika observed her daughter without a word of response.

Then she turned to the window, her eyes lost in thought.

Kat sincerely started to worry that she had broken something in her mother's mind.

After a long while of no one moving or making a sound, Annika addressed Fin.

"At what point in learning about this did it dawn on you she's taking after me?"

"It took a lot longer than I'm proud to admit," Fin confessed while risking a small smile.

Annika's stare lowered and an eyebrow raised. "The Gods have a funny sense of humor."

"Are you angry?" Fin asked quietly.

Annika scoffed. "I don't have much of a right to be when I'm the same way."

The house witch stared at his wife in open awe. "Gods, you're amazing."

Annika reached over and clasped her husband's hand before once again facing her daughter.

"Come over, you two, I think we all have quite a bit to discuss."

Kat glanced at Eric, unable to mask her astonishment at how well her mother handled the news. Though, admittedly, she *had* just drank what would've knocked the average sturdy Troivackian man unconscious.

Kat made her way over to her chair with her husband following close behind.

"If I'd known it was going to go over this well, I wouldn't have bothered wearing a dress."

Annika balked. "What would you be wearing if not— Oh no. Katarina, have you been wearing *trousers* here in Troivack?!"

"*That* you take exception to?!" Kat had been in the process of laying a napkin in her lap as she stared incredulously at her mother. "Yes, I wear pants! But only after I was ranked the top of my class, and it is an official uniform!" Kat snapped back indignantly.

Caught off guard by this tidbit of information, Annika leaned back in her seat. "Top of your class? Truly? Who is your teacher?"

Kat grinned. "Leader Gregory Faucher. It took a while, but the old grump likes me now! He even walked me down the aisle for our wedding!"

"I still haven't forgiven you completely for robbing me of that experience," Fin grumbled in his seat while he ladled some small seasoned potatoes onto his plate.

"Leader Gregory Faucher . . ." Annika frowned. "Does he happen to have a wife named—"

"Lady Nathalie, yes! She mentioned you two knew each other years ago." Kat nodded eagerly, hoping that they were moving onto far safer and more pleasant conversation.

However, the duchess suddenly looked mildly irked. "She did, did she?"

"Yeah . . . Did you two know each other well?" Kat queried next, though she was starting to grow wary again.

"We crossed paths once or twice."

Kat decided not to mention how Lady Nathalie had indicated that she actually knew her mother quite well . . . Not when Annika Ashowan had handled the most shocking piece of news so swimmingly!

"Ah . . . I see . . . She has a daughter, who's wonderful. Her name's Dana. I'll introduce you tomorrow morning!"

Annika bobbed her head vaguely, her true emotions and thoughts unclear.

Sensing this, Fin eyed his wife before addressing his daughter.

"After we eat here, Kat, your mother and I are going to look for Likon, but I'll have to leave her on her own for a while. I learned earlier today that there have been rumored sightings of sirins."

Everyone's attention snapped to the duke.

"Another ancient beast?" Eric leaned forward.

Fin nodded. "Yes. There were four types of ancient beasts that legends say used to dominate this world, each one aligning with an element. The stone golems were for earth, the imps were for the water, the dragons for fire, and the sirins for air."

"What do sirins look like?" the prince insisted, his eyes intent.

"They have the head of a woman, bird claws for feet, and wings for arms, though there are claws on them as well as working hands. Usually, they have white or gray hair, and red or blue eyes. They're the size of an average person, and they have great control over the wind . . . At least that's how the old texts described them. It now makes me wonder if maybe they have something to do with the terrible weather we were experiencing over the Alcide Sea, which could also explain the strange winter Troivack is having."

Kat cringed. "Gods, as if the nobility here needed more fuel for their hatred of magic . . . I'm shocked they even let Mage Sebastian into the meetings."

"That was a bit different. They aren't really aware of how much magic he can wield. They are treating him more as an academic who knows about magic rather than a magic user. At least they were. Alina's coronation changed everyone's view of him, and people have been wary of Sebastian ever since. However, with all this speculation about Duke Icarus's heir . . . things might get even nastier for him," Eric expounded.

Fin nodded. "From what I've heard, there is a chance that Duke Icarus's next of kin may even relinquish the title, as it is going to be more hassle than the prestige is worth, what with all the duchy's finances being tied up. With the people he enslaved having been released, there aren't enough workers to help in the vineyards, and his ships are docked for the foreseeable future."

Annika turned to her husband. "Do you like Mage Sebastian?"

Fin tilted his head back and forth thoughtfully. "He seems alright. What about you two? What do you make of the man?"

"Annoying as hell, but a decent fellow. Why are you asking that though, Mum?" Kat wondered while loading her dinner plate with half a rack of mutton and potatoes.

"I'm debating if we should help him." Annika gave a dignified shrug and took another drink from her teacup, though when she finished, she noticed the prince giving her a hard stare.

"Is there something you wish to say, Your Highness?"

Eric looked at Kat, his eyes asking the silent question.

She gave her head a small shake.

"Not presently, Your Grace," Eric responded tightly.

Annika watched the exchange between her daughter and new son-in-law and recognized that there was definitely something the future king of Daxaria wished to say, and surprisingly . . . her daughter was navigating the situation and deciding to bring the matter up at a different time.

The duchess couldn't resist giving a discreet smile toward her plate, unable to say what she wanted to in Eric's company.

It looks like my daughter has grown up quite a bit since I've last seen her . . .

CHAPTER 35

A DEVIATED DIRECTION

Fin and Kat stepped into Lady Elena's keep, which was swarming with knights. His Majesty King Brendan Devark was already speaking with Leader Gregory Faucher by the grand staircase, both looking intent and serious.

As they approached, however, the two men moved their attention to the witches.

"Your Grace, Lady Katarina." Brendan nodded. "How was the duchess?"

Fin let out a sigh and shook his head, still in a state of disbelief over his wife's unexpected reaction to all their daughter's news.

"She took everything a thousand times better than my da did," Kat explained bluntly.

"I never thought I'd be the sane one in our family," Fin muttered with a partial grumble.

Brendan nodded, relief bright in his eyes over the news.

Leader Faucher, unaware of the gravity of everyone's stress surrounding Annika Ashowan, brushed this exchange off.

"That is good. Now, we have yet to go into the tunnels, but Mr. Kraft is ready to take us down to start our investigation."

Kat smiled, unable to hide a glint of excited interest in the mysterious passageways that allegedly ran under Vessa.

"Have you seen the raccoon yet?" Fin asked suddenly while looking between Faucher and the king.

The two men gave him blank looks in response. "No, Your Grace. Though you've been talking about it at length as of late."

"You'll see what I mean." Fin waved off their lackluster reactions while already peering around the entrance hall for the familiar he had not been able to stop thinking about. "Where is Lady Elena?"

"She is in her experiment room explaining to the Royal Physician what they have been studying."

The duke frowned. "Is someone other than knights and the physician with her?"

Brendan gave the duke a mildly irritable look. "She is potentially facing charges for plotting treason or at the very least illegal construction."

"Yes, but if everything is handled as though she is going to be burned at the stake, I don't think it'll be a very fair trial when she may have just been trying to protect the remaining witches here in Troivack," Fin argued vehemently.

Brendan regarded the duke coolly.

The king didn't appreciate the implication that he would be anything but fair in his judgment, but he couldn't deny the previous years of witch-hunting in his kingdom.

"Very well. Lady Katarina, would you mind joining Lady Elena?" Brendan turned to address the noblewoman.

Kat's shoulders slumped. She'd been excited to join the exploration of the tunnels.

"Actually, Your Majesty, given that Lady Katarina has her abilities and sword expertise, I believe it is safer if she is the one to join us in the tunnels," Faucher interrupted.

Fin straightened.

It had never happened before that his daughter's presence and magical abilities had been chosen over his own, though when he glanced over Kat's uniform and the sword at her side, he couldn't stave off the swell of pride.

She really had earned respect in Troivack.

"That does make sense," the duke acquiesced before his daughter could respond. "Well then, I better go tend to Lady Elena. I look forward to hearing about what you all discover, Your Majesty." Fin bowed and turned his toes to make his way up the stairs to the experiment room.

"What in Gods' name is that?!"

Fin whirled around, a beaming smile already on his face.

Faucher was staring over the king's shoulder, and the house witch had no doubt about what had earned such a reaction from the military man.

Sure enough, Reggie the rotund raccoon was waddling toward the stairs.

"I told you!" Fin crowed excitedly.

"How does it move?!" Brendan exclaimed with more emotion than anyone had seen from him in months.

"That cannot be healthy. My Dana would be in a fit if she saw a creature in such a state under someone's care," Faucher rumbled.

Even Kat was watching the familiar with her mouth hanging open, utterly speechless.

As the small group watched the raccoon climb the stairs in shared astonishment, they found themselves struggling to wrap their minds around the creature's existence . . .

So much so that for a brief moment, all thoughts of tunnels and witches disappeared from their minds altogether as they, too, became acquainted with Lady Elena's familiar.

Likon sat curled in a ball, his hands pressed over his ears and his eyes firmly shut.

He felt like a child again . . . hiding by the stairs from the lascivious acts of the brothel he lived in after his parents died. Back then, he had wanted to be glued to his sister's side at all costs, but after the first month, he couldn't bring himself to go back down from his room no matter how much he hated waiting alone in the dark quiet.

The beast that he had seen the previous day was prone to random shrill shrieks, and when one of the people or beasts—he wasn't sure which, as they'd never revealed themselves—came to deliver him his food, he had insisted on being untied so that he could cover his ears that, even in silence, would continue to ring.

Surprisingly, his captors had acquiesced, though Likon had still been forced to be blindfolded during his mealtimes.

He continued waiting in the cavern-esque prison, his mind at last cleared of the effects of Witch's Brew.

There was a chance he could rush the next person to come check on him and make a run for it, but with the presence of the screeching creature, he wasn't certain how far he'd get.

He was just about to consider this possible escape plan more carefully when yet another ethereal scream echoed around him, forcing him to clamp his hands down over his ears even harder.

It was a struggle to even remember to breathe against the piercing noise . . .

Then it suddenly stopped.

Likon's eyes opened. It had been the quickest outburst yet.

"Good morning, Likon."

He jumped in shock and turned slowly . . .

There was his captor sitting in his vacant chair. He blinked in shock.

"I don't think we've been properly introduced yet . . . Feel free to call me Aradia."

"You . . . I've—"

"Sorry about the sirins, they are quite the noisy bunch. I like to jest that they are a perfect representation of why having birds as pets can be problematic." Aradia shook her head with a brief laugh.

She wore black trousers, a black tunic, and a leather corset. There wasn't a speck of jewelry on her, and surprisingly, her hair only touched a short way below her collarbone. Most women wore their tresses long enough to reach their hips . . .

Her elbows rested comfortably on the arms of the chair Likon had been tied to before as she stared down at him with a kind smile.

"Don't worry, the sirins won't make a ruckus while I'm here. If I had another place for them to hide, I would move them to torment you less."

"I don't believe for a second that this casual torture is accidental." Likon unfurled himself to sit more comfortably, propping his right arm atop a bent knee and leaning back against the earthen wall of his prison.

"Believe what you want." Aradia sighed while eyeing the hole in the ceiling. "I don't have the stomach for even regular Troivackian torture methods. You'd think I would after all this time . . ."

"Why are you here?" Likon asked coldly.

Aradia lowered her gaze to him, her expression still gentle. "We'll be sending our demands for your release soon. I just thought you'd like to know."

Likon frowned. "What proof of life are you going to give?"

"Mm, I was going to have you sign your name to a letter, but if you refused that, I'd probably take a bit of what you're wearing or a lock of your hair." Aradia settled back into the chair as though intending to stay for a while.

"You aren't worried about getting caught?" Likon bit out next.

Aradia tilted her head back and forth thoughtfully. "I don't intend to stay hidden much longer, so I'm not too worried."

Likon's lip began to curl.

Aradia noticed this and raised a wry eyebrow. "You know, Likon, I'm not all that concerned about you coming after me either, because I think we want the same things."

He didn't hide his disbelief.

"I just want Lady Katarina to go home. What's so terrible about that? Wouldn't you prefer it as well?"

Likon straightened. "If that were true, why were there so many attacks on her?"

Aradia leaned forward. "A lot of that was thanks to Sam getting involved in politics in the castle. The poisonings? His assassins. The attacks on her carriage? His mercenaries. Kidnapping the prince and prying open her magic abilities? Again, him. Aside from kidnapping you and trying to bind her magic the one time, I haven't done anything all that terrible."

"Yet." Likon's eyes narrowed. "What if she doesn't go home regardless of the ransom letter?"

"You think she'd cast you aside just so that she could fight the devil?" Aradia queried with a crease of concern between her eyebrows.

"You aren't going to succeed in turning me against her."

"I'm not trying to turn you against her. I'm asking because it would be problematic if abducting you didn't propel her out of the kingdom," Aradia explained simply.

Likon felt a small tremor run through his heart . . .

The woman before him was disconcerting for many reasons.

The biggest one of all being that . . .

Everything she said rang with truth.

She wasn't trying to deceive him.

He had worked near and with liars his entire life, and either she was the best liar in the world . . . or she wasn't bothering trying to hide anything.

But why?

"Who gave Aidan Helmer a dragon?" Likon wondered suddenly.

Aradia blinked in surprise, then gave another tinkling laugh. "I did. Aidan liked to parade that poor dragon around as his familiar, but the beast was merely doing my bidding . . ."

"Why the hell did you do that?" Likon felt a rush of relief.

He needed to validate that the woman before him was indeed a villain.

"I needed to sabotage the war." Aradia reached up to rub the back of her neck thoughtfully. "Paiste was supposed to turn on the Troivackians if they made it too far, then retreat back to the mountains."

"Paiste?"

"That was the dragon's name. Paiste," Aradia's expression saddened. "I . . . He was my friend. I . . . I never thought he would die."

The pain in her eyes made Likon hesitate.

He almost felt sorry for her for having sent a dragon to kill thousands of innocent people.

Then again . . . The Troivackians would have done that regardless.

So . . . what was her true motivation? Was it really all to get rid of witches in some odd, roundabout way?

"While I can guess what has made you so loyal to the Ashowan family, I do wonder if you're happy with your life. I heard you had a rather . . . concerning reaction to the news of the prince and Lady Katarina's marriage."

"Because I didn't want Kat to end up like Dena," Likon blurted before he could stop himself.

Aradia tilted her head. "Dena?"

Likon bit his tongue, refusing to say more.

"Well . . . even if it was for some noble reason, it was undoubtedly amplified by the fact that you've been terribly in love with her for years. Aren't you tired of the suffering?"

Likon felt his shoulders round as he stared up through his eyebrows at Aradia. He didn't like how the woman seemed to know so much personal information, and the way she looked at him as though she could see every inch of his soul . . . It was off-putting.

"Look, I understand. The Ashowan family has become the pinnacle of all that is good in Daxaria. Wholesome while also powerful, thanks to Annika Ashowan. It's a deadly but effective combination, and they've been good to you," Aradia reasoned aloud. "However, there is nothing wrong with wanting to create a life for yourself outside of them. Sometimes, even if there is nothing inherently wrong with a situation or relationship, it just isn't the right fit. In a lot of ways, it makes it that much harder trying to break free, because there isn't a reason to motivate yourself."

Likon felt exposed.

The woman's words tore at him and reached his very protected, wounded heart . . .

All because everything his captor was saying . . . accurately struck the feelings Likon had struggled to confront for years.

Even as it pertained to his relationship and love for Kat. She hadn't felt the same way he had for her. Not because there was anything wrong with him, but because it simply wasn't meant to be . . . And sure, he knew Annika, Fin, and Tam loved him like a son and brother, but . . . there was still something that didn't feel quite right. A sense he couldn't name that there was always a missing note to what should've been a harmonious family life. They were wonderful. All of them, but he wasn't quite like them . . .

Likon had struggled with that sense for years. Waiting and hoping for it to change . . . but Aradia was right.

It *was* a special kind of torture.

"Likon, regardless of what happens, whether Lady Katarina leaves or stays . . . You will be freed at the end of this, and you can make your own decisions then."

He didn't answer. A firm lump had formed in his throat, and he knew if he spoke, the emotion in his voice would be heard.

Aradia gave him a single, sympathetic, tight-lipped smile before rising from her seat and turning toward the door.

"I'll see about getting you some beeswax to stuff your ears with," she called over her shoulder while she knocked on the door to be let out.

"Who . . . are you really?" Likon heard himself ask while belatedly thinking how he should get up and hold her hostage to be let out with her.

But his limbs felt heavy . . . and something in him . . . didn't want to leave.

Not yet.

Aradia turned back, her eyes bright and her smile gentle.

"Sister of the devil, daughter of the Gods . . ." She trailed off and let out a weary sigh, as though tired of the title. "I am the first witch. Now, get some rest, Likon. I'll come visit you again soon."

CHAPTER 36

CONFRONTING A COVEN

K at stood, her right hand clasping the hilt of her sword, her left a lit torch, as she and Faucher stood at the head of the entourage that was to go down into the tunnels beneath Lady Elena's keep.

"Ashowan, are you frightened?" Faucher asked with the faintest note of disbelief and humor in his voice.

"Gods no. I'm excited!"

"Of course you are." Faucher sighed while shaking his head. "You know that this could be a trap and there may be the people who have attempted to harm or kill you down there, right?"

"*Or* these are people with magnificent Gods-given abilities who have been hunted their entire lives and forced into hiding and will just need a bit of coaxing," Kat countered loudly.

"That may be true for some of them, however—"

A loud throat clearing from the back of the entourage interrupted the teacher and student.

Both Faucher and Kat looked over their shoulders and back through the rows of knights toward Mr. Kraft, Brendan Devark, and his assistant, Mr. Levin. The king was giving Faucher a flat look before jerking his chin up toward the knights between them.

It was only then Faucher realized that his discussion with Katarina was starting to make the men anxious.

He barely resisted grumbling that Kat had permanently altered his own sense of what was outlandish and what was normal . . .

Instead, he turned to face the troupes that had all crammed themselves into Lady Elena's wine cellar, where there had been a false wall filled with wine bottles that opened to reveal stairs that led underground.

"Alright men, do not act aggressively toward these people. We are not certain there is a traitor in their midst, and many of them will be frightened. Do your best to de-escalate the situation before using force."

The men chorused back a "Yes, sir!" and then, with one final nod to Katarina, they began to descend into the tunnels.

At first the stale air smelled a bit of moisture, but the farther they descended . . . Other scents came forth.

The smell of cooking. Bread baking . . . Broth simmering . . .

Kat's stomach growled, and Faucher shot her a subtle look of incredulity.

She raised an eyebrow in response but bit her tongue, once again displaying that she had learned some modicum of discipline under his command as they marched down the stairs that fortunately were wide enough for two people to step side by side and had a high enough arched ceiling that it didn't feel like they were being buried alive.

Then the faint glow of light softened the darkness ahead of Kat's and Faucher's torches, and the murmuring of voices could be heard.

Faucher held up a fist, halting everyone.

From the back, Mr. Kraft called out.

"Goddess of our people!"

The voices below fell silent, and an uneasiness plucked at the knights.

Until at last someone responded, "Antlers of the Green Man!"

Faucher tried to peer back through the crowd to see the king's nod of confirmation to continue, but in their enclosed space, the shadows were too heavy.

"He's nodding," Kat whispered, her gleaming eyes only making the knights slightly uncomfortable—a small yet promising sign she had made strides in making them less fearful of witches. A crucial detail in that moment.

Faucher faced frontward again without issuing a thanks and continued leading everyone down the rest of the stairs.

When they stepped onto the bottom level and moved through the rounded doorway, Faucher and Kat halted at the sight before them.

A tunnel ran as far as the eye could see, and on each side were circular wooden doors, some had stairs built going up their sides to apartments on another level. Torches were lit by the main entrance and between the doors. The most stunning sight of all? The crowd of unique-looking men and women that froze and stared at the entourage.

A family to the right appeared to be leaving their apartment, their son with dark green hair, and the man who presumably was his father carried a pot of soup in his hands.

To the left, there was a pair of women that had a basket filled with dark bread with steam still wafting from the loaves.

"Attention!" Faucher roared, and Kat almost flinched. She could hear how his voice was terrifyingly loud in the confined space, but she gripped the hilt of her sword tighter and moved back with the other knights to make room for the king to walk forward with Mr. Kraft at his side.

There was a flutter of movement through the crowd as a figure approached . . .

A man with shoulder-length wavy black hair threaded with gray, brown eyes, and a hooknose peered at Mr. Kraft, his panic barely hidden.

"Mr. Kraft, what . . . what is happening?" Despite his alarm, the man managed to ask the question loudly enough for everyone nearby to hear.

The coven leader's throat bobbed before he lowered his gaze mournfully.

"His Majesty King Brendan Devark wishes to hold interrogations of everyone here, but there is nothing to fear. They are not here to hurt anyone who is innocent."

"My Shandalle was innocent! But knights still cut her down!" An older, shriveled woman hobbled free from the crowd, tears in her eyes as she stared at the king, the pain in her wrinkled face palpable. "My daughter did nothing! To no one! S-She grew flowers! She just wanted to bring a bit of beauty to the world, and yet knights murdered her, and *nothing* was done!"

Another person in the crowd reached out and seized the elder's arm to pull her back and stop her from speaking. While the old woman wasn't strong enough to fight back, her anger and grief-filled stare bore into the king.

Brendan didn't bat an eye as he regarded the sea of faces that appeared either hostile or terrified.

"Troivack lost its way, for many years. It is not right that many have suffered, which is one of the reasons why I will not be forcing anyone to leave this place of safety or alerting the public of its existence for the time being. *However*, there are forces that are threatening the entire kingdom now, and it is possible that there are people down here who are instigating this."

"What do we care what happens to the rest of Troivack? *They* turned on us! We've been hunted, slaughtered, and chased from our homes. My own mother tried to bury me alive, saying I was going to bring hell upon our family." A new man stepped forward, his front teeth half an inch longer than was the norm, and the entirety of his eyes were black, yet he peered at the king and his men with no problem in the low light.

Brendan regarded the new speaker, again, without any outward reaction. "This conflict could bring about the demise of not only Troivack, but it could be the start of a war between the ancient beasts and the rest of the world. While your reaction is understandable, we will begin our questioning immediately."

Faucher joined Brendan's side then. "I want two lines. Women on the left, men on the right. Children can sit before the king in the middle. The knights behind us will call you forward one at a time to ask you questions."

Despite Faucher's authoritative tone, no one moved.

In fact, many people crossed their arms.

Kat bit the inside of her cheek, wishing she could say something, being well aware of how Brendan's coldness was not serving him well in such a moment . . .

With her thoughts consuming her attention, Kat was unaware that the small boy with green hair was staring at her interestedly, and after a moment of observation with squinted eyes, broke free from his parents and shuffled closer. His mother immediately dove for him, dragging him back, but the action snapped everyone's eyes over to them.

"H-Hey!" the boy shouted. "*She's* a witch!" His mother had already begun exerting effort to cover the child's mouth, but his declaration and pointed finger made her stop. Slowly but surely, all gazes found their way to Kat, who they then could see had golden, glowing eyes, and . . . was a woman . . . wearing a knight's uniform.

Murmurs began to hum around the tunnel.

Kat leaned forward to the king and Faucher. "Permission to speak to them?"

Brendan studied Kat, his eyes hard.

She fully expected him to say no. Especially given the last time he had allowed her to speak openly in a crowded room, she had caused more headaches than the king cared to count.

However, as the whispers around them began to rise in volume, Brendan listened to his gut and nodded to her.

Kat let out a quick sigh of relief and moved in front of Brendan, who hadn't realized that she intended to take center stage to deliver her message . . .

"Everyone!" she shouted, and the room fell quiet as they gaped openly at her. "My name is Lady Katarina Asho—"

"Reyes."

Kat blinked and looked over her shoulder at Faucher, who had interrupted her and wore a sardonic expression on his face. "Your last name is Reyes now."

She grimaced in response. "Gods, this is wildly annoying to get used to," she muttered before rounding back to the crowd that was growing confused. "My name is Lady Katarina Reyes! Oh. No. No, no. That doesn't sound right. I wonder if Eric would change his last name . . . I think I could persuade him."

Brendan let out a grumble and crossed his arms behind Kat as she continued talking to herself.

"Alright! Well . . . My last name was Ashowan, now it's Reyes! There!" She paused, smiling at everyone, who stared back at her blankly. Her grin faltered. "Now . . . What was I going to say again . . ."

"Oh for the love of—"

"Right! I am a witch from Daxaria, and His Majesty King Brendan Devark has been tasked with not only keeping me safe but also has allowed me to learn to defend myself with a sword under Leader Gregory Faucher!" Kat had cut off Faucher's irate words and at last finished her introduction.

"W-Wait . . . Are you . . . Are you related to the house witch?" A woman in her sixties inched closer, her dark, wide eyes bright with hope.

"That I am! I'm his daughter, and I am pleased to make your acquaintance!"

"Oh! Thank the Goddess! We're saved!"

"Come again?" Kat leaned forward, her brows lowering as the woman looked to the heavens and clapped her hands together.

A man with a pronounced hump on his back dove for Kat's hand, bowing and kissing it.

"Lady Katarina, you can deliver us to Daxaria! We can be taken there as refugees!" the woman who had asked the question heralded, tears already rolling down her cheeks.

Meanwhile, everyone was talking excitedly again while Kat was distracted, trying to free her hand from the old man without actually harming him, though she did shoot a look toward Mr. Kraft for assistance.

He was a mite dumbfounded himself by the reaction.

"N-Now, let us stop for a moment!" Kat hollered after successfully detaching herself from the hunchbacked man. "I am here because there is a threat that could destroy not just humans here in Troivack, but everyone. Witches included! In all kingdoms! We need to find whoever is helping . . . someone . . . a woman in the castle here in Vessa. Someone with connections to Witch's Brew!"

Thankfully, everyone fell into a thoughtful quiet, and so Kat took the opportunity to add, "We have additional questions that might help bring some light to the situation, so if you could please line up, that would be appreciated."

The same woman who had declared Kat their savior drew even closer until she stood in front of the redhead, revealing that she was incredibly tall, hovering an extra five inches over Kat.

"If we cooperate, will you save us? Please. Please take us to Daxaria. To the Coven of Wittica."

"I—er—we can discuss that. My father is here in Troivack as well. He will be able to listen to your requests, but *only* if everyone here cooperates with questioning!" Kat raised her voice again while trying to call out to the very back of the crowd.

However, the older woman tugged Kat's hands, pulling her attention back to her.

"My name is Esther, my lady. Thank you. Thank you for coming for us." Esther's round eyes still watered with tears; her skin, while pale due to living underground, was well kept and sprinkled with freckles. However, there was an intensity about her that unnerved Kat . . .

And the longer Kat stared at Esther, the more pronounced her discomfort grew. It was like the woman was making her insides itch . . . and yet she couldn't look away.

Kat's aura burst from her body, making everyone around her save for Brendan and Faucher leap back.

"Ashowa— Reyes? Damn, that *is* annoying," Faucher admitted under his breath as he stumbled in addressing his student.

Kat wondered why her hearing felt like it was starting to turn inward . . .

It wasn't like when the devil had broken down her defenses and freed her magic, but there was still the sense that she was being pulled far away . . .

"Esther!" Mr. Kraft snapped, though he did so only after Brendan shot him a concerned look. While the exchange appeared tense, it didn't seem threatening, aside from Katarina's aura making an appearance.

Esther blinked, and everything stopped.

"It is good you have controlled it. Be careful not to let it grow too powerful without release," Esther warned in a whisper.

Kat felt dizzy . . . What had Esther done? Did she have the ability to see magic like Mr. Kraft . . . ?

Her dazed thoughts were interrupted as Esther's gaze then filled with sadness as she continued staring intently at Kat. "Death is hardest on those that remain living. Remember that, and value what you can offer the world before making a choice, child."

Esther released Kat's hand and bowed her head.

Shaken to her core, Kat could neither speak nor move in response . . .

Had . . . that woman . . . just seen her future?

CHAPTER 37

FINE-TUNED FORESIGHT

Yes, Esther can see images of the future . . . Her grandmother had the same gift, but her powers are far more strange and unique than a simple mutated witch's power," Mr. Kraft explained to Kat, who was sitting with her elbows braced on her knees off to the side of the rows and rows of people being interrogated.

"How . . . do you mean?" Kat managed, though she still felt like she was going to vomit.

"Well, didn't you find it strange that your abilities weren't able to absorb what she was doing? Up until now, you have been able to have your aura consume any magic directed toward you, but she was able to look into your future without any interference."

Kat swallowed and finally succeeded in lifting her eyes to peer toward Esther, who sat near the base of the stairs being interrogated by the king himself.

"What is it that makes her abilities so special?"

"We don't think she's a descendant of the first witch."

Kat looked up, while stilling. "What? How is it possible that she can see into the—"

"Lady Katarina, your father's account of his time in the Forest of the Afterlife has been well documented, and he was gracious enough to share said accounts with me since arriving," Mr. Kraft recounted carefully. "I admit, my theory pertaining to Esther is new in light of what your father has shown me. However, I'd always thought it odd, her abilities . . . They don't clearly align with any element, and furthermore . . . well . . . I didn't want to say this in front of the others, but"—the coven leader leaned forward and quieted his voice—"it could be argued that it is intruding upon one's free will to be observed by someone without consent. This could incite a great deal of danger, as you can imagine."

While Kat frowned, she lowered her eyes in silent agreement. She didn't want to admit that she was already worried about what impressions the knights were getting of the witches when they were so openly hostile, let alone from one who could see the future . . .

"The other peculiar piece about her power is that it has run in her family for three generations. Her grandmother traveled the world telling fortunes, and her mother did the same until she met a Troivackian man and settled down here with him . . . Never has a mutated ability been passed down with the exact same properties and the exact same amount of power. There have always been variations if the power is passed down at all to begin with."

Kat gradually lifted herself to sit straight as she continued listening to the coven leader's words.

"Then there is the fact that I can't see her ability at all until she is in the middle of a vision. Normally, I'm able to see any small use of power, or if I touch them, I can understand completely. I cannot with her."

"What does this have to do with what you mentioned about my father's time in the Forest of the Afterlife?"

"Your father said the crystal that the Green Man wore around his neck cast images that revealed the past, present, and future."

"You think Esther is a mage?!" Kat exclaimed a little louder than she intended to, making Mr. Kraft shush her fearfully while looking around nervously to ensure no one heard.

"No. Esther doesn't require a crystal, nor does she require the language of mages either, but I do wonder, if perhaps the Green Man bestowed a select few with this ability to align with what is happening presently."

Kat frowned. That hadn't been her guess at all, so she turned to Mr. Kraft with a slight tilt of her head. "I thought you were going to say it indicates they are the descendants of the devil."

Mr. Kraft's expression fell.

The man looked utterly stunned.

"I . . . I confess I'd never considered that."

"Well, wouldn't it make sense? The first witch had children. I doubt the devil has been celibate the whole time he's been on earth. He probably has offspring of his own, and given that he obviously has abilities, doesn't it make sense his own children would have them as well?"

Mr. Kraft held up a finger while inching forward excitedly. "Then why have we not heard of anyone else—including in Daxaria—having abilities outside the norm?"

Kat gnawed on her tongue thoughtfully. That was a tough one to answer . . . The descendants related to the first witch each had a piece of her original power though nowhere near what legend said the daughter of the Gods had been capable of doing.

Following that pattern . . . Wouldn't it make sense for the devil to only pass along a portion of his ability?

Wait . . . but the devil couldn't see the future . . . Could he?

"A decent theory, Lady Katarina, but I am still of the mind that, like mutated witches, this new ability is the Gods' way of interfering to help things along."

"Help what along exactly? Are we supposed to defeat the ancient beasts? Are we supposed to defeat their son? What is it that they want from us?"

Mr. Kraft leaned back on the old stool he sat upon to rest his back against the tunnel wall.

"That . . . no one can truly know."

Kat's knee began to bounce rapidly as her mind raced through everything. "Why didn't you tell anyone about Esther?"

"I didn't because no matter how I looked at it, I couldn't see how revealing her could be of any help."

At this, Kat stared incredulously at the man. "Oh. You're right. Someone who could tell us everything that is going to happen is absolutely useless."

Mr. Kraft rolled his eyes toward the ceiling wearily before closing them. "She sees two or three images at most. Sometimes it is only of the present, sometimes the future, sometimes it's a mix of past, present, and the future. The farthest ahead she has seen is up to a year, but that only happened once or twice. Usually it is within a few months, and the visions don't always come to her. Sometimes she is able to see something, and sometimes she can't. The unreliability of her powers could create an even bigger discordance with everyone's views of magic here in Troivack. Do you see how it could be far more dangerous than helpful to introduce her?"

"Even once you learned of the devil's presence? Didn't you think this skill would be something that we should take into account with all the other strange things going on?" Kat asked almost angrily.

Mr. Kraft met Kat with a level stare. "I did ask her to look into the future after our encounter with the devil. She tried and saw nothing but blackness. She screamed the entire time she tried and took days to console . . ."

He shook his head at the memory. "Even more reason not to bring her into things."

Letting out a long, exhausted breath, Kat slowly pushed herself to her feet. "What're the odds that she will tell me what she saw in my own future?"

"You are welcome to try, but with a fortune like yours, I doubt she will share it."

"Wonderful. I just have to think about who is going to die. Which is great, honestly. I don't have *anything* else stressful going on. Nothing. I am just fat and lazy these days. Not a serious thought in my head at all!" Kat retorted sarcastically while throwing her hands into the air and walking back toward the knights so that she might help with the interrogations since she was feeling a little more like herself again.

Mr. Kraft rose as well, though he shook his head at the redhead's rant.

Despite her usual unrefined, unguarded behavior, Lady Katarina *had* brought up a very interesting question . . .

Did the devil have any offspring?

While the old records said he roamed the world trying to corrupt humans, there was nothing about whether he had sired any children . . . Or was he unable to? Had the Gods condemned him on earth for eternity to walk alone and repent?

Mr. Kraft looked out over the sea of witches, when a new idea occurred to him as he pondered the devil's influence in history . . .

I wonder if the devil had something to do with mutated witches appearing in the first place . . . ?

The room was dead silent save for the occasional clinking of porcelain.

The three women didn't even lift their gazes to one another.

With the suffocating tension, even the stoic maids could feel sweat dampening their backs as they worked to set the private meal.

Lady Annika Ashowan, Lady Nathalie Faucher, and Lady Rebecca Devark sat around the small round table in the solar.

Given that Lady Rebecca was not permitted to dine with the rest of the nobility due to her exile, the alternative dining plan had been presented so that the women might converse on recent events . . .

However, no one was speaking.

When the maids completed their work and politely curtsied, they waited to see if they'd be dismissed . . . But it dawned on them, they were not entirely certain which of the women present had the most authority in that situation.

Was it the former queen Lady Rebecca Devark, even though she was technically still serving out her punishment?

Or Lady Nathalie Faucher, the wife of the new acting captain of Troivack's military, even though she was technically a guest at the castle?

That left Lady Annika Ashowan, a foreign guest, but a duchess . . .

It was a circumstance that there hadn't been explicit training for.

In the end, while Lady Rebecca Devark raised her eyes as though she were about to speak, it was Lady Annika Ashowan who said the words.

"That will be all. Please leave us," the duchess ordered softly without looking up while taking a sip from her teacup.

Rebecca Devark's gaze cut to Annika, a spark of fury in her eyes that could almost be passed off as a trick of the light.

Lady Nathalie saw this, however, and reached for her own cup, her attention sharp, and her fingertips prickling with anticipation.

She hadn't felt such a thrill like this since . . . well . . . Since the last time she had been in the presence of the Dragon.

"I'm pleased to see my daughter-in-law has been so gracious and that you feel at home here, Your Grace." Lady Rebecca addressed Annika with her head held high. Her words were thinly veiled.

Annika calmly set her cup down.

"Her Majesty has been quite welcoming. It is wonderful to see her again. Have you been well, ma'am?" Annika's polite, friendly tone made a corner of Rebecca's mouth twitch.

"I have. Though I must confess, your daughter's presence has certainly brought more excitement than this court has seen in many years."

Annika tilted her head and settled back in her chair, making no move to start partaking in her dinner.

"I imagine my daughter forever making her mark in Troivack's history *would* be something noteworthy."

Lady Nathalie proceeded to pick up her cutlery and carefully began cutting into the seasoned chicken breast on her plate without interrupting.

"She has indeed made a name for herself during her time here. As I'm sure she will when she returns to Daxaria in the near future," Rebecca speculated airily.

"Oh? I was under the impression Her Majesty wished my daughter to stay here for the remainder of the year as was agreed upon by both kings," Annika continued, staring unwaveringly at the former queen, who didn't falter for an instant.

"I would have thought she would have wanted to take care of her pressing responsibilities as the future queen of Daxaria." Rebecca raised her eyebrows and casually reached for her goblet.

"Given that there is still an attempted murder trial that needs to be wrapped up, as well as great instability in the kingdom, my daughter and son-in-law feel it is also in Daxaria's best interest that they offer their assistance," Annika returned with a graceful bow of her head.

Rebecca picked up her own cutlery, and Lady Nathalie eyed the tightly gripped knife in her hand.

"Yes, speaking of His Highness Prince Eric, I hope his father the king won't mind terribly that his nuptials with your daughter were so *hurried*. Though I know my son His Majesty did his best to ensure it was a beautiful ceremony."

"Oh? Were you a part of the planning? It was terrible that I wasn't able to make it in time, but the dress she wore I heard spared no expense."

Lady Nathalie almost choked on her chicken.

So . . . Annika Ashowan knew her daughter had worn trousers on her wedding day.

Nathalie would have been worried about the duchess's reaction over such an occurrence were she not wielding the information as a weapon to check the former Troivackian queen within the next two exchanges.

"His Majesty King Brendan Devark and I have managed a great deal of matters together through the years," Rebecca returned vaguely while spearing a turnip with her fork.

"Of course, of course . . . Ah. Though, I think I misspoke just now. Lady Nathalie?"

The Troivackian noblewoman froze. She should've known she'd get caught in the crosshairs at some point . . .

"I believe it was actually *your* husband who spared no expense on my daughter's wedding attire and . . . Oh dear. While I said dress, I meant to say uniform. I must confess, Leader Faucher's students do look dashing when in their official uniform."

Lady Rebecca froze, and all color drained from her face.

Nathalie watched Annika cast her eyes to the ceiling with practiced innocence before brushing her fingertips along her mouth. "While I would have fought against such an idea at first, I must confess, the uniform does represent much of who my daughter is as someone with a respectful position in both Daxaria's and now Troivack's courts. Don't you agree, ma'am?"

Rebecca Devark looked as though she were ready to stab Annika Ashowan right then and there. Duchess or not.

Whether she would act on the urge remained to be seen.

Lady Nathalie busied herself by downing the rest of her goblet of wine and reaching for the decanter to refill it while the former queen and duchess stared each other down.

Gods, she'd missed this.

CHAPTER 38

ONE-ON-ONE

Lady Annika Ashowan left the solar after her meal with the former queen of Troivack, accompanied by Lady Nathalie Faucher.

The two women proceeded down the halls while making idle, polite conversation.

However, once they reached the duchess's chamber, she regarded Lady Nathalie with a demure tilt of her head. "Would you care to join me for a moment? I'd like to hear more about my daughter's time in your keep."

Nathalie felt her stomach flip but lowered her head in assent.

They entered the chamber quietly and closed the door before making their way over to the two armchairs that sat before the fire.

But while Annika sat, Lady Nathalie remained standing, adjusting her posture.

Annika stared at the woman stonily. "Why did you not contact me when you realized my daughter was in your care?"

"I tried, Dragon. My husband had our keep under tight surveillance, and when I did reach out to our point of contact, I heard you were already traveling to Troivack."

Annika raised an eyebrow, her reaction to the recounting unclear. "I hear my daughter has made both a great and terrible reputation for herself here."

"Yes. She is infamous for her mischief but also has earned respect for her skill with the sword."

"What is your opinion of Broghan Miller? I hear he is now indentured to serve her."

"It was your daughter's decision that, rather than forfeit his life to death's carriage, he forfeit it to her. I believe it was a fair decision. Broghan Miller seems to be repenting and changing, though still arrogant in many ways. It also has brought great loyalty from Lord Milo Miller."

"And how *is* Lord Milo doing? He has been quiet as of late. I can't even remember his last report."

"He, too, has been under great scrutiny—particularly from Duke Icarus. The duke kept trying to pressure Lord Milo to send his adopted son, Sir Cleophus, to handle the rebels. However, given Cleophus's prowess and the state of things here in the castle, he was able to refuse—though it was not easy, as the former Captain Orion aligned himself with Duke Icarus ages ago."

"So I've heard." Annika's finger slowly tapped the armrest of her chair.

"What is happening with the trial of Sir Seth Herra?"

"Currently His Majesty suspects that Sir Seth Herra is under the influence of Witch's Brew. His behavior is different from the norm of the drug's users, which is why your husband, His Grace, has been investigating the powdered form of the drug. This is especially important given that it was what Sir Herra tried to dose Lady Katarina with."

Annika nodded in understanding. "I see. Is Lady Rebecca Devark suspected to have her hand in any of this?"

"There are suspicions," Lady Nathalie confirmed, albeit carefully. "However, no one is certain."

"Where was Lady Rebecca Devark staying during her brief time away from court?"

"In her old family estate, a quarter day's ride due west from Vessa."

"Isn't your keep southwest of Vessa?"

"Yes."

Annika raised a thoughtful eyebrow. "Curious."

The duchess thought about these details in silence.

"Have you been keeping an eye on Mr. Levin's wife, Caroline?"

"I was, until Rebecca Devark was removed from court. It must have concerned Mr. Levin, as he has his wife moving around various residences with their daughter regularly."

"Jocelyn Piereva still lives?"

"As far as I know, though she has been quiet for many years."

Annika frowned. "Caroline is behaving as though she has something to hide, or as though Mr. Levin is hiding her *from* something. I want someone monitoring her at all times, or . . . better yet . . ."

Annika rose from her chair and let out a long breath as she eyed the window. "Perhaps I should officially meet my niece. Please see that an invitation is sent out to Mrs. Caroline Levin. I believe it's high time I faced the past."

"Dragon, there is one thing I would like to say, if I have your permission to speak freely?"

Annika's brown eyes drifted back to the woman, her expression at last gentling. "You may."

"I've missed you. I was so worried when your brother sold you off to the viscount . . . I'm relieved that you've done so well. And, if I may . . . your daughter is just like you, only—"

"Better at getting herself into trouble than out?" Annika asked with a wry smile.

Lady Nathalie shook her head, a rare upward curving of the mouth gracing her own elegant face. "While true, that is not what I was going to say. What I was going to say was that she is how I imagined you would have been had you grown up in a different household . . . perhaps in Daxaria."

Emotion filled Annika's eyes. "Thank you. That is . . . That has been a goal of mine since the moment I became a mother. That she . . . be free of some of the hardships I endured. Though it was difficult at times curbing her more wild expeditions."

Lady Nathalie laughed quietly. "Yes . . . my sons told me the details of the story about the donkey."

Annika's foray into an improved mood dissipated instantly. "I don't want to talk about Harold right now."

Unable to contain herself, Lady Nathalie let out a snort that caught both Annika and her off guard.

But when the duchess met her former friend's wide eyes, sighed. "Alright, I grant you, it's a little funnier now that it's been a few years."

That was all the permission Lady Nathalie needed to allow herself a brief bout of hysterical laughter while the duchess rolled her eyes and succumbed to a smile of her own, though after a moment it was touched with sadness.

The exchange was reminding her of Ainsley Reyes, the former queen of Daxaria, her best friend, who had passed years ago . . . And it made her miss her horribly in that moment, especially when she recalled how their two children were, in fact, married.

Annika's throat tightened, and she turned away from Lady Nathalie to not spoil her moment of fun.

Gods . . . Ainsley would've . . . loved having Kat as her daughter-in-law. I wish . . . I wish I could tell her all that has happened.

"You realize because you are wishing for your status as a Zinferan prince to remain a secret that you are also forgoing more comfortable accommodations, yes?" Brendan asked Eli, the Zinferan prince Eric Reyes had discovered, enslaved, at Duke Icarus's home.

The lad, who still had not confirmed his age, though looked no older than sixteen, nodded, his chin almost touching his chest as he did so while seated in shackles before the Troivackian king.

Brendan had gone to visit Eli in the cells of Lord Miller's home, where it had been decided the boy would be safest for the time being while Duke Icarus and Sir Herra were dealt with.

"Your information has proved helpful, particularly your detailed report of the duke's expenditures and his safe combinations. I'm surprised he trusted you with such information."

The tips of Eli's ears turned red. "He wasn't always aware that I was watching him."

"And you were watching him to find a means of escaping?"

"I was hoping the opportunity would present itself."

Brendan nodded carefully while taking his time in asking his next question, his black eyes remaining fixed on the reedy young man before him.

"What is it you want, aside from being free?"

"I-I want to go to Daxaria and work, Your Majesty. To . . . To make a life for myself where I am in charge of my own fate and I have nothing to fear."

"Oh? What kind of work do you think you are suited for? Or is it that you simply wish to join the Coven of Wittica?"

"My hope is to . . . to perhaps become a magistrate, and . . . as I said to His Highness . . . I don't wish to use my magic. I would much rather live as though I am a complete human than a witch."

Brendan felt his eyes narrow.

There was something about the boy that made him think of Tamlin Ashowan's attitude toward magic, and so he ventured a guess.

"Do you happen to know of the Ashowan family?"

Eli risked a glance at the king, his features still. "O-Of course, Your Majesty. Lord Finlay Ashowan came on several diplomatic visits to the Zinferan court during my childhood."

"He is now a duke. His title is now His Grace."

"My a-apologies, Your Majesty."

"There was no way you could've known otherwise," Brendan dismissed calmly. "What is your opinion of the duke?"

"His Grace has always been kind and respectful, i-if a little obsessed with food."

Brendan nodded along.

A fair assessment overall, but still . . . the way the boy had tensed at the mentioning of the duke's name was curious.

"His Grace is currently here in Troivack at my court. Would you like to speak to him given that you are a witch trying to make your way into his kingdom? You would be expected to register with the Coven of Wittica regardless of whether you wish to use your magic."

"No, thank you."

The swiftness and surprising firmness that came from the boy only deepened Brendan's reservations.

"Given he is the diplomat to all countries and their covens, you will have to speak with him at some point."

Eli remained quiet.

After the long day of interrogating the witches cloistered beneath Vessa, Brendan found he had little patience for this final appointment—particularly with so much secrecy everywhere he looked.

"If you are not cooperative and forthcoming, I see no need to expedite your request to leave Troivack." Brendan stood and turned toward the cell door where two guards waited at the ready.

"The Ashowans . . . I . . . I have no issues with, but . . . but I'm worried if I get entangled with them, then the people who wanted me dead might discover my whereabouts and renew their efforts to find me. There are a great many people who take exception to the duke."

Brendan stared down at the lad coolly. "What is it that makes you so valuable? You should at least confide this to me. Besides, having a meeting or two with the duke hardly indentures you to him."

"I've heard of many people falling in with the Ashowan family for one reason or another, and I don't want to risk it."

Brendan was feeling more irritable as the daylight from the cell's small narrow window began to fade and the dining hour neared.

"If you wish for help, then a measure of trust must be given. I'm told His Highness advised you to be cooperative with me, and if you trust him, then you should trust his judgment. I know this decision is being made out of desperation, but that is your fate at present. Will you choose to be stuck in Troivack for the foreseeable future, or will you do as His Highness suggested so that others may help you?"

Brendan eyed the boy's bony hands as they fidgeted and flexed.

"My ability is mutated, and while it seems simple at first, I can assure you it is not. If I . . . If I show Your Majesty, do I have your word that you will never ask me to show it again, and you will keep it a secret?"

The king wanted to reiterate his earlier point that the Zinferan was not in a position to be making demands, but the way Eli was reacting was sparking his interest, and perhaps if he knew the boy's magic, he could better understand him.

"Very well. You have my word that, unless it is information that needs to be communicated for the sake of the greater good, I will not share it."

Eli was quiet, and Brendan briefly wondered what he was waiting for . . .

"Please ask the guards to look away."

Brendan considered refusing the request, however, his instincts told him things would be alright . . . So he obliged.

Then, he waited.

What burst from Eli then had him leaping back, slamming himself against the bars in shock as the clang of the boy's shackles rang out loudly.

"Your Majesty?!" The guard on the king's right moved to turn around, but just as the man caught the king in his peripheral vision, Brendan held up his hand to stop him, though the king's gaze never left the sight before him.

"I'm fine. Do not look."

The guard visibly bit back arguing against the order, but he did as commanded.

Brendan continued staring at Eli, his face pale, utterly bereft of words, until Eli stopped using his magic, and he once again sat with his head hung before the king as he had moments before.

Letting out a subtle, calming breath, Brendan made his way back over to his chair and sat down in front of the boy.

"I think I'm starting to understand how you came to be where you are. I will think on what you've shown me today, and I will let you know what I believe should become of your fate."

Eli remained silent, his hands trembling.

Brendan didn't comment on this, as he silently came to an important realization.

Eli was interesting but traumatized, and it was easy to see how he could be. He was also naïve of just how powerful the Ashowan family was, and how, should he choose to reveal his state to the Ashowans, he would become one of the best-protected witches in the world—even from the emperor of Zinfera himself and his bloodthirsty harem.

Despite Eli's reasonable misgivings about the duke's family, something in Brendan told him that the boy's complicated story and abilities didn't belong anywhere else but within the safety and chaos of the damnable care of the newest dukedom in Daxaria. Though it would potentially take some time to make it possible to place him there . . .

CHAPTER 39

TEATIME

Ihaven't seen him eat, but I may order that I be privy to the event. There just has to be an explanation."

"Brendan."

"Lady Elena insisted that even if she didn't feed him, he found other means of getting into anything and everything, so she simply ensured he ate healthy items. What purpose could a familiar have being so large? How would it theoretically help his witch?"

"Brendan, I swear to the Gods. You need to stop talking about this raccoon."

The king and queen of Troivack were strolling toward the throne room that had been converted to a space where Alina could hold a luncheon with the Troivackian noblewomen of the court.

While the queen had been delighted at first that she would get to spend a few extra minutes with her husband that morning, she found her good mood swiftly plummet as talk of Lady Elena's rotund raccoon familiar dominated the conversation.

"Alina, once you see him, you will understand what a perplexing creature he is. I didn't even know raccoons could live in Troivack. I'd only ever heard of them in Daxaria," the king insisted with his usual stern tone.

"I really . . . sincerely, do *not* need to meet this raccoon."

"But—"

"Brendan? I love you, but I think we have enough on our plates right now without trying to solve the mystery of a raccoon's digestive abilities." Alina turned and clasped the king's hands in her own, her gaze imploring.

The Troivackian king took a breath, and for a dreaded moment Alina wondered if he was going to insist that they keep discussing the matter, but luckily, he decided that it wasn't the time to argue.

Instead he said, "Are you confident about the meeting with the noblewomen?"

Alina smiled beautifully and looked down at their clasped hands. "As ready as I'll ever be, I think. I can't keep holding them off—I'm sure I'll hear a jibe or two about how it's taken me this long already."

"Be sure to lean on Lady Sarah should you wish to rest," Brendan ordered firmly.

"I will. It's quite fun seeing her so excited about something for once." Alina turned back toward their destination and resumed walking.

"She was handpicked by my mother to lead the young women of Troivack," Brendan mused thoughtfully.

However, his words made Alina pause in her journey once more and round back to her husband.

"Brendan . . . Did your mother want you to marry Lady Sarah?"

The king stiffened and refused to meet his wife's eye.

Alina laughed softly. "I should've known. It's alright. I'm not angry, and Lady Sarah has always conducted herself respectfully."

Relaxing with relief, the king gently tugged his wife back along, deciding that he should remain silent until they parted to avoid getting himself in trouble.

Upon reaching the throne room, the royal couple straightened their postures and forfeited all emotion from their faces as the guards saw to opening the doors to reveal the transformed space. Now filled with noblewomen, the room was brightened by round tables adorned with shimmering gold tablecloths, fresh greenery, and gleaming cake towers ladened with desserts and sandwiches.

The women all rose and curtsied to their king and queen.

"Good day. I trust you all will conduct yourselves well in the company of your queen," Brendan greeted gruffly.

"Yes, Your Majesty," the ladies chorused.

Pleased with the response, Brendan nodded, then gave a slight bow to Alina before excusing himself.

Ladies Sarah and Wynonna rose from their seats and guided Alina to her seat at the farthest table, which was the only one that sat in the middle of the room.

Once standing in front of her ornate dark wooden chair, Alina faced the room.

"I thank you all for coming to this event. It has been a meeting I have longed to do since arriving in Troivack, but given affairs out of my hands,

His Majesty felt it was best to delay. I look forward to getting to know you all a bit better today." Alina held out her hand at the end of her speech for a goblet to be placed in her grasp. She was already feeling a small warning rattle in her lungs. She had forgotten to talk to Kezia about magically setting up the amplifying bowls. "To Troivack!" Alina toasted as loudly as she dared.

"To your health, Your Majesty!" Lady Sarah added while accepting a goblet of her own from a footman and sweeping into a curtsy.

The rest of the nobility present murmured the same while curtsying again.

Once that was finished, Alina nodded, satisfied. She proceeded to sit and tuck herself in close to the table.

Given that she was meant to form connections with the women she was not yet familiar with, she had Lady Sarah and Lady Wynonna sit farther from her, and Lady Kezia was seated at another table entirely.

Instead, on Alina's right was Lady Camille Selby, and on her left, Lady Elyse Ball.

Two women who were known to be more neutral in their opinions of the new Troivackian queen.

The meal passed by pleasantly enough with polite conversation being made, but by the time the young women were starting to mingle around the grand room, Alina was suspicious.

No one had approached her, but they all seemed chatty enough with one another . . .

They are either afraid to talk to me or don't want to bother. I'll never be able to appeal to them while they avoid me.

Well . . . there *was* a way to start engaging people. Though Alina had hoped it wouldn't have had to come to it.

"Lady Camille, I hear your daughter, Miriam, is partaking in Lady Katarina's lessons. How is she finding them?"

The quarter of the room that heard Alina's question fell silent.

Lady Camille Selby, with her long face and lined, puffy eyes, regarded the queen sharply.

Alina did her best to feign a docile expression.

"She . . . is enjoying them, though I'm encouraging her to stop in the near future."

"Oh, what a pity. I know even Lady Elyse here was interested in signing up. How is your husband recovering by the way, Lady Elyse?"

Another section of the room fell quiet.

"Lord Ball is . . . is suffering from persistent migraines and troubling dreams at this time, Your Majesty," Lady Elyse responded with her eyes downcast.

"I'm terribly sorry to hear that."

"Why was Lady Katarina not punished?"

The one who spoke out was a woman perhaps only a few years older than Alina. Her arms were folded, and her long black hair was styled over her right shoulder in sculpted waves.

"Why would Lady Katarina need to be punished?" Alina asked while giving her head a regal tilt.

"She's the one responsible for Lord Ball having to fight a bastard who would use underhanded tricks in a fight."

"Given that Lord Harriod Ball insulted Lady Katarina and refused to greet her respectfully, she was well within her means of challenging his offensive behavior. As for permitting Mr. Joshua Ball to spar on her behalf, she felt it was a fairer fight that way." Alina reached for her goblet casually. "Though perhaps I've missed something in my account of the events?" The queen continued to eye the noblewoman over the rim of her cup.

"Lady Katarina could have chosen Caleb Herra or one of Leader Faucher's sons," the noblewoman countered, though her cheeks had deepened in color.

"She could have, but then again . . . we have servants who are of illegitimate birth, and yet they still work in close quarters to us legitimate offspring. So why should she not have chosen him?"

"Because now Lord Harriod Ball's honor and dignity is in shambles! Why, I heard he even tried to have a cat arrested after his savage beating! He has clearly had his mind addled as a result of the match!" Lady Camille burst out, her eyes flashing dangerously at the queen, who was alarmingly calm throughout the confrontation.

"Why would his dignity be in shambles? He accepted the challenge as a consequence for his actions, as a man should. If anything, I would think he's more respectable now. Unless you think perhaps he should have simply been made to *apologize* to Lady Katarina. Though I was under the impression that would've been far too extreme a punishment." Alina waited to see what her baiting words would bring.

She felt guilty when out of the corner of her eye she saw the embarrassed hunching of poor Lady Elyse's shoulders and Lady Sarah's frantic gulping from Lady Wynonna's cup, but . . . she had to see it through. She could make it up to the two wronged women, but only if she won.

"A bastard beating a legitimate sibling is—"

"Is a great point of evaluation when we begin to consider the merits of a person and what their talents may offer. We now know Mr. Joshua Ball has the makings to be a knight that could serve Troivack well," Alina cut the noblewoman off while slowly rising and setting her drink back down on the table.

She then proceeded to glide over to the antagonist who had first spoken out and stood before her.

"We consider bastards lesser than, and yet Joshua Ball has beaten a legitimate sibling. We consider women fragile, yet most of you bore witness to Lady Katarina's duels, and not only stomached it, but found enjoyment. Some of our women have even begun to train like her—so it isn't merely because Lady Katarina is a witch that she can handle such things. And women allegedly have no place in the council room, except that now three women have sat in those meetings and contributed. Does change frighten you, Lady . . . ?"

"Sanchez. Arette Sanchez," the woman replied though her breathing had quickened, and anger gripped her face.

"Lady Arette Sanchez. Are you frightened?" Alina questioned again, softly.

It had been Reese Flint who had taught her the most powerful leaders and teachers didn't need to scream or shout to be feared or heard, but rather, they should be able to command the room with a single look.

Alina had worked hard at developing such a skill, and in Troivack, it was especially difficult, as she was significantly shorter than the average woman, but she held her ground and stared up at Lady Sanchez sharply.

"I am not frightened of what will not last. These occurrences . . . They exist because our kingdom is on the brink of civil war."

Alina smiled coolly. Her face was so devoid of warmth that no one could mistake it for a friendly expression.

"These are events that some said would never happen, and yet they have. Things have already changed, Lady Sanchez. Not all change is bad. Imagine if a woman such as yourself was able to express her opinions and be heard? What if your words carried importance not just amongst women, but amongst the men? Would that not be a change you'd like to see?"

Lady Arette's upper lip began to curl. "Troivackian women still control their men. We just prefer to do so with class and restraint."

Alina raised an eyebrow, still not reacting to the noblewoman's outright insult.

She let silence settle over the party, allowed Lady Arette's words to rest over her as a small tremble developed in her long fingers.

Lady Sarah stood up as though to intervene, but Alina held up her hand, stopping the movement, her eyes never leaving Lady Arette's face, though the noblewoman was starting to squirm even more noticeably.

"Your husbands do not tell you everything. You are left scrambling and investigating. You use your energy and brilliance to deduce what decisions are being made about your lives and your homes. I am proposing a world where you do not work to command your men with whispers at their backs but in a dialogue to their faces. Just like we are having now."

Lady Arette was about to open her mouth to say more when Alina lifted her chin, cutting her off.

"Tell me, do you feel more respected when I look you in the eye and listen to what you have to say, or shall I turn around for you to talk to the back of my head to better show it like you say your husband does?"

Lady Arette's eyes widened, and before she was able think about her retort, she started to say, "Y-You d—"

But again Alina prevented this by sweeping her gaze out over the noble-women, who watched the scene frozen in shock. Many of them pale, a few angry to their core, but some . . . Alina could see their hands gripped into fists, or their shoulders straightened and their faces eager . . . Hopeful . . .

"I want a better life for you all. Troivack's strength is astounding, and its women are no exception. You should *all* be given the honor and decency owed to you. While you may not like me or believe that I will accomplish what I am working on, I'd say I've made more than enough progress to have earned a bit of your faith."

Alina gave another rueful half smile. "I've survived more assassination attempts than I'd like to count. Thanks to both luck and Lady Katarina. Whether you like it or not, even should I die suddenly, or while giving birth as many of us women do, I *have* changed Troivack and made a mark in its history. Now, would you like to be a part of this chapter I am writing? Would you like to see how far I can go? If so . . . come, talk to me."

Alina rounded back to her table, and in the deafening silence after her speech, she sat herself down while giving off an air that nothing of consequence had just taken place.

Inside, she had quaked and raged, but thanks to the months of lessons with Annika Ashowan prior to her wedding, Alina had held her own.

And so, as she reached for a raspberry tart to place upon her plate, she added a final note to Lady Arette, who stood like a statue with her emotions showing on her face.

"Ah. If you simply wish to fight with me more, I'll welcome that too. Your husbands have already had their turn against me in the council room, and I happen to have a soft spot for people who are passionate about their home and kingdom. So please, don't be shy. I myself have no intentions to be docile as others expect me to be so I don't expect you to be either."

CHAPTER 40

POST-PARTY PARTICIPATION

Kat pushed open the doors to Alina's tea party, well aware that she was incredibly late, but she *had* alerted the Troivackian queen she would be running a tad behind as the interrogations of the witches of the coven continued.

However, instead of a room filled with Troivackian noblewomen, Kat instead found the serving staff cleaning up and two guests speaking with Alina, who sat primly as ever, her hazel eyes intent on them.

Lady Sarah had her head in her hand and was pointing unsteadily at Lady Wynonna as she slumped back into Kezia, who stood behind her fellow handmaiden with her hands on Lady Wynonna's shoulders as they waited for their queen to finish speaking to her remaining guests.

"Ah, did I miss the whole thing?" Kat approached the noblewomen while Alina wrapped up with her conversation.

"Mm-yeah. Yeah, you did." Lady Sarah turned blearily toward Kat. Her right eye closed then, as she appeared to have difficulty seeing only one Katarina in that moment.

"Lady Sarah, I've never seen you properly sauced before!" Kat chortled delightedly.

Even Lady Kezia was smiling over the development, though Lady Wynonna looked as though she were already asleep.

"Well, you know . . . Is because I've had to . . . to do all this work . . . alone! *You* are off with . . . swords and such, an' *you*." Sarah turned to Kezia. "Jus' had a beautiful baby!"

Kezia laughed, her eyes warming at the mention of her son. "That I did. Thank you for all your hard work to make Her Majesty's first official gathering such a success, Lady Sarah. I know she could not have managed everything without you."

Kat smiled at the Troivackian noblewoman appreciatively as a pang of guilt thrummed in her gut. She really hadn't been doing much to help Alina directly as of late.

"The throne room looks lovely!" Kat cited while casually gripping the hilt of her sword out of nervous habit.

"You!" Lady Sarah brandished her finger at Kat suddenly. "You—*hic*—have a brother, right?"

Already sensing where the conversation was going, Kat looked wide-eyed to Kezia, who pressed her lips together as she barely staved off another laugh.

"Er . . . Yes. Yes, I do."

"Is he good-looking?" Sarah insisted, her eyes fluttering.

"Well, I'm a bit biased against the ninny, but some women show an interest." Kat cringed and shook her head as though already trying to rid herself of the thought of her brother being appealing to anyone.

"Then les' do it! Les set up—*hic*—a wedding!" Lady Sarah tried to stand in a commanding manner but instead slipped and fell back into her seat. "Huh . . . Someone musta washed the floors."

Lady Kezia couldn't hold back any longer, her chin dropped to her chest, her beautiful waving black hair falling over her shoulders, curtaining her face as she laughed.

Kat, on the other hand, was already letting out a sigh. "Lady Sarah, I sincerely doubt that he's your type. I'm sure there are some halfway decent men in Troivack . . . somewhere."

"I used to think so!" Lady Sarah whirled around in her seat with surprising quickness. "But then *you* showed up, an' now, an now . . . Ugh. I have . . . *opinions!*" The noblewoman dropped her face to her hands, ashamed.

Kat frowned but was also starting to smile simultaneously in shock and amusement.

By then at least, Alina had bid farewell to the other two noblewomen, who were holding each other's hands while whispering back and forth excitedly.

Once they were gone, Alina seemed to deflate in her seat while letting out a long breath, but then noticed Kat.

The redhead held up her hands. "I'm sorry, I know I missed it. Faucher insisted I help finish questioning the witches. His Majesty is compiling the findings, and I also have to—"

Alina waved, effectively stopping her friend's apology with a weary smile. "We're both working hard. No need to worry. Thank you for everything you're doing, Kat. Truly. And thank you, Lady Sarah, for arranging this. I wouldn't have known that long tables were not used for these gatherings had you not told me, nor that lighter colors are expected to be used for the first gathering after the solstice.

Lady Sarah had rested her head on her forearm while Alina and Kat were talking, and it seemed that she had joined Lady Wynonna in falling asleep.

"Well, if it isn't the *dream* team!" Kat crowed happily.

Alina groaned at the terrible pun while Kezia shook her head, still laughing.

"I think Lady Wynonna's drinking habits are rubbing off on Lady Sarah," Kat added while pulling up a chair beside Sarah.

Alina tilted her head side to side thoughtfully. "She does now tend to drink during times of high stress or after an important meeting or event . . . Though in a way she's also a lot more relaxed in general."

Kat nodded while reaching up to rub her eyes.

"Good Gods, are you actually *tired?*" Alina asked in astonishment.

"Give me a break. After a month of training and no sleep, I got married, then have been running all over, training, facing my parents, and probably other things too . . ."

"The first few months of being a newlywed are tiring," Kezia recalled with a feigned innocence.

Kat looked up at her flatly while Alina blushed and averted her gaze.

"That's enough of *that* topic . . . But . . . I will say . . . before attending the next council meeting, I think I might actually try for a nap."

"Gods, now I know you really are pushing yourself." Alina looked at Kat, her concern deepening.

"I'll be alright. I just need three days where nothing major happens— Oh. By the way, His Majesty is going to be interrogating the handmaidens tomorrow."

Lady Kezia tilted her head. "Are we suspected of having ties to Witch's Brew?"

Kat grimaced. "There's a woman close to Alina who we've been warned has a hand in causing all this chaos, so we're being cautious."

Kezia's former good mood faded as she nodded seriously. "Of course. Her Majesty's safety comes first. I have faith that we are all good women here."

While opening her mouth to agree with the sentiment, Kat was interrupted by the arrival of Lady Nathalie, who came through the servant's hallway.

"Ah! Lady Katarina! I'm glad you're back, but I must insist that you go speak with that man named Dimitri who fixed your sword. He has been getting more and more adamant that there are things you need to know about its history."

Kat let her head flop forward before she pushed herself to her feet. "Is he here at the castle at least?"

"I'm afraid not. He is at his shop in Vessa. His Highness has also returned from searching for Likon, so if you would like to go with him, it might be for the best in order to be cautious."

Kat bobbed her head in understanding and gave Lady Nathalie an appreciative smile before the Troivackian noblewoman curtsied to Alina and took her leave.

Kat reached up and scratched the back of her neck, then her scalp.

"When was the last time you bathed?" Alina rose to her feet with a hand on her rounding middle and her eyes stern.

"Hm . . . Two days ago? Wait . . . Before the wedding? Oh Gods . . ." Kat's tired eyes widened briefly before she gave a sniff and yanked her hair free of its tie so that she might retie it properly again, the red roots slick with oil, her skin sallow.

"Take a bath. Have a nap. And *then* go see the blacksmith before dinner," the queen ordered softly.

Kat stifled a yawn while attempting to shake her head. "No, no. If I go now, it's done with and I can—" She was unable to finish the thought as yet another yawn overtook her.

Alina moved to stand in front of Kat and gripped her friend's upper arms with surprising strength. "You aren't any use to us if you're too tired to do anything. Go. Rest. It doesn't take you long to recover your strength anyway."

Kat smiled down at the queen, who was looking at her firmly.

She inclined herself to the small blonde. "This errand won't take long, Your Majesty."

Giving a tight-lipped smile to the queen and a quick wave to Kezia, Kat didn't allow anyone else to try and stop her.

Making her way back toward the throne room doors, Kat proceeded to tie back her long hair as she walked, though the women all noticed that her steps were a mite less graceful and energetic than usual.

Kezia leaned over to Alina. "I'm very concerned about her. Everyone has relied so much on Lady Katarina, and she has seemed to bear it well, but perhaps she is reaching her limits."

Alina watched her friend's back disappear through the throne room doors.

"I know. It honestly scares me how much we rely on her right now, especially with everything happening. If only her father had his abilities or we had more magical power in this court, we could maybe give her a rest. But the council . . . They are barely permitting me to get away with the progress pertaining to the rights of the noblewomen. Pushing the agenda for more witches in the castle on top of that?" The queen closed her eyes.

"I think Lady Katarina isn't the only person who needs rest." Kezia eyed Alina, and then the two noblewomen behind her.

"Lady Wynonna has been the one logging all council notes and records *and* collaborating with the king's assistant even on the meetings Your Majesty cannot attend. Lady Sarah has been managing your events, schedule, and diet. I have been of very little help. I'm sorry, Your Majesty."

Alina turned, grasping her sister-in-law's hands. "Do not apologize for taking care of yourself and your son. The fact that you have returned to your duties so soon speaks volumes of your loyalty."

Kezia lowered her gaze demurely. "Hopefully I can now lessen the load for both Ladies Wynonna and Sarah. Then . . . who knows? Between the three of us, maybe in the years to come we can all better help create the progressive court you dream of and have started to craft with your own hands today, Your Majesty."

Alina took in a deep breath. "I'm certainly going to do my best to keep going, though hopefully we can wean ourselves away from leaning so heavily on Kat, otherwise things will start falling apart once she leaves for Daxaria."

"I think you are stronger and more capable than you realize, Your Majesty. Lady Katarina's powers have been integral, it's true, but I think it speaks of the uniqueness of events taking place. The first witch, daughter of the Gods, could not best the devil. To say things would fall apart without Lady Katarina, well . . . I think without the devil present? That wouldn't be the case at all. I know you're still learning, but your passion, effort, and sincerity for Troivack and its people are what is changing this court."

Staring at her sister-in-law, tears welling up in her eyes, Alina had no choice but to hug the woman.

"Thank the Gods I have you as my sister-in-law."

Kezia accepted the embrace. "You have an army on all sides, Your Majesty. Don't worry. This all will pass."

"I hope so . . . I wake up fearing that people will die when everything comes to a head."

"Let us pray that it does not come to that." Kezia released the queen and stepped back with her hands on the queen's shoulders.

Peering up at the impossibly beautiful woman, Alina sighed. "How are you so lovely?"

"I wasn't always." Sadness shone in Kezia's eyes. "I used to run away from things . . . and I used to resent that my family and I had to hide our knowledge of magic . . ."

Alina listened, her surprise undisguised.

"It wasn't until I met a witch who had been hunted all her life, and she told me that while I had every right to be angry, not to dedicate my life to it. She told me how we are responsible for finding our own happiness, and how allowing my life to be consumed in anger means I've allowed everything to be taken from me by those who persecute us. Those words have changed how I've lived. Your Majesty, I want you to know, the reason I like you so much is because you were treated as if you were weak due to your health difficulties. However, the fact that you found your strength and continue searching for how to build it? It's similar to my own journey, and I have nothing but admiration, respect, and complete confidence you are going to do great things. "

Alina reached out to hold Kezia's hands once more, unsure of what she could say to such a thing when, off to the side, Lady Sarah proceeded to vomit on the floor.

Both Kezia and the queen looked at each other with a wince, then turned to the nearest serving staff, the profound moment between them broken.

"Perhaps a jug of water for Lady Sarah."

When they looked back to the two handmaidens, they were taken aback to see Lady Wynonna sitting up once more as well, the noblewoman then proceeded to rise from her seat with impressive grace.

She looked to the queen and Kezia, her eyes still glassy. "Good day, Your Majesty, Lady Kezia. I'm afraid I might be sick myself."

Lady Wynonna proceeded to curtsy, and then she departed while walking in an impressively straight line.

"For a woman not born in Troivack, her alcohol tolerance is incredible," Kezia chuckled softly to Alina.

"I fear for her liver."

"We all do. Though, I heard Lady Katarina's mother may be the one woman who is able to put her to shame."

"Oh Gods, don't bring it up to the duchess. She's oddly competitive about her alcohol tolerance . . ."

The two women were starting to get sidetracked in their conversation again when another retching sound from Lady Sarah drew their attention to the more pressing matter of getting the poor noblewoman back to her chamber to rest.

CHAPTER 41

THE BLACKSMITH'S BENEFIT

K at barely managed to cover her mouth as her twenty-fourth yawn of the day claimed her. Despite this, she did not falter in her stride as she and Eric made their way down the alleyway toward the blacksmith's shop in Vessa.

There was a damp smell in the warming air that teased of the coming spring, which would normally have Kat feeling rejuvenated and excited . . . yet this time it only made her body feel heavier.

"After this, you are going to bed and you aren't leaving our chamber until tomorrow at luncheon hour," Eric informed his wife firmly.

"Gods, don't say that. That'll be torture!"

"Hardly. You need to catch up on rest. As impressive as your endurance has always been, you've hit your limit. If there is a battle in the next few weeks, you need to be ready. And if you insist on pushing yourself, I'll make sure you're locked in a cell."

"What a loving husband you are."

"It'll be the best cell money can buy."

"Still not better, but fine, fine. I'll go back and rest, but if I wake up tomorrow morning feeling like myself, I want to be able to leave. We still haven't heard anything about Likon, and His Majesty is talking about trying to persuade members of the Coven of Aguas to help should any magical beasts attack—you know that could make a massive difference in how the witches are perceived by everyone in Troivack."

"Gods, look at you. Being responsible and enjoying working as a noble." Eric raised an eyebrow at her with a wry grin.

Kat stuck her tongue out at him, making him laugh.

"Good to see you aren't entirely different."

"I heard my da went through a similar change when he first was ennobled . . . Though everyone lately keeps saying I'm like my mum . . ."

"Believe it or not, you can have traits from both parents." Eric knocked on the door of the blacksmith's shop.

"You sure are snarky today," Kat remarked while eyeing Eric up and down. "What died in your ale?"

The prince ignored her and continued waiting by the front door.

When no movement came from inside, Eric knocked again.

Kat sniffed in the cold as they stood silently.

At last, the door opened and revealed . . . a shriveled old woman.

Her long white hair was unkempt, and her back hunched, bringing her closer to the ground.

"Err . . . Hello. I'm here because Dimitri has been asking for a meeting for . . . well a long time, I suppose." Kat awkwardly showed the rolled message that the blacksmith had sent most recently.

The woman didn't bother introducing herself and instead snatched the parchment from Kat's hand and unfurled it.

She scowled at the message, then looked up at the couple, her brown eyes sharp. "It's taken you long enough. He's been waiting for you before fleeing to Daxaria."

Kat straightened in alarm.

"Why is he fleeing to Daxaria?" Eric interjected with a frown.

The woman didn't answer, merely rolled her eyes and made an irritable sound before turning back to the shop and disappearing inside, then closing the door in their faces.

Looking at Eric, Kat made sure to lower her voice. "Do you think this has anything to do with the devil? Didn't you say he approached you the last time you were in Vessa? What if he has been following you every time you come into town?"

Eric didn't have time to answer his wife's speculations before the old woman reappeared, only this time she was wearing a gray traveling cloak.

"This way." She waved to them as she shuffled toward the end of the alley.

"Pardon me, ma'am, but what is your name?" Eric queried politely while he and Kat fell in step easily behind her.

"I'm not telling either of you that," she bit out hostilely. "You two are more trouble than you're worth."

Neither Eric nor Kat bothered trying to argue the point.

Instead, they proceeded to allow her to take them to the end of the alley, where there was nothing but a stone wall spanning three stories high and two stone buildings parallel to each other with windows boarded shut.

Kat was starting to wonder if the woman was perhaps unaware of her surroundings, when she let out a short, shrill whistle, followed by an imitation of a pigeon call . . .

One of the boarded windows to the left creaked open.

The woman nodded to it as though it were obvious what they should do.

"Do all those boards swing open?" Eric asked slowly.

The elder glared up at him. "Figure it out for yourself but keep quiet."

She then stormed off as abruptly as she had come.

While the prince stared after her, amazed at her feisty yet rude attitude, Kat was already stepping forward to investigate the boarded window.

She gave it a small push and watched as, sure enough, the boards all swung open as though it were a shoddy shutter.

Kat leaned in carefully and peered around the darkened room.

Thanks to her golden eyes being able to see through the darkness, she easily found Dimitri sitting beside a fire that was little more than embers, a goblet clasped in hand.

Waving her hand, Kat drew Eric's attention while already sidling up to the wall, then hoisting herself up and over the window ledge to enter the building.

Inside was a relatively sparse, dusty room with two dirty tattered armchairs by the fire that at one point may have been gold but now took on a tragic mustard yellow color. A wardrobe sat in a dark corner, its left door hanging slightly ajar. To Kat's left was a large, rounded doorway that led even deeper into the seemingly abandoned building.

Eric landed behind Kat and squinted, unable to see their surroundings in the same detail as his wife.

Kat strode forward confidently while Dimitri reached beside his chair and procured a well-loved bottle of moonshine that he poured into his cup.

"Dimitri Phendor," Kat greeted with a bow.

The blacksmith grumbled.

Kat noticed that he was still wearing the peculiar darkened goggles around his eyes despite the darkness of the room and being nowhere near his forge . . .

"Sit," he ordered gruffly.

Kat obliged.

Eric, his eyes finally adjusted to the low light, made his way over to where the blacksmith and Kat sat and stood behind his wife, his hand casually gripping his sword hilt.

"What took you so long?" Dimitri asked after taking a gulp of moonshine.

"Had someone try to poison me, got married, my parents showed up, you know. Normal things."

Dimitri set his cup down and leaned forward.

"I know who tried to poison you."

Kat blinked and sat up straighter. "Well, technically, I know his name too. Sir Seth Herra."

"He's a puppet. That woman did it, and you need to stay far away from her, or you will help her unleash Gods know what upon the world."

"Who is this woman?" Kat demanded next.

"The one who has been alive for centuries. Doomed to live alongside the devil until they make amends," Dimitri rumbled, his darkened goggles turning toward the weak flame that struggled to rise from the coals in the hearth.

"You can't mean the first witch. He killed her! In no record has she survived their last battle!" Kat insisted while shifting to the edge of her seat.

"In a sense he *did* kill her."

"Speak clearly." Eric's voice, while quiet, was intent. "We have been searching for this information for—"

"Did I not try and contact you multiple times?" Dimitri barked irritably.

Eric fell silent once more as Dimitri refilled his cup.

"The devil . . . He took the first witch's magic. He sealed away her abilities and, therefore, her means to go home to the Forest of the Afterlife. But by doing this . . . he also cut her off from her sense of balance. Her sense of self. She is not what she once was. However, the devil sees it as a proper punishment for her after she sided with humans over the ancient beasts they were raised alongside. In other words, he condemned her to humanity."

Kat balked. "But . . . Why would the devil be afraid of her now if she doesn't have power?"

"Connections," Eric interrupted softly. "He . . . He said she had connections."

Dimitri barely looked in the prince's direction.

"That she does."

"If she's been alive for centuries though, and it's his sister, wouldn't the devil bloody well know who she is then?! Why in the world is he saying he doesn't even know what she looks like!" Kat continued frantically.

Dimitri stared at Kat, not saying anything . . . as though waiting for her to calm down.

"Because he *doesn't* know what she looks like. While the devil lives and dies and then is reborn from his ashes like his father, the Green Man, the first witch continues to live as her mother, aging from a young maiden to a matron to a crone without dying. Her features change as she grows from crone to maiden once more. She could look Troivackian, Zinferan, Daxarian, or Lobahlan, and no one would know."

"How . . . How do you know all this?" Kat whispered as she absorbed the story.

"Because with your sword finding its master, it isn't hard to guess the devil is near . . . And as for the other details of the first witch . . . There was a reason my grandfather crafted your sword. He was . . . close with the first witch many years ago."

"He loved her," Eric guessed.

Dimitri cleared his throat, then continued. "She recognized the power in his work. Saw that his weapons were capable of magical properties."

"Magical properties? Like the mage crystals?" Kat interrupted curiously.

"In a way, but they had to be connected to their master. Whoever wields the weapon or item Theodore Phendor crafted has to have a master that possesses some sort of ability for it to have magic." Dimitri paused but neither Eric nor Kat interjected with any questions. "The first witch asked my grandfather to make her a dagger. One that could absorb power. Even though her own magic was cut off, she still had the space in her being to have magic; she simply needed a means of obtaining it. He wanted to help her, to see if she could perhaps feel whole again . . . so he crafted the dagger."

"Why a dagger? Why not a necklace? Or something infinitely less ominous? How did he not see where this was going?" Kat pointed out glibly.

Dimitri growled, and Kat held up her hands in surrender, immediately backing down.

"He made it a dagger so she could defeat the devil. She claimed that if she could absorb his abilities, she would then be able to unlock her own power once more and take them both home."

"Buuut she got power hungry and started stabbing people?" Kat hypothesized while leaning back in her seat.

Dimitri shook his head. "No. She was careful, but the problem was the devil is clever, and if he ever worried she was about to catch him, he simply killed himself to be reborn elsewhere."

"Can he predict where he would be reborn?" Eric queried interestedly.

"That, I do not know. While I know he is reborn of ashes, I do not know if it must be the ashes from his previous body, or if there is another component to it. Through his centuries in this world, he accrued loyal followers who aided him—though most didn't know his true identity, so even when she would interrogate them afterward, she'd learn nothing."

"How is it that this all ties in with my sword? And why are you fleeing to Daxaria?" Kat wondered next.

"The first witch used to be predictable. Her motive was to overpower her brother so they both could go home. However . . . that is not the case anymore. When she created Witch's Brew and started bringing over the ancient beasts, it was so uncharacteristic, that it makes one wonder if she is after something else. Perhaps she thought they would help her subdue the devil, or if she swayed their alliance with a different kind of promise, but I can't speak to that either." Dimitri grunted. "I'm leaving Troivack because now that you are aware of the first witch's past, you will need to inform the king, and it will not take her long to find out who told him. She'll come for me. So it is best I disappear. As for your sword, Lady Katarina . . . Your sword was the original weapon my grandfather crafted for the first witch."

Before continuing his speech, Dimitri plucked up the moonshine bottle and drained the last of its contents into his cup. Both Kat and Eric shared a look of amazement as he did so.

"He thought that if he simply made a weapon that could amplify the power the devil had locked away or hone the magic and power that still lingered in the first witch, that would be all she needed as opposed to a weapon that stole or borrowed another witch's power."

Kat went still. She remembered how when she'd drawn her sword while the imp was attempting to bind her that she had grown stronger as she pulled it free from its scabbard . . .

"Your sword feeds off your power and hones it to your intent."

"Wait," Eric interjected. "Does that mean it drains her magic more when she uses it?"

"It would allow her to use more of her magic in a single use, but it also helps stabilize her magic, as it will pull from the areas of her abilities that are strongest before it pulls from the weakest."

"That's why you're tired." Eric turned to Kat eagerly. "You used the sword how many times since getting it?"

"Erm . . . The imp and my duels are the only times I used my magic while wielding the sword."

"You started getting tired after that," Eric pointed out. Then he addressed the blacksmith. "Wouldn't that make sense . . . ? Is the sword slowly draining her power?"

Dimitri made a rumbling sound in his chest as though irritated. "No. You might have had less power at the end of the day, but it wouldn't still be draining you beyond the times you unleashed its full power. If you want my guess? You are spreading your power too thinly."

Kat raised an eyebrow as Eric fell quiet again.

"How do you mean?"

"A . . . A seer visited my grandfather years ago, and she foretold your coming. Your ability feeds off people or magic around you, however you also are able to redistribute what you absorb, helping to amplify energy, strength, endurance . . . You are most likely doing this subconsciously by wishing to help those around you." Dimitri shifted awkwardly and even turned his chin away . . .

Kat felt her hands tighten. "How do I control that if I'm not aware?"

Dimitri snorted. "I don't know everything."

"Could've fooled me," Eric countered evenly. "You know quite a lot for a mere blacksmith. How did you even know the first witch created Witch's Brew and brought over the ancient beasts? That is classified information."

Dimitri's finger tapped his cup carefully as though calculating what he should say.

"A seer told your grandfather all this? We just discovered a seer the other day, and it's quite a convenient answer." Eric drew closer to the blacksmith, his expression icy. "Tell the truth, or I will carry your head out of here."

Kat rounded on her husband in alarm.

The blacksmith must've seen the sincerity in the prince's eyes, however, because he gripped his cup with an air of resolve.

"Fine. Have it your way. It would've been better for you if you'd just turned a blind eye." Dimitri leaned forward, his upper lip twitching. "The devil came to see me. I already knew about the history of the first witch and the sword from my grandfather, which is why I had already been trying to find you. But he was the one who shared the details of Lady Katarina's power and about the beasts and Witch's Brew. He is the one who is telling me to leave Daxaria."

"Why would he tell you anything? Unless"—Eric's eyes narrowed—"he wants a weapon."

Dimitri said nothing. Only set his cup down.

"He sent you to tell us all this instead of coming himself. Why hasn't he reached out to me directly?"

At first, it didn't seem like the blacksmith was going to answer.

Eric started to draw his sword, but Kat's hand shot out and stopped him, her aura softly growing in light.

"He has given us a wealth of information." Kat turned patiently to Dimitri while ignoring Eric's hardened countenance. "Do you know where Likon is?"

Dimitri frowned. "I don't know who you're talking about."

"What weapon does the devil want you to make?" Eric continued after both he and Kat studied the blacksmith but could see his confusion was genuine.

Dimitri snorted. "Once he learned of my limitations, nothing. I can't make magic-infused weapons like my grandfather."

"You do . . . have magic though," Kat started while eyeing the Troivackian knowingly. "You're hiding your eyes in the dark for a reason."

Dimitri smiled bitterly, revealing yellow stained teeth. "That I do. Not entirely unlike your own eyes, I am highly sensitive to sound, light, smell, even touch. It allows me to make exceptional weapons, but not magical ones."

"I take it the devil didn't like hearing that." Eric released the hilt of his sword and crossed his arms.

Dimitri shrugged. "He was glad enough that I could talk with you. He is suffering. He doesn't want anyone to know, but I could hear the stressful beats of his heart, and troubled breaths."

Both Kat and Eric exchanged looks.

Despite learning information they had been desperate to get their hands on, there was so much still unknown . . .

Taking in a deep breath and letting it out, Kat tried her best to wrap her head around the situation and what the blacksmith was telling her.

The scale of this feud between the children of the Gods was frightening . . .

But if it was going to help them stop a possible supernatural war, then she needed to ask the question that she was already anxious to hear the answer to . . .

"You mentioned how my presence will bring calamity. I need you to tell me exactly how it will, and then I'll be more than happy to see about helping you escape to Daxaria once you tell us *when* the devil said you should leave by."

CHAPTER 42

AN ALLEYWAY AFFIRMATION

K at, I know you don't like it, but you have to admit that if you are the key to the first witch's plans, then you should go home!" Eric trailed after his wife as she stormed through the streets of Vessa.

Kat ignored him and continued her determined trajectory back to the carriage.

"This isn't just your fate we are talking about anymore—" Eric was cut off as a snarling Troivackian man in a long coat stumbled by him while carrying three sacks of grain over his shoulder.

The prince didn't bother trying to apologize as he was forced to continue chasing after Kat, hollering at her back.

"Will you just stop so that—" Two children bolted out of a nearby house into the street and looped in front of Eric, once again intercepting him on his mission. Though after they were gone, the prince took a moment to check to see if any of his belongings had been pickpocketed. Surprisingly, they were all accounted for.

Finally fed up with having to stumble after Kat and being unable to finish a sentence, he sprinted. He caught up to her near the end of the street. Just as Kat was getting close to the bend in the road that would take her back to the carriage that awaited them, Eric seized her wrist and pulled her into a nearby empty alley before she could stop him.

"Eric! Wha—"

Grasping her shoulders and herding her toward the wall of the abandoned building, Eric leaned close to Kat, his nose a mere inch from hers.

"No running. We're talking about this. Right here. Right now. Because I know the second we get back into the castle, everyone is going to come at us for one problem or another, and we won't get a chance to speak alone again until who knows when."

Kat started opening her mouth to protest, but Eric silenced her by kissing her, pinning her to the wall.

It caught Kat so off guard that it succeeded in making her mind go blank.

Especially when his right hand moved to cup her face as he deepened the kiss . . .

Kat felt her aura warm to life, and her body eased into his.

She suddenly was feeling incredibly relaxed . . .

When Eric did break the kiss, he stared at her in such a way that made it obvious to Kat that she happened to be the only one he could see in that moment . . . but that didn't change the fact that he had things he wanted to say to her.

"Kat, if the first witch gets your blood on the dagger as well as the devil's, then she may have enough power to open a portal to herd the devil through. And given that she's summoned the ancient beasts? It sounds like she's going to be forceful about it, and that means there will be casualties." He paused and watched as his wife's momentary lapse into peace disappeared and was replaced by upset. "We don't even know how this whole thing will go with the rebellion tied in . . . but if you leave, then—"

"Why does she want me to leave if she needs my blood?" Kat interrupted. "That doesn't make sense! First she wants me out of Troivack, and now she wants my blood!'"

Eric didn't answer immediately as his eyes searched her face and his hands drifted to her waist where he pulled her into an embrace. "She probably didn't know she needed your power back then. You heard the blacksmith. She probably thought it'd be enough to open the door if she had the blood of a water, air, fire, and earth witch along with the devil's. Your power is like her dagger's, and if it means the blade can absorb more magic in a single dose, and you are a mutant witch with technically all four elements . . . it seems reasonable to assume she'd change her tune. Even if it isn't just for opening a portal, if she could get your blood it'd amplify any other power."

Kat's hands fluttered into fists at her side, and her eyes trailed away from her husband's face. He was looking so earnestly at her that it made it hard to think . . .

"He could be wrong though. I mean, first the blacksmith tried to tell us about a seer, and then he admitted the devil told him everything. How did the devil or blacksmith even know we would believe in seers when they had been little more than legends until we met Esther? How could they have known?"

Eric opened his mouth to offer a perfectly reasonable explanation but found that the question had in fact stumped him.

She was right.

He lowered his own gaze with a frown, though he didn't relinquish his hold on his wife.

"Godsdamnit . . ." He proceeded to drop his head on Kat's shoulder and let out a weary sigh. "He probably has spies of his own in the castle."

"Or what if *he* is the one making this all up? What if it is just the devil who wants me out of Troivack? The blacksmith even said the devil was unwell!"

Eric pulled back, and after his tired eyes roved over her face lovingly, he reached up with his gloved hand and brushed one of the stray strands of fiery red hair that had escaped her cap away from her face. "You're right."

Kat stared back, stunned. "I-I'm sorry, what?"

Eric chuckled softly. "I said you're right. I'm not saying it again. You heard me just fine. I'm starting to think that the entire castle is filled to the brim with spies. If not the devil's, then his sister's, and if neither of theirs, most likely the ones belonging to all the other nobles."

"So who can we absolutely trust?" Kat mused while chewing on the inside of her lip.

"Well, you, me, Alina, your father, Kraken — as long as no one offers him a dinner roll in exchange for our lives — "

Kat laughed, and Eric grinned, but then continued his list, "Faucher, Brendan Devark, and . . . that's it. Maybe Sir Cleophus Miller, given his devotion to your familiar."

"My mum," Kat supplied idly, not at all anticipating that her husband would stiffen in response.

At first, she simply assumed he was trying to be funny again, but then she remembered the talk they had had before their wedding.

Eric had said her mother was feared in several circles and was wildly powerful . . . She hadn't had a chance to ask the duchess anything about that . . .

"I know you have your doubts about my mother, but . . . I do think she is going to be on our side against the Troivackians, the devil, the first witch, and anyone else," she told her husband slowly.

Begrudgingly, Eric let out a long breath. "I know. It isn't my place to request this, but, Kat, do you think we could talk with her today?"

Nodding, Kat twisted her mouth in understanding.

Eric mirrored her nod, then closed his eyes and leaned his forehead to hers. "By the way, in case I haven't mentioned it, I'm in support of running off, forgetting all about this sodding nonsense, and us having a yearlong honeymoon instead."

Kat smiled. "That sounds lovely, but I feel like I'd get bored after a year."

"There would be no paperwork."

"Let's go. Right now. I don't need to pack."

Eric laughed while pulling his wife into a full hug and kissing the side of her head as he did so.

"Are those really all the people we can trust?" Kat asked quietly after taking a moment to enjoy the hug and breathe in Eric's comforting smell.

The prince grimaced, and while Kat couldn't see it, resignation was present in his voice when he replied with, "Afraid so. It could be one or all the handmaidens, it could be Prince Henry, it could be any of the nobles, Rebecca Devark, even Lady Nathalie Faucher."

"It's not Kezia."

"Kat . . ." Eric pulled away again though kept his arms around his wife so he could fix her with an apologetic yet serious look. "She hid the fact that she was a mage for years. She traveled nomadically. No one other than His Majesty or His Highness has met her family. There is no way to be absolutely sure she is who she says."

Unable to hide the woundedness in her eyes, Kat gripped the prince's cloak. "Well, what about Ladies Sarah and Wynonna?"

"Lady Sarah has been well-known from birth in this court. Everyone has seen her grow up, but that doesn't mean she doesn't have a hand in anything. As for Lady Wynonna, she was thoroughly vetted by Lady Rebecca Devark and other noblewomen in the court. They interviewed her family back in Xava where she grew up in Daxaria, and again, there were reports and several eyewitnesses who saw her since childhood and have attested to her character. If what the blacksmith says is true, that means she couldn't be the first witch."

Kat blinked. "I . . . I won't lie . . . I'm a bit surprised by that."

"That Lady Wynonna, the infamous drunk in the court, isn't the first witch?" Eric asked dryly.

"No, that her character was vetted and approved. Also that she isn't suspicious at all. She *is* Daxarian . . . And she also had mentioned once a long time ago that she was looking for her brother here in Troivack."

Eric raised an eyebrow and cast his mind back. "Ah. We found her brother, actually. He's a merchant who does quite well for himself here in

Vessa. He purchased a great deal of the abandoned buildings here in the city, intending to use them to craft his wares. I heard they had a falling out because Lady Wynonna's now-deceased husband wouldn't loan him money to purchase a ship. A poor call on her former husband's side, given what the man is now worth. Her brother is actually one of the few successful merchants who didn't have ties to Duke Icarus."

Kat's jaw dropped. "Then . . . Then that leaves . . . Kezia," she uttered with a croak.

Eric kissed his wife's forehead again, saddened to see her in pain at the thought of her friend being a traitor.

"How did you . . . know all this . . . ?"

"After the devil approached me and said the woman was close to Alina, I've been digging up as much information as possible. I had honestly thought it'd be Rebecca Devark, otherwise I wouldn't have let Lady Kezia remain close to Alina. But hearing that the first witch can only be in one of three forms also rules out the former queen, as she would've also been closely watched while growing up and most likely has hundreds of eyewitnesses still alive to attest to her character—your mother being one who we can trust completely."

"Gods." Kats hands came up to cover her face as she felt sick to her stomach. "Kezia . . . But . . . I just can't . . . can't believe it. I love the handmaidens . . . Lady Wynonna is bloody funny, and . . . and I even love Lady Sarah, but Kezia is the one I suspected the least."

"I know. It makes it even worse that she's Prince Henry's wife . . . This could drive a deep wedge between the prince and His Majesty."

"This is awful . . ." Kat trailed off while succumbing to her horrible heartbreak. "What do we do now?"

Eric stepped back from his wife reluctantly and slumped against the wall of the other building that was perhaps only four feet from the one Kat still rested against. When they'd past it, it wasn't clear whether it was still used for any kind of business . . .

"First, we speak to your father. Then I want the most recent update on the rebellion's movements. That should tell us when they are supposed to attack and what time frame the first witch is considering. Next, I want to lay out a plan with a bit of bait to see if we can lure out either the devil or the first witch."

"Wasn't the devil supposed to be in contact with you again for information?" Kat recalled.

"He was . . . He had also said he was going to send me something the last time we spoke, but that didn't happen either . . . Believe it or not, the devil doesn't seem all that reliable." The prince scoffed humorlessly.

"What about Likon?"

Eric winced and found himself unable to meet his wife's eyes. "The best I can say is he's hidden somewhere in Vessa. It's odd how we haven't heard anything about ransom or any other demands by now. Last I heard, Kraken was starting his own investigation. It sounds lazy on our end, but he has the best chance of finding him, knowing his success rate."

Kat was all too aware how capable her father's familiar was, and so the news was actually comforting. "Do you know what my father found out about the sirins?"

Eric shook his head. "They are still interrogating the rediscovered coven and Lady Elena, though I know Fin was trying to find out more. I don't know if Kraken had a chance to visit the tunnels before he started hunting down Likon."

Kat stood up from the wall, though her shoulders still sagged. "For everything going on, we don't have nearly enough people we can count on . . . I wish we were back in Daxaria."

Despite smiling at his wife's wistful thought, Eric's eyes were filled with defeated agreement.

"It's hard being a hero," he said instead.

"Not to mention I now need to talk to my da and Mr. Kraft about unknowingly using my magic to bolster other people . . . I have no idea what that could even mean. Do you feel any different being around me?" Kat asked while folding her arms over her middle.

Eric considered the question carefully as he cast his mind back.

He *had* started to feel differently . . . But when had it started? He'd felt something small stirring after the night they had first met . . . However, when had it *really* started to —

The prince's eyes widened. "Oh. Gods. That's what he meant."

Kat looked in confusion at her husband's stricken expression. "What?"

Before answering, Eric rubbed his face. "Godsdamnit."

Kat continued waiting with increasing impatience.

"You kissed me after the devil broke down your walls. After that, I started feeling different. I had more energy. I felt motivated. More clearheaded and awake . . . The devil had said you were a boon to me, but I think . . . you might be feeding power to me and possibly others as well. Maybe after he broke free your power, it started leaking out. Then when we had our first night in the closet, you kept sending me power without realizing it. I've been able to work tirelessly this whole time, and I've barely craved my vices since we got married."

"And because I was already pretty drained after my month of training . . ." Kat joined in quietly.

"We need to talk to Mr. Kraft about this. Now." Eric turned toward the mouth of the alleyway, intense purpose burning in his eyes.

Kat reached out and grabbed his hand before he could leave, though he flinched when she did so.

She could already see what he was terrified of . . .

"You. Aren't. Hurting. Me. I'm happier and feel better than I have in years. I probably just need to . . . to feed on other people's magic, and I'll be fine again! Or maybe it's just that the devil messed up how I manage my power!"

Eric's face had turned stony. He didn't look at all swayed by his wife's words as he was faced with his worst fear.

Seeing this, Kat wasted no time.

She grabbed Eric by the front of his tunic and brutally slammed him against the other wall, her eyes flashing.

"Don't you *dare* run or start avoiding me," she raged at him despite not raising her voice. "We fight at each other's backs no matter what. Eric, I need you. I need you like I've never needed anyone in my life. I don't care if my energy levels go down to what a normal person feels. We'll find a way to manage it so it doesn't get any worse. But you are worth . . ." She trailed off, tears rising in her eyes, startling both herself and Eric, whose impassable expression broke into worry and heart-wrenching love as his wife spoke. "You are worth more to me than my magic. I love you, you Godsdamn idiot! Don't you even think of—"

"Okay, okay! I'm sorry, Kat." Eric's hands came up again, this time to hold Kat's face. "I'm sorry. You're right. Again. I never want you to feel . . ." he trailed off, unable to find the words as tears fell from his wife's golden eyes. He wiped them away, then kissed her softly. "I won't run from you. You have me. Completely. I promise. I *am* scared of hurting you in *any* way, but I am always yours. No matter my state."

"You better be! You swore that I'd see you love me more than was reasonable, and I need that!" she spluttered, hating that she was reduced to tears. Sometimes it snuck up on her just how important Eric had become to her . . .

Her husband smiled, still staring at Kat with a look that burned through to her soul and made her feel whole, leaving no room for doubt that that was exactly what he felt from her as well. He kissed her again. "I love you. More than anything, alright?" He held her close again.

Kat sunk into the embrace gratefully.

They hadn't had much time together as of late on top of the extraordinary stress surrounding them. The distance their schedules had caused made it all feel like everything was too much, and so despite it seeming as though the world were ending just outside the alleyway they stood in, and knowing that they needed to rush back into the fray, both Kat and Eric allowed themselves a moment of solace with each other. Both were well aware that such moments may be even harder to come by in the near future. And so they took as much effortless relief, understanding, and strength from each other as they could.

CHAPTER 43

A NETTLING NIECE

Annika waited.

Her back was straight and her ankles were crossed as she sat primly in the solar. She looked as composed and untouchable as ever.

However, her lifelong maid and friend, Clara, could tell the duchess was stressed and nervous just by looking at the two shadowed lines running down her forehead toward her nose. As the duchess aged, her face betrayed more of her true reactions, as it took very little to deepen the lines caused by often used emotions.

"How has the search for Likon been going?" Annika asked softly while raising her teacup to her lips.

"According to the duke, Kraken says he has been able to pick up his scent down in the tunnels. However, when they followed the trail, they only found a dead end. Kraken speculates that the tunnel was blocked off, and there is no telling how far it goes on the other side either."

Annika raised an eyebrow. "Who is it that built the tunnels in the first place, and how long have they been there?"

"Lady Elena says the tunnels had been there when she married her husband. The baron allegedly had them built in the years prior to the Tri-War as a precaution in the event of eventual conflict in Vessa.

Annika turned her chin toward her maid. "That is a massive undertaking for a mere baron. Was he bankrupt after?"

"No. The duke showed me the records of their financial situation that he had obtained during Lady Elena's interrogation, and it seemed as though they had someone assisting them with the costs . . ."

Annika's finger tapped once against her fine porcelain cup before she set it down. "If it weren't for the fact that Baron Souros knew his wife was a witch and didn't begrudge her the fact, I'd suspect Duke Icarus. If not him, one of the other powerful courtiers here at the time. I'd wonder about Lord Milo Miller's father, but I'm sure Milo would've reported anything suspicious like that . . ."

The duchess's gaze grew distant as she cast her mind back. Then she reached up to touch her forehead with a small smile on her face.

"You know . . . given the general loyalty of the king's current court, I find it hard to believe that anyone would willingly omit the knowledge of these tunnels underneath Vessa. Other than Duke Icarus, I can think of one other possibility that would make everything all the more . . . interesting."

Clara's blue eyes sharpened knowingly. "You think your brother funded it?"

Annika looked to her maid. "If it had been Phillip, and they were discovered, he could've blamed the baron. If they needed to hide an army or offer an escape to the king, he'd claim the credit. However, I'm skeptical, given that the plan is a little too smart for him, and those tunnels would've taken years to build. Maybe my father or—"

"Your grandfather could've done it. Was he alive during Baron Souros's time? The baron was a good deal older than Lady Elena from what I've gleaned."

Annika tried to count back to when her grandfather, Georgio Piereva, had still been alive . . . He was the last member of the master spy family, and he had conceded to teach his granddaughter his legacy, as she was the only one to possess the skill set for the trade.

Georgio had died two years before Annika had been sent to wed her first husband, having retired from his work three years before that when Annika had been twenty-one . . .

With how extensive the tunnels were, it would've taken decades to accomplish . . .

"It very well could have been him. Though he was meticulous about hiding his activities, there would have still been suspicious amounts of money being moved, and the only remaining family members in the Piereva family would've been able to access those documents. However, there is a chance that the age of the deal made it so that whoever inherited the title wouldn't have noticed. Particularly if the tunnels had been finished prior to my father, or John, or Phillip taking over . . ."

Annika paused, her gut fluttering with the sense that she was on the right track.

"If it had been my grandfather, he would've built those tunnels for the sake of sneaking around better, but that begs the question of why he would have made the deal with Baron Souros to begin with. Why him?"

"Assuming you are right that the anonymous backer was in fact the Piereva family, then that means there were two other people who would've known about the tunnels."

Nodding slowly, Annika opened her mouth to respond, when a knock on the solar door cut her off.

"Your Grace, Mrs. Levin has arrived to meet with you."

The duchess looked to Clara, and the two shared a meaningful look.

Unfortunately, it seemed the reunion between Annika and her niece was not going to be a warm one.

Caroline Levin sat across from Annika, her furious emotions barely concealed.

Her dark eyes remained fixed on the wall opposite the one Clara stood against, her light brown hair half swept back in a style that had been popular nearly ten years prior, which was about the similar age and style of her dark yellow dress.

During the silence between them, Annika took the time to try to control her own emotions.

She was staring at one of her few remaining blood relatives.

The daughter of her brother Charles, or Charlie, as she had affectionately called him . . .

He had been one of the only decent Piereva men in the family, and his death had been horrible to endure.

And there sat his daughter.

She looked a great deal like her mother, Janelle, in the shape of her eyes, mouth, and nose, but the sloping and width of her face . . . was Charlie's. The large knuckles on her fingers were also Charlie's . . .

Annika cleared her throat. Incredibly, her emotions were getting the best of her.

"Mrs. Levin," she started, hoping that once she started speaking, she'd be able to stifle her feelings better. "I thank you for coming to meet me. It has been too long since I've seen you."

Caroline's eyelids fluttered downward. "It is an honor to share tea with you, Your Grace."

The response was wooden.

Raising an eyebrow, Annika decided to see if a direct attack could shake some honesty from her niece.

"I heard you were quite intent on debasing me to your king. I take it your mother's misguided anger toward me has only thrived since I last saw her."

Caroline's eyes snapped to Annika's relaxed face, her expression contorting with fury.

"You dare say such things about my mother when we've only discovered more and more of your despicable dealings the deeper we dig?"

The duchess tilted her head, nonplussed. "Which dealings are you referring to?"

"Your investment in brothels is well-known," Caroline bit back instantly.

"Of course. Their improved states have bettered many unfortunate lives, so I'm unsure how they are seen as 'despicable.'"

"You use them to gather information!"

"Information that is freely given and then shared with the Daxarian king to better serve and protect his kingdom. Again, I fail to see how this is as untoward as you believe it to be."

"You dare sit there guiltless?! Have you no remorse for getting my father killed?!" Caroline was on her feet, tears already in her eyes as she bore down on her aunt.

"Your father came to see me in Daxaria regularly so that I could help support you and your mother. He had to visit me in person because if I simply sent the funds, not only would that have been more suspicious, but our older brother, Phillip, would have taken them. Your former king decided to use this information to blackmail me and, subsequently, the king of Daxaria. My part in this is that my future husband at the time volunteered to go bring you, your father, and your mother to safety. Sadly, the king had Charlie killed before we could do anything. I then kept you and your mother safe in Daxaria until the Daxarian king negotiated with the Troivackian court to not enforce that your mother remarry and instead be left with the remaining Piereva title and wealth. It was the only exception to the inheritance law at that time, and it happened because of my influence. So, tell me. What grave and terrible thing did I do?"

Annika held her niece's gaze levelly.

"Y-You didn't even cry when my father died!" Caroline flung out passionately.

"I did, actually. However, given that at the time my priority was caring for you and your mother, in addition to the fact that war was days away, all of which prevented me from showing my emotions openly."

A bite entered Annika's voice then, one that was unlike her. Though it did succeed in conveying that she did in fact have feelings regarding that dark time . . .

Caroline shook her head, tears spilling over her cheeks. "I don't believe you! You have informants everywhere! You-You're known as the Dragon, and everyone is afraid of you for good reason."

"Who is afraid of me?" Annika asked softly. There was a subtle, dangerous glint in the duchess's eyes that Caroline, despite her emotional state, noticed.

"Everyone who knows you as the Dragon!"

"Oh? And what type of *characters* are the people who fear this person called the *Dragon*?"

"Lowlifes! Slave traders! People who-who—"

"People who, if you were alone in an alley with, you'd want to be afraid of *you*, because Gods know what would happen if it were the other way around, yes?" Annika asked lightly, though a very ominous aura seemed to fill the air around her.

Caroline paled and her hands began to shake. "You've killed people."

Annika lifted her chin gracefully. "I don't know about that. Though I am curious about what makes you think you know everything about me and my dealings, since we haven't spoken since you were a babe in your mother's arms. For all the support I offered your mother, for everything I did for your family, your determination to see me as the villain is quite narrow-minded and dangerous in and of itself."

"Are you trying to frighten me?" Caroline's voice dropped to a hush, though her eyes showed she was anything but fearful.

"Hardly. I'm merely defending myself and giving you a warning."

Caroline frowned and blinked, but before she could make another accusation, the duchess continued, "It is one thing to hold a grudge against me, but if you are endangering *anyone* I care for, you will be declaring yourself an enemy of mine. I have done nothing but wish to be of help to you, my niece, but if you spit on my face and strike another of my loved ones, I will not let the matter be." The icy edge in Annika's tone made Caroline swallow, but the duchess wasn't through with her yet. "I'm well aware your husband is at the king's side, saying all manner of things he devoutly believes because you have convinced him. I'm also well aware that since his trip to Daxaria, the king came to know my family and formed his own opinions. Since then, Mr. Levin's relationship with His Majesty has never been the same."

Caroline took a shuddering breath. "This is a threat, not a warning."

"This is not a threat. Unless, say, you knew something about some tunnels that were recently discovered, and perhaps, also knew something about my adopted son, who is missing."

Caroline wasn't quick enough hiding her reaction. She flinched.

She must not have been anticipating Annika's blunt approach . . .

The duchess rose from her seat, making Caroline stumble back a step.

Clara turned and glided toward the solar door.

The lock rattled shut.

Annika slowly rounded the table and stared down at the young woman. When she stood nearly nose to nose with Caroline, she allowed some of her genuine emotion to shine through while her niece floundered upon realizing she was blocked in with no means of running.

"I-I-I'll report you to my husband, and he will—"

"Caroline," Annika cut her off, her eyes were filled with sadness, but the set of her mouth was firm. "You may not believe me, but I do love you."

The young woman opened her mouth as though she were about to start spewing accusations again but didn't get the chance, as Annika raised her hand and touched it to Caroline' damp cheek, making the younger woman tremble.

"I will do my best to protect you from the king if you did know about the tunnels, and I will even be open to forgiving you for taking part in abducting Likon, depending what state he returns in. However, if you want my help, then you will tell me everything. Otherwise, your treasonous actions will face the full wrath of not only Troivack but also Daxaria, and you and your husband will both suffer."

Someone started pounding on the closed solar door, making Caroline jump, but Annika and Clara remained as steady as ever.

"What will it be, Caroline?"

With her hands trembling at her sides and slowly closing into fists, Caroline spat on Annika's skirts.

"Go to hell, Dragon."

Silence filled the air, and Caroline's shaking worsened.

"Your father would be disappointed in you." Annika spoke quietly, and yet the words had Caroline hunching over as though they were a punch to her gut. "You should've protected your daughter from what is now to come. Caroline, do you know what is next? The Troivackian Jigsaw method may be discussed for both you and your husband."

"H-H-His Majesty will believe—"

"King Brendan Devark is now the brother-in-law to my daughter and will not risk a war with Daxaria when he needs their help. I understand you have not been aware of what has been happening in the castle, as your husband has been moving you around in an effort to protect you, but that is your current position."

Annika turned, proceeded to move away from her niece toward the exit while giving a nod to Clara, who unlocked the door. By the next breath, it swung open to reveal Mr. Levin, who was panting and ghostly white.

Annika regarded him with her previous mask of coolness once again affixed.

"Good day, Mr. Levin. I believe you may wish to sit with your wife while I report to your king what I have just discovered."

The assistant's lip curled, but when he saw his wife's tearful state, concern overtook his face.

"I want you to know"—Annika lowered her voice to a whisper—"I gave her the opportunity to confess the information willingly. I was more than ready to offer any assistance I could to protect your family. She has quite literally spit on that offer, and so you now have until I reach His Majesty's office door to settle this matter between you two."

The duchess then swept out of the room with Clara bowing her head and following behind her mistress without another look back.

Things had not gone as well as they'd hope.

Annika wouldn't admit that seeing her niece's ire and how accurate her guess had been about the Piereva house's involvement with the tunnels wounded her deeply.

It was a sickening, wretched feeling to have to doom her brother's one and only child . . .

The duchess did her best to push such thoughts aside, however, as she reminded herself that Likon was still being held captive somewhere, and she would see him home safely no matter what. Even if another corner of her heart writhed in agony for her former family.

CHAPTER 44

COMPILING CONCERNS

Fin, Kat, and Eric stood in front of the king's office, waiting for Brendan's previous appointment with Faucher to conclude in order to relay to him what had been discovered in Vessa from the blacksmith.

The house witch turned to his daughter, murmuring something that had her nodding along sternly, and Eric opened his mouth to add something . . .

However, the trio was distracted from the conversation when none other than Annika Ashowan turned down the corridor and headed straight toward them.

As he regarded his wife's expression, Fin turned slowly and placed his hands on his hips.

He had known she was meeting with her niece, and despite the fact that anyone else who looked at the duchess would have thought nothing was amiss, Fin knew his wife was feeling a mixture of hurt and anger.

Once Annika had reached them, she gave a bow of her head toward Eric before looking at Fin.

"I take it that the meeting with Caroline didn't go well?" Fin guessed softly.

Annika took in a sharp breath and briefly glanced at Eric as though debating whether to share what had transpired in his presence. However, when she observed her daughter's perplexed and worried face, she conceded that Kat would most likely want to know any information about Likon.

"Mr. Levin and his wife seem to be embroiled with the tunnels *and* Likon's disappearance."

"What?" Kat's eyes flashed dangerously.

Fin frowned. "How did you find out so quickly?"

"I'll explain everything to the king. I've already alerted the guards to keep an eye on them, though whether they will obey my orders as I am a woman of foreign nobility, remains to be seen."

Fin nodded sternly. "We have news as well. Depending how close the rebel group is to coordinating an attack, everything might be breaking out a lot sooner than we'd like."

As if on cue, the door to the king's office opened, revealing Leader Faucher and Brendan.

"Did I just overhear you saying something about the timing of the rebellion attack?" Brendan asked somberly.

"Yes." Eric squared himself with the king. "We have reason to believe that everything is coming to a head with the devil and ancient beasts, and the only notice we'll receive is when those forces arrive."

Brendan and Faucher shared a look before sidling back inside the office.

"Then we must do everything we can to prepare," the king explained stonily.

Dread brewed in everyone's stomachs as they filed into the privacy of the office.

Once the door was closed, Brendan and Faucher exchanged one final knowing look while everyone gathered around.

"Leader Faucher has received reports today that Duke Icarus's own knights along with several units consisting of mercenaries are headed for Vessa, and they are expected to be here in three days."

No one could say anything at first, the shock and gravity of the situation temporarily overwhelming their minds.

The king continued, "Your Highness, Mr. Levin informed me that you and Lady Katarina had important information to share with me?"

"On the note of your assistant, I'm afraid I have more bad news," Annika interjected, though her eyes remained downturned.

Brendan hesitated, his hands briefly twitching as though he wanted to make a fist. "One thing at a time. Your Highness, what is it you and Lady Katarina discovered?"

The Daxarian prince shared a look with his wife, then proceeded to relay exactly what they had learned from Dimitri Phendor.

By the end of their story, Fin was staring at his daughter in open panic, and Annika Ashowan had reached out and grasped her daughter's forearm.

Even Brendan's eyebrows shifted upward in a show of rare surprise at the news.

"Lady Kezia may be the first witch . . ." Leader Faucher repeated, his gruff tone gentling as he understood the news had weighty consequences for the Devark family.

The king said nothing, his black eyes lost in thought as he processed what he'd just heard.

"Kat, have you experimented purposefully absorbing people's intentions or magic before?" Fin wondered aloud while looking at his daughter.

Kat shook her head. "Every time Mr. Kraft and I practiced, we worked on *not* doing that. Why?"

"Well . . . Similar to how I grow power from feeding off the collective sentiment of home, you grow more powerful by absorbing abilities and intentions. If you openly absorb these things, instead of hanging on to them and overwhelming yourself, what if you were able to magically enhance others around you like you are saying you have been doing subconsciously? Only this time it would be for larger groups of people?"

Kat frowned thoughtfully. "It's . . . an interesting idea, but we don't have a lot of time to experiment with it, and someone could get hurt."

"Indeed," Brendan added while lifting his face to the group before him. "However, it may be worth working on during whatever time we have left. Tonight you rest, and tomorrow you practice this with some of the men staying behind to protect the keep."

"Pardon me, Your Majesty," Annika called everyone's attention to her. "This attack from the rebels may be a trap, and we still do not know whether it is the devil or the first witch who is commanding them. On this, I'd like to now offer you my own discovery from this afternoon . . ."

And so the duchess recounted the startling encounter that had taken place moments before. At first, Faucher had seemed surprised that the imperious duchess would be so bold as to address the monarch first, however, as she spoke, he recalled how Katarina had insinuated long ago that there was a reason she wasn't scared of much for a reason. Though any mention of a certain underground lord named Dragon was omitted from the story, the duchess's interrogation of her niece was executed ruthlessly enough to be noted.

Brendan was starting to look a mite sick as he discovered that yet another person close to him may be betraying him . . .

When Annika had finished repeating the details calmly, Brendan looked to Faucher, and the two men shared a very telling moment as the military leader gave him a pained yet understanding look, while Brendan found strength in his dear friend's steadiness.

"Faucher . . . please bring both Mr. Levin and his wife here."

Faucher bowed and without another word moved to carry out the order.

"Once I am able to speak sense into my assistant, then we can get to the bottom of—"

The king didn't get to finish his thought, as Faucher had opened the door to the study and found Clara, Annika's maid, standing there with her fist held in the air.

Brendan stopped talking and stared at the woman, prompting everyone else to look at the newcomer as well.

Clara dipped into a hasty curtsy.

While she didn't betray any sign of stress, her movements were quick . . .

"Mr. and Mrs. Levin have disappeared."

Annika turned fully at the news while releasing her daughter's arm.

Brendan drew himself perfectly straight.

"They were in the solar and as you ordered, Your Grace, I stood outside to see if they would go anywhere. They didn't. However, after a while, I could not hear them inside, and so I checked and discovered they were gone."

"The tunnels must be under the castle . . ." Annika breathed while turning toward Brendan. "Maybe the tunnels connected to Baron Souros's keep used to reach all the way to these grounds."

"I can go with Kraken to the solar right away to see if he can smell where the entrance to any sort of secret passage may be," Fin offered instantly.

Brendan nodded, his throat bobbing as he did so. "Please do, Your Grace. I also now plan on interrogating Duke Icarus to learn more about his men that are allegedly about to attack us." The king addressed Kat next, and she was more than a little alarmed to see a pleading light in his eyes. "Lady Katarina, please stay with Alina. She was feeling unwell this morning, and with everything happening, I want her protected."

Kat bowed formally. "Of course, Your Majesty."

"Your Highness, I need you to share with me your findings on every powerful person connected to Duke Icarus to see if any of them had the financial means to take over funding the army," the king added to his brother-in-law.

Eric bowed in response.

"Excuse me, Your Majesty. I understand this is a difficult time but, what is this rebellion's objective? Is it solely to dethrone Her Majesty? If it is being backed by the first witch or the devil, that means that there may be another motive," Annika proposed urgently.

Brendan considered her words and nodded to himself.

"Your Highness, the devil never did get back in touch with you after his initial offer, and you say that this blacksmith indicated he was not doing well. Is there a way you can ask to meet with the devil directly?"

Eric folded his arms. "I was considering this after the meeting today . . . but I think if we ask Mr. Kraft to speak to the imps or half fey that his magic gives him the ability to see, they should be able to deliver a message. Or at the very least they should be able to let him know we're looking for him."

Brendan tilted his head in agreement. "Very well. Leader Faucher, you will start organizing the knights, I will go speak with my brother, Henry, to see if we can isolate Lady Kezia from the queen, and then I will speak with Duke Icarus. His Highness will get the information he has on Duke Icarus's allies; Duke Ashowan, you will take your familiar to inspect the solar; and Lady Katarina, you will guard Her Majesty."

Everyone bobbed their heads save for Annika, who lowered her chin and said, "Would Your Majesty permit me to also join the queen's side?"

Brendan hesitated, but after a moment of quiet appraisal, acquiesced. "I believe Her Majesty would appreciate that. She has spoken very fondly of you from her time in Daxaria."

"I am very fond of Her Majesty as well," Annika returned without hiding the warmth in her voice.

That was all Brendan needed to hear to affirm it was safe to permit the duchess's presence near his wife, and so they all departed from the office.

Though Kat and Eric hung back to say their final farewells, the group hadn't gotten very far when Rebecca Devark came rushing up the hall, her normal ceremonial walk closer to a stomp, and her face revealing her to be in a soured mood . . .

She stopped in front of the group, curtsied, and then her gaze cut to Finlay.

Rebecca opened her mouth to say something, however, was cut off when the fluffy black familiar, Kraken, ran over to his witch.

"Duke Ashowan. I am here to insist that you mind your familiar." Rebecca's voice was pure acid.

Fin blinked in surprise. "Has Kraken done something . . . ?"

Rebecca's glittering glare turned downward to the cat. "He defecated in my shoes."

A long, drawn out snort coming from Katarina Ashowan as she struggled not to outwardly howl was the only noise in the silence. Even Eric was biting his tongue.

Rebecca Devark glared.

Fin looked down at his familiar he had just summoned. "Kraken, why in the world would you poop in her shoes?!" There was a pause as Kraken chirped up at the house witch.

Fin's face fell. "What do you mean Pina did it?"

Kat couldn't contain herself.

She turned around and clamped her hand down over her mouth.

"Kraken, that isn't something you should compliment her on! Kat!" Fin turned to look angrily at his daughter.

Kat held up a finger, her back still turned, having sensed her father's attention.

Eric lowered his chin as he, too, hid a tight smile that held back a laugh.

"Lady Katarina, you will mind your familiar in my castle," Brendan called with a rumble toward the woman whose shoulders still trembled.

Kraken mewed again.

"I don't care if this improves your opinion of Pina! She shouldn't have done such a thing!" Fin lectured his familiar sternly.

By then Kat was finally turning around, though her eyes were suspiciously wet, and she hadn't fully eradicated her smile.

"L-Lady Rebecca." She cleared her throat. "My . . . regards . . . to your soiled footwear . . . I . . . will . . . speak. To Pina. About that."

Lady Rebecca did not look in any way placated.

When Fin peered back at his daughter during her response, he shot her the most subtle of winks that only she and Eric might see, his previous disapproval vanishing during the brief exchange.

"P-Pardon me . . . Lady Rebecca . . . I will go talk to my familiar right . . . now . . ." Kat turned in the opposite direction everyone else was heading and moved away swiftly . . . A short way down the hall, the sound of loud hysterical laughter rang back up to them, making Brendan stare ahead of himself flatly, willing himself not to scowl or stare after the woman who *had* just agreed to guard his wife . . .

Fin glanced back at Rebecca and shrugged.

There was nothing he could do about it.

The former queen eyed the group of people in front of the king's office more pointedly, but when no one had anything else to say to her, she rounded back the way she came and took her leave after issuing a curtsy to her son.

With the former queen gone, Fin risked a quick look to his wife while casting a cheeky grin her way with a partial shrug.

As dire and serious as everything was . . . having a good laugh wasn't the worst thing in the world in that moment.

A corner of the duchess's lips twitched.

That was the extent of her humor over the situation, however, as the group once again resumed executing their designated tasks, all hoping that they could properly prepare . . .

They also made mental notes to check their shoes before putting them on in the future.

CHAPTER 45

A BIG BANG

Brendan stared at the wretched state of Duke Sebastian Icarus before him.

He sat, still and bloody.

Were it not for the wheezing, wet sound of his breaths, one could almost assume he was dead.

"Did you really think going against me was going to end well for you?" Brendan questioned icily, his voice barely more than a hush in the dark, grim surroundings of his dungeon.

The air stank of blood, decay, and excrement, while the only light came from the lone torch on the wall behind Brendan.

"I . . ." Duke Icarus trembled with the effort it took to speak, then coughed. "I only wanted . . . what was best for Troivack."

"*Your* idea of what Troivack is, perhaps. That is not the Troivack I am working toward creating."

"That is just . . . because of the . . . damned Daxarians." At last, the duke seemed to have given up on insulting Alina explicitly.

Brendan's obsidian eyes didn't waver for an instant. "I was implementing changes even before I wed your queen. For example, *making slavery illegal.* Which you also ignored."

"Slavery . . . is the only way to keep this kingdom working."

"Daxaria has shown that collaborating with their coven has negated a great deal of the need for such practices. However, I am not here to have a discussion about economics. I am here because I want to know what your hired mercenaries want. Did you tell them that you intended to overthrow the queen, or was there another motive behind your dealings with the devil?"

Despite the pain it would place him in, Duke Icarus jolted his face upward, his one remaining eye staring in shock at the king.

"Yes. I knew about your dealings with the creator of evil," Brendan informed the duke while remaining perfectly still in his seat.

"I didn't . . . know . . . he was the devil until . . . until *that* woman . . ."

"Which woman?" Brendan asked a little too quickly. "The first witch?"

Duke Icarus's bloodied lips twitched. "As much . . . as I loathed . . . working with her . . . she . . . at least had a . . . reasonable vision for the future."

Brendan's eyebrows lowered, but he remained silent.

"She . . . might be the one . . . to bring Troivack to its proper glory . . ."

"What is it she wants?"

The Troivackian noble's eye fluttered shut as he gave a quivering, weak laugh as an answer.

Brendan gave a terrifying smile. "It would seem my queen has had a positive influence on you for you to place stock in a woman to bring about glory for Troivack."

The duke's tenuous smile fell. "She is the daughter of the *Gods*, not a mere mortal."

Brendan waited as the duke coughed before repeating his question.

"What are the mercenaries going to do when they attack with your knights?"

The duke fell silent.

Having anticipated this reaction, the king changed his tactic. "I suppose once we suppress them, I'll have to appoint new knights to the Icarus dukedom. Of course, they will be under Sebastian's rule."

Duke Icarus twitched. "Surely . . . sire . . . you do not mean . . . that *bastard* child."

"Of course. None of your other family members wished to pick up the tatters of your duchy. As a son, he does have some claim. Then again, if you wished it to instead go to one of your legitimate daughters, as a favor, I could see to that."

Drool and blood dribbled out of Duke Icarus's mouth as he quivered with rage. "The council will never . . . agree to that."

"You would be wrong there. Everything is different now, Duke Icarus. There is no returning to the old ways."

The Troivackian noble spat on the floor more out of necessity than insult. "You may be surprised, Your Majesty."

Brendan tilted his head, glad to at least be riling up the man. "Even if the council doesn't agree, I can just as easily break apart the dukedom and sell it off to the nobles. That certainly would fill my coffers. I see no downside, and even if your mercenaries and knights come, they will not win against an army under the command of Leader Faucher."

"While . . ." Duke Icarus licked his lips. "While I have the greatest respect for Leader Faucher, even he cannot win against ancient beasts."

"The first witch cannot keep the beings here without an equivalent exchange, and those creatures are worth more than a lone life or two."

"An army is worth quite a bit . . . as is a powerful witch . . . or . . . say . . . the devil."

Brendan stilled.

"How would she simultaneously kill enough people to summon those forces? Or the devil for that matter?"

Duke Icarus swayed in his seat despite his remaining hand being bound behind his back. He didn't have legs to chain any more. "All will come to light soon, Your Majesty. Don't . . . worry. She promised me . . . she had no designs on harming . . . you. Just don't . . . count on the coven or . . . the Ashowan family to save everyone . . ."

Duke Icarus coughed yet again, only this time, his remaining eye closed, and his head hung before him motionless.

Brendan stared at what remained of his once loyal vassal, emotion surging through him, though he hid it behind his formidable defenses.

He wasn't certain if the duke had fainted or died.

Either way . . .

Brendan rose from his seat and exited the cell with his thoughts racing.

His talk with the duke had only made the coming events all the more terrifying . . . Brendan found himself at a loss at how best to calculate what he needed to win, or just how massive the coming threat truly was. One thing seemed certain . . . The first witch wanted more than just to send the devil back to the Forest of the Afterlife; she wanted the power to change Troivack. So the subsequent question and problem became, what did she want to change, and why?

As the king stalked through the halls, his expression warding away any serving staff or nobility that happened to enter the same space, he directed his feet toward his office where he intended to meet with Faucher to start organizing their men. Afterward he would summon Mr. Kraft and Finlay Ashowan to discuss what Duke Icarus had implied . . .

However, he was distracted by a swish of long red hair . . .

"Lady Katarina?" Brendan called out, the sharpness in his voice making several unfortunate souls who were carefully padding around behind him jump.

Kat had been striding down an intersecting corridor when she had passed Brendan, and she turned at the sound of voice.

"Yes, Your Majesty?" she asked after bowing.

Brendan noted she was in her full formal uniform . . .

"I thought you were with the queen?"

"Ah, Her Majesty is having a word with Prince Henry. He wished to speak with you, but you were occupied with Duke Icarus," Katarina recounted, and Brendan could tell by the uncomfortable tightness in her voice and strained mouth that his brother was still enraged and distraught after Brendan had told him what they had learned . . .

"Where is Lady Kezia?"

"She and Elio have been escorted to a private holding in Vessa for the time being. She was incredibly gracious and understanding about everything . . . as usual . . . She's the one who calmed Henry down the most," Kat explained glumly.

Brendan's gut roiled. "I see. Where are you going right now?"

"Ah, I was summoned by your council to sit in on concluding arguments for Sir Herra's fate."

Brendan straightened his shoulders in alarm. "I did not hear anything about such a meeting."

Kat blinked and lowered her eyes thoughtfully. "Wait . . . Was this maybe arranged by Mr. Levin before he left?"

Brendan felt like his world was crumbling around him.

He wished he could kiss Alina again before tackling this new suspicious danger . . .

"We will both go and find out," he informed her with a faint rumble. "Where is His Highness, your husband?"

"Ah, I think he went to visit Eli to get more information, but I told Poppy where I was going so he should be joining the meeting soon."

"He wasn't invited explicitly?"

"Er . . . no, come to think of it."

"What about your father?"

"I was told he would be in attendance, yes. He found the tunnel with Kraken in the solar and is letting Faucher know before joining." After she finished her recounting, Kat noticed how pale the Troivackian king looked.

"I know something is off, but you've got the Ashowan family here, Your Majesty. Don't worry. You even got Kraken, so everything is bound to turn out alright." With a half grin, Kat reached up and lightly slapped Brendan's arm.

"Lady Katarina, I think that you and your father might be walking into a trap," Brendan informed her sternly.

"Pfft. Of course we are. But not one person has been able to set a trap that has ever stopped me."

Brendan shook his head. "This is different."

Kat shrugged. "So what do you propose we do?"

Lowering his own gaze to the ground, Brendan considered all the information they had . . .

This opportunity of willingly walking into a trap could reveal who was helping the first witch or the devil in his council . . . It could reveal who Mr. Levin was working with . . . But Duke Icarus had hinted that Katarina and Finlay wouldn't be much help for what was to come.

Given that there had been an attempt to exclude him from the meeting, it sounded like someone or *something* was going to try to eliminate Kat and Fin without the Troivackian king's interference.

Finlay Ashowan would be easy enough to take care of without his magic, but Katarina was a different story. Then again, who aside from Faucher's family and Alina would know how capable she truly was?

It didn't even seem like the first witch or devil knew her true prowess.

Brendan then considered the promise the first witch had made . . .

If she kept her word, she would not harm him, which shrank the likelihood of a full-out attack in his presence.

Brendan nodded to himself. "Alright. You will go to the meeting, but we are telling your father everything going on before we enter the room—and yes, I am going into the meeting. I want to know who the traitors in my court are so that I can take care of them myself." He didn't need to explain his troubling conversation with Duke Icarus just yet.

Kat jerked her chin down in understanding. "Sounds good to me."

"Be on high alert. I don't know what their plan could be, and it seems as though a coup is happening even sooner than we thought."

"Yes, Your Majesty." Kat bowed.

Brendan eyed her quietly. "You are genuinely unconcerned about being in the middle of a civil war where both the devil and the first witch are participating?"

Kat's upbeat air dwindled, and Brendan was given the rare sight of a somber Katarina.

"I've been dreading something like this ever since returning to the castle from Faucher's, but—and it probably makes me seem like a child to admit this—but my da's here. And I don't know . . . I guess between him, Kraken, and Faucher, I really do think everything is going to work out."

A small, sharp prick of grief nudged at the king's memory . . . the memory of how once upon a time, he, too, thought his father was invincible . . .

He didn't want to destroy Katarina's morale, however, so he kept that thought to himself, and instead he turned and gestured in the direction Kat was heading.

They would go wait for Fin, let him know what was happening, and then, well . . . It felt like the war was starting.

The doors to the council room opened and in stepped Brendan Devark, donning his crown and a chest plate.

He instantly observed which nobles looked shocked and worried and which ones looked relieved.

Those who looked shocked? Lord Ball, Lord Herra—not much of a surprise there . . . Then there was Lord Sanchez and Lord Edium . . . Those two were a bit more surprising . . . Anyone who appeared openly relieved negated suspicion for the time being, as it meant they had found it odd the king wasn't in attendance.

"Your Majesty, what are you—" Lord Ball began as Brendan's long strides got him to his empty seat at the table before his vassal could finish his thought.

"This is a council meeting. Should I not be here?" The king's voice thundered in the hall.

Everyone averted their eyes.

They all could see their king looked fit to kill.

"We had all just received word that Your Majesty was busy with Duke Icarus's interrogation. Given the uncertainty going on in the castle, we thought we would at the very least handle the matter of my son." Lord Herra stood and addressed the king calmly. There wasn't a trace of guilt in his demeanor.

Brendan's gaze bore into the man's round face, making Lord Herra involuntarily twitch.

Then in walked Katarina and her father, Finlay Ashowan, who looked every bit as furious as the Troivackian king.

They took their seats near the king without saying a word to anyone.

"Well?" Brendan thundered. "Aren't we deciding Sir Herra's fate?"

Lord Ball cleared his throat and nodded to the guards.

It took a little while, during which uncomfortable silence seized the council. When Sir Seth Herra was at last escorted into the room, his eyes were glazed over, and his face slack . . . he looked like a puppet more than he did a man.

Fin shot an alarmed glance at the king.

"Sir Herra, this is your final moment to confess and beg for your life," Brendan informed the knight, who stood a short way from the back of Katarina's chair. The king had grown quieter when he beheld the alarming state of the man in front of him.

The former elite knight swayed on the spot.

Then his eyes slowly swiveled over toward Kat.

She raised an eyebrow at him.

He appeared relaxed. Not at all like he was about to attack or jump into action . . .

And yet, that's what happened.

He didn't have a weapon in his shackled hands, but he did have a fistful of white powder that he threw directly into Kat's face.

The guards instantly tackled him to the ground while the king was on his feet and looking at the council members who were staring hungrily at the redhead.

He didn't get the chance to let out any sort of bellow or warning before Kat stood from her seat unsteadily.

She stumbled back from the table, hastily wiping the powder off her nose, but her knees buckled as she did so . . .

"Kat?" Fin was also on his feet, already at his daughter's side, his hands gently touching her upper arms. "What's wrong? Was that powder Witch's Brew?" The duke directed this last question toward Lord Ball as though he already knew the man was guilty of the attack.

The nobleman flinched in surprise but was saved from having to respond, as Kat sneezed . . .

And when she did, her aura exploded, filling the room. However, instead of it merely being a startling display, the aura exploded with actual force. Everyone was blown off their seats and sent flying back into the walls, knocking many of them unconscious as though the aura was acting as a shield around Kat herself . . .

Fin had been blown the farthest, landing with a hard thump beside Brendan as men and guards shouted and hollered in shock.

Sitting back up with a wince, Fin's eyes went wide.

His daughter, with her golden, light-filled eyes, was staring around the room with her aura still growing like hungry flames, heat thrumming off her body in waves, making the room feel increasingly like it *was* on fire.

Her inhuman gaze turned toward Lord Ball, then Lord Sanchez, Lord Herra, and finally, Lord Edium.

Only Lords Ball and Edium were awake after the explosion, and they cowered in dawning horror over the sight before them.

If they had thought they were in control of the situation, they found themselves sorely mistaken as Kat prowled toward the long council table that had been flipped onto its side—which had also most likely saved the council members from the worst of the initial explosion.

"KAT!" Fin roared and leapt onto his feet, his mother's curse of healing taking care of his fractured tailbone instantly.

The burning witch didn't even acknowledge hearing him.

Instead, her aura grew and pulsed yet again, raising the heat of the room.

Fin staggered toward his daughter, but her aura was still repelling him, making him slide back slowly as he tried to press himself through it despite its heat searing his face.

"KAT! LOOK AT ME! IT'S YOUR DA! KAT!" Fin shouted as loud as he could, but Kat remained intent on reaching Lord Ball.

She bent down, seized the council room table, and snapped it in half, then proceeded to step closer to the lord who was sweating, crying, and had even wet himself . . .

Fin's hand curled into a fist.

He spared a lone, apologetic glance over his shoulder at Brendan, knowing that what he was about to do most likely would cause some trouble down the line, but there was no choice.

He closed his eyes.

Wherever my family is. Is part of my home.

A ringing filled the air around everyone like a bell tolling, making the air reverberate . . .

And then . . . his eyes snapped open, but this time, Finlay Ashowan's own eyes were filled with blue lightning, and a blue shield of lightning wrought with symbols surged from his outstretched hand with a shout of effort. The shield expanded bit by bit until it completely encased Kat, though it wasn't an easy feat.

Once entirely encumbered in her father's shield, Kat turned toward Fin, her eyes still aglow, but her aura had at least been smothered from the rest of the occupants in the room.

She moved toward him, but Fin could see that she still hadn't returned to herself yet . . .

"Kat, my love . . . my girl. Come back. I know Witch's Brew is doing this to you, but you're always telling me you can handle poisons and drugs," Fin pleaded, all too aware that containing his daughter was far harder than he had hoped as her magic sought to escape its new confines.

He could tell, as far as she was concerned in this state, that he was only an obstacle in the way of getting rid of a threat . . . Plus, he didn't have an entire kingdom of people fueling into his 'home'—it was just him . . . and his daughter.

Kat moved closer and raised her hand to her father's throat.

Fin could tell if she tried to kill him right then and there, he could do nothing to stop her while maintaining the shield . . .

He stared down into his daughter's face, the blue magic lightning in his eyes turning white and a tear escaping down his cheek.

"Forgive yourself, Kat. I know you will blame yourself, but I know this isn't your fault. I love you, Kitty Kat. No matter what."

He felt her grip tighten against his throat, and he closed his eyes.

He had no way to knock her out or seal off her powers with his current power level, and even though she wouldn't kill him if he just let down his shield, he knew that she would never be permitted back in Troivack if she murdered the noblemen responsible for this in her current state. And if she killed someone without meaning to . . .

Fin knew she would never be the same.

So, banking heavily on the small chance that he could survive somehow . . . Fin accepted his fate. Whatever it may be.

CHAPTER 46

SPELL SHOCK

Eric had been on his way to the council room after his meeting with Eli when he'd heard the explosion.

He heard the shrieks, the cries . . . Then over the din of noise, he'd heard Fin shout, "KAT!"

The prince broke out into a sprint and, once he had reached the open council room doors, saw the entire room engulfed in magical chaos.

He recognized Fin's shield filling the room, encircling himself and Kat. The room was blistering hot, and several council members were trapped inside on the other side of the shield.

Despite his wife's back being to him, Eric could tell from the way she moved that she wasn't in control.

Just what the hell had happened?!

Taking a single step into the room, the prince froze again when he saw Fin's shield start to turn white.

Eric darted to the shield, ignoring the hollering from guards within for him to stay back and squinted through the lightning and ancient symbols. He watched as Kat put her hand to her father's neck . . .

"KAT!" Eric roared.

Her magic shouldn't be able to still work in Fin's shield! Why isn't she feeding off his intention?!

The prince then watched in horror as Kat hoisted her father into the air by his throat.

Eric didn't care about risking death by running through Fin's shield. He lunged in an attempt to break through, but it held tight. At least it didn't repel him with as much force as it had been capable of doing in the past.

"KAT, WAKE UP! WAKE UP, KAT!" Eric was screaming by then as he watched Fin's face turn purple, his magical white eyes fluttering . . .

And then his shield disappeared, and . . . Kat lowered her father back onto his feet, though he immediately crumpled to all fours, grasping for breath.

Kat, on the other hand, swayed.

Eric was already at her side, and so when she collapsed, it was right into his arms.

"Kat? Hey, hey! Kat? Hey! You alright?" Eric lowered Kat to the ground, his eyes roving her motionless sickly gray face. "Hey, you need to answer me!"

Fin spluttered and gasped on the floor, but after a moment, he, too, managed to crawl over to his daughter's side, though he looked on the brink of passing out.

"She was dosed with powdered Witch's Brew," the house witch rasped.

Eric's gaze snapped up. His eyes sought out Brendan's. The prince looked murderous with black rage, and Brendan didn't need to hear a word from him to know what he was demanding.

The king, looking a mite battered himself from being magically thrown back, stepped over to Sir Seth Herra and executed him then and there.

"That's not enough." Eric growled in the heavy silence that filled the room.

Brendan nodded, then strode over to where Lord Ball remained pressed against the wall, unable to stand as he trembled.

The man couldn't even speak after what he had just seen.

And so he had no final words before his shoulders were relieved of his head. Brendan strode past the council members, and without ceremony, without a question, he proceeded to execute Lord Sanchez even though he was only just coming back to consciousness. He left Lord Herra and Lord Edium alive. They were going to give answers no matter what.

The remaining council members cowered in shock. They had never seen something so terrifying in their entire lives.

However, both Fin and Eric weren't all that attentive to the gruesome executions taking place behind them.

The duke was grabbing his daughter's wrist to check for a pulse, as her complexion had begun to turn even more ominous.

"PHYSICIAN! GET A PHYSICIAN!" Eric ordered, his grip on Kat's shoulders tightening.

"I think . . ." Fin interrupted softly, his eyes fluttering. "I think . . . she depleted a lot of magic . . . I couldn't . . . Even I couldn't completely subdue her . . . She may . . . need to . . ." The duke collapsed beside Kat, unable to keep himself awake.

Brendan joined at their sides, staring down at the father and daughter who both looked on the verge of boarding death's carriage.

It was the first time that Katarina had been wrong about her capabilities.

She had been able to survive so much . . . Was incredibly strong . . . But . . .

Brendan felt cold sweat trickle down his bruised back as Duke Icarus's words came back to him.

Duke Icarus had known that the Ashowans wouldn't be able to support them in the coming attack because he knew that this trap would work . . . He had also said Brendan couldn't count on the coven . . .

The king looked to the guards who had brought Sir Herra up from the dungeon and stalked over to them just as the Royal Physician came bolting into the room and over to where Eric sat with his wife and father-in-law.

"Who had access to Sir Herra?" Brendan demanded of the two men who were still pale as they gathered their wits.

"N-No one! We guarded him day and night! There was no way anyone could have given him anything. The guards were handpicked by you and Mr. Levin— Oh."

Brendan felt his heart drop to his stomach. News of his assistant's betrayal had spread throughout the castle, but Mr. Levin had been a part of nearly every important decision and had contributed to almost every deal Brendan had executed . . . for years.

He needed to get his hands on the man and kill him himself . . . But with how little time there was before the rebellion arrived at the castle doors, he knew he may not get the chance. First and foremost, he needed to find Mr. Kraft and tell him everything that had transpired with Finlay and Katarina, then warn Faucher—

The king was distracted by movement out of the corner of his eyes from the doors to the council room.

He looked and found himself watching Kraken and Pina darting over to their witches.

Things definitely weren't good.

With the physician attending to both Katarina and her father, he sent one of the knights who came after the commotion had been settled, having been tardy to the original meeting, to go fetch more physicians from Vessa to attend to the injured council members.

Brendan left the room, stopped five knights that were rushing to the scene, and ordered them to keep anyone that was not a physician out unless he ordered otherwise and to detain Lords Edium and Herra.

The king then stormed back up the corridor to where people were starting to gather in concern—many of them being wives or children of the men inside.

Brendan vaguely noted Elyse Ball standing outside the council room doors, wringing her hands. He would tell her about her husband's treachery and death later.

As the king moved, he wasn't surprised to see Faucher come barreling down the corridor with Sir Cas on his heels.

"Sire! What happened?" Faucher demanded as shrieks began to ring out around them.

Someone must have seen the corpses.

"Not here. We need to see the queen."

Faucher looked as though he wanted to argue the fact as even more knights bolted by but he had never seen the king look so . . . disheveled.

So he obeyed without question.

The three men made their way up to the queen's chamber, the journey becoming easier as the occupants of the castle rushed to the commotion and left the halls empty.

Brendan didn't even bother knocking on the door when they reached their destination; he just burst in without slowing his pace.

Alina jolted in her bed in alarm, while Lady Annika Ashowan had already been on her feet—most likely sensing something wasn't right in the castle.

"Your Majesty?" Alina breathed, her hand flying to her belly. Ladies Sarah and Wynonna rose hastily from their seats at the queen's bedside and curtsied.

Brendan swallowed and turned to the duchess. "Your Grace, I regrettably need to inform you that both your husband and daughter are unconscious in the council room. There was a trap set, and Lady Katarina was dosed with Witch's Brew. She had a magical outburst that the duke managed to subdue by . . . well, I'm not sure if he declared Troivack as part of his home or not. However, he was able to contain Lady Katarina to a degree though it taxed him, and as I said, the two are now unresponsive but are receiving treatment from the Royal Physician."

Faucher hadn't heard Brendan ramble since he was a boy, and he had *never* seen the king so shaken.

All color drained from Annika's face as she proceeded to curtsy to the king and then queen.

"Pardon me, Your Majesties, but I would like to please attend to my family."

"They will be transported to their chambers in the near future; I recommend you wait for them there."

Annika lowered her chin briefly, her dark eyes glittering and hard as she swept out of the room.

"Gods, are they going to be okay?" Alina asked, tears filling her eyes.

"Your Majesty, who did such a thing?!" Lady Sarah spluttered, forgetting her manners in light of the shocking news that she was not to speak first.

"How did this happen?!" Lady Wynonna wondered fearfully, her hands clutching her dress while glancing back to Alina.

Brendan didn't answer.

He didn't know what to say.

"I am going to go speak with Mr. Kraft and Mage Sebastian to see if they might offer some insight on what has happened. Alina, I am leaving Sir Cas here to guard you."

Alina opened her mouth to ask another question or say something more but didn't get the chance, as the king charged out of the room before she could.

It wasn't until they were in the corridor and had made their way a good distance from the king and queen's chamber that Faucher stopped Brendan by clasping a hand on his shoulder.

"What else happened?" he asked quietly.

The king stared ahead blindly then turned his chin in Faucher's general direction after a moment of deliberation.

He repeated the events, including his discussion with Duke Icarus.

It was Faucher's turn to go temporarily catatonic.

"Then the plan was one way or another to get Katarina and her father out of the picture . . . So the new information we received from the blacksmith about the first witch needing Katarina's blood was incorrect?"

"I don't know." Brendan gave his head a slight shake. "There is too much confusion. When I speak with Mr. Kraft, I want to ask how successful he was in convincing the half fey we cannot see to send a message to the devil. At the very least, I'd like to discern if the devil is lying or not."

Faucher didn't bother pointing out that while Brendan was an intelligent and shrewd man, if the devil felt like lying, there was a strong chance that he would be exceptionally good at it.

The king probably knew, but . . . they were running out of time and options.

"I've organized the men. I'm sending two units to the north of the castle to intercept the mercenaries that were reported being spotted. I have a unit guarding each of the other directions on the outskirts of the city, and one unit remaining here in the castle. The men in charge of the warning bells have been informed to remain on high alert."

"What of the Coven of Aguas?"

"The witches refuse to fight for Troivack. We have another unit guarding them in the tunnels, but aside from them . . . we are out of men unless we send and wait for soldiers from Norum, Rozek, Biern, or Taliez."

"Taliez would get here the fastest," Brendan reasoned, his heart gradually calming as he turned over the familiar strategies he'd memorized since childhood.

"They would, and they could come behind the mercenaries and Duke Icarus's men to cut them off if they run."

Brendan nodded. "I don't have a lot of supporters in Taliez since I banned slavery, but there should be at least three viscounts and a marquess willing to spare me their knights."

Faucher raised an eyebrow as he, too, silently reviewed a list of their allies who wouldn't drag their heels under the king's orders.

"Get the messages sent out quickly, but quietly, and make sure the knights don't share the news with anyone in Vessa. I don't want to cause undue alarm in the city just yet." Brendan took another three steps, intending for them to move back into action, however, Faucher stayed behind.

"Your Majesty isn't prone to being taken aback," the military leader observed carefully.

Brendan paused, his right hand gently closing, then relaxing again as he took a slow, steadying breath.

"I've never seen magical power like that in my life. When Finlay Ashowan blasted me into the sea last year, I thought he was an exception. That he would be the most powerful witch I'd ever meet, but Lady Katarina would've bested him today if given the time. It . . . It's made me realize how utterly pointless fighting against witches in a life-or-death battle would be. If it weren't for the fact that the Ashowan family is decent, they'd be an abhorrently large threat."

"Perhaps that is why the Gods bestowed them with such abilities. Because they are good people."

Brendan's mouth twitched and looked at Faucher over his shoulder. "Whatever the reason, I don't think we can count on them for what is to come anymore, and given that there may be more powerful individuals out there and we do not have any witches offering aid, this war is starting with us at a significant disadvantage."

Faucher's brows crashed down.

He was struggling to imagine Katarina, his star pupil, being in any type of poor condition that would stop her from fighting . . . and found he suddenly was feeling every bit as rattled as Brendan had first appeared.

"I'd like to go see Asho— Damn. Reyes. I'd like to go see Lady Katarina Reyes, Your Majesty, before I give the orders."

Sympathy and appreciation flashed across Brendan's face.

Faucher really had grown to care for the mischievous redhead.

"Yes, but quickly."

The military leader bowed briskly, then turned and retreated down the corridor, once again leaving Brendan alone.

The king let out a final breath before setting himself back into motion.

He pressed his concerns for Alina's best friend to the back of his mind, along with his worry over the physical pains the queen had been experiencing all that morning, and instead focused every ounce of mental energy on how he could potentially win a war that included ancient magical beasts capable of flattening a keep without any assistance from the house witch or his daughter.

CHAPTER 47

DIRECT DEFENSES

Annika stood perfectly still as Mr. Kraft studied her daughter's sleeping form.

Eric watched at her side with his arms crossed.

The coven leader had already examined Fin and determined that the duke's magic was recovering incredibly slowly—most likely due to only a few members of his "home" being present. Therefore, it could be up to a full week until he regained consciousness . . .

Kat, however, was a different story.

After several silent moments had come and gone, Mr. Kraft at last let out a sigh and turned to the duchess and prince, sweat shining on his forehead from the extensive effort and pressure he was experiencing.

"I believe she will awake by this evening or tomorrow morning. However, I can't say what the state of her mind will be. In all our research, we've never encountered a witch who has consumed Witch's Brew in this new powdered form. At the very least, her magic appears stable, albeit extraordinarily weak, and it isn't consuming any intentions at this time."

"What about when Witch's Brew is eaten by a witch in its original state as the mushroom? Have there been instances of that happening?" Annika asked with a frown.

"Unfortunately, no. Because witches here in Troivack have been hiding underground, there haven't been any cases of anyone who's taken it. I would've thought you would have some records of such a thing," Mr. Kraft reasoned aloud somberly.

The duchess shook her head. "Not that I'm aware of. All the cases we investigated were for average humans."

Mr. Kraft looked back at Kat, who still wore her official uniform, her face slack and peaceful.

"Lady Katarina is a remarkable woman; I'm sure she will recover swiftly. My guess is that because of her constitution burning through the drug, she could have been under its influence for far longer—as humans are—so already things are not as bad as they could be."

Neither Eric nor Annika said anything in response.

It was hard to see any kind of bright side to the current situation.

Without there being anything else he could say or do to help ameliorate the heavy atmosphere, Mr. Kraft took his leave after issuing the proper bows.

Annika and Eric stood in silence after the door closed behind them, both staring at Kat without sparing so much as a glance at each other.

Eventually, the prince moved over to his unconscious wife and gently began untying her hair and letting it lay down loose over her shoulder.

He then started carefully pulling off her boots.

"You should go be with Fin," Eric addressed his mother-in-law quietly as he worked.

Lowering her dark eyes, Annika let out a long breath. "Eric, I know you've investigated some of my dealings and that you are wary of me as a result."

"This is not the time for that." The prince's voice was sharp, and he didn't even bother looking at the duchess as he set Kat's boots a safe distance from the crackling hearth.

"It *is* the time. After seeing the nature of your relationship with Kat, I'm sure you would've wanted to discuss this with my daughter present and conscious, but I believe it may be better for us to speak more candidly with just you and me present." Annika's tone was soft, yet when Eric finally locked eyes with hers, he saw that she was as assured as ever, though the tension in her expression betrayed her stress.

He faced the duchess squarely, his hazel eyes steely.

Annika clasped her hands in front of her skirts and lifted her chin.

"Your Highness, how much of my work are you aware of?"

Eric slipped his right hand in his pocket. "I know you own most of the brothels in Daxaria and a substantial amount here in Troivack. I know you have a web of informants and participate in other underhanded dealings."

"And do you believe I am engaging in any treasonous actions?"

The prince took his time considering this. "I don't know. I'm aware how close you were with my mother, but I don't know how transparent you have been with her or my father."

Nodding at the reasonable response, Annika's expression saddened at the mention of her lost best friend, Ainsley Reyes.

"Well, your parents and I had long discussions about when it was best to enlighten you on the nature of the deal we have . . . However, after Her Majesty's passing and your disappearance, the discussions ground to a halt."

Eric frowned but didn't interrupt.

The duchess met his eyes evenly. "Your Highness, here in Troivack, my family was infamous for their behind-the-scenes work in aiding whoever wished to pay their fee. My brothers were not a part of this legacy, and when I moved to Daxaria, for a time, I, too, stepped away from it. However, I . . . started resorting to my familiar methods after a few months of my marriage with Viscount Hank Jenoure. That is, until your mother noticed . . ." Annika trailed off, a warm smile lighting her face. Her love of Ainsley Reyes was indisputable. "She was sharp. She noticed some of my activities, and we formed the foundation of our friendship. As I got to know her and your father, I realized I wanted to use the skills and tools at my disposal to help and protect them. As a result, I entered into a lifelong agreement with them. Your parents are aware of any and all my activities, and we have been in constant communication regarding them. Some they don't know simply because it isn't necessary, but the information is available to them should they ever ask."

The prince's eyes widened fractionally. He hadn't considered the idea that the powerful positions the duchess and duke held would be surrendered and disclosed so readily to the crown. That type of loyalty wouldn't exist in Troivack . . . And even in Daxaria, it was hard to come by as it meant the dukedom's fate was perpetually in the hands of the monarchy.

"I will continue to serve the crown until I pass, and Tamlin has started resuming these duties as well, and training with me should you wish for our family to continue its work."

"Would my father even be able to hold you accountable should you choose to act of your own accord?" Eric asked pointedly. "Between your wealth and connections, not only with your brothels but also with the Coven of Wittica, you could successfully seize the throne or control the kingdom however you see fit."

"We have become a powerful family; I won't even bother trying to say otherwise," Annika countered bluntly. "However, this has carried on for so long and with such great success because of the great trust between your parents and our own household. Should you wish to put an end to this relationship, there is a significant amount of work that would need to be sorted.

Now, I must ask, do you think nullifying this arrangement is wisest when, by marrying our daughter, we are now a highly invested ally?"

"Do you expect an answer right now?" Eric questioned with a bite to his voice.

Annika shook her head. "Not at all. While you may feel uneasy about the agreement and power we hold, it does warrant careful thought. I will of course abide by whatever Your Highness wishes once you assume the throne."

"While you had a strong bond with my mother, you're essentially asking me to trust Tam in the same manner, and I know next to nothing about him."

"That is accurate. What you may like to do is get to know our son before making your decision. Even with your return to court, you will not be taking over the throne for at least a few years, especially with Katarina being required to learn more about becoming a queen. So until then, you can consider how you would like the relationship between the crown and the Ashowan duchy to be."

"A perfectly reasonable suggestion," Eric responded stiffly.

Annika eyed the prince calmly. She could see he was not at all convinced of trusting her, and she knew the feud that had taken place with Fin had done significant damage to his opinion and outlook of them . . .

She gave a lone shoulder shrug. "There is no reason to worry about this now, Your Highness. My loyalty is with your family regardless of this answer—though in a sense I suppose through marriage, it is by extension also *our* family . . ."

Eric's expression hardened momentarily before he closed his eyes and tried not to respond emotionally.

"I dislike the duplicitous nature of your work while presenting yourselves as the epitome of a wholesome family," the prince stated frankly. "I also know I am not biased to think favorably because of the state of my relationship with Fin in recent years. That being said, I'm given to understand you have been a prominent figure in my sister's life and she thinks incredibly highly of you, Your Grace.'"

Annika lowered her gaze in demure thanks to the prince's acknowledgment.

"I will of course have to carefully consider what our relationship is going to look like in the future."

The duchess curtsied. "Of course. In the meantime, I will attend to Fin."

The prince inclined his head. With a graceful turn and careful exit, the duchess left the chamber.

Once alone with Kat, Eric slowly turned back around, nervous to stare at her still face in the silence of the room where his more potent feelings could run rampant . . . His anger and suspicion toward the duchess had actually been a reprieve to the dark consuming terror he had been feeling prior to their talk, but when alone with Kat, that all faded away and he was left back in the cold, quiet reality where his wife was far away from him.

His hand gripped into a fist in his pocket.

Then he made his way around to the empty side of the bed where he climbed in beside Kat and carefully pulled her into him.

The faint aroma of amber touched Eric's nose, and before he knew it, tears were gathering in his eyes.

"Godsdamnit, Kat . . . You knew it was a trap . . ." he murmured into her hair while hugging her even more tightly. "We should've just run away when we had the chance."

By the following day, the king had finished sending out the units of men to guard Vessa and ensured that their supplies were well stocked should the city be surrounded and merchant routes be cut off. He was feeling far more in control of the situation.

Faucher of course being the steady and reliable presence he always was helped immensely.

Preparing for war or skirmishes was like second nature to the two men, and for a brief window of time, it felt as though things were once again as they should be . . . until the messenger came.

The wanted mercenary, Leochra Zephin, showed up at the castle, claiming he had something to relay to the king himself.

All at once, Brendan found himself plunged back into the unpleasantness of uncertainty.

He permitted the man entry, however, with the knowledge that he was a witch, summoned Mr. Kraft and Mage Sebastian to be present for the meeting in his office along with Faucher.

The king sat behind his desk and waited.

When at long last the infamous mercenary leader swaggered through the office door, he briefly smirked at the sight of Mr. Kraft before he swept into a theatrical bow before Brendan.

"Your Majesty, I come bearing a message from Samuel Zephin, or as you know him, Satan."

"Samuel Zephin? You two are brothers?" Brendan's eyes glinted with interest.

"My parents adopted him." Leo waved off the king's question, making the monarch's eyes narrow at the flippant attitude. "The devil wished to convey to you that the men coming to attack Vessa are no longer coming in order to murder the queen."

Brendan sat up straighter, the air around him turning dangerous.

"They are coming because they intend to trap the devil. We ask permission to leave the city, and as a result, this should negate the threat to your citizens. We would've done so sooner but noticed that the roads leading out of Vessa were blocked this morning." Leo bowed again, his tone magnanimous.

Brendan rose to his feet and fixed his black stare on the man, whose disrespectful behavior was bringing the king's tenuous control of his violent urges to a boiling point.

"If you knew the purpose of the rebels' attack, why didn't the devil leave sooner?"

"Ah, because his fate is tied to Katarina Ashowan, and so it is . . . difficult for him to put distance between him and her."

"The rebellion has been breathing down our necks, trying to assassinate Her Majesty. Why has their objective changed? Do you mean to tell me all of them are now aligned with the first witch?"

Leo's eyes sharpened. "You've learned of the first witch? Do you know who she is?"

Brendan raised an eyebrow and schooled his expression. "That is not business you have any right to know."

Leo ran the tip of his tongue over the point of his canine tooth before he nodded slowly.

"I see . . . Well, the reason the rebellion is following that *woman's* orders is because she promised to cripple the Ashowans' influence in your court, bolster their coffers, and to add the final nail to the coffin, she swayed Duke Icarus to join forces to give the rebellion better odds of winning, but most of our own men have still withdrawn, so you shouldn't be too overwhelmed." Leo all but rolled his eyes.

Brendan's lips curled upward coldly. "Your master isn't aware that she is prepared to use magical beasts and the rebels to sacrifice thousands of my soldiers and militia so she can not only open a portal and thrust him through, but then possibly keep the beasts she's summoned to assert even more of her own control over my kingdom?"

At last, Leo looked taken aback. "What do you mean?"

"Witch's Brew. She's using it to exchange lives from the Forest of the Afterlife to open a portal to send the devil back, yes, but she also may intend to impose her own will." Brendan watched as Leo's face paled but took no pleasure in seeing it.

"That cannot be right."

"Is the devil certain he knows exactly what the first witch might do or be after, or is there some room for interpretation? Because if that's the case, and I am now understanding there is some kind of magical bond to Lady Katarina, *who was attacked and is now unconscious*, I would say your master should prepare to return home to the Gods."

All former arrogance in Leo's countenance had dissipated as he first looked to Faucher, then Mr. Kraft, and finally Mage Sebastian.

When he saw no signs of deception on any of their faces, he swallowed.

"I will . . . speak with the devil and . . ."

"No. You will take my men to the devil, and you will bring him back here so that we can settle this once and for all." Brendan loomed over the mercenary, who tensed.

While he had been relieved of his weapons, they knew he was a water witch. Mr. Kraft watched him warily in that moment while glancing briefly at Faucher in warning.

"If you bring the devil here, you are serving him up to that woman." Leo slid closer to the door.

"This matter between the devil and the first witch is jeopardizing the people of my kingdom. So they will confront each other *now* and finish their business between them. Besides, I'm sure your master is anticipating that I would react in this way. There is only one of you here, after all."

"Are you really going to give the devil to the woman who holds your people hostage?" Leo snarled while noticing Faucher's hand go to the hilt of his sword.

"The way I see it, unless we know *who* the first witch is, we are sitting ducks. Now, are you going to cooperate, Leochra Zephin? Or will things become violent?" Brendan stood inches from the mercenary leader and awaited his answer.

At the very least, despite facing down a technical witch and seeing the fear in his eyes, the king doubted that Leo was anywhere near the same level of power as the Ashowan family. Despite the two members in his castle being unconscious, the thought did comfort Brendan just a tad.

CHAPTER 48

READY TO RALLY

S he was warm . . . and relaxed . . . Her thoughts were muffled, and her tongue was dry . . . She even felt a bit queasy . . .

Kat's eyebrows twitched.

Was someone saying her name? She couldn't make out the words.

But . . . she could smell sandalwood and bonfire smoke . . .

Eric was nearby.

The corners of her mouth quivered, and the voice near her seemed to get louder.

She wanted to open her eyes and see her husband. She wanted to see his hazel eyes staring at her, and then she wanted to say something outrageous that would make them crinkle, maybe even have him hold her while she listened to his heartbeat.

But her eyes weren't working. They didn't want to open . . .

Kat turned her attention to her magic. What was it doing that she felt so strange?

That was when she found that in place of the usual burning chaos within her being, struggling against her control . . . was a highly manageable flicker. One that reminded her of when she was a child and life was simpler . . . But . . . her body wasn't used to having so little magic.

Gods . . . What the hell happened?! She struggled against the weight of sleep, struggled to power her mind into functioning. What was the last thing she remembered? Talking to the king in the corridor . . . But there was more, yes?

Hadn't she gone to the meeting?

Why couldn't she remember the meeting?!

Panic started to rise, and that fueled her enough that, with a very grand effort, Kat managed to open her eyes. Though upon doing so, she immediately felt the urge to be sick, and in turn discovered she lacked the strength to roll over.

She stared at the ceiling above feeling absolutely horrible, when suddenly, the muffled murmuring she had been hearing blared loudly in her ear.

"Kat?! Kat are you alright? Can you hear me?!" Eric's frantic voice behind her sent Kat rolling onto her side and retching on the floor as pain engulfed her skull and a cold sweat broke out all over her body.

Kat felt Eric get off the bed and could hear the sound of him pouring her a cup of water, only even the sound of the water was torture to her and had her getting sick yet again.

Taking slow, shallow breaths, Kat focused on staying conscious, as she then became acutely aware of how the rest of her body ached horribly—it felt like she had slept in a contorted position the entire night.

She couldn't even speak . . . All that remained was pain and nausea . . .

"Kat? Can you say anything?"

She barely fought off getting sick again.

"Godsdamnit," Eric cursed from somewhere in the room Kat could not see.

Even moving to lie flat on her back again was out of the question.

However, Eric appeared in her vision with a towel and proceeded to cover her sick on the floor.

He studied her pallid face, his eyes desperate.

"Kat, if you can understand me, can you blink twice?"

Blinking! That I can do!

She blinked twice.

Eric let out a loud sigh of relief, his eyes closing. "Do you think you can move again?"

She didn't blink.

"Shit." Eric's momentary relief turned back to stress. "Do you remember what happened?"

Kat didn't blink.

"Sir Herra drugged you yesterday with powdered Witch's Brew. Your magic went wild, and you tried to kill anyone who wanted you dead . . . Your father stopped you."

"Nrraaw!" was the only sound that was able to make its way out of Kat's mouth, and it was more of a frog-like croak than a word. Fortunately, Eric understood the meaning.

"Fin, he . . . he expounded his home . . . or . . . or something like it. We don't know exactly. He's asleep after using so much of his magic, and because he's here in Troivack and not in Daxaria, it's harder for him to recover."

"Shrri."

"I know. It's not good. His Majesty did execute a couple of the people we are certain were behind this attempt. Though now the council is demanding you be sent back home immediately. They may be a bit traumatized . . ."

"Wh ese?"

"I don't know; I've been here with you." Eric chuckled while carefully cleaning the mess on the floor to the best of his ability before tossing the soiled towel into the fire.

Kat grumbled and Eric smiled. His eyes crinkled, and she felt her agitation over her inability to move or to figure out what was happening momentarily dim. Though she still was determined to make her tongue work again.

"Trs awr . . . we . . . ned . . . t'feet."

"You aren't fighting anyone. Kat, I swear to Gods, I thought you might've died."

The look of intensity and pain on Eric's face as he stared at her made Kat wish she was capable of making a witty quip or even just a crude comment . . . She wanted to lessen his worry somehow . . . to drive away the darkened thoughts . . .

"I'm invcissble . . . 'neet klll me."

"You aren't invincible. I think today proved that—and I don't want to test the limits of what is able to kill you anyway," the prince pointed out firmly.

With a painstaking amount of effort, Kat lurched forward, forced her hand to move to her side, and pressed herself up. As she struggled, Eric's gentle hands quickly assisted her as she managed to sit upright on the bed.

The movement nearly made her sick again, but by the time she was vertical, she felt her head gradually begin to clear, which encouraged her to battle through the unpleasant sensations going on in the rest of her body.

"Why . . . arnt . . . cllllng . . . fr phiiiisssshan."

"I've handled the aftereffects of Witch's Brew more than any of the physicians currently in the castle," Eric answered wryly. "You feel like you're going to be sick any time you move, you're aching all over, and your head feels as though a hundred nails were pounded into it, yes?"

Kat responded with a grumble of annoyance that had Eric smiling again as he reached up and tucked her hair behind her ears.

"What . . . helps . . . it?" Kat was gloriously pleased over the fact that she was able to complete a coherent sentence.

"My solution was always a good dose of moonshine, but I think in your case we need to get your magic to absorb something . . . At least, according to Mr. Kraft. That way you can finish burning through the drug's effects and regain some stamina," Eric explained, still crouching in front of his wife.

Taking a long, ragged breath in, Kat nodded while Eric reached to the small table beside the bed where he had placed the cup of water for her and pressed it into her hand.

He watched as she drank the water tenuously, then when she realized just how thirsty she was, finished downing the entire cup.

"Kat, you scared the hell out of me." Eric's voice rasped as he stared at her drawn face vulnerably.

Kat shifted uncomfortably under such a look.

"I know you like to try to take on the world, but if anything happens to you? I'm going to lose it."

"You aren't . . ." Kat struggled against her tongue that felt swollen. "You aren't going to . . . lose . . . your mind. And I'm . . . not going anywhere."

"I damn well *am* going to lose my mind. Do you remember our talk in the desert after you'd been stabbed? When I said that you pushing aside other people's feelings isn't fair? I really need you to hear me this time, Kat. I'm not a well-rounded individual, and I'm far from healthy. If I lose you . . . ?" Eric shook his head while holding his wife's widening gaze. "Kat, I didn't want to *live*, and it wasn't until you started annoying me that that changed. So please . . . Please can you promise me you're going to be more careful and sit out the war that is coming?"

Kat stared at Eric, both at a loss for how to respond and having to battle against the remnants of the drug in order to articulate her words.

"I'm going to fight. I'm going to . . . absorb as much as I can . . . and I'm going to protect everyone I love, but . . ." Kat reached her arms out, and Eric dutifully leaned into her embrace, allowing her to hold him and hunch her body around him comfortingly, her fingers tangling in his dirty blond hair. "I'm never going to leave you, and you . . . aren't allowed to leave . . . or give up either. Okay?"

Eric didn't say anything at first. Really, he was just taking as much joy and reassurance as he could being in her arms, surrounded by her smell, her hair tickling his nose.

"You're essentially refusing my request and just reiterating that you are hard to kill, and I just need to deal with it."

"Yes, but I said it nicer than that."

Eric chuckled softly and pulled free from her. "Will you at least agree to be more cautious about walking into situations you *know* are dangerous?"

"I'll think about it for three extra breaths. Deal?"

"If you aren't going to stay out of the battle then you need to promise that during the fighting you are by my side. Always."

"I can't control the things that happen in a fight!"

The prince's eyes narrowed. "You do realize you're going to be the one responsible for what I do if anything happens to you, right? This time, three people got their heads cut off. Next time, who knows? I might sign the kingdom over to Kraken and just see what happens."

Kat grimaced at the mention of three people losing their heads, making Eric hesitate again. "Kat, if you're determined to fight against the rebel army, you know you'll have to kill people, right? It's going to be all around you. It isn't as heroic as some think . . . Most of the time it feels wrong no matter which side you're fighting on."

Kat fidgeted, and her gaze fell to her hands that were presently held in Eric's. "I know. I guess I . . . I just need to remember that they are going to hurt innocent people if I'm not standing there."

"You also have to try to find any opportunity to end it. To stop the fighting and negotiate something peacefully even after watching them cut down a friend or family member."

The redhead's eyes rounded as she considered this new scenario the prince laid before her.

Not enjoying the warning he had to give his wife, Eric was at the very least glad that she was finally listening to him and taking his words to heart.

He knew firsthand how war and brutality changed a person . . .

"This is going to be hard, and . . . I do promise that I'll fight beside you."

"Thank you . . . and yes. Yes, it will be hard . . ." Eric lifted her hands to his mouth and kissed them. "Now, do you think you can walk? We should probably get you to your father to see if maybe another member of his home can help his recovery."

Kat stilled then, her gaze boring into the floor as an idea flashed in her mind.

"Eric . . . Where are the council members right now?"

The prince frowned. "A few of them got injured when you chucked a table at them. So some of them are getting treated, and others are writing to their households to summon their knights. Why?"

"I chucked a table at— Never mind. I'll find out about that later. Can we please summon them? I think I have an idea that might help."

Eric raised an eyebrow skeptically at his wife's suggestion but wasn't in any position to question her request further, as her face split into a dazzling, if a bit worse for wear, grin that left him perfectly helpless to her whims.

Likon stared at the inky night sky through the hole above while lying on his back, his hands cradling his head as he listened to the whistle of the wind through the land outside.

He couldn't remember the last time he had so much free time to think.

There was nothing to do, no work to be done . . .

The first witch had said the ransom letter had been passed along, but no one seemed to talk about it . . . which was odd . . . Likon wondered if someone had intercepted it, as he refused to believe that the Ashowans would ignore it.

The question then became who had stopped the letter from being delivered, and why?

He closed his eyes briefly with a sigh.

He hoped Kat was alright . . . He'd noticed a few days prior that the sirins had disappeared, which could be a sign that people searching for him were getting closer to where he was being kept . . .

Sitting up, Likon peered around the room that was lit with several torches that were also helpful in keeping the space comfortably warm.

He was even given a blanket and pillow at night after the first five days.

All in all, his captors hadn't been mistreating him other than keeping him locked in a room . . .

Though the first witch hadn't come to see him in a while. Most likely with everything going on, she couldn't afford to leave the castle and risk cluing people in to her true identity.

Coming to his feet, Likon began to stretch in the hopes that maybe he would force his body to relax enough to sleep soon, when lo and behold, the door opened, and in came Ansar.

"You are coming with me," the man declared in a brisk, business-like tone.

"Why?" Likon scoffed back, his heart rate already picking up speed as he readied himself for the opportunity to fight and free himself.

"The war has started, and given that the Ashowans are still in Troivack, despite them being incapacitated, we aren't taking any risks."

"What do you mean they are incapacitated?" A wave of anger and panic flooded Likon's senses. "You better answer me, or—"

The same imp that had been there when he had been abducted appeared magically behind Likon, covering his face with the same foul-smelling cloth as before. Without being able to finish his threat, Likon fell into darkness, though prior to doing so, all he could think about was how he was going to slaughter anyone who had harmed a hair on any of the Ashowans' heads, daughter or son of the Gods—or not.

CHAPTER 49

A DEVILISH DEBUT

Kat had stumbled thrice by the time she reached the stairs to summon the council members. The first two times, she had grumbled and pushed off Eric's assistance, but by the third time, he didn't care whatever she said or squawked as he slipped an arm around her waist and grasped one of her hands.

"Give yourself a break; you were drugged and unconscious," he whispered in her ear as maids passed by and paused to gawk at them.

"I need . . . to hurry though!" Kat retorted while barely hiding her panting.

Eric looked at the intent frown on his wife's face as she attempted to take two more shuffling steps.

"If you really want to go faster, then get on my back."

Her head snapped round. "That isn't proper though . . ." While she said the words, a mischievous smile was starting to climb her face.

Eric didn't bother pointing out the obvious fact that she was wearing pants and an untucked shirt with her hair looking like she had just come from being bedded. Instead, he rolled his eyes, released her, then crouched down in front of her.

Once loaded on, her arms around his neck, Kat leaned in close until her breath tickled Eric's ear. "Giddyup!"

"We aren't doing that."

"I'm just having fun." Kat pouted.

"Say it again, and I'll take you back to the chamber."

The huskiness in Eric's voice made Kat blush scarlet as she then understood what her husband was getting at.

"*Now* of all times? Weren't you just saying how I'd almost died?!"

"We men are complicated creatures."

Kat gave an embarrassed chuckle and buried her burning face into Eric's back. "Come on. Let's get going. We need to wake my da up as soon as possible— By the way, have you seen Pina?"

Eric stood with a grunt and started walking quickly toward the king's chamber.

"No, not since you first collapsed. Both she and Kraken took off, and I'm not sure where."

Kat frowned, unsure what her and her father's familiar could be up to, but she decided that in the very worst case scenario she could endure an awkward conversation with Cleophus Miller to find out where Pina had run off to. Gods knew the man kept better tabs on the kitten than she did . . .

With Eric's assistance, the couple made it to the king's office only to learn that he wasn't there.

He was in the throne room awaiting a guest.

So they rerouted.

"Who is the king expecting?" Kat wondered aloud.

"I know as much as you do," Eric explained as he descended the final set of stairs far slower than he would've at the beginning of their journey as his wife was starting to feel heavier than when he'd first picked her up. "How is it that you're taller than me and I'm always the one carrying you?"

"Life just works out for me like that."

Eric half laughed, half moaned. While it seemed outrageous that they were bickering and bantering as they usually did when the tension in the castle air felt both oppressive yet delicate at the same time, the prince was just happy to have Kat awake again to care too much.

At last, they reached the throne room where two guards stood waiting.

"We need . . . to speak with His Majesty." Eric had to swallow while speaking. His throat had gone dry from all the heavy breathing.

He was moderately shocked his wife hadn't made fun of him for it.

The guards looked at each other uncertainly.

"Chop-chop! My elderly husband is on the brink of a death rattle from carrying me like this!" Kat barked.

Eric rolled his eyes.

He should've known it was coming.

He pretended to drop her and made her squeak.

The guards were even more put off by such a display.

"His Majesty said no one is to enter," the guard on the left explained slowly.

"Really? Would he have said that if he knew I was awake?" Kat asked once she had hoisted herself back up to a position where her arse wasn't dangling close to the floor, which had made Eric stagger.

"I . . . will ask, Lady Katarina." The guard nervously backed away from Kat, a move that was not lost on her. Nor was the shiftiness in the other guard's eyes.

She could tell they were frightened of her.

That meant that the rumors of what had happened in the council room had already spread . . .

After a few moments, the great door opened again, and the guard slipped back out.

"His Majesty says you may enter."

Kat could tell by the guard's stiff face that he was not in agreement with the king's decision.

She lowered her head with a tight smile of thanks.

The guards' reaction to Kat had sombered the temporarily bright mood between her and Eric, so they proceeded into the throne room with serious expressions fixed in place.

Brendan sat on his throne with Mr. Kraft, Mage Sebastian, and Faucher standing nearby. They looked . . . tense.

Though seeing Katarina conscious did bring a bit of relief to both the king's and Faucher's faces, it was short-lived when they registered that she was being carried in . . .

"Lady Katarina, we are glad you are awake," Brendan called with a stoic nod and questioning gaze.

Kat tapped Eric's shoulders and slowly slid from his back so she could bow to the monarch. In doing so, she revealed her disheveled appearance.

"While I am grateful to be alive, I am concerned at—"

"Gods—her magic!"

"That. Yes." Kat grimaced at Mr. Kraft's outburst.

The king turned to look at the coven leader expectantly.

"I . . . I inspected her before and could see her magic was stable if depleted." He regarded the redhead in morbid awe. "It really did become a part of your everyday life. I can see how it flickers uncertainly in you now." Mr. Kraft almost sounded apologetic.

Kat lowered her chin and clasped her hands in front of herself, already avoiding the look of concern Faucher was giving her.

"That is why I came here, Your Majesty. I wanted to ask a favor of you."

The king leaned forward and gestured for her to continue, though his eyes drifted to the door expectantly . . .

"I would like to meet with the council members. The ones who are still alive."

Everyone froze in alarm.

"I need to absorb as much hate as possible to regain some magic. Or . . . if we capture a magical beast that we need killed, I can absorb something from them? Or maybe I could go for a quick bit of regular hunting . . ."

The men stared at Kat, looking collectively concerned.

"While it may sound a tad risky to greet the council given my current reputation, I'm hoping that if I regain some of my magic, I can maybe try and bolster my father's own power and help him wake up. I know it really has just been a theory until now, but if it's possible, I think it's worth a try."

"Are you certain that the hate the council feels for you will be enough?" Brendan questioned "If not, I recommend we let them rest. They are not thinking favorably of you at this time, so if I antagonize them by forcing your presence, it may end poorly."

"I don't know for certain, but—"

Kat didn't get the chance to finish her argument.

The doors opened, and in stepped none other than Leochra Zephin followed by . . .

The devil himself.

Eric instantly stood in front of Kat, blocking her from view as the two men entered with the doors closing behind them.

"Why wasn't I notified he was coming?" the prince furiously asked Brendan over his shoulder.

"Your Majesty, Your Highness," the devil greeted breezily as he walked. He wore a burgundy coat and all black underneath, his long black hair still partially tied at the back of his head in a very similar manner to most Zinferans.

Though . . . he looked like he had lost weight since the last time Eric had seen him, and there was a certain eagerness in his countenance that was directed toward Kat after he had bowed to the king and prince.

"Lady Katarina, I see that you chose to stay and have paid a hefty price already," the devil observed, his tone lazy, but his eyes sharp despite Kat being mostly hidden from view behind Eric.

"I have summoned you here, Samuel Zephin, because I am under the impression that my citizens are going to be slaughtered in large part due to the feud between you and the first witch." Brendan's voice boomed imperially in the room.

The devil raised an eyebrow, and the corners of his lips quirked upward at hearing the use of the surname he had received from Leochra's parents. He glanced at his subordinate by his side, Leo, but the man had his eyes dutifully lowered to the ground.

"Yes, well. It seems my sister wants me out of this realm no matter what. She's finally gotten desperate, though we'll see if she can honestly wipe out thousands of people. She never really was good at widespread evil doings."

"She has already been drugging thousands of people to death. Whether she is or is not capable of an all-out war is not a gamble I am taking with my people's lives." Brendan's voice had lowered dangerously. "I want whatever this feud is settled between the two of you outside of Vessa."

The devil stared at the king and slowly folded his arms. He looked humored . . . and interested . . . but the manner with which he addressed Brendan was as though he were still a seven-year-old child king.

Mage Sebastian took a step back, Mr. Kraft was rooted to where he stood, remaining perfectly still, and Faucher was doing everything in his power not to grasp the hilt of his sword.

"I take it Your Majesty isn't all that war-hungry since seeing the stone golems?" the devil asked with a faintly taunting note.

Brendan's gaze darkened. "To you, this moment of time is most likely similar to many others you have already experienced in your eternity, and it may already be forgettable to you. However, I don't intend to spend the rest of my days rebuilding my capital city or battling for control of my kingdom with the offspring of the Gods." There was a rare passion in the king's voice, and it most likely came as he knew deep within his bones that should his army face a horde of magical beasts, they would not survive.

The devil sighed and looked to the ceiling as though already weary and bored of the exchange.

"Rest assured, Your Majesty, if you can tell me who the first witch is parading around as, I'd be happy to escort her away from Vessa. But you don't know, and unless she comes forward herself, I have no way of knowing either."

"Wouldn't you be able to see the threads of fate tied to her?" Kat interrupted while sidling out from behind Eric.

The devil dropped his hands and then clasped them behind his back, while turning to look at Kat, as a teacher would a favored student. "Excellent question. I am not able to see anything strange about her, thanks to one of the many annoying details of my punishment here."

Gods, the devil's time here sounds more like a— A rush ran through Kat as a sudden realization dawned on her . . .

"You . . . You weren't banished by the Gods from the Forest of the After-life. You were *cursed* by your sister. She lost her powers by binding you to this earth forever, except she can't die like witches should when a curse is cast . . ." Kat reasoned out, her eyes rounding.

The devil raised an eyebrow and then beamed a smile in her direction. "You aren't far off. I was trying to suppress her magic, she fought against me until she reached her limits, and well . . . here we are. I got what I wanted, but . . . as your family well knows, there must be an equivalent exchange. I paid my price. In my books, I still count it as a punishment by my parents, as this all is happening under their laws and power."

"Why didn't you tell us *any* of this sooner?!" Kat demanded, throwing her hands in the air only to become light-headed and have her left knee buckle.

The devil's cavalier expression momentarily turned to concern, but by the time Eric had steadied his wife, the look was gone.

"If I told you everything from the beginning, I was risking a lot of problems. For one, I was trying to convince Lady Katarina to leave, but knowing her family and their terrible habits of taking on the protection of others, I assumed she would stay to stop a war. Oh dear. It looks like I was right."

"Oh yes, because knowing the devil was here wouldn't raise any concern, and I'd be happy to abandon my best friend here," Kat snapped back sarcastically.

"For another reason," the devil continued a little louder to the king. "I prefer to live relatively inconspicuously. My sister is the one changing things, and I wanted to avoid becoming embroiled in it. However, as I'm given to understand from the message Your Majesty sent with Leo . . . you believe she intends to kill thousands of people to transfer even more ancient beasts here *and* to not only open a portal and 'defeat' me, but to enforce her own will over the kingdom of Troivack."

"Yes, and so what we are going to do is bring the woman we suspect of being your sister, and you two can settle this once and for all and keep my vassals out of it before she gets the opportunity to do either of these things," Brendan informed the devil with a rumble.

Sam scoffed. "Sure. If you think that is a good idea given that we know so little about what weapons she does have, and you don't know exactly what she wants to happen in Troivack, by all means. While my sister does have connections, she is technically powerless. Go right ahead, Your Majesty." The devil held out his arms and smiled elegantly. "Let us have a family reunion between the devil and the first witch right here in your throne room, though I believe the best thing to do is simply let me leave as she will have no choice but to abandon her plans and chase after me. I sincerely think that even she wouldn't proceed with a full attack just for the sake of obtaining more magical beasts. It simply isn't in her nature."

"I'll be sending you both outside my city to handle each other however you two see fit."

Brendan did not care at all for the devil's smugness, but if at the end of the day he had at least determined which of the women nearest his wife he could trust, that would be a small blessing. Especially if it did once and for all prove Kezia's innocence.

He waved to Faucher, and the military leader descended the steps obediently, kept his eyes ahead, and gave a wide berth between himself and the devil when he passed.

While nothing terrible had happened yet, there was still the serrated blade of unease in the air that something horrible was nearing . . .

Sam tilted his head as he stared at Kat, still smiling. "So tell me, how is that father of yours? I must admit, I've been incredibly curious to meet him and of course, the infamous Emperor Kraken himself in the fluff."

Kat's hand curled into a fist at her side.

She wanted to punch the devil in the face.

She wanted to do it so badly . . .

But . . . She bit down on her tongue and held his gaze as levelly as she could.

She wouldn't let him coax out an explosion of any kind from her ever again. And so instead of responding to him, she merely folded her arms across her chest and glared.

CHAPTER 50

WHICH IS THE WITCH

The throne room was becoming more crowded, or at least it felt that way as Alina, Ladies Rebecca Devark, Sarah, Wynonna, and Kezia had all arrived. It had been a lengthy wait getting them assembled—one that had been done in a smothering silence.

Kat had been forced to sit on the stairs to the throne, as she couldn't handle standing for very long in her weakened state.

Surprisingly, the devil didn't try to antagonize anyone as they waited . . . though his dark eyes were disconcerting as he took his time studying everyone.

When the sun began to lower in the sky and cast the throne room in a weak glow that hinted of brighter days to come, the king had a bench brought in for the devil and Leo Zephin to sit on. Shortly after, the women and Faucher arrived.

The noblewomen faced the throne and had collectively curtsied to the king and queen.

Alina nodded regally in response, though she still looked pale from the pains she was experiencing during the previous few days.

The devil eyed the back of the noblewomen from his position on the bench with a subtle smirk . . .

Brendan and Alina watched him charily as he did this, and upon noticing that the king was staring so pointedly at him, the devil stood and issued a bow to the two monarchs.

Despite the mysterious man behind them, the noblewomen kept their faces downturned. None of them had been told why they'd been summoned.

Kezia had a grim air about her, her wavy black hair was draped and pinned over her right shoulder. There were dark lines under her effervescent blue eyes—but that could have been due to the stress of being ejected from court and tending to her infant son.

She wore a deep red velvet dress to combat the wintry cold, and, as always, looked wildly stunning. The only piece of her normal visage missing was her pendant containing her mage crystal threaded on a black ribbon, as it had been confiscated the previous day.

"I have gathered you all here, as I believe one of you is guilty of treason. A noblewoman in this court is plotting to bring an army of men and ancient magical beasts here to Vessa with the goal to slaughter thousands. I have Mr. Samuel Zephin here to help me determine which of you is responsible for these events," Brendan announced loudly. His anger and anxiety brewed together in his gut slowly but steadily.

Lady Sarah and Lady Wynonna looked to each other with wide, fearful eyes, and Lady Kezia straightened, her gaze snapping to the devil with dawning realization.

Brendan, Kat, and Alina felt their hearts sink to their stomachs when she did this . . .

"Kezia . . . ?" Kat asked, her voice warbling with pain.

The noblewoman looked at Kat, her brows lowered and her full lips pursed. "No, *ryshka*. No, I am not a traitor." She then looked to Alina and gave her head a brief shake before once more facing the devil, who had brought his hand up to his mouth, his thumb touching his lip as though his cloying smile may turn into a laugh. "While His Majesty hasn't announced who this man is, I know he is the devil. I can feel it in my bones."

"What a marvelous intuition you have." Sam dropped his hand and took a swaggering step forward. "Usually, it's only *witches* who are capable of sensing that so easily."

"His Majesty has been looking for the devil for months. It makes sense that a man who dares act so arrogant in the king's presence is him." Kezia stood her ground as the devil started to circle her. He eyed her up and down, though Kat could see Kezia's hands were trembling while clasped at her front . . .

"Tell me, Your Majesty." Sam turned to look at the king, his hands held behind his back. "If I declared this was the first witch, would you cut off her head here and now?" He reached out and flicked a wisp of Kezia's hair, and Brendan let out a warning rumble while Kat was sorely missing the presence of her sword.

She looked to Faucher, and he met her gaze knowingly and raised an eyebrow.

"Do not touch her." The ominous warning came from Alina, who stared down the devil as she gripped the armrests of her throne.

"No need to be angry. That would be the best way to determine who is the traitor after all. The first witch may be powerless, but she *is* still immortal. If you tried cutting off everyone's heads, you'd find out the answer rather quickly by who just happens to morph into a brand-new young woman with a perfectly intact head."

"What is he talking about?" Lady Sarah whimpered while holding Lady Wynonna's hands fearfully.

"The first witch doesn't die. She ages and lives like her mother, the Goddess. When she dies or reaches the end of her years as a crone, she returns to the state of a maiden, then continues to age to matron, and so on. Over and over. Her appearance morphs each time she becomes the maiden once more," Kat explained as she stared at Lady Rebecca Devark, who had remained impressively stoic and silent during the whole exchange.

Kat tilted her head, still observing the older woman. "Lady Rebecca, are you simply one of the most hardened women I've ever met, or are you also not surprised that this is the devil?"

Sam laughed and looked at Kat. "It's interesting, isn't it? How quickly people become suspicious and read into any little detail they can."

"Oh, so she absolutely *isn't* the first witch?" Kat asked, pointing at the older woman while directing an unimpressed stare at the devil.

"Well, I'll tell you why I have my doubts that she is," the devil drawled. "For one, she has been one of the most protected noblewomen since birth. For another, everyone would have seen her grow up."

Eric cast a very brief look at Kat. He had said the exact same thing . . .

"Enough with your games. Who do you believe to be the first witch? You don't seem concerned that she has been amassing great power in order to banish you to the Forest of the Afterlife," Brendan barked while shifting to the edge of his seat.

Sam sighed and rolled his eyes, but then . . .

He froze.

His expression turned serious, and he peered around the room with keen alertness. "What just happened?"

Everyone blinked and frowned in confusion.

Leo rose from his seat on the bench and moved to stand beside his master, making Faucher draw his sword.

"Just now . . . there was magic . . . but . . . not witch magic . . . it . . . it felt almost like mage magic, but . . . it . . . wasn't . . ." Samuel turned to look up at Mage Sebastian, who faltered under the sudden attention from the devil.

"Nothing happened. You're stalling," Eric interjected with his voice rising in frustration.

"No, no. Something happened that none of you noticed . . . I don't know how to explain it . . . Something . . . Some magic occurred . . . but I see no traces of it . . ." This time when the devil regarded the noblewomen under investigation, he did so with what some could mistake as mild panic.

Ladies Sarah and Wynonna cowered, Lady Rebecca held her ground, as did Lady Kezia, though she breathed a little more quickly . . .

"You know . . . Your Highness . . ." the devil started while turning toward Eric. Do you happen to remember how I said I'd send you a little gift last we spoke in Vessa?"

The prince's eyes narrowed in response.

"You never received it, did you?"

Faucher began to descend the throne steps quietly, his sword at the ready, making Leo move in front of the devil protectively, his weaponless hands raised.

"He's a water witch, Faucher. Be careful," Mr. Kraft warned loudly.

Leo made a hissing sound of annoyance between his teeth, and it made Faucher slow his descent.

Kat stood up from the steps and joined Eric's side as this happened.

"I had tried to let you know that your assistant, Mr. Thomas Julian, is loyal to a certain man named Likon, and he seems to tamper with correspondence when he sees fit . . . Or it could be that Likon is the one feeding him information and telling him what to do."

"What the hell does Likon have to do with the first witch besides the fact that either she or you kidnapped him?!" Kat almost lunged for the devil, but Eric held up an arm to hold her back, the prince's stare had turned hard at this piece of information.

"Well, I'd be interested to know a few things about him, like whom he spent time with, how often he was meeting romantically with Lady Katarina's maid, or possibly interacting with these noblewomen here . . . I know my own sources saw him gathering all kinds of information."

"You haven't a clue who the first witch is, do you?" Katarina laughed indignantly while listening to the devil change the course of the discussion with news of Thomas Julian's betrayal.

"I don't," the devil confessed instantly, startling everyone into silence. "But I have a hunch that the prince's assistant, who has been moonlighting as an informant to his *uncle* Likon might have some insight."

"Where did you even hear about this?" Kat insisted while moving the rest of the way around Eric's outstretched arm as she bore down on the devil, who ambled over to stand in front of her with an unimpressed eyebrow raise. Her fury over his implication toward Likon's shady activities was eclipsing any sense of danger.

"I noticed the boy writing a letter to your dear Likon back when we first met. This was when I was posing as a wine merchant and your carriage had stopped. It didn't take long to figure things out from there once I looked into everyone named Likon associated with the Ashowan family. And Likon's nephew, Thomas Julian, just so happened to be serving the prince!"

Brendan's fist pounded against his armrest, drawing everyone's attention to him as he glared down at the devil. "Enough. We are wasting time as an army marches closer. Go fetch the boy, and we will see if he can point out who is the—"

A gurgling, gasping sound stopped the king's words.

Everyone turned to see Leo Zephin with his eyes wide, his face ashen, words cut from his body from an attack that came from behind . . .

"LEO!" The devil rounded in alarm to see the final moments of the man who had grown up beside him as a brother for his 142nd life. By the time Sam had processed what he saw, however, Leochra Zephin, the legendary mercenary, was dead.

His body fell to the floor in a heap. In the next instant, a blade whipped through the air, a stream of water wrapped around its handle, that then plunged the dagger into Kat's side. She let out a yelp and half leapt, half fell back into Eric, who caught her just as the blade was yanked free of her and snapped back into the hand of its owner. Kat gasped as Eric slowly lowered her to the floor.

"Oh Gods, Kat? Kat, you'll be alright!" Eric immediately said as he looked at the location of blooming blood beneath her tunic and at least had enough clarity of mind to see that it wasn't a fatal injury. However, the prince didn't have much time to process or say anything else as his wife lay in his arms, her hands grasping her new wound.

Meanwhile the devil stared into the new face of his sister.

His sister, whom he hadn't seen or spoken to in centuries. He was pale, but a small space beside his nose twitched as he tried to jeer but didn't succeed. When he squared himself to her, his movements were clumsy with shock as he watched her reach up and tear off her hair covering.

"It's been a few years, Aradia."

She gave a breathy laugh, her eyes wild as she still wielded the dagger in her hand. "Sam, you look awful. You should've known better than to interact with a family our parents bestowed so many gifts to."

"Me? *You* just stabbed one of them."

While the otherworldly brother and sister shared a charged exchange, Faucher finished descending the steps stealthily. Brendan rose to his feet, his hand drawing his own sword, while Alina also stood with a shaky breath as she tried to process the shock, her hand reaching behind her back toward something hiddin on the throne.

"Oh . . . Gods . . ." Kat was panting in pain as she said the words, but she couldn't help it.

There, with her hair unbound, wearing an expression no one had ever seen on her face as she stared with a mixture of hate and coolness at the devil, was the first witch.

Though while the devil had called her Aradia, everyone else had come to know her as . . .

Lady Wynonna Vesey.

CHAPTER 51

A CURSED CAUSE

The infamous drunken noblewoman who waited on the queen . . .

As it turned out, she had red hair, though a more subtle tint than Katarina's, but no one had ever seen it before as she'd always kept it hidden, and for good reason.

With her face turned upward and her hair unbound, there was a certain familial resemblance to Katarina, which was a peculiar turn of events given that the first witch could've looked any variety of person . . .

However, there wasn't much time to ponder this, as Katarina proceeded to shout, "WHY DO I KEEP GETTING STABBED?! HONEST TO GODS, THIS IS GETTING RIDICULOUS!"

The devil and first witch each looked at her with small grimaces.

"Our parents do like to work in threes . . ." Aradia explained apologetically. "I tried to make it less painful—but if I'd aimed any lower, you would've kicked it away."

"YOU STILL WERE TRYING TO STAB ME!"

Aradia sighed as though explaining herself would be too tiresome. So instead, in a series of three movements, she shed her black dress that acted as a sheath and revealed black trousers, tunic, and corset while wielding her dagger.

"Why aren't you doing anything to stop her?" Eric ground out while eyeing the devil.

"Give me a break, Your Highness, I haven't seen my dear sister in ages," Sam drawled while continuing to stare at his sister with a predatory smile.

"Yes, not since you told me I hadn't suffered enough here on earth because I refused to renounce all humankind. Complex creations have complex problems. You always were too lazy and thought too highly of yourself to see that!" Aradia accused, though she lowered the dagger fractionally.

The devil rolled his eyes. "Complexity excuses all the disgusting things humans do?"

"You know, as the person who helped plan the murder attempt on the queen," Kat panted in the devil's direction, "and you, who stabbed me," she continued toward the first witch while glaring. "Neither of you is really coming from the moral high ground," she finished.

Behind her, Kat could feel Eric's tension ease as his wife proceeded to behave exactly like her usual self, save for the gasping breaths and pale complexion.

"Why aren't you doing anything?" Rebecca Devark startled everyone then as she stared at the otherworldly siblings with an arched brow.

While she may have seemed terribly calm, she hadn't so much as twitched since all the violence commenced, the stiffness in her countenance betraying her own fright.

"Oh, so you all waiting for a grand fight?" Aradia asked with a derisive chuckle.

"Well . . . Yeah!" Kat blurted indignantly. "Or did you attack me for the fun of it?"

Aradia glanced at her brother, who rolled his eyes, shaking his head as though the two had shared a brief, wordless conversation . . .

"Lady Katarina, my brother is unable to use his abilities against me, so there isn't much he can do as he knows I now have both your and his former ally's magic. Right now, he's making chitchat while waiting for me to make the first move so he can decide what to do," Aradia explained while sidling a little bit closer to the devil.

"Why won't his abilities affect you?" Alina questioned while leaning toward her husband.

"When he sealed away my magic, particularly strong emotions were sealed away as well. Love. Fear. A few others . . ."

"How does he expect you to learn how depraved humans are if you cannot empathize with them?" Eric interjected flatly while staring at the devil's back and silently wondering just how intelligent the children of the Gods truly were.

"I didn't know that sealing away her magic would have that particular cost. It may have also been caused by her subsequent curse." The devil shrugged, nonplussed, without turning around.

While the two siblings were managing to sound casual, there was still tension in the air that only seemed to increase with every passing moment.

"If you both want to go home, why don't you just unlock her abilities? Why are you dragging the rest of the world into your petty feud?" Eric wondered, his voice icy as he watched the siblings size each other up.

"Petty feud is an insulting description given how I was abandoned, injured, and made powerless. A state the women here should know that left me open to all manner of horrendous acts," Aradia retorted stonily. "And I'd like to try to set this world back to rights after he has scarred it so horribly. Though even that will of course come at a cost."

"It doesn't give you the right to kill thousands of people," Kat argued angrily.

"Do you know how many people *he* has killed? Do you know how he has manipulated and twisted the humans over centuries?! The Troivackian king here will even admit that sadly, sometimes there are sacrifices to be made for the long-term greater good," the first witch defended, her tone steady as she recognized the growing hostility in the room. "Sam doesn't want to return to the Forest of the Afterlife because then he would have to face our parents. But enough of this stalling. Are you going to help me or the devil?"

"You see . . . I would've absolutely jumped on that wagon and even been happy to help brainstorm a means of opening the portal without the death of thousands had you not kidnapped Likon and just *stabbed me!*" Kat lurched as she shouted and winced in pain as a result.

Aradia sighed. "Well, luckily for me, I suppose, I'm more interested in hearing what His Majesty has to say. The devil, the one responsible for trying to kill the queen countless times, is here. He is defenseless, and we can send him far from this world." Despite the first witch addressing Brendan, she never moved her sights from her brother, who took a long sidestep away from her.

"You would be open to finding an alternative solution to slaughtering my people?" Brendan asked slowly, but his voice was still an impressive rumble.

Aradia gave a partial shrug. "It can be discussed. Though I doubt you can. Your coven will not offer help no matter what you say. They have been wronged for too long. I'll need more lives in exchange."

"You don't need all the blood of the witches, only some?" the king continued while watching the siblings.

"She will have to kill people no matter what if she has to keep the portal open for a long period of time. It's more a matter of killing a handful of witches or thousands of humans, unless she means to bring over more beasts to gain more power here in Troivack, in which case she would need both," the devil clarified when his sister didn't respond immediately. "Also, don't forget she is the one who manufactured Witch's Brew and distributed it with the intent of killing people to start bringing the ancient beasts here in the first place. She hasn't explained at all what 'putting the world to rights' means either."

Aradia waived off the observation casually. "There is a lot to fix since the devil is the one responsible for centuries of wars, coups, and . . . the creation of mages."

"What?!"

"You son of a bitch!"

Mr. Kraft and Katarina burst out in fury at the same time, the redhead obviously being the one to have sworn.

Then she remembered Kezia and looked past the devil. "No offense, Kezia, but you are the exception, not the rule, generally."

Kezia didn't bother responding to Kat as she stared at the devil in alarm. Seeing this, Sam smiled coyly at her.

"It was fun to irk my sister's descendants."

"Eric, please kill him for me?" Kat murmured to her husband.

"Actually, about that," Eric spoke up again while speaking to the devil's back. "Don't *you* have any descendants?"

The devil couldn't resist looking over his shoulder at the prince, his eyes glittering in delight, but he didn't offer a response . . .

Nothing more could be said anyway, as the first witch flicked her dagger, and a stream of water wrapped itself around the devil, binding his arms.

In an instant, the room was plunged into darkness and menacing shadows that made everyone shrink back or fall to their knees in all-consuming terror.

Kat's magic flickered to life against her will, weakening her even more . . .

No one had the presence of mind to reason out what was happening, but they could hear the devil's voice in the abyss of tangible fear surrounding them. "I'll force the burning witch to use the rest of her powers and kill her, Aradia. She'll curse this land. That's what you want to avoid, isn't it? You're trying to take over this world for yourself in some skewed sense of justice . . . ? Well, good luck with whatever curse *she* produces."

A sudden movement and a sting along Sam's throat had his head snapping around to stare up at none other than Alina. The Troivackian queen was holding a small crossbow in her hands that must have been hidden by her throne . . .

"Don't kill him! If you do, we'll lose him again, and I won't know where he will be reborn," the first witch boomed.

Alina still aimed at the devil with watering eyes and trembling hands, even though her weapon needed to be reloaded. It had been an impressive shot given everything going on . . . The devil smirked at her, then directed more potent power toward the queen, reducing Alina to a weeping mess as Eric clutched Kat, muttering nonsensically as though in a partial soldier's spell. Mage Sebastian, Mr. Kraft, and Faucher were all doubled over. Ladies Kezia, Sarah, and Rebecca huddled together . . .

The first witch stared at her brother's triumphant face as he turned back to her.

"You are trying to cast me out so that you can rule peacefully in this world again without me, but if the burning witch dies, Daxaria and Troivack will be thrown into chaos, and you know it."

In the past, Aradia would cry, seethe, shout . . . She had come close to getting her way many times before, but usually Sam just had to dangle a few meaningful deaths in front of her to make her back off . . .

However, the fact that she had already killed people with her manufactured drug and was also prepared to slaughter thousands in a war to be rid of him, should have reminded the devil that she was not going to utilize her old approaches.

Aradia laughed.

While the throne room was permeated with her brother's frightening abilities, she sounded giddy as she tugged him closer by using her rope of water.

"I guess it's a good thing I have a backup plan. Sorry, Lady Sarah." She looked over her shoulder at her former fellow handmaiden. "Our recent friendship really was lovely, and I meant what I said to you." Aradia managed a hint of an apology in her gaze during the mysterious message before she returned her brilliant smile to her brother. With her free hand, she reached inside her pants pocket and procured a peculiar brass item that emitted a ticking noise that only the devil could hear in its proximity. It had a faint white glow emitting from its round seams that reminded him of mage crystals . . . and he could even feel the same sort of power starting to fill the throne room . . .

The first witch clicked a knob on the top and then . . .

Something strange happened.

Aradia and the devil disappeared in an instant.

The shadows vanished just as suddenly as they had appeared.

Sniffles and shaking breaths filled the gloriously restored peace.

Despite the throne room being cold, its absence of evil made it feel like it was bathed in the warmest light the Goddess herself could create.

"W-Where'd . . . they go?" Brendan demanded raspily, his hand bracing against the marbled floor in front of his throne.

It took everyone else far longer to collect themselves, but finally Mr. Kraft responded.

"There is no trace of them or any magic. We could . . ." He paused to swallow. "We could ask the guards outside if anyone left . . . but I see nothing. It's as if they disappeared."

Brendan let out a shuddering breath as a bead of cold sweat rolled down his spine.

"Alina, are you alright?" he asked, completely forgoing proper formality in light of the living nightmare they all had just suffered.

Brendan had closed his eyes and was taking calming breaths after asking the question, but when he didn't hear his wife's response, his eyes flew open. Looking to his left, he could see Alina curled on her side, trembling.

"Alina?" Brendan dove for her, carefully turning her over to see her face white as snow and scrunched in pain. His gaze dropped to her hands that were grasping her middle.

"Gods—PHYSICIAN!" Brendan roared loud enough that it felt as though the windows rattled.

"What's wrong?!" Eric called from his place at the bottom of the steps where Kat was working on standing with his help.

The king didn't respond as he held Alina closer. Ladies Kezia, Sarah, and Rebecca moved to the bottom of the stairs to the thrones and froze, unsure of whether to move closer or not.

"Alina, love . . . What is . . ." Brendan was whispering hurriedly, hoping he could get a response out of her, but she only gasped as though physically unable to respond while hunching even farther over her middle . . .

Lady Rebecca turned and flew out of the room, shouting again for a physician as everyone else waited with growing dread over what they suspected may be happening to the beloved queen.

CHAPTER 52

LOST LOVE

Aradia dropped the devil beside Likon's unconscious body and sheathed the dagger.

She didn't need to worry about subduing her brother given that they happened to be in a large, drafty abandoned building containing a stone golem, an imp, and a sirin.

Pulling out her watch, she clicked it again, and time resumed its usual course.

Sam jolted in alarm and instantly sprang to his feet while looking around frantically.

Aradia chuckled. "I haven't seen you this flustered since that time I got you stuck in a tree leagues up in the sky."

"What magic was that? That wasn't witchcraft." The devil breathed, then startled into stillness once more when he laid eyes on the ancient beasts that stood behind his sister.

"Tak?!" he stared up into the glowing eyes of the golem before dropping his astounded face to the sirin. "Hafey . . . and . . . Viellen." The devil fell into a brief shock as he gaped at the imp in particular. "Viellen, it's been . . . How are . . . Why are . . ."

The imp shook his head sadly. "We just want you to come home."

The devil's right hand quivered. "You . . . You really opted to work with *Aradia*?! After she told our parents you should just return to the Forest of the Afterlife?! This world was supposed to be yours! *She* betrayed you!" Sam was becoming more emotional than he had been in years.

"Not anymore." Viellen the imp's eyes lowered sadly, his pupils only spinning once. "This world is corrupting you, master. Mistress is right."

Sam stalked up to his former friend and didn't stop until his nose nearly bumped into the imp's chest. "You really are going to let these horrid creatures win this world? After you created the waterways of Lobahl's capital? After you crafted the infamous waterfall outside of Sorlia in Daxaria? Those were things of beauty for *our* kin to enjoy! Not to let the humans ruin!"

"Master, it is the will of the Gods that this place be left to the humans."

"NO!" Sam roared and whirled around to stalk up to the golem. "Tak, you were as furious as I was! You helped bind Aradia! I know you do not change easily or surrender your grudges! What has she done to you?!"

"I didn't do anything, Sam. Why didn't you just have faith in our parents that there was a better place for them somewhere?" Aradia spoke to her brother's back quietly.

Sam rounded on her and moved quickly back to seethe down into her face while seizing the front of her tunic. "Then what? The Gods create some new creature that cannot control its selfishness and greed, and they are chased out again?"

"You are thinking of this all wrong." Aradia reached up and gently wrapped her hand around her brother's wrist. "I already know humans aren't as worthy as our kin. That is why the beasts were asked to leave. To punish the humans. Without the golems, earthquakes have decimated their cities and sinkholes have swallowed their homes. Without the sirins, thousands of ships have sunk, and the weather is difficult for humans to predict because they can't read the winds. Without the imps, there have been floods, tsunamis, and so, so much more. Lastly, they do not have the wisdom and warmth the dragons could provide . . . Humans *are* suffering. "

"They don't even see their absence as a punishment! They see it as a war won!"

"You could've helped them to see the truth and conquer their fears. But you chose to push them deeper into their chaotic anxiety," Aradia bit back, her eyes turning hard.

"Humankind was a lost cause long before the ancient beasts retreated. You should already know this though."

"Following your logic, was your recent loyal follower, Leo, a disgusting being who you loathed and had no faith in?"

The devil snarled terrifyingly. "He was prone to violence and greed. He was prideful, arrogant, and—"

"He loved you like a brother. Just like generations of your other followers have loved you as a son, nephew, uncle, and even *husband*. Oh, yes.

I know all about your two marriages. Were those people disgusting and undeserving too?"

"That first marriage, she left me. The second —"

"He died. Hardly some large betrayal," Aradia finished while boring down on her brother. And sure enough, his grip on her tunic weakened . . .

"He — Kalwen — was an addict. He was selfish." Sam's eyes narrowed, but he wasn't able to properly glare . . .

"You could have helped him, but instead you let him kill himself slowly."

"*He made me swear not to use my abilities on him. He chose to struggle and die alone and leave me!*" the devil roared, his shout ringing around the large empty space.

Aradia merely tilted her head and raised an eyebrow.

"He wanted you to feel equal to him and not like a caretaker. He did his best until the end. For you. How is it I can't feel love and yet you can't see that?"

Sam was silent as he stared hatefully at his sister, who remained infuriatingly calm.

"I'm really going to kill you this time."

"No, brother. You won't. You're going home. You're going to let our mother and father take care of you. I am going to fix the mess you made with these humans, and even though I don't have your abilities, I know they can be better than they are. I'm going to take power from the witches of Daxaria to avoid them disrupting the balance, and Troivack will progress without any witches as it could've done years ago if it weren't for your meddling and turning it into an oppressive land."

"Are you saying you intend to kill thousands because you think you can save the world?" Sam studied his sister's unnervingly unemotional face. "You think you can act as a sort of demigod to them and fix it all? Is this for control? For you to feel powerful again? Who are you to say they should be anything than what they are?"

Aradia raised her eyebrow, and then with an expert hit and kick sent her brother sprawling onto his back.

She stared down at him dispassionately. "I'm going to make the world *and* you better."

"That . . ." the devil wheezed, his back aching. "Is a load of fucking nonsense. You just miss . . . being the golden child of the Gods. You can't even feel love anymore. You can't possibly want anything good for others."

Aradia crouched down, noticing out of the corner of her eye the imp flinch and look away from the scene.

"That's where you're wrong. I see the benefits of a kinder, more balanced world for everyone involved. A cruel world is destined to eat itself until there is nothing left. I don't need feelings to know that. I just need to not be an idiot blinded by pain like you."

Kat sat in the corridor on a chest with her left hand pressing a mound of gauze to her wound with Eric at her right side, his elbows braced against his knees, his eyes gazing blindly ahead.

Lady Rebecca stood staring at the closed chamber door belonging to the king and queen with her hands clasped in front of herself in silence.

Meanwhile, Lady Kezia was reunited with Prince Henry and her son, Elio, elsewhere in the castle, and Lady Sarah was resting in her chamber with her father, who was still recovering from the shock of Kat's earlier magical outburst.

Faucher, Mage Sebastian, and Mr. Kraft had all excused themselves to go make further preparations for the attack that was to come, following the carefully laid plans that had been set by Brendan . . .

Presently, the king was in the chamber with the court physician, along with Duchess Annika Ashowan, who had been summoned by the queen between gasps . . .

None of the trio that waited outside could tear their minds away from what was happening to Alina, despite the time for battle nearing.

For once, Rebecca Devark didn't hide the genuine fear and worry in her face as she awaited news of the fate of her daughter-in-law and grandchild.

As time drifted on, nighttime crept across the windows, prompting the servants to light the torches as they passed through the halls. Many of them cast concerned glances at the quiet chamber as they moved.

Word was traveling quickly through the castle that there had been an attack from a rebel group. According to the news, Lady Katarina was injured trying to protect the monarchs, but the queen was in a precarious state with the unborn prince or princess as a result . . .

It was a partially fabricated rumor made up by Faucher to ensure no one blamed Kat or learned that the children of the Gods themselves had been present.

His plan seemed to be working too, as servants bowed reverently toward Kat when they passed and carried on their duties quietly.

When smells of dinner started wafting through the castle, Kat's stomach let out a faint gurgle.

"You should eat something. Do you mind if I summon Lady Kezia to take you?" Eric asked softly, his darkened hazel eyes gentling when he turned to his wife.

She sat up as straight as her fresh stitches would allow, her gaze defiant. "I'm staying right here until I hear everything is alright."

A pained knowingness filled Eric's face as he shook his head and reached out to grasp Kat's hand.

"It isn't alright, Kat. It only takes this long when . . . when the babe needs to come out," he finished with a rasp.

Rebecca's head snapped to stare at the prince, tears filling her eyes, but she still didn't say anything.

The prince met the former queen's gaze somberly. "I remember it with my mother well enough." He swallowed. "No, what we are waiting to hear . . . is whether Alina is fine and can make a full recovery."

Kat felt a lump harden in her throat before she looked at the door, grief rising in her chest . . .

Which was when the chamber door opened and out stepped Brendan wearing a loosened black tunic and pants, his face ashen, his dark eyes fixed on the floor and looking suspiciously red.

"Your Majesty." Rebecca reached toward her son. But without looking at his mother, Brendan's hand clenched into a fist, stopping her.

"The physician needs privacy with Her Majesty. I'll be back in a moment."

"Is Alina alright?" Kat insisted while pushing to her feet, though the movement made her vision temporarily spin.

Brendan's eyes fluttered. He swayed as though he were about to walk away without bothering to respond, but in the final moment decided that his wife's brother and best friend deserved to know. "She . . . will recover. Eventually. I'll see to the burial rites in the morning."

Then he strode away, incapable of saying anything else.

"Gods . . . Alina . . ." Kat faced the door and reached for the handle.

"Give her time," Eric called out, though his words sounded strangled. Tears fell from his eyes and ran down his nose until they fell to the corridor floor. Kat looked to Rebecca, but she was staring after her son while she, too, openly wept.

She then left in the same direction Brendan had headed.

Kat felt her lip quiver as she cried in the heartbreaking silence.

Without knowing what else there was to say, Eric covered his face with his hand and mourned his sister's loss.

In all her life, Kat had never experienced sadness or grief as poignant as what she felt in that moment. She stared helplessly at the door, wanting to be with her friend more than anything . . .

She instead sat down and pulled her husband to her, and the two grieved together, wishing that the fates didn't have to be so cruel to someone they loved so much . . . or to the innocent life that they had loved unconditionally without having ever met in this lifetime.

Rebecca found her son staring out a window at the starry night, his hands braced against the window ledge.

She watched him. Her heart felt as though it were being clawed to pieces in her chest as she sensed the devastation of her eldest son. Her entire being ached with restrained emotions that she had no idea how to express with words.

"Alina didn't want to know . . . if it was a daughter or a son," the king said without turning to face his mother.

"She may wish to know later," Rebecca supplied softly.

"It was a son."

The former queen flinched at the roughness in Brendan's voice, instantly recognizing that he was succumbing to tears of his own.

"It . . . was . . . *my* son. *Our* son . . ."

Rebecca barely managed to take in a shuddering breath.

And then Brendan, the child king who had grown to be a man so stoic, so strong and steady, that he was compared to mountains . . . crumbled.

The heels of his palms came to his eyes as he crouched down and surrendered to his broken heart.

Rebecca, before she could think of what may or may not be proper, had him in her arms.

She hadn't done anything motherly toward him in two decades . . . but none of that mattered.

Not when her child, who had done everything right in his life, had been beaten so mercilessly.

"Brendan," she whispered while she held him, her voice thin and weak as it never was.

"I'm so sorry."

The two remained in the corridor, undisturbed, attempting to find comfort for a wound that was deeper than any physical or emotional one that could be dealt.

There never was anything but pain and silence after the loss of a child.

Brendan did his best not to collapse when he knew he needed to return to his wife, whom he had left muffling her screams into the shoulder of Annika Ashowan as the physician herded him out to give both him and the queen a moment apart to grieve.

Alina had cried and bit down on their bed linens to stop herself from causing a breathing attack, all the while asking the Gods why they would do such a thing . . . And yet no answer had come.

Nor would it ever.

All that would come of it was her ravaged heart that would never be the same again and the barbed memory of another loss she would never fully recover from.

Why did she have to lose a life she was prepared to love wholly? Why, when she had done all she could, been all she could . . . Why did she have to pay such a price in exchange for a hole in her soul?

It was an injustice she knew countless other women felt, and yet despite knowing she was far from alone in experiencing it, it still changed her and broke her in a way she never could have imagined.

CHAPTER 53

AN UNBURDENED UNION

Night had wrapped the castle in its embrace, and within its starry arms, a heavy, solemn mood rested as news of the queen's miscarriage and the attack that caused it spread throughout the corridors.

There was much to do, but they were running out of time . . .

Brendan Devark had returned to his chamber after gathering himself, but learned from the physician that his wife insisted he didn't need to stay with her and should instead see to the preparations for the coming battle.

Katarina and Eric stared at the king, who nodded sternly at the news through the crack of his chamber door, then he turned to stare at his brother-and sister-in-law. Rebecca Devark had already taken her leave to see about ordering a hearty broth for the queen from the kitchens.

"Your Highness, Faucher is already seeing to last-minute preparations. Most have left for their posts around Vessa with a unit remaining here. I trust Faucher to lead the men in the north where the rebels are predicted to arrive from. I will be with Faucher unless there is a sighting in the west facing the desert with the intention of flanking Faucher's men once the fighting begins. Dante Faucher will be leading the east, and I have tasked Sir Cleophus Miller with leading the men in the south, though should the rebels break through the walls of Vessa, Sir Miller will return to the castle," Brendan explained in his usual gruff tones.

Eric stood as the king spoke, his saddened face hardening to one of dutiful resolve.

"I understand. Who will be tasked with managing the unit left to guard the castle?"

"Duke Siata—you've met the man. Though you may not have spoken at length, as he is a quiet—"

"I know him," Eric interrupted while nodding in understanding. "He is quiet, but intelligent. However, I never could discern his relationship with Duke Icarus."

Brendan drew his shoulders straight as his mind slipped back into the all-consuming ways of war.

"While I suspect he did succumb to some pressures from Duke Sebastian Icarus, I do not believe him a traitor. I ask that you assist him and keep an eye on him."

Eric bowed. "Yes, Your Majesty."

Brendan jerked his chin down in thanks, then looked at Kat . . .

She was staring dazedly at the closed chamber door.

Brendan's stomach lurched sickeningly, his anger and pain over events outside of his control surging forward once more.

"Lady Katarina, I believe you will be fine to see the queen. I also ask that you stay by her side during the coming battle. I understand you are injured and, therefore, your options for combat are limited, but I still trust that you will do all you can to keep Her Majesty safe. I will summon the inner council as you requested to see if we can regain some of your power."

Kat turned to the king, her troubled countenance remaining for a breath before her golden eyes drifted down to the floor. Then in the next moment, she lifted her chin with determination. "Thank you, Your Majesty."

Brendan lowered his eyes in thanks, then stalked back down the corridor.

Kat turned to Eric, and the two of them shared a long, heartfelt look whereby they understood each other perfectly.

Things were grim, but they were going to fight until the end no matter what.

Eric gently pulled Kat toward himself and planted a kiss on her forehead before saying, "Tell Alina I love her and am here if she needs anything."

"I will. Keep Duke Siata in check."

Eric grimaced. "He had better not be a traitor. I think we've all experienced enough betrayal these last few days to last a lifetime."

"Agreed." Kat let out a huff of annoyance. "The only bright side I'm seeing is that the first witch hinted that I'm finished being stabbed."

"That would be nice," Eric remarked idly.

Kat gave his shoulder an affectionate shove. "See you."

He gave her an equally small push back. "No more injuries?"

"That's the plan."

Eric bobbed his head in satisfaction, and then the two turned to tackle their set tasks.

With her heart leaping to her throat, Kat reached for the door handle to Alina's chamber while distantly hearing her husband ordering the guards at the end of the hall to take their posts back in front of the queen's chamber. With Brendan and Eric no longer there, the guards' services were required again.

Kat stepped into the room and first saw the physician with his sleeves rolled up, scrubbing off his arms in front of the fire using a white washbasin. His dour expression was indicative of the tragedy that had just taken place.

The redhead barely resisted wrinkling her nose at the smell of the room . . . The metallic scent of blood, sweat, and unidentifiable others told the unfortunate story of what had just taken place.

Closing the door behind her, Kat took the extra moment with her back turned toward the bed to school her expression before facing Alina.

Once she had accomplished this, she faced the Troivackian queen, and discovered Alina looked sickly, with dark stress lines under her eyes. She kept her gaze lowered while Annika Ashowan finished braiding her hair as she sat in a clean white night shift.

Kat cleared her throat, not trusting herself to give a proper greeting.

When Alina's eyes lifted, she stared at the wall across from her rather than at her friend, her face hardening.

"Did Brendan go check on the knights?" she asked, her voice rasping as she spoke. The hoarse state of her throat revealing she had spent a great deal of time shouting and crying throughout the night.

"He did. Most of the knights are already marching to the borders of Vessa, and Duke Siata will be directing the unit in the castle. Eric will stay behind to help," Kat repeated stiffly as the physician finished packing up his tools, then picked up a box covered in a white sheet . . . Kat pointedly ignored that last part as well as the bloody towels in a pile by the fire.

"Duke Siata? He couldn't command the most obedient dog in the world. His Majesty is probably trusting Eric to take care of things."

Kat nervously shuffled a little closer to the bed as the physician closed the door behind him.

"You've been stitched up? You're alright?" Alina continued, her head turning toward Kat but her eyes not yet fully finding her friend.

"Oh, I'm fine. Still a bit weak from the drugging, but I have a tentative idea about how to get back some power."

"I'm glad to hear you're safe." Alina met Kat's gaze at last, and the redhead almost flinched.

The crushing despair in Alina's eyes . . . The sadness that ripped through her. Kat could feel echoes of the trauma from Alina's look alone . . .

It was hard, but Kat somehow managed to swallow and speak again just as her mother finished braiding the queen's hair.

"I'm sorry, Alina."

The queen's eyes fluttered, and she moved her attention back to the wall. "It wasn't meant to be. Besides, at least I can help with preparations without worrying anymore." She glanced over her shoulder in thanks at Annika, who gave a subtle, warm smile.

Kat fidgeted. "You can rest. I'm sure we all can handle—"

"The children of the Gods are making us their pawns, and your father is unconscious. The coven refuses to help us because of how they've been treated. It's too late to summon help from Daxaria or the Coven of Wittica. This is not the time to wallow in grieving." Alina pushed herself off the side of her bed and stood.

Kat braced herself to run to Alina's side in the event that she collapsed, but she didn't.

"Lady Annika, do you happen to have a spare pair of trousers I may borrow?"

The duchess curtsied gracefully. "I do, Your Majesty."

"Good, please fetch those for me."

Annika rose without another word and left to retrieve the clothing, though she looked at her daughter with a raised eyebrow and softness that Kat interpreted to mean that it was alright . . . that it wasn't a bad thing that Alina was making such a request.

When the door had closed behind the duchess, Kat allowed her shoulders to sag fractionally. "Gods, Alina, are you sure—"

"They made me lose my child. I am not going to lie down and do nothing when the devil and first witch threaten my citizens as well. If I can survive what I just went through? I can survive them."

Kat didn't respond straight away. She was too taken aback. Beneath her friend's intense mournful suffering, rage burned, and there was a steeliness to it that gave Kat the distinct impression that Alina had made up her mind. But more than that, she had had enough of being beaten down.

The redhead crossed her arm over her middle and bowed. "Of course, Your Majesty."

"Kat?"

The redhead righted herself and met the queen's stare to find a rather startling shift in emotion.

"Yes, Your Majesty?"

Alina's eyes drifted away before she took in a deep, trembling breath and let it out again.

"Thank you. Thank you for being my friend. For . . . For working so hard for me. For protecting me. I'm sorry if I haven't been as appreciative of you as you deserve. I have needed you . . . Your strength, your terrible humor . . . All of you. You've always given me everything you can, and I see that now. I wasn't as respectful as I should have been to your boundaries or to your struggles with opening up, and I'm sorry. You've been there for me from day one, and I . . . I don't think I can honestly say I've done the same for you. I'm sorry."

Kat blushed scarlet. "Good Gods, what in the world—"

"No, no. Please don't say anything." Alina waved off her words. "I have been able to count on you and your mother more than some of my own flesh and blood. I don't know how to be a good friend to someone as amazing as you, so thank you again . . . Thank you for being patient."

Opening and closing her mouth, Kat wasn't certain if she was allowed to speak yet, so she raised her hand like a student in lessons.

Alina couldn't help but give a smile. "Yes?"

"Can I ask what prompted this wildly . . . kind . . . speech?"

Amazingly, the queen's smile remained as she dropped her eyes to the floor in thought. "I guess . . . while I was going through the absolute hell of passing the child . . . I realized if everything burned down around me, you'd be there. Brendan will have to tend to the kingdom as he should and I want him to, but you, no matter what, I know you will do your best to support me, and it dawned on me then that I have not properly thanked you."

"Well, uh . . . thanks, and . . . you know I love you . . ."

"I know. I love you too."

"Good, good . . ." Kat cleared her throat awkwardly, then reached up and rubbed the back of her neck. "Are you sure you're able to move around?"

"The worst of it was a while ago. I've mostly just been monitored while crying and recovering the past little while. The physician says everything seemed alright for me to move around at least, though there will be some aftereffects. I've taken some pain relievers for now."

Kat's hands gripped periodically into fists.

"I . . . I'm going to be a little weaker than normal, but at least . . . erm . . ." Alina fumbled uncharacteristically, her voice turning to a croak. "I shouldn't have . . . other issues with . . . another pregnancy . . . that the physician could see . . . Godsdamn, I swear . . . I'm done with crying." The queen turned, her hands on her hips as she looked to the ceiling and blinked back tears. "Now's not the time. Later. I can think about this later," she breathed the words roughly to herself.

Kat felt her mind flounder for what to say to help, something to make her friend feel better . . .

"Would you like to see me piss off your inner council so that I can hopefully get back some of my magic?"

Alina let out a choked laugh that had her looking back at her friend's desperate expression. Tears were falling down her face, but she did seem as though she were calming down again. "Gods, yes. Shall we go once I put on a pair of pants?"

Kat nodded while giving a tentative smile. "Of course. I think seeing you dressed as a man is going to help rile them up."

Alina wiped the tears off her face while giving another chuckle.

"Can I hug you?" Kat asked as her chest ached.

"Of course," Alina responded, her voice a mixture of happiness, relief, and sadness.

That was all the permission Kat needed as she swept over to her friend and wrapped her in a tight embrace.

"You're amazing, you know that? Everything is going to be fine because you're acting exactly how a queen should." Kat knew she was babbling, but she couldn't help it. Her emotions were overwhelming, and she wished she had some other means of offering even more strength to her friend.

"I don't feel amazing right now, but . . . you'll be beside me during this, right?"

"Of course. I'm here as long as you want me," Kat reassured her friend.

"You'll have to go back to Daxaria one day."

"You're sending me mixed signals."

Alina laughed and hugged Kat tighter. While it felt like her world was falling apart, at the very least she had the brilliant warmth of Katarina Ashowan at her side. And with a woman like her? Well . . . even the children of the Gods should be nervous.

Which was a very good thing, as that was when one of the warning bells lining the gates of Vessa clanged through the night . . . making the two women pull apart and listen, wide-eyed.

"Oh Gods . . . The rebels . . . The first witch . . . They're already here." Alina rounded back to Kat, her previous fury burning bright in her eyes once more. "We better get you some of your magic back, and quickly. I don't know if we'll all survive without it."

CHAPTER 54

AN INVIGORATING INITIATIVE

Everyone was alarmed to hear the quickness with which the rebels were approaching. They had been under the assumption that they at least had a few days to organize . . .

However, it made the most sense on their opponents' end to attack while the king and his army were unprepared.

Kat had her armor on and her sword attached to her side, though she moved far more slowly than she usually did thanks to her injury and weakened magic; she sincerely hoped she'd be able to absorb enough hatred from the council to recover more . . .

She had agreed to meet Alina in front of the council room doors and happened to be the first to arrive.

Serving staff, still working despite the pending conflict, rushed by her. As she waited, husbands of the servants and noblewomen passed with their arms around their wives and daughters, commanding them to the king's cellars to wait until the fighting had concluded.

Children clutched onto hands or skirts belonging to their mothers, fathers, nannies, or grandparents. Some cried amidst the chaos erupting around them, some had fallen into silence out of fear.

Kat leaned her shoulder against the wall, taking long, slow, deep breaths and thinking she may have to sit down on the floor soon when at long last Alina appeared.

The busy corridor stopped its harried movement, and everyone parted for their queen in stunned silence.

Alina wore black pants, a black tunic, a brown leather vest, a small crossbow over her back and her braid coiled into a tight bun at the back of her neck. She didn't wear a speck of jewelry, and while she still looked poorly, there was a determination and iciness in her expression that discouraged any comments from the vassals she passed. Instead, the nobility and servants bowed and curtsied as was expected.

Ladies Sarah, Rebecca, Kezia, and Annika followed behind the queen . . .

Each of them also wore trousers. Even Katarina's own mother had a crossbow on her back and knives on her hips.

Kat gaped in astonishment.

She was so stunned that she almost forgot to bow when Alina finally reached her.

"Ready to do what you do best?" Alina asked with an arched eyebrow.

Kat couldn't help but grin as she leaned around Alina to stare at Lady Rebecca. "How does it feel to wear pants, ma'am?"

Lady Rebecca stared back irritably, and that was when Kat belatedly noticed something else shocking . . .

The former Troivackian queen, the exemplary traditional Troivackian woman . . . wasn't wearing her hair wrap, and as it turned out . . . she had short hair.

The same length as a man's. Cut close to her scalp. It was dark and streaked with white . . .

But it only made her appear bolder, more daring . . . even younger in age . . .

"Actually, how *did* Lady Rebecca end up in pants . . . ?" Kat turned to Alina, who was staring at her friend flatly.

"We can discuss the pants later."

"Where did you even get pants for everyone? I know my mother's size fits you, but they all—"

"Kat. We are about to be in a battle. Focus. Now, what do you say? Let's go aggravate some councilmen." Alina gave a dry smile, and while it didn't have its usual brightness, Kat could still see the flicker of the kind soul of her friend.

"Well . . . it *is* a hobby of mine to be annoying . . ."

Brendan stared at the army of men drawing closer to the walls of Vessa, the sky had only just started to lighten as daybreak approached. Dusty pinks and pale blues blushing over the horizon revealed the size of the army before him.

"We've beaten worse," Faucher noted gruffly beside the king.

"I don't see the magical beasts, and that concerns me," Brendan returned levelly. "Though at least it appears they are only coming from the north. We can focus more of our efforts here. Unless the beasts show up elsewhere."

Faucher nodded. "We'll keep a good portion of the men at their original posts. They know to wait for the signal before joining us if we end up need-ing aid."

Brendan grunted.

"Where did you choose to station Sir Cas and Sir Vohn?"

"At the castle. They are guarding Her Majesty and will follow His High-ness's orders."

"Lady Katarina can help," Faucher said more to himself than the king.

Brendan slid a sideways glance at his teacher. "She was stabbed and drained of magic. While she can still manage better than the average sol-dier, even *her* power has limits."

A defeated yet fond smile filled Faucher's face.

"Oh . . . I don't know. She told me before we left that she had a gut feel-ing that things would be alright."

"She was stabbed in the gut. That is concerning, not comforting," Bren-dan retorted glibly.

Faucher's grin dimmed, but he tilted his head thoughtfully over his shoulder as he recalled Kat's intense determination and then thought about how his own daughter had turned into a confident, willful young woman, capable of shouting at the most terrifying knight in the entire kingdom because of that outrageous redheaded woman . . .

"I suppose she's made me a bit mad as well, but I think she might be right. Things will be alright."

Brendan didn't dismiss Faucher's out-of-character musings a second time. Rather, he stared at the military leader with softening eyes.

"Are you pleased to have gotten to teach her after all?"

Faucher cleared his throat, then scowled. "She's still a pain in the arse, and I want a tax exemption on the amount of food we had to purchase in bulk because of her."

Surprisingly, Brendan gave a brief, low chuckle.

"I suppose we shall see if we make it through a skirmish against the chil-dren of the Gods."

Faucher suddenly stilled, color draining from his face . . .

He rounded on the king, the sharp wind on his cheeks stinging.

"Your Majesty, the gates to the city have been closed since the devil was brought to the castle."

Brendan frowned . . . until he realized what Faucher was getting at. "The first witch could still be in the city . . . The tunnels!"

"MAGE SEBASTIAN!" Faucher roared over the heads of the archers that already had their arrows notched.

Mage Sebastian hurried over, his ponytail fluttering in the wind. "Yes, Leader Faucher?"

"Send a missive to Mr. Kraft. *Now*. The witches need to get out of the tunnels. They are in danger—the devil and the first witch might be nearby, and she may intend to gather her sacrifices while keeping us distracted. Make them scatter! No more than two witches can stick together at a time!"

The mage's eyes widened, and without a word, he turned and sprinted back to the nearest tower where he might be able to magically send the missive.

"How did I not think of that?!" Brendan's hand gripped the hilt of his sword, his eyes wide as he stared at Faucher.

"Everything is in chaos right now, Your Majesty. Sometimes we miss the obvious. But we can't change the past. Remember, don't get bogged down from an error; just keep fighting. You'll be overwhelmed otherwise."

Brendan swallowed with difficulty while slowly shaking his head.

"Gods, help us . . . I hope we get them out in time."

"Tak, are you ready?" Aradia peered up at the stone golem, who didn't verbally respond but nodded his great head slowly, the vines hanging around his head swinging as he did so.

"Viellen, you have Likon? Hafey, how is my brother?" Aradia called back to the two ancient beasts who stood a short way behind her with their charges unconscious. Viellen carried Likon gagged and bound, while the sirin merely floated the devil along, his head rolling limply on his shoulders.

Aradia popped open the brass device she kept in her pocket and smiled at it lovingly. She had called it Chronos, and it was her finest creation ever, even if it did burn through magic at an alarming rate when she needed to stop the flow of life . . .

A single mage crystal allowed her to stop time for two minutes, a hefty price given the rarity of mage crystals, but in her estimation, it was worth it. She could move about freely, as could anyone who touched her when she initially cast its magic.

Though even when she wasn't using it to move between moments, it was a damn useful thing . . .

It quantified time. It measured it, broke it down, and it was never wrong. It took her centuries to develop, and when she had succeeded . . . ? Gods, it was incredible.

"We are prepared, mistress." Viellen lowered his head and stepped protectively in front of Sam, who floated innocuously beside Hafey.

The first witch battled back a twinge of bitterness in her chest.

It never mattered what she had said or done since their first battle centuries ago . . . The ancient beasts always adored her brother.

She turned to face the rock wall before her and raised her hand.

Tak lifted back his great arm, swung it powerfully, and with a great crushing boom, he broke through the barrier that he himself had built a few decades ago.

"Mr. Levin," Aradia hollered after the dust had settled. "How many witches did you say had been discovered?"

The king's former assistant shuffled toward the first witch, his shoulders hunched fearfully when the sirin's beady red eyes followed him.

"Two hundred sixty-three."

"Excellent. We should at the very least be able to catch five." Aradia proceeded deeper into the tunnel. Her hair was tied back in a high ponytail and swung back and forth as she climbed through the wide opening effortlessly.

Everything was going according to plan.

Katarina Ashowan would have no way of absorbing enough power to be a threat, and Finlay Ashowan was unconscious, which meant his familiar couldn't share any of his information with anyone. The king would be trying to hold off the rebel army, and that meant Aradia could open her portal after sacrificing a few witches, return her brother, and then retreat to her own hideout to continue reshaping the country. If she managed to kill a few extra thousand men, she could bring over even more ancient beasts to help build her power as well. She knew she'd need them if she were going to make the changes she wanted to as efficiently as possible.

It would've been better if the king had simply offered up the witches and she could've attacked Vessa since she'd already received what she wanted, making it a surprise and giving her army an advantage. She wondered what would've stopped him from falling for her trap and so decided to bait the king's former assistant.

"Was there any particular reason the king wouldn't want to sacrifice five witches to avoid the war?"

"H-His Majesty knows that powerful people offering a cheap solution to a valuable problem is always more costly than it seems," Mr. Levin defended his former employer, his hands clenching at his sides as sweat rolled down his back.

Despite the assistant knowing his wife Caroline was safe with their daughter back at the other end of the tunnels the first witch could tell he was struggling with his betrayal . . .

"I appreciate your admiration for your king, Mr. Levin. It's a shame you two had to part ways," Aradia noted lightly as she heard distant shouts down the tunnels where the few remaining Coven of Aguas members had lived for years. "I wish I could have taken the time to convince His Majesty and his council, but . . . well . . . my brother was always the one who was patient and persuasive."

She continued striding through the tunnels, waiting for the bravest and ideally strongest witches of the coven to rush at them, making everything perfectly easy to continue with their plans.

But no one came.

Her eyebrows twitching toward a frown, Aradia, Mr. Levin, and the ancient beasts continued following the tunnels only to find . . .

They'd been abandoned.

"T-They may have decided to evacuate into Lady Elena Souros's keep!" Mr. Levin suggested hastily when he noticed the first witch's expression darkening.

Her eyes slid over her shoulder toward the assistant, making the man want to cower even more than he already was, but she didn't say a word.

It was hard to believe the bumbling, awkward Lady Wynonna Vesey was the very same woman before him. She had acted the part of a drunken, well-meaning, airheaded noblewoman so perfectly . . .

They continued, the silence thick around them. Being so far underground, there wasn't any sound they could hear that could indicate anything about the battle that waged north of Vessa, meaning by the time they reached the stairwell that would lead them up and into Lady Elena's keep, the first witch was impatient.

"Tak?" Aradia looked back at the poor stone golem that was already nearly doubled over to fit in the narrow tunnel. "Do you think you can dig upward safely so that we can all pass through?"

The golem rumbled a response that wasn't quite coherent, but the first witch understood nonetheless.

Aradia and the other ancient beasts with their captives ducked into the nearby doorways of the apartments, allowing Tak to squeeze through to peer up the stairs.

Tak let out two short clacking noises.

"It's alright if you burst through part of the floor as long as we don't get crushed," Aradia responded reasonably, though she was getting more tense with every moment that passed.

That was one downside to her invention of Chronos . . . She was all too aware of how precious time was.

The sound of stone grinding and crumbling started echoing down to Aradia and the others as they waited.

Small rocks rained down on the stone golem as he worked, reshaping the stairwell, making it wider until . . .

He broke through the cellar wall and a bit of the floor above.

Tak opened his mouth to inform the first witch that he was finished, only the golem was distracted . . . by the fattest raccoon he had ever seen in his exceedingly long life. It was staring at him, its teeth bared as if smiling.

He had never seen such a creature . . . How was it still alive? Could it move? It was somewhat cute . . . Back when he lived in that realm, he had seen raccoons before, but none ever as large as that one . . .

Tak tilted his massive head, intrigued by the creature, but that was when the large raccoon opened its mouth and let out a savage shriek.

The next thing the golem knew, the ceiling collapsed over him, burying him back under the ground of what had to have been three floors of Lady Elena Souros's keep.

Reggie the raccoon chirped and waddled away.

There was much to see to for his dear decay witch. Though of course there were two other familiars nearby that were going to help.

Kraken the empurror and Piña Colada.

CHAPTER 55

PUSHING POWER

Kat stood before the council already lightheaded.
She wouldn't be able to last long . . .

Especially given that the men before her were more fearful than angry.

"Good to see you all. How do you like the new fashion choices of the ladies here?" She opened with a great deal of forced taunting.

The noblewomen shared looks of confusion and apprehension over her graceless attempt but didn't say anything.

Meanwhile, no anger could be sensed from the council . . .

"Godsdamnit," Kat uttered without trying to be quiet.

At least that made one or two of the men stiffen.

"The lot of you are bloody stupid, you know that? You're scared of me when I wasn't able to control myself thanks to being dosed by one of your very own elite knights. I've seen men shit themselves when they drink! Well . . . not really," Kat added when she noticed her mother shift behind her. "But I've certainly heard about it! I get drugged against my will and you think I'm some evil spawn of the world because I didn't have perfect control of myself under one of the most potent drugs in existence?"

"You tried to kill us!" One nobleman stood from his seat, his hands reaching for the council table that was no longer there, which made him balk for a moment.

"Correction! I only tried to kill the people who tried to kill me first! It was self-defense!"

"What about your father?" another nobleman burst out.

Kat whirled on him, scowling, while also trying to ignore that the room spun for a moment before her.

The fact that she hadn't slept the night before probably wasn't helping either . . .

"I didn't try to kill him." The words didn't sound entirely convincing even to Kat's own ears.

The councilmen at least weren't as fearful as they had been at the start of the discussion . . . but they were more exasperated than angry . . .

"Your Majesty, is there a reason for this meeting? Our city is being attacked, and there are significantly better uses of our time." This time it was Duke Siata. The Troivackian nobleman was a hunched, lean fellow with a neatly cropped beard and short straight black hair with white touching his temples that he wore slicked back. While normally a quiet man, his new position of power seemed to feed his self-confidence. Though when he peered around Kat at Alina, her hollowed stare made him recoil instantly.

"Kat, any improvement?" Alina called out instead of responding to the nobleman.

Kat gave an impatient sigh and closed her eyes to evaluate whether she was sensing any change to her magic . . . Alas. She was not.

"No," she responded to the queen irritably.

She had known it'd be a long shot, but . . . it was all she could think of. That being said, she sadly wasn't able to give it as much of her all as she'd have liked. A free pass to torment her brother-in-law's inner council? When would such a golden opportunity come again?! However, her weakening state was damning any kind of solid effort she wished she could muster.

A pounding on the council room doors distracted everyone. Surely the enemy hadn't already crossed the castle's threshold.

The door opened a crack, and Mr. Kraft's head appeared. "Pardon me, everyone. Lady Katarina, I believe I have a solution to your . . . issue. Would you be able to meet me in the throne room?"

Kat shared a brief glance with Alina. "Sure. You're dismissed," she called out flippantly over her shoulder at the Troivackian noblemen, which actually did succeed in angering a number of them. While it didn't seem to do much to restore any of her magic, at least it was mildly amusing.

However, the brief spell of humor was short-lived, as Alina then stepped forward and stared down her small nose at them all.

"Before you go, lords, I have a few matters I myself would like to discuss presently. Though I will do my best to keep it short."

"Your Majesty, we really—"

"*Silence.*"

Everyone was shocked when it was none other than Rebecca Devark who had shouted at the men.

Everyone save for Alina, that is, who, quite honestly, looked as though she wouldn't mind standing in the middle of a battlefield with her eerie, despondent stare.

"While we are preparing the castle in the unfortunate event His Majesty and Leader Faucher's efforts do not keep the rebel units out, I want to be apprised of what means we are using to defend the castle."

The men shared dark looks with one another.

"It wasn't a request. What are the plans for defending this castle?"

"Your Majesty, that is not your role as queen. I understand His Majesty has— YOUR MAJESTY!" One of the lords had begun to argue against Alina, only she had slung the crossbow from her back into her hands and casually started to load the weapon while lining up her shot at the man who dared to defy her.

"I may have been a little too kind as of late, so let me refresh your memories. The day I was crowned, I told you all I would be accepted as your queen or I would sit atop the bones of those who opposed me. But you all have seemed to forgotten, so here is a brief reminder. If you accept me as your queen, as a leader of your kingdom, we will have no issue," she explained lightly while raising her weapon.

The lord, an elderly man with a mole on his left cheek, stared furiously at Alina while also pressing himself back as far as possible in his chair.

"Your Majesty, I think grief has made you lose your mind—"

Faster than anyone could have expected, Alina fired the arrow toward the new speaker . . . and it lodged into the chair right beside his left ear, which immediately began to sting horribly.

"Anyone else have something to say that isn't information regarding our defenses?" she queried while already reloading her weapon with intimidating swiftness.

One or two noblemen rose from their seats as though with the intention of running away from or stopping her.

"Come now, no need to be so squeamish. This is how power and respect is earned here in Troivack. That's what you all like to preach. I'm merely doing my best to accommodate your lofty ideals." Alina casually waved the weapon around, and the two noblemen that had stood seated themselves back down.

"Ma'am, surely you cannot condone—" One of the noblemen darted a look at Rebecca Devark, though he faltered when he noticed her shorn hair . . .

"I condone keeping this castle safe. His Majesty did not marry a fool, and nor did I raise him to be one himself. Now, I, too, would like to hear what is being planned, my lord." While Rebecca may have lowered her eyes and given a somewhat respectable bow to the nobility before her, the imperial air about her was far from submissive. The council took stock of the group of women that remained behind the queen . . .

The duchess from Daxaria was carting a weapon of her own, and Lady Kezia was wearing her silver locket, her blue eyes just as disturbingly calm, yet vigilant, as Alina's . . .

The fight left a great deal of them.

Sensing this reluctant surrender, Alina gave a triumphant nod. "Wonderful, now, let's see what you have in mind. I have a few ideas of my own."

When Kat entered the throne room already feeling her eyelids becoming unbearably heavy, she tried to fathom what kind of solution Mr. Kraft could have come up with, but she found her mind turning sluggish and foggy . . .

Her feet started to drag . . .

"Oh, Gods . . . Lady Katarina, do I have your permission to assist you?" Mr. Kraft moved forward hurriedly, his eyes glinting as he noticed the dying flicker around Kat.

"Ssssure . . . Myeah. Fine . . ." she slurred while already zagging from her original trajectory.

Mr. Kraft carefully grasped her arm and guided her along.

Thanks to her declining mental state, Kat was unable to comprehend that there were more people than just herself and Mr. Kraft in the room . . . until her blurring vision revealed several sets of boots . . .

"Whasss . . . Whas going on . . . ?" Kat tried to get a better look at her surroundings but found that it made her lose her ability to stand. Mr. Kraft let out a small *oomph* as he did his best to keep holding her up.

Whispers whirled around her . . . or was she imagining them . . . ?

"Help her!" Mr. Kraft called out, his voice uncharacteristically impassioned.

"Why should we help her when she is just going to go out and fight alongside the Troivackian army?"

Kat heard someone ask the question to her left . . . though her head was beginning to thrum with pain. She really just wanted to sleep . . .

"Because she would save you if you were in the same position! Didn't she already start the process with her father to allow for you all to become refugees belonging to the Daxarian coven?!"

"We've been treated like prisoners this entire time! We don't owe her anything yet!"

"Arnez, you do realize that if the rebellion and first witch reach this castle, you will be in just as much danger as everyone else, yes?!"

"I don't buy it! The first witch is probably on her way to save us, and you . . . You're just being threatened!"

Mr. Kraft grunted under Katarina's growing deadweight. "Are you just going to let her fall into this state? She could be unconscious for weeks at this rate! Do you really think Daxaria and its coven will proceed with helping you after you turned your backs on their future queen and daughter of the coven's diplomat?!"

That certainly made everyone pause.

Kat was more asleep than she was awake, but she was at least able to somewhat realize that the people around her must be witches given the way Mr. Kraft was talking to them . . .

"We have nowhere to go now! The tunnels have been discovered, Troivack is about to battle magical beasts, there is every excuse in the book to slaughter us along the way, *but not if we save Katarina Reyes!*" Mr. Kraft insisted as his knees buckled underneath her weight. "Celeste! Please, won't you help her? You like Lady Katarina."

The air witch was quiet.

But then . . . a slight movement behind one of the other witches distracted everyone.

Pina, Lady Katarina's familiar, was trotting forward to her witch, her eyes wide, her nose twitching uncertainly.

The witches swallowed uncomfortably as they watched the sweet feline move to her witch, her head lowered in concern as she approached.

Mr. Kraft, unable to keep supporting Kat, did his best to set her down gently on the floor.

Kat's eyes were already closed, and her every limb became limp . . .

Even when she felt Pina's nose press into her ear and her tongue worriedly lick her hair, Kat couldn't bring herself to stir.

Pina kept bumping her witch's head and nuzzling her cheek, trying to get her to respond . . . Then she let out the most heartbreaking mew.

Mr. Kraft, still on his knees, stared at the circle of witches around them. There wasn't a single person present who didn't feel immensely guilty as they watched the distressed kitten try to rouse her witch.

A few even started to feel their throats tighten . . .

Several witches looked away, as the heartbreaking scene of the kitten becoming more and more distressed by the state of her witch was bringing tears to their eyes.

"When did we start turning our backs on one of our own?" Mr. Kraft's voice rasped.

He no longer seemed like the refined man he had always presented himself to be . . . His eyes always bright with knowledge and sight no one could understand had dimmed . . . His grizzled cheeks, his unwashed long hair, and the deep exhaustion lines in his face humbled his appearance greatly. He looked up at the five members of his coven, broken.

"Lady Katarina . . . has fought harder than anyone I've ever met to protect others. To be stronger. To be better. To bring . . . light to this world. I was afraid of her power when we first met . . . but . . . I see now . . . she simply had too much goodness that she didn't know what to do with it, and so it came out in ways that didn't truly show how great she was. She has supported the Troivackian queen, yes. Not because she is power hungry, but because Her Majesty Alina Devark is her best friend that she loves dearly. She risked her life to face the devil to save her husband. She keeps diving headfirst into any situation if someone needs help. Even when she learned of your desires to go to Daxaria, she did what she could to start the process. You should all be ashamed that you refuse to offer her aid. There . . . are few people I've ever met who deserve to have an army fight with her. I believe Lady Katarina fights for the goodness in life. For fairness and the balance that the Goddess wishes for us. I have faith in the burning witch. She should be who we follow to brighter days, but should you decide to keep dwelling in the darkness of our history . . . then I can't make you help her."

The witches stared at the redheaded woman on the floor and her sweet familiar . . .

"We just . . . have to throw magic at her?" It was Celeste's quiet voice that broke through.

Mr. Kraft gave a weary smile at the young witch. "Yes. A small amount at first, but I think if we keep casting at her, she can regain her power. She feeds off it. Like a raging fire."

"What strange abilities . . ." one of the witches murmured while shaking her head. "Well . . . I'm willing to give a *small* amount."

Mr. Kraft smiled at the witch and slowly pushed himself to his knees. "Thank you."

"Fine. I'll help too, but only because I'm getting to Daxaria no matter what."

"I'll throw as much fire as I want at her, and no one can get angry? Might be fun . . ."

Mr. Kraft felt his heart swell, and so . . . he crouched down and held out his hand. "Come here, Pina. I think it's time we healed your witch."

The familiar looked uncertainly at the coven leader and then at Kat. After taking a brief moment of consideration, she proceeded to make her way over to him.

Once Pina was safe in his arms, Mr. Kraft proudly looked around at the handful of the most powerful coven members under his command. It finally felt as though they were doing something worthwhile . . . not just hiding underground, trying to weather a storm that would never cease.

"Celeste, could you please start with a light wind?"

The air witch bobbed her head, sending the white strands of her bangs swinging.

She held out her hand and released a subtle gust at Kat, who lay perfectly still on her back.

Nothing happened other than the rustling of a few loose wisps of Kat's hair.

Mr. Kraft felt dread claw at his throat.

"Again."

Celeste obeyed, but . . . still . . . nothing happened.

Pina looked at Arnez. The man with straight brown hair that brushed the back of his neck had golden eyes that were amazingly like Katarina's . . . The kitten mewed at him.

He smirked at her. "Guess the familiar thinks we should break out the strongest power!" Arnez pushed his sleeves up, his expression turning excited and hungry.

"W-Wait— Arnez, *wait!*" Terrified, Mr. Kraft stepped forward just in time for Arnez to cast a stream of fire right at the redhead, his eyes shimmering in the light of the flames as he relished in releasing his magic. . .

"ARNEZ!" Mr. Kraft roared as he flinched away from the heat, his arm coming up protectively to cover both Pina's and his own face.

Gods . . . what if Lady Katarina was burned alive?!

The second the flames disappeared, Mr. Kraft uncovered his eyes.

"ARNEZ! I SAID TO EASE INTO—"

Kat coughed, snapping everyone's attention to her . . .

Her eyes slowly opened, and she stared at the ceiling. She still looked tired and pale, but . . . she was awake, and better yet . . . her aura was emanating softly around her.

"Lady Katarina, are you alright?" Mr. Kraft called frantically from the sideline.

"Er . . . Yes? I think . . . ? Whoever did that, can you please do it again?"

Arnez stared dazedly at Kat on the floor for a moment before a manic grin broke out across his face.

"Lady Katarina, I have to confess . . . You're starting to grow on me," Arnez chortled affably.

Weakly, Kat lifted her thumb in the air. "Glad to hear it, whoever you are . . . Also . . . If anyone else wants to jump in, feel free . . . That might be the most efficient way to help me along."

"Won't that possibly kill you?" A woman asked from the opposite side of Arnez in the circle.

"Eh, who's to say? Now, how about on the count of three. Ready?"

The members of the Coven of Aguas stared at each other with vague humor in their eyes and wry smiles.

Well . . . At least helping the future queen of Daxaria was going to be a little bit interesting . . .

CHAPTER 56

A CATAPULTED COMEUPPANCE

Duke Siata stood before the knights that had been placed under his command and let out a weary sigh.

The Troivackian queen had had a plethora of ideas on how to hold off the rebels should they happen to break through the king's defenses outside the city . . . But all her methods relied heavily on traps and avoiding as much confrontation as possible. It was not the Troivackian way. The knights would never agree to it, and besides, if they built the traps she suggested and the rebels didn't break through the king's defenses, which was far more likely, then they'd all have to dismantle them safely.

The duke let out a soft grumble. He had been content to let Duke Icarus go head-to-head with the queen in the past. While he himself didn't take as much exception to her, he did strongly believe she had no place advising the army. Even if she said she was basing her stratagem on Daxaria's when they had won the Tri-War . . .

She doesn't understand that this isn't how things are done, but if I send the men out now, she'll have no choice but to continue with the tried-and-true defense that has worked for Vessa for decades. She had to be checked by the physician again, so I should have time . . . The other noblewomen are waiting for her with their guards, so they won't know, and Lady Katarina last I heard isn't fit to fight . . . This is how it should be.

"Alright, men, I want a quarter of you guarding exterior doors, another quarter guarding the wall with the archers, then the rest of you—"

"Duke Siata, were you momentarily deaf when the queen explained her plans, or are you being treasonous right now?"

Duke Siata froze.

Then slowly turned around to find His Highness Prince Eric standing four feet behind him.

"Your Highness," he greeted warily while also lowering his voice so the unit of knights behind him wouldn't hear. "I am merely trying to save Her Majesty's life. I understand she is moved by her grief to act unpredictably, however, we are talking about the lives of hundreds of people and the stability of the crown."

"Her Majesty told me her plans, and I agreed that they were well thought out. And *I* am of perfectly sound mind," Eric retorted levelly, his dark gaze boring into the duke, who met it with the same expression one might give a child making unreasonable requests.

"Pardon my saying so, Your Highness, but this is a matter outside your jurisdiction."

"Well, how about this!" A new voice sounded off behind Eric from the shadowy depths in the castle.

Both Eric and the duke turned, but only the prince grinned when he saw the glowing woman approach them.

Kat's eyes were magically sparkling, her aura was flickering wildly, and she looked as though she was bursting with energy.

She wore her official armor, her sword at her side, Pina perching perfectly on her shoulder.

"How about we ask the knights if they would like to listen to Her Majesty's orders or yours, Duke Siata, given that if they follow *your* orders without knowing they are treasonous, they also face charges and title strippings."

"Feeling better?" Eric asked, his eyes crinkling and his shoulders relaxing as he took in the healthy state of his wife.

"I had an overzealous fire witch try to set me ablaze during most of breakfast time—I feel better than I have in ages."

Eric opened his mouth at first in concern but chuckled instead before the couple readjusted their sights on Duke Siata.

The man looked as though he were a word away from rolling his eyes at the Daxarian duo.

So Kat didn't waste a word on him. Instead she stepped before the knights, kissed Pina on the cheek, and held up a hand.

Instantly whispers broke out amongst the men.

"Pina!"

"Gods, she looks cute today."

"She looks cute every day!"

"But she's smiling today!"

"Must be because her witch is with her."

Kat smiled at the men, who no longer stared at her as though she were strange or a nuisance but exactly as though she were one of them, and she felt her already soaring mood rise even higher, even though she knew a great deal of their acceptance was because of her kitten . . .

"I really need to know what you did to them one of these days . . ." she murmured.

Pina's only response was a purr.

Kat reached up and scritched her kitten's cheek appreciatively before returning her attention to the army.

"Knights of Troivack! Her Majesty has crafted a new plan in order to catch the rebels off guard should they break through your king's defense! The reason for this is that Mr. Levin, the king's assistant, betrayed His Majesty and, therefore, knows better than anyone what the court's go-to strategy would be in times of war!" she shouted over them.

The exuberance the unit had exhibited when Kat and Pina had first arrived died down instantly as they were reminded of Mr. Levin's treachery.

"Duke Siata here wants you to use the original plan! Now, do you want to follow the queen's orders and *not* commit treason by blatantly ignoring her command? Or would you like to catch those bastards off guard?" Kat roared, pumping her fist in the air, which had Pina craning her neck forward as though trying to encourage the men to agree.

Sensing this, Kat glanced at her kitten. "And what do you say, Pina?"

Pina opened her mouth and let out a squeaking mew that was both adorable and also impactful.

"WE FOLLOW OUR QUEEN!"

"AND PINA!"

Kat shot them all a flat look.

"AND PINA'S WITCH!" At least one knight tried halfheartedly to placate her.

After letting out a disparaging breath, Kat gave the knights a relaxed smile that they all returned.

She even spotted Sir Cas and Sir Vohn standing in line to her right, and once she locked eyes with Sir Cas, he pumped his fist in the air and let out a loud "HOH!"

The army soon followed in kind, and so Kat turned and faced the duke, who looked like he was experiencing a terrible headache as he winced against the army's shouts.

"I think I'll take it from here, Duke Siata." Eric clapped a heavy hand on the duke's shoulder that made the man's knees buckle. "Though I will say, before you go inside and perhaps have a cup of moonshine . . . I would've thought you'd all have learned by now what happens to those who oppose Her Majesty. If you'd like a reminder, I hear Duke Icarus is still breathing, though he wishes he wasn't."

Impressively, Duke Siata did not cower or flinch, but he did submit to a look of utter defeat, as though this recent attempt at undermining Alina were the one and only silent protest he could manage.

With the duke slinking off into the shadows of the castle without another word, Kat gestured with her head for her husband to come forward before once again addressing the knights.

"Alright, everyone! Here's what we're going to do!"

Aradia strutted through the abandoned streets of Vessa.

There was a balmy breeze that brushed her cheek that the three sirins flying above her had nothing to do with. It carried the scent of warming earth and softening water . . .

The first witch smiled to herself.

She'd always liked spring.

Especially after escaping Baroness Elena Souros's keep . . .

Poor Tak had had to burrow out of several more feet of rubble for them, then they had discovered a most horrendous stench filling the air. Aradia had recognized that there was a startling amount of garbage that must have been piled up on the floors that had collapsed. To add insult to injury, there was an acidic odor that told her the destruction of the keep had most definitely been intentional.

It was particularly suspicious when they had exited the reeking remains and there wasn't a soul in sight.

Not even an alarmingly massive raccoon that Tak couldn't stop trying to understand or describe to his allies.

Sure, there was a bit of a hiccup to Aradia's plan, and the longer her brother remained in her care, the more likely it was that he would figure out a way to escape, but she was determined this time. Her brother would not best her again.

She could live free of his shadow over her once and for all, and to her, that was sweeter than even the faint aroma of spring.

Rather than following the road to reach Vessa at its western gate, Aradia had simply barreled through the city's wall with Tak's help and proceeded north toward the castle.

No doubt that was where many of the witches had relocated. If not? Well . . . she may just have to kill more people than she had wanted to. Unfortunate, but . . . it was for the greater good.

She reached the castle with a surprising lack of resistance . . . So much so that she halted in her steps and turned toward Mr. Levin.

"You said they divide their men among the sides of the castle walls while leaving a few inside. Where are they?"

Mr. Levin's normally sharp brown eyes rested on the castle gates nervously as he thought through the various possibilities.

Meanwhile, there was a loudly clanging bell sounding off to their left.

"Sounds like the unit in the west heard about our detour," Aradia voiced aloud with her eyes calmly drifting over the assistant's head. "If they get in my way, I will kill them all. Now tell me, is there another strategy His Majesty could be using? Traps? Boiling oil? The coven was adamant about not helping the king, so I'm doubtful we have a plethora of magic power to combat."

"W-Well, I . . . He . . ."

"You have no idea." The first witch sighed. "Very well, I guess we'll have to get new eyes on this."

Aradia lifted her hand to her mouth and let out a shrill whistle, making the sirins above them dive down to her and hover above as they waited to hear from their mistress.

"I want to know what's going on inside the walls. If you see any archers, scream."

The sirins, all three looking identical to the human eye save for their slightly different hair colors, grinned, revealing sets of matching pointy teeth before they took to the skies again, their white robes rippling against the winds.

Aradia watched from the ground with the imp and Tak and shielded her eyes against the sun as she waited to hear their screams or to at least see them again . . .

They were gone for an exceedingly long time . . . But then . . .

An explosion of blue light erupted from within the castle walls, and all three sirins were blasted out of the vicinity and sent flying a league northward away from the castle . . .

Aradia's hand and brazen expression fell.

"The house witch."

Her hand curled around the handle of the dagger at her hip as her mood blackened, and she started to move purposefully toward the gates. She'd now have to leverage her hostage to get in, but so be it.

Things had just become infinitely more complicated.

"There's my da." Likon's soft broken voice was only heard by the imp, Viellen. He hadn't even noticed the young man return to consciousness or remove his blindfold and work his mouth free of the gag. Yet he was there, squinting against the daylight, his body weak, but his smile filled with confident relief. The imp didn't have a chance to even think about retying the blindfold or shoving the gag back in place, however.

"Ka?" Tak pointed a finger to the sky.

Confused by what the stone golem was trying to say, Aradia stopped and looked up.

Her jaw dropped.

"What . . . in the living *hell* is—"

Soaring through the air as though having been catapulted from the castle courtyard were three figures.

An adorable kitten in the middle, her small paws splayed out with her claws extended, a second cat on her right with a magnificent tuft of chest fur fluttering in the breeze, his body fully outstretched, and lastly, what looked like . . . a pillow-shaped raccoon careening through the air.

Aradia wasn't positive, but she was relatively certain the raccoon was shrieking . . .

And then all three landed on Tak—Pina on top of his head, Kraken on his left shoulder, and Reggie, being significantly less agile and considerably heavier than the other two, landed closer to the golem's stomach, but managed to grasp onto the vines that swung from its body.

The impact of the raccoon's landing was loud enough that it echoed down to Aradia and the others on the ground.

The first witch was at an utter loss as to what the possible purpose could be to such a move, until . . . the golem wavered in the air.

He flickered . . . in *existence* in that realm.

Aradia's eyes widened as she realized what was happening.

The cats were capable of moving between realms, and if there was another being not entirely of the earthly world like Tak, they could push them *back*.

She rounded on Tak and shouted up at them, "YOU WON'T BE ABLE TO SHOVE HIM BACK ON YOUR OWN! HE'S TOO BIG!"

"That might be the case! Though he's going to have a difficult time helping you if he can't see *and* keeps disappearing."

Aradia slowly turned back around.

Katarina stood just outside the castle gate, looking perfectly strong and full of magic, grinning and wearing her armor. Her father was standing behind her in the courtyard with his eyes filled with lightning.

"Why is the raccoon involved then?" Aradia wondered bluntly.

"Reggie? Oh, Reggie is a very awkward handicap to have. Take a look for yourself." Kat jerked her chin toward the stone golem.

Aradia risked a quick glance back to see that the raccoon was swinging on the vines hanging off Tak and he was squealing like a demented child having a marvelous time as he wrapped the vines around Tak's legs despite them all flickering in and out of the realm.

The first witch looked back at Kat and shook her head disparagingly. "Your father can't hold the shield forever."

"That's true, but we don't need him to hold it forever. We just need to take that dagger of yours, and we'll go from there."

"The sirins will be back soon, Lady Katarina, and furthermore"—Aradia waved her hand casually over her shoulder, and the imp half-lifted Likon, then gave him a small shake—"either let me in and give me five witches, or I'll cut Likon's throat here, which would be a great pity."

The redhead's jubilant expression hardened instantly.

"You kill him, and I'll make sure you spend the rest of eternity buried in the ground with nothing to eat, see, or feel, and I don't care if I burn in hell for eternity for it."

"KAT, SHE CAN STOP TIME!" Likon suddenly roared, shocking everyone with the strength of his voice. "I DON'T THINK SHE CAN DO IT FOR LONG, BUT—" The imp blurred into a cloud of steam and disappeared with Likon in tow.

The sirin that had remained behind the first witch and who was still levitating the devil let out a kettle-like hiss.

Kat looked at the first witch in alarm at Likon's news.

Aradia tilted her head casually. "I guess we are at an impasse at least until the rebels break through and we simply camp outside the castle . . . and that should be in about . . ." she held up three fingers and counted down, and then sure enough, as her last finger lowered, there was the sound of a trumpet . . . a trumpet that had been carved of rough bone and not brass like the Troivackian army's.

The rebels had broken through one of the gates and were coming toward the castle.

Kat stared at the first witch, who smiled. "Sorry, Lady Katarina, I had to be exceptionally prepared. So even with you and your father in fighting shape, I'm afraid you will not win this war. Though I *am* surprised you don't want to banish the devil. I fear for the future of Daxaria and Troivack," Aradia informed Kat disappointedly. "Brendan Devark should've known better and one day could have come to his senses, but you . . . You're a hero. You save the one, but a queen needs to save the many, even if it costs a few lives. I understand though. You and I . . . the Gods made you like me after all. Down to the very fact that I no longer feel fear. You know what that's like, don't you? Being reckless and taking risks because you don't fear the possible repercussions. I used to use that to help any poor soul in need, but it means nothing if you aren't fixing the bigger problems. "

The first witch's words made all color drain from Kat's face, and a ring of magic pulsed in Kat's eyes.

"I'm nothing like you."

"Of course you are. Otherwise, my brother wouldn't have found you so interesting."

"I don't casually sacrifice people."

"You are willing to casually sacrifice thousands of men fighting on the rebellion's side, as well as the ancient beasts. The beasts are creatures purer than you could ever realize. I wouldn't be mounting that high horse just yet."

Kat swallowed, and for a moment it looked like she was starting to doubt herself . . . until she stared through her eyebrows at the first witch with a demonic smile.

"Well . . . The way I see it, we have more differences than similarities. For example, I have my family, and better yet a cute cat, while even your allies prefer your brother. I have two kingdoms who love me and will help me become the greatest queen I can be. You don't even have one person who likes you, which should tell you something, and the fact that it doesn't is a shame. And just for the record? Neither you nor your brother has anyone to blame for your situations other than yourselves." Kat pulled her shoulders straight and her sword free, flipping it in her hand, and making the blade ring in the air.

Aradia's eyes snapped to it and widened in recognition.

Kat grinned. "Even Theodore Phendor crafted *my* blade first, and that's how this war will end. With me coming in first, so . . . Sorry, Great-Great-Great-Great-Great-Great-Whatever-Great-Grandma, but . . . I'd say the odds are actually stacked in my favor."

CHAPTER 57

A RELIEVING REVIVAL

T*he morning before the arrival of the first witch . . .*

Kat stared over her father's sleeping body, her magic humming, and her energy levels unparalleled.

Her mother, Lady Annika Ashowan, stood silently behind her with the Coven of Aguas's leader, Mr. Kraft, at her side.

"Right . . . Mr. Kraft, I've apparently been bolstering other people around me without realizing it . . . Shouldn't I be able to direct it more specifically if I want to?"

"In theory, yes," the coven leader began. "You recall how you are able to feel and sense your magic within yourself? Have you ever tried to examine how it flows from your body and interacts with people or things outside of yourself?"

Kat furrowed her brows, though she didn't look away from her father. "I can't say I have."

"Then try starting with that. You see, I believe that if you identify this flow of your power, you can manage how it is routed."

"Your father has said his magic has a relationship with all the items in the home, and, therefore, they work with him. It could be your magic connects to others," Annika volunteered quietly to her daughter.

While Kat had been feeling significantly more confident since regaining her strength thanks to the efforts of the Coven of Aguas, her mouth twisted to the left worriedly while she closed her eyes. What if Mr. Kraft and her mother were wrong and she couldn't sense anything?

She focused on the brilliant, blazing ball of magic in her chest that was whirling and dancing merrily. It was happy to once again burn as brightly as it wished to.

Part of Kat felt afraid to even attempt seeing what her magic could do outside of her body, as though prodding it would somehow make some new catastrophe occur . . .

So when she turned her attention to the faint threads of her magic she hadn't ever given much thought to, the ones that drifted free of the core of her power that she considered the same as sparks that would burn to ash away from her, she half expected to find nothing.

Only . . . she found they weren't ash . . . Not at all . . . She could feel . . . tiny, easy to ignore tugs on the wispy lines drifting away from her power.

She felt a thread going toward . . . Alina.

Kat recognized the feeling of her friend on the other side of her magic. She wasn't sure how, but it was as though . . . she could sense her friend's presence there with her . . .

Resisting the urge to blink her eyes open, Kat shifted her focus to another thread . . . This one burned hotter than many of the others . . .

Eric.

She could feel her love for him, but could feel that as she freely gave her love, her magic blended in with the emotion quietly . . .

At this she couldn't help but open her eyes and look to Mr. Kraft.

"What was it that triggered a great output of my magic to these other people? I could feel my connections with Alina and Eric, but his is stronger than hers."

Mr. Kraft tilted his head thoughtfully. "It could have something to do with how much you want to help or protect them, or how much of your emotional energy you expend on them. Similar to how you can absorb intentions toward yourself, you can send power out. Honestly, I would not have considered this were it not for your father's insights, but . . . really, the Goddess knew what she was doing when she crafted you." He chuckled in awe. "She made it so that as long as you yourself were balanced, your abilities had the means to balance themselves as well. I imagine your coven had no idea how to approach this, as it is completely different due to your technically being a mutated witch." The coven leader's colorful eyes started to shine a little brighter.

"What do you mean so long as *I* was balanced?"

Mr. Kraft shifted and looked a little sheepish. "Lady Katarina, it could be that you are more . . . open with others now, and more transparent in your true thoughts and feelings. Leader Faucher expressed concern that you wouldn't be able to do such a thing, but I had no idea it would go so far as to affect your magic. I was so focused on the intensity of what you had locked within you, that I never thought to look at the threads of what left you."

Kat was at a loss for words. On one hand, she felt horribly, ridiculously embarrassed. On the other, the coven leader wasn't wrong. She *had* started opening herself up to more people. She'd been honest with Faucher about her feelings more times than she could count. The same happened with Sir Cas, Alina . . . And of course, she'd been the most open with Eric . . .

She knew in that moment, that while she hadn't meant to expend quite so much power, she wouldn't have been able to come as far as she wanted to in every other area of her life had she remained as guarded as she had once been before.

Feeling bolstered by the coven leader's insight and her own self-reflection, Kat returned her attention to her father. If she could find her connection with him, then maybe she could push enough magic at him and wake him up.

Kat closed her eyes again and searched for the magical link between her and her father . . .

At first, she couldn't sense anything, and she started to panic . . . But then, there was a fluttering ribbon of blue wrapped around a faded flicker flowing from her magic.

She turned her power toward it and almost started weeping with joy. There he was, and . . . his own magic was encircling her own like a bow that had been tied there her whole life.

With her eyes still closed, Kat smiled.

Alright . . . Easy does it now . . .

She pressed a tiny bit against her thriving ball of magic near where her father's wisp dangled and all but jumped in surprise as a healthy amount of power gushed out. The thread thickened to the likes of a vein, rushing full of her power toward her da.

There was a slight shifting beneath her hand . . .

Might as well give him a little more. We are less than a day away from actual combat.

A fraction more of her magic poured out. It wasn't anywhere near enough to hinder her own abilities, but it was hot, and—

A warm hand grabbed her wrist.

"Kat."

The croaking voice of Finlay Ashowan made Kat's eyes snap open.

When she stared down into the waking face of her father, she burst into tears in an instant.

"Da, Da, I'm so sorry!" Kat flung her arms around her father.

Fin let out a small *oomph* but returned his daughter's embrace, though he was still bleary and trying to fully wake.

"It's alright, Kitty Kat," he soothed gently. "I know it wasn't your fault."

Kat couldn't respond, she just kept weeping . . .

Fin kissed the side of her head, then slid his gaze over to his wife, who was smiling in relief. She gave him a small nod. He returned it in understanding.

Mr. Kraft cleared his throat and bowed. "I will go inform His Highness that Duke Ashowan has awoken."

Once the chamber door had closed behind the coven leader, Annika rounded the bed to the opposite side her daughter stood on and climbed on so that she, too, could join the embrace.

While the duchess had been able to manage on her own, her world only turned right when she could see her husband's beautiful blue eyes glimmering back at her.

She held his gaze as their daughter sobbed into his shoulder and thought some well-worn words . . . *Man that I love . . . man of my dreams . . . father of my children . . . Thank the Gods you're back. We would not have won this battle without you, and life is unbearable without you at my side.*

Eric stepped into the duke's chamber wearing armor he had thankfully packed for his time in Troivack, though in putting it on he was unpleasantly reminded of his young assistant's alleged betrayal as he struggled with tying on the more difficult pieces. While Sir Vohn was fortunately available to help the prince . . . the traitorous Thomas Julian weighed heavily on Eric's mind.

The young, naïve boy, who had been so eager to help and serve him . . . was Likon's nephew, and he had been reporting on the prince's activities and tampering with his correspondence.

A massive, surprising breach of trust.

When it came to keeping tabs on him, Eric could have possibly forgiven him if it had been done at Likon's orders to ensure Katarina was protected. However, when he discovered that his assistant had in fact tampered with his correspondence and disappeared somewhere during the first witch and devil's confrontation, he was in far less of an open-minded disposition.

Despite the news that Finlay Ashowan was once again awake, Eric could not entirely free himself of these dark thoughts, even when he had received news that the duke had summoned him to his chamber.

When Eric laid eyes on Fin, he found him pulling on a navy blue coat. While the house witch had a sword at his side, he didn't wear a speck of armor.

While some people may think this a foolish move, the truth was Finlay Ashowan found he could fight better without it. Between his ability to heal and his shield, he rarely missed having that layer of protection.

"Glad to see you've recovered," Eric started as a greeting while closing the door behind him.

Fin briefly glanced over his shoulder as he finished pulling the collar of his coat straight, a peculiar expression on his face when he looked at his son-in-law.

"Thank you," the house witch responded casually. He then moved over to a long sturdy chest in his room. "I know I called you here when we are about to be attacked, but there was something I wanted to give you before the fighting started."

Eric's brows twitched together, his mind slowly pulling free of thoughts of betrayal and war.

Fin crouched down, unlocked the chest, and lifted from its depths . . . a sword.

It was a magnificent weapon. Its sheath was made of black leather and decorated in silver, the hilt already polished to a gleam.

Eric's stomach flipped when he recognized exactly which weapon it was.

"This is the sword Captain Antonio gave you the day you became a master of the sword. You were sixteen. An impressively young age to have earned that title, but it was because you loved it. You spent hours every day studying, and even helping your friends improve and learn. Captain Antonio had this made for you with your style and size in mind. It was crafted specifically for you, and I know . . . he was proud. He knew you'd be a great king just from seeing you learn this discipline alone."

Eric swallowed with difficulty.

"You sent this sword back to Austice shortly after your mother died and a few months later you went missing. I'm given to understand you haven't touched this sword since."

The prince's hands gripped into fists.

"Why do you have that?"

Fin had been slowly walking back over to Eric as he spoke of the late Captain Antonio.

"I brought this because I hoped that maybe . . . you'd come back to yourself during your time here in Troivack. And the way I see it, as of right now, you're a married man aiding your sister's army to defend against beings from another realm. I'd say you've more than regained the right to wield this sword."

Eric was starting to shake his head, his heart pounding. "I'm not—"

"Eric . . . I'm sorry, again, for how I've failed you, but just as my daughter has grown as a person and has every right to be proud of what she has accomplished, you have the same right. It's okay to forgive yourself."

"I'm not a better person than I was, Fin."

The house witch's face hardened as he stopped a foot from the prince. "Just because you forgive yourself doesn't mean you aren't finished working on yourself, Eric. It just means you don't want to be the same person you were before or make the same mistakes, and you will continue to try to improve. That alone is enough to be proud of."

Eric's thumb rubbed the side of his fist before he gingerly raised his hand, uncurled it, and grasped the handle of the sword Fin offered to him.

His heart raced as he stared down at the weapon and thought back to Captain Antonio the day he had gifted him the sword . . . his one clear blue eye proud and bright . . .

He could still hear his mother and father cheering from the sidelines with Alina, who had no idea of the significance of what was happening at eight years old, but who had clapped just as enthusiastically as everyone else.

For years, it had been the proudest moment of his life.

Fin's hand rested on his shoulder. "I think it's time we rejoin everyone."

Eric swallowed and lifted his eyes to meet the duke's.

After years of nightmares and pain . . . he was staring at his best friend . . . holding his own sword . . .

Before he could say a word, however, an excessive stroking noise at the door interrupted them.

Knowing exactly what was making such a sound, Fin stepped around Eric and opened the door to stare expectantly down into Kraken's face.

"*Witch, come. The daughter of the Gods is nearly here, and I have a new plan.*"

Fin looked over his shoulder at Eric, his warm expression morphed to one of seriousness.

"It's time. Are you ready, Your Highness?"

The prince faced the doorway. "Yes. I'm ready to get this over with and take Kat on one hell of a honeymoon."

Fin recoiled. "Keep those plans to yourself, please."

Eric smiled mischievously. "What? I would've thought the house witch would love the idea of becoming a grandfather."

"Eric, we were having a nice moment just now, do you really have to—"

"I could ask Mr. Howard to babysit."

Fin paused at the mention of the king of Daxaria's assistant, who infamously loathed—though respected—the house witch thanks to his antics and a certain rumor about the two having been in a torrid love affair years ago . . .

"He did escape being around Kat and Tam growing up because your family was in Rollom on the other side of the kingdom . . ." Fin grinned to himself.

"Exactly. Now imagine you as a grandfather, Kat as their mother, *and* they are now part of the royal family."

The two men exited the chamber, momentarily distracted from the battle that was fast approaching the castle doorstep, as they couldn't help but enjoy a shared reprieve from the heavy atmosphere as they further reflected on dear Mr. Kevin Howard's future. The poor man didn't even know Eric and Kat were married . . .

It was important to remember there were happy times yet to come as they descended into battle.

CHAPTER 58

A HELL OF A FIRING

S ire! The rebels have almost broken through the western gate!" Brendan
cursed over the clamor of battle below him.

As if things weren't bad enough, they had discovered that the rebels who
met their front lines were using poisoned weapons . . .

The poison didn't react instantly, but within a few moments, the affected
men fell to the ground either dead or barely alive.

From what was screamed back and forth on the field, it sounded as
though the weapons were coated with a form of Witch's Brew . . .

"Godsdamnit. Mage Sebastian! Start lighting the oil on fire! We are
going to be launching this as far and wide as possible. We have to resort to
distance attacks!" Brendan bellowed toward the mage, who was in the midst
of magically halting the enemy's arrows from cresting the castle wall.

"Yes, sire! Though please pass the order for everyone to duck while I do so!"

Brendan grimaced. He knew even with everyone taking cover that they
wouldn't be completely successful in avoiding being hit. He hoped that they
were able to at least take out a hefty number of enemies with the catapults
that were already being loaded along with the oil to at least offset those
losses . . .

However, even if those assaults went well, things were not looking hopeful, and the king couldn't help but turn his mind to the civilians in the city
behind him that would be subjected to the rebels who were about to plague
their streets.

Gods, I hope Alina is safe . . .

"MEN, TAKE COVER!" Brendan bellowed once Mage Sebastian gave
him the signal confirming he was ready to send out the first wave of boiling,
flaming oil.

The men ducked and within minutes, they could hear the shouts and cries of their enemies in pain.

"At the very least because we had to retreat, we have less casualties when we do this," the king muttered as he pressed himself into the stone wall behind him.

"Sire, I've finished!" Mage Sebastian called out.

Brendan still waited an extra moment before ordering the archers and knights near him to stand once more. It was the most he could give Mage Sebastian as far as a rest went.

The mage's voice was already hoarse from casting so many spells, but his eyes were ablaze with ferocity, the crystal dangling from his ear burning constantly . . .

"Sire! An urgent message from the castle has arrived along with some crates!" a squire on the stairs to the wall hollered up.

Brendan's heart dropped to his stomach, but he didn't waste any time making his way across the wall while still crouched, passing behind his archers.

Once he reached the squire, he looked back and was relieved to see that most of the men had lived through the moments during which they had lost their magical protection.

"MEN! RISE AND FIRE!"

After giving the order, the king turned around to receive the message that the squire brandished to him.

Unfurling the parchment, Brendan's eyes flew across the page.

At first his eyebrows shot upward in alarm, then he let out a breath of relief. But at the last part of the message . . . he looked confused.

Until a sudden explosion of blue lightning erupted behind him, drawing everyone's eyes as they then witnessed three creatures no one had ever seen the likes of before launch through the sky at an alarming speed and disappear into the distance.

Brendan dropped his attention back to the note, reread the last line, and gave a bloodthirsty smile.

He hurried down the steps to the crates and lifted off the lid to see the bottles and barrels of Troivackian moonshine and piles of rags . . .

Within several sacks were globs of . . .

Small bits of beeswax.

Hope swelled in Brendan's chest.

"MEN! NEW ORDERS!"

* * *

Kat had lunged forward, intending to cut down the first witch or at the very least incapacitate her while she was surprised by the presence of a sword crafted by Theodore Phendor. While the former handmaiden had once upon a time even been the one to deliver the weapon to Kat fully repaired—thanks to it at the time being fully wrapped—she had not been aware of its true origins.

Despite this unexpected twist of events, however, Aradia still dodged Kat's initial strike and then the second. In fact, she continued evading each cut and stab easily, but after leading Kat away from the castle, she didn't need to worry about dodging again, as the imp Kat recognized from the attack on Faucher's keep appeared in front of her with Likon once again gagged and blindfolded, and now with a knife tip pressed firmly at his throat.

"That's enough, burning witch." The imp's set of three pupils spun as he bore down on Kat.

She snarled in response, her aura burning higher so that it spanned nearly twice her height.

"Your magic cannot—"

The imp wasn't able to finish his sentence, as through Kat's aura, an arrow was shot, and because Viellen was not able to see through the wild flame-like magic surrounding her, he could not stop or avoid it.

The moment the arrow pierced his skull, Kat severed the arm clasped around Likon from its shoulder with a leaping swipe from the ground.

Now free, Likon crumpled to the ground as the imp fell back, dead.

"NO!"

Kat paid no mind to the first witch's shout as she hastily, while using her inhuman strength, bent down and flung Likon over her shoulder before starting to retreat toward the castle gate where her father's blue lightning shield still shone brightly.

To her left, the stone golem was stumbling in and out of the realm, struggling to stay upright and present. She managed to dodge its right foot that was ambling off toward the east side of the wall as she darted toward the safety of the shield and castle walls.

Kat was almost at the gate when three sirins landed in front of her.

She halted in place and gritted her teeth.

The three creatures were beautiful and nightmarish with their red eyes, silvery hair, and pointed teeth.

"Likon, cover your ears!" Kat shouted over her shoulder.

Hearing this order from Kat, Likon wasted no time in obeying and was just in time as the three sirins opened their mouths and let out a chord of hellish shrieks that would've most likely rendered someone temporarily if not permanently deaf if caught unawares.

Yet, interestingly, Katarina Ashowan only flinched as she kept barreling toward the castle, sword in hand.

The sirins attempted to blast her away, their hands outstretched and releasing streams of hurricane-force winds, but Kat's aura devoured their power greedily. She smiled, her golden eyes shining as she drew back her sword and was about to cut through the sirins when they flew up out of the way. But then two crashed down beside her and seized her arms while the third grabbed Kat's waist from behind in the span of a breath.

Kat let out a feral growl and tried to wrench free from their hold, but they had sharpened claws that pieced her skin, latching firmly on to her.

Letting out a shriek, Kat lunged for the lightning shield with the sirins in tow, but they instead dragged Kat up into the air, her skin tearing under their viselike grip.

With her waist and arms restrained and Likon on her shoulder, Kat had no space to move. As the ancient beasts flew higher while she struggled, she could see the top of the castle wall rise before her. And so with a surge of strength, she managed to lurch her body enough that Likon was able to roll through the shield and onto the top of the wall as they passed where the archers and Annika Ashowan awaited.

Free of Likon's deadweight, Kat tried to fight against the sirins more aggressively despite knowing they could drop her.

Arrows whistled out of the shield near them, but the winds the sirins produced stopped any from hitting their mark. Kat could tell they planned on dropping her from a great height; she hoped that her abilities would prevent her from being hurt too badly . . .

However, things took a surprising turn when out of the shield, jumped Eric. His armor gleamed in the stray beams of light that broke through the cloudy day.

And it was thanks to his heavy armor, that he was not as easy to blow off target as an arrow. While he wasn't able to tackle Kat and the sirins out of the air, he was able to latch on to both Kat's waist and the sirin who held her there.

The sirins let out another earsplitting set of screams, but Eric, like Kat had done before, only flinched.

While they tried to burst his eardrums, Eric fumbled around his wife's side, procured the dagger she had at her belt, and proceeded to plunge it into the side of the sirin's head that still clung to Kat's waist.

The sirin had opened its mouth to let out another terrible shriek just as the blade sliced through its pointed ear, but the sirin wasn't able to make a sound as its red eyes turned black . . . and its body then went limp as it fell from the sky like a ragdoll, dead.

Without their third sirin holding up the couple, the remaining two let out another bout of screams and released them. On their descent, Kat at least had the presence of mind to shove Eric back to land on the castle wall as she plummeted to the ground below, her aura blazing.

She landed with a crash against the stones, her armor unpleasantly bending from the impact, the gashes she'd received from the sirins bleeding heavily. Her shoulder piece dug into her rotator cuff, making Kat wince as she pushed up to a sitting position.

As she started to get her bearings back, she looked around, expecting to see more chaos, thanks to the stone golem that she had last spotted near the north side of the castle. However, she instead found herself staring at a wall of men on horseback, dressed in black.

The rebels that had kept their horses through the initial attack had reached the castle before their foot soldiers, it seemed.

The first witch stood nearby. "Pardon me, Lady Katarina, I believe I will need to go elsewhere for the time being, but these men are more than happy to fight with you."

Kat grimaced as she pushed herself, bloodied and bruised, to her feet. Thankfully, her sword was still in hand . . .

"Where do you think you're going . . . ?" Kat pointed her sword in Aradia's direction as the first witch had turned around and began striding away from the castle. "We're not finished."

Aradia raised an eyebrow and blinked. "Mm, we are for right now. The sirins are telling me there are other witches hiding in the city. The Troivackian king, or the coven leader, I don't know which, must've had them scatter, but no matter, I'll find them one way or another."

"If I promised to help you open that gate, would you go back to the Forest of the Afterlife with your brother?"

Aradia turned back around, looking completely amused by Kat's suggestion.

"I need to finish the task the Gods sent me here for before I go back. I just can't do that if my ridiculous brother keeps getting in my way."

"So to convince Troivack that you, the first witch, can help them . . . you . . . you are killing people . . . ?" Kat questioned while hoping that the first witch wouldn't notice she was buying time . . .

Aradia shook her head, suddenly appearing morose, though whether that sentiment was genuine was hard to say. "No. I am trying to lessen the influence of witches, but to do that I need a position of power. Witches are taking over Daxaria, and that is not at all what they should be doing. Troivack is the perfect place to gradually spread this teaching."

"We're not taking over Daxaria though! We're working with humans as we should!"

"You're helping them with their inventions and civilization, you are not connecting them to nature. Now, I'd love to elaborate, but time is somewhat of the essence here."

The first witch pivoted away while giving a wave over her shoulder, uninterested in anything else Kat had to say.

However, that was when an arrow struck Aradia in her shoulder.

It would have been a deadly hit if it hadn't been for the short burst of air that interfered from the sirin still holding the devil.

With a paling face and clutching her wounded arm, Aradia swiftly located her assailant.

The Troivackian queen, Alina Devark, stared at her, having just stepped from a nearby alley.

"Good day, Lady Wynonna. I have a few things I'd like to discuss," Alina called out while reloading her weapon and pointedly ignoring the knights on horses who were turning toward her with their swords drawn.

The first witch yanked out the arrow with a quiet grunt as she started to stalk closer to Alina.

From the other end of the castle wall, more crashes and cracking could be heard as the stone golem continued his struggle with the familiars, but aside from that, all was silent.

"Your Majesty, you should remain inside the castle. I honestly don't want to see any harm come to you."

"I'm afraid that I honestly can't say the same."

Aradia managed a tight smile while she shook her head and drew her dagger, the sirin carrying the devil fluttering closer to her mistress's side. Aradia reached into her pocket, looking for something else . . . only . . . she couldn't find it. Giving a quick frown, the first witch realized she didn't have the luxury of searching more thoroughly for her beloved Chronos.

"Is there some grand plan other than you and Lady Katarina fighting magical beasts, me, and an army?" she asked while recovering from her startle, twirling her blade expertly in her hands.

"I have a parting gift for you, as I take it you will not be returning to your position as my handmaiden," Alina explained evenly. Her lifeless eyes bore into the first witch.

"Oh . . . ?" Aradia was only fifteen feet from the queen. "What is this gift?"

"Well, I remember how much you like your moonshine."

Aradia was about to roll her eyes and continue walking away, though still eyeing the weapon in Alina's hands, when all a sudden, several barrels of moonshine crashed to the ground in a circle around the castle, right behind the rebels and right between Alina and the first witch. All of them had been magically launched and upon impact . . . burst into flames that roared high.

And as though it were the first strike in the tentative stalemate, a war cry from Katarina filled the air as she charged at the wall of men before her.

Alina stared at the first witch through the flames, who merely shrugged and grabbed hold of the sirin's arm at her side, intending to be flown over the fiery barricade, when the earth abruptly opened up and ate the sirin, first witch, devil and all, then just as quickly closed once more.

Alina smiled emptily at the patch of churned earth they'd disappeared beneath, then turned toward Kezia, who stepped out from the discreet doorway she'd hidden in, her locket aglow, and the ancient mage words flowing seamlessly from her lips as she proceeded to magically stack the broken rubble around them from the stone golem's demise to continue to bury the first witch, devil, and sirin deeper and deeper underground.

"How long do you think that will hold them . . . ?" the queen asked her sister-in-law as the shouts and clangs of Katarina fighting with the men carried over the flames.

Kezia shook her head seriously as she continued uttering spells. She was in the process of melting and solidifying the stone over the ground into a molten sheet.

A hiss of steam emanated from somewhere, indicating that just as they had anticipated, the first witch had tried using her stolen water abilities to blast through.

However, all that it accomplished was cooling the molten lava to a rock-hard state, making their underground tomb all the sturdier.

With that finished and the liquefied rock starting to singe the tips of Kezia's and Alina's boots, they each took a step back.

"I spun the earth around them a few times, so it is likely they will have trouble directionally . . . We have maybe an hour?" Kezia explained uncertainly. "She'll most likely find a loose patch of earth and crop up somewhere."

Alina nodded. "So we have that long to figure out how to stop her from channeling the deaths of our army into opening a portal?"

Kezia nodded. "Come, Your Majesty. We need to get back to the tunnels to return to the castle."

Alina followed her handmaiden quickly. They needed to stop a portal opening and the deaths of thousands as quickly as possible.

Despite the tunnels they had discovered in the castle being an issue during Mr. and Mrs. Levin's betrayal and subsequent escape, the queen had seen it as an excellent opportunity to come and go from the protected castle during the battle.

"Hopefully, by then both Duke Ashowan and Kat can take on the first witch together, and then . . ."

Kezia raised a smile at the queen over her shoulder. "Then it would be lovely if this could be over once and for all."

CHAPTER 59

THE PORTAL PROBLEM

W eapons poisoned with Witch's Brew . . . So that's how they are funneling souls into the Forest of the Afterlife," Alina recounted while reading from the magical slip that had been delivered to her and Kezia before they returned to the tunnels. They had luckily sent to His Majesty their own note along with the provisions just before intercepting the first witch. Upon their return they had found a response waiting for them in the form of a parchment magicked into a folded bird that had flown right into Alina's hand, though they had waited until they were back in the castle courtyard before reading it.

Rebecca Devark and Kezia looked toward Finlay Ashowan, who stood only ten feet from where they convened in the courtyard, though the house witch was a mite occupied with sustaining the shield around the castle.

"Sir Cas!" Alina shouted up to the blond knight, who was in the process of commanding archers.

"How is Kat?"

"She's getting bored!" the knight responded after a moment of surveying Kat fighting the remaining stragglers.

Admittedly, when Kat indulged her magic-infused persona, she seemed more like a savage animal ripping through each man and sending their horses on their way . . .

"Gods, that is terrifying," Rebecca Devark uttered before she could stop herself. She didn't need to see the carnage to know that for someone to be bored from taking out a group of armed men meant things wouldn't be pleasant.

Alina ignored this. "Has Sir Cleophus Miller arrived from the southern gate?"

"He should be arriving around the same time as the rest of the rebels from the west gate by the looks of it! Judging from Sir Cleophus's formation, Your Majesty's men might be moving to encircle the castle!" Sir Cas called back after consulting Sir Vohn, who was tracking the movement of both their allies and the rebels.

"Any change with the first witch?" Alina wondered aloud.

"No other movement under the stone! My guess is she is going to pop up elsewhere!" Sir Cas leaned toward Sir Vohn in conference.

Meanwhile, Eric had been watching Kat's decimation of the rebels to determine whether she would need any assistance. His concerns turned out to be unfounded as, unlike her duels with a sword, she had wisely not held back. With her magical abilities raging, she quite efficiently dealt with the men that had arrived thinking the castle would be easy to seize.

To make matters worse for the rebels, the more she battled against them, the more powerful she grew . . .

While on every other occasion such displays of her power were terrifying, it was serving the defense of the Troivackian castle and its occupants wildly well. Seeing this, the prince had made his way down the stairs of the castle wall to approach his sister.

"Hopefully, she'll get a spare moment to send more power to Duke Ashowan." Alina nodded to herself thoughtfully.

"What next, Your Majesty?"

Alina turned toward her brother, his hazel eyes sharp and ready as he approached.

His presence further confirmed that Katarina was in absolutely no danger, otherwise the prince would not have left his position on the castle wall.

"What do you think, Eric? We still don't know where the first witch will reappear, those sirins are figuring out we aren't as affected by their screams thanks to the beeswax in our ears, and last we heard the stone golem is . . . ?"

"He's sitting down. Still flickering in and out of this realm, but he seems really enraptured with Pina."

Alina nodded.

"Personally, I'm a bit surprised he isn't more interested in the raccoon," the prince muttered before giving his head a small shake to bring him back to the present. "Ah, and from the explosions beyond the north wall we can see that His Majesty received the crates we sent."

"Do you think Brendan should've manned the west wall? Would that have made a difference?" Alina questioned worriedly.

"Given the numbers we saw approaching from the north, it was a reasonable assessment. No use dwelling on it now. My suggestion for the first witch? Get Fin to shoot Mr. Kraft in the air. With his magical sight, he should be able to vet the nearby surroundings of any abnormal magic or pixie presence to find where the first witch may be."

"And the rebel army that is coming?"

"You have the castle rigged with traps, the knights lined against the wall so that they can't be seen from overhead . . . It isn't a bad idea to have them split up should we be breached, depending on the size of the next unit that attacks. My suggestion? Position Fin with his wife in the front entryway to take out whoever Kat and I don't. Leave half of your knights hiding beside the gates and send the rest in the main halls. Katarina and I will stay in the center of the courtyard, drawing attention, you retreat to the solar with access to the tunnels, and Sir Cas can be the messenger and guard for your orders."

The queen nodded. "What about magical beast sightings? The first witch might have killed enough of our army to summon more and open the portal as well, and we both know those sirins are plotting something. They've been too quiet."

"With the stone golem distracted, I think we—"

An ethereal squawking shriek rang through the air, making both Eric and Alina look at the sky just in time to see Kraken pouncing from the castle wall and tackling one of said sirins out of the sky, as though it were nothing more than a bird.

They also noticed what at first seemed to be a black cloud cutting across Fin's shield but was actually . . . a thick swarm of pigeons.

The queen and prince proceeded to watch as the sirin Kraken had latched on to flicker out of their realm. The other sirin that had been diving toward the fluffy cat in order to pry him off her kin was intercepted by the pigeons that clawed and pecked at her, muffling her cries.

"Kraken's taking care of the sirins," Eric announced flatly.

"I might ask to borrow Kraken from Daxaria on occasion in the future," Alina remarked, her tone matching her brother's.

"Keep in mind if you do that, he will most likely expand his reign of power and claim Troivack as his while taking over the cats, rodents, and pigeons."

"I don't mind."

"He most likely will keep pooping in shoes."

"That's fine."

"I beg to differ," Rebecca Devark, who had been silently listening throughout the entire exchange between the siblings, jumped in loudly.

The pair looked at her, then back at each other, both deciding not to continue discussing the sensitive topic just then.

"If any more imps, stone golems, or Gods forbid, a dragon come through, we can reorganize then," Eric continued. "For now, though, let's just try and get that dagger from the first witch."

The prince scanned the courtyard for Mr. Kraft, and as he did so, Kat strode through the front gate. She was covered in blood that mostly wasn't her own, but her aura was blazing, and the magic light consuming her eyes was already fading.

She didn't look as though she had relished killing the men outside, but her countenance was in no way discouraged.

Seeing his daughter's reappearance, Fin released the shield.

Sweat was pouring from his forehead, and his knees buckled, making Kat rush to him, grasping him under his arm.

"Sorry, Da, I tried to be fast."

"Don't worry about me, Kat, I— Oh."

Fin blinked as his daughter closed her eyes and already saw to restoring her father's magic.

"Kat, don't overextend yourself!" As he spoke, the duke steadied and stood tall once more, looking instantly revived from his previous exhaustion.

"Da, I have too much power right now after what I just did. You're helping *me*," Kat explained without an ounce of sarcasm.

The house witch regarded Kat seriously but said nothing more as he realized the part of his daughter's ability that received more power when she killed bothered her enough.

"Where's Likon?" Kat looked around the courtyard hurriedly.

"There." Fin nodded toward the steps to the castle wall with a relieved smile climbing his face.

Kat whirled around to see that sure enough, Likon was being led down the stairs by her mother, though the duchess appeared to be supporting him . . .

Rushing over to save them steps, Kat threw her arms around Likon.

"Are you okay?!"

Likon let out a grunt thanks to her bone-crushing embrace, but after a moment to gather himself, he released the duchess and returned the hug, dropping his forehead to her shoulder.

"Fine. Just sprained my ankle when you chucked me on the wall."

"It was that or have you break both legs from the fall."

"Excuses."

Kat laughed and leaned back, looking into his brown eyes that were tired, his face pale and full of shadows.

"I'm sorry we couldn't find you sooner."

Likon shrugged. "Honestly, it was like a vacation compared to what your mother and brother make me do."

Annika cleared her throat.

Likon shot her a wry smile that the duchess couldn't help but return.

Seeing this, Kat released him so that he could face the duchess more squarely.

"Your Grace," he greeted.

Annika blinked, her eyes looking suspiciously wet as she then hugged her adopted son.

"Be more careful with yourself, or I'll make you do another year of training. You scared the wits out of us."

Likon blinked as he bent down to accept Annika's hug, a lump rising in his throat. He couldn't say anything at first as he realized then just how much the Ashowans had become his family . . .

"The way I see it, you could use less wits, Your Grace, you're too smart for your own good. Oh and . . . Kat, remember when I said the first witch can stop time . . . ?" he asked suddenly, pulling free from Annika's hold.

"Yeah! What the hell is that about?!"

Likon shook his head with a smile. "I honestly said that more so to distract her at the time . . . You see . . . I kind of stole this thing she calls Chronos . . ." Likon reached into his pocket and withdrew a peculiar brass item that ticked . . .

Kat grinned. "Likon, you trickster you, did you pickpocket the daughter of the Gods?"

"She didn't notice my blindfold had lowered ages ago. She was an easy mark." As he shrugged innocently, Annika laughed and proceeded to reach up and cup Likon's face, pulling his attention to her.

She didn't need to say anything, but everyone could see how she loved him.

Fin had started making his way over to his family with Eric at his side.

While the house witch was equally relieved to see Likon returned safely, he and the prince knew they needed to reconvene for the next attack.

However, just before they reached the reunion taking place, an eruption of stone and dust broke through the middle of the courtyard.

Everyone turned, Kat and Eric already drawing their swords free.

A crater appeared in the courtyard, and from its depths floated the first witch, sirin, and the unconscious devil.

The first witch scanned the courtyard, unimpressed. Kat charged forward, Eric on her heels while Fin started levitating some of the rocks that had been blown out of the ground with the intention of pelting the sirin back down into the hole.

However, the ancient beast had already anticipated this, and instead shot the rocks right at Fin, Annika, and Likon.

Thanks to his daughter rejuvenating his magic, Fin was able to erect the shield in time to stop them, but it did impede his sight.

The first witch, seeing Katarina charging and the archers already turning their arrows toward her, sighed.

"While I didn't want to have to use my emergency plan and forfeit getting more magical beasts, I guess I don't have a choice . . ." Aradia reached into the inside of her pocket and procured a slim vial with a black liquid inside.

Kat and Eric had almost reached her while the sirin kept Fin occupied and blocked both the archers and Kezia's magical attacks from the other side of the courtyard, when Aradia poured the liquid over the blade of her dagger.

The blade sparked and vibrated, then Aradia turned to face the castle gate that stood twenty feet away, and she plunged the dagger into open air . . . or so everything thought.

The ground trembled.

Then it rocked.

A deafening crack echoed, and then a hot, white vertical seam tore through the air starting from the dagger.

Aradia was uttering words no one could hear over the din of the commotion . . .

Kat and Eric stumbled to their knees as the courtyard lurched beneath them, and they barely managed to fling themselves out of the way when the sirin attempted to fire an additional attack at them.

The glinting tear in the center of the courtyard sparked and screamed before a pair of large stone hands slipped through the slowly widening brightness. It gripped either side and tore open a hole.

Another stone golem.

Kat and Eric shared a single look of panic and resumed running toward the sirin and first witch.

Any time the sirin managed to cast a spare burst of air or stone at the couple, Kat's eyes would glow, and with her inhuman strength, she'd either deflect a missile or absorb the magic while making sure Eric was near enough to her side that she could cover him.

The stone golem stepped out of the portal, and as Kat and Eric approached, they could see through to the Forest of the Afterlife . . .

The stone golem turned toward them and blocked their view not only of the portal but also of the first witch and devil.

"Shit," Eric said breathily as he stared at the giant creature that could easily wave its hand and decimate a castle tower.

"I'll handle him. If you can't shove the first witch and the devil into the portal, kill the devil so he can be reborn! We need someone who can fight the first witch here in our world—that bitch is too much of a problem!" Kat shouted to him, her eyes wide and frantic.

"Kat, you can't handle a—" Eric didn't get a chance to finish his thought as the golem attempted to crush him. He was forced to dive through its legs, narrowly missing being flattened into the broken stones.

Kat sheathed her sword and noted that the archers were refocusing their efforts toward the golem's eyes as Faucher had instructed them to do in such a circumstance.

Once again releasing her magic to allow it to course freely through her being, Kat's aura surged, her eyes filled with light, and she started climbing up the golem, intent on stabbing its eyes out once she got up there.

The ancient beast noticed her doing this, however, and so swung around in an attempt to shake her off.

Luckily, not only was he unsuccessful, but he accidentally knocked over the sirin.

Eric bolted toward the devil, who had fallen on the ground, hoping to the Gods that it was alright that he wasn't watching where the golem was stumbling as he focused on cutting off the devil's head as quickly as possible.

The devil had fallen to the ground when the golem had shoved the sirin aside, and so Eric landed on his knees beside him. Seizing a fistful of his hair, Eric yanked the devil's head back, his sword swinging down in preparation to kill him, when the first witch leapt onto the prince's back, her arm around his throat, her dagger slipping between his backplate and shoulder armor. Eric yelped in pain, his sword falling from his grasp. The first witch had stabbed his back more than his arm, making Eric fall to a knee. However thanks to Aradia's injured state, the prince's wound wasn't incapacitating.

Aradia grabbed Eric's hair, her dagger moving to cut his throat much in the same manner Eric had almost done to her brother, albeit significantly less gracefully than before as blood dripped down her arm from her arrow wound.

It was during this extra time that the first witch required that allowed Eric the opportunity to turn and punch her in the gut with his left fist.

She grunted, and her blade changed position as she doubled over. She prepared to stab Eric through the eye, though his hand was already coming up to stop her, when she suddenly let out another shout and collapsed on her side.

Eric looked down, baffled at what had happened . . . then noticed the arrow protruding from her arse. He stared dumbly at it, then looked up to see his sister with her crossbow in hand and Lady Kezia murmuring words beside her.

For a moment that felt longer than it was, Eric smiled at his sister in both appreciation and admiration. He leaned down and grabbed the first witch's blade, slipped it into his belt, and picked his sword up from the ground. He plunged its tip into the first witch's neck, pinning her to the courtyard. It would've killed a mortal being, but the first witch merely trembled.

The golem, with Katarina clinging on to his torso, swung around to see what had transpired.

Kat grinned down at her husband when she realized that Aradia was incapacitated, triumph rising in her belly.

But . . . a powerful gust of wind cast by the screeching sirin that had turned and seen what had happened, hit Eric from the side, lifting him up off the ground and sending him flying back . . . into the portal.

"NO!" Alina screamed.

Kat felt the world fall silent, her heart leapt into her throat as she watched her husband be cast back . . .

In an instant, she knew what to do . . . and what it could cost. A certain seer's words rang in her ears . . .

She launched herself off the golem, diving into the portal, her aura burning to a white gold as she flew at a speed that was beyond what any human could see.

To her, the world slowed, and she watched the shock in Eric's hazel eyes as she reached for him.

He didn't reach back as though refusing to accept her help as he fell to what was sure to be his death, but Kat seized him by the tunic that peeked out of his chest plate and flung him back out of the opening.

With how fast it had transpired, it wasn't until Eric was flying outside of the portal that he registered what was happening and started to shout . . . He saw Kat smile . . . as though everything would be alright . . .

But before Eric even hit the ground, he watched as the portal started to shrink; hungrily closing its mouth around the witch that had just come through.

When Eric hit the ground, the impact of the crash radiated through his shoulder and ribs, assuring him that he had broken several bones. Despite the blinding pain that came from his rough landing, he forced himself to turn his head and watch with horror as the seam crackled but did not reopen. The portal had accepted too much payment from the earthly realm from the Troivackian army and the burning witch . . . Something else needed to be returned from the Forest of the Afterlife for the order of the universe to balance . . .

This meant Kat was trapped in the Forest of the Afterlife unless she could figure out how to get back . . . and there could be other ancient beasts waiting to come through . . .

Eric looked up as a shadow fell over him. Although he was already shaking with fury and shock, the stone golem stared down at him.

The prince gave a breathy, dark laugh and smiled up at the ancient giant beast as the furious screams and mayhem of the battle echoed around him.

Closing his eyes slowly, he took in a deep breath before shouting, "Go on! Send me to her! You'd be doing me a favor."

CHAPTER 60

A WITCH'S WIN

Kat landed with a thud amongst the moss, ferns, and mushrooms, a thin, wispy fog hovering around her.

She sat up hurriedly, ready to charge back through the portal, but . . . she instead found herself staring at a large stone with a long glowing crack in it that resembled the portal when the first witch had created it moments before.

"Godsdamnit, this isn't good." Panic fluttered in her throat as she drew her sword and tried to tap the glowing crack only to have her blade be repelled off, making the steel ring. "Reeaaaally not good. Damn, damn, *damn!*"

She lifted her chin and looked at the clear blue sky bordered with lush trees.

"Come out."

Kat jumped, then swung around to find herself staring at several ancient beasts standing and waiting eerily outside the stone circle.

The one who had spoken appeared to be another imp, though this one had short pale blue hair and eyes the same color. Similar to the imp she had just seen die, his eyes had three pupils and was extraordinarily tall. He stared emotionless at the redhead.

"Go join the others that have come through. They have found peace in the forest. We must try to open the portal again."

Kat let out a long breath and turned around to stare at the beastly faces.

"I agree that this portal needs to be opened, but only because *I'm* getting out of here. You lot need to stay here. The devil isn't coming back today. Not unless we can get both the first witch and him through this stupid thing."

She gestured over her shoulder and watched as the imps and sirins narrowed their eyes.

Kat blinked. "Wait . . . No more stone golems? What about dragons? Not that I'm complaining, but it's odd."

"We just sent a golem," the imp who had first spoken to her retorted defensively, his icy eyes watching her unnervingly and his pupils slowly spinning. "Come out, or we will force you out. You've died; you need to pass."

"Like hell I will! I'm not dead! My body came through with my soul. Nice try!" Kat gripped the hilt of her sword even more tightly.

The creatures murmured amongst themselves at this development.

"That does not matter. You are dead," the imp tried to reiterate, though he didn't sound as certain.

"Look, I get you're loyal to the first bitch, I mean witch, but I have a husband who is slightly codependent, a familiar who isn't even fully grown, an emotional father, a brother I haven't annoyed in months. And if I die, my mother might come find me and make me regret dying in the first place! Gods, you have no idea what she'll do to you if I tell her about this! Hell, even *I* don't know what she'd do . . ."

The creatures grew angry over her insult of the daughter of the Gods, and Kat watched warily as both an imp and a sirin started approaching her from the sides of the stone circle.

She readied herself.

They aren't using magic to cast me out . . . Maybe they can't use it inside the circle . . .

Kat stood perfectly still, then when the sirin and imp crossed into the circle, she lunged to the right, stabbing the sirin and throwing a knife at the imp.

The imp fell back, the blade lodged deep into his chest.

Kat kicked the body of the sirin off her sword and recentered herself by the portal. When she had gotten close to the border of the stone circle, she could feel an unpleasant pulling sensation in her body . . . An instinct in her told her that if she crossed the stones, there really wouldn't be any going back.

Her heart pounded in her chest.

There were enough of the beasts that if they rushed her, they could crowd her out, even if she unleashed her magic . . . She needed to find some way, some hope that she could open the portal again, and fast.

Wait!

Kat took a risk and closed her eyes.

She could still feel her connection to everyone! She could feel it flowing through the portal . . .

There really was a chance! She did her best to push a little magic through. She needed her da to at least feel that she was still alive while she sorted things out, and maybe he could help get her out, and she needed to make sure Eric wasn't too hurt after his fall.

Kat only had just enough time to press a little spark through her connection to Fin and Eric when she heard the rustle.

Her eyes flew open, and she gritted her teeth as the beasts all ran toward her.

I just have to beat them all, I guess . . .

Her eyes glinted, and she bared her teeth.

At first it was easy. She cut down two sirins who swiped at her with their claws, but then the imps joined, and they could reach over the sirins that packed the circle, trying to grab Kat from above, which meant she had to try to cut the sirins and dodge the imps simultaneously . . . Her aura burned, but they just kept coming and coming . . .

Then two imps worked together, each reaching down and grabbing an arm of hers and hoisting her up. Though Kat still gripped her sword, she could tell they intended to simply chuck her out of the circle.

"I will sic my father's cat on you, you sons of—"

A dagger lodged itself in one of the imp's heads, making him crumple to the ground, and without his companion helping him, the other imp instantly dropped Kat as well.

The magical beasts turned and found themselves staring at a small cluster of people . . .

Kat looked to see who her savior was as well, and her jaw instantly dropped.

"C-Captain Antonio?!"

There, with his blue eye glinting and wearing a comfortable periwinkle tunic and brown pants, was the former captain of Daxaria's military. He smiled fondly at her and was already drawing another dagger from his belt.

"Hello again, my little spitfire."

Kat laughed in disbelief, her eyes watering in an instant as the man she had thought of as a grandfather smiled at her kindly while already prowling closer to the horde in the circle.

The imp that had been holding Kat suddenly doubled over as he found his groin crushed by a long staff . . .

"Mage Lee?!"

Kat gawked toward her left at the elderly mage with his well-muscled arms, who had served as the Royal Court Mage under King Norman Reyes for decades, as he effectively wielded the staff without its mage crystal.

He grinned back at her without saying a word as though even in death he were still trying to be mysterious.

"Katarina?"

The redhead whirled around to see two women. The shorter one with wavy brown hair and who had called out to her had something familiar about her . . .

"Gods, you look like Fin!" she uttered with a watery smile.

Kat blinked, stunned, but when she regarded the other woman and recognized her as Queen Ainsley Reyes, everything clicked.

"You . . . You're my grandmother, Katelyn Ashowan." Kat stared in awe at the shorter woman, who beamed proudly back at her and nodded. Then the redhead turned to Ainsley Reyes. "You . . . You are . . ."

"Your mother-in-law, from what I last heard." Ainsley smiled, then proceeded to wind her arm back and chuck a stone at a sirin near the outskirts of the circle.

"Katarina, do your best to get through that portal! It will be harder for it to exist if fewer soldiers are coming through!" Katelyn Ashowan shouted urgently right as Kat narrowly dodged a sirin's claw swiping toward her face as the brawl resumed.

"It seems to repel my sword!" she hollered back while punching another imp in the groin. From outside the circle, Mage Lee clubbed the same imp on the backside of the head.

"Fuse your magic with it! If you can absorb it and become part of it, you just need to find a way to pull yourself through to the other side!"

Kat drew her sword again to cut down another three sirins who reached out and yanked at her hair and tried to cut her throat with their sharpened nails.

She knew she didn't have enough time, but she wished she did . . . She wished she could've said thank you to all her dead loved ones for helping her . . . She wished she could've told her grandmother Katelyn Ashowan how everyone adored her and still talked of her often . . .

One day I guess I will get the chance . . . It just won't be today.

While both saddening and humbling, Kat couldn't spare another thought. With her aura rising again, fully rejuvenated thanks to the magical creatures and their fury toward her, she shoved her hand into the glowing seam and willed her magic into it. She could feel sharp teeth bite into her legs, but she had no choice but to close her eyes. She belatedly remembered her sword could help hone her abilities, and so she channeled her power into the weapon until it reverberated in her hand while praying that it would help, then lunged with her entire body into the portal. She could feel the push and pull of the intense magic surrounding her, more powerful than anything she had ever encountered. She took one step and another and then . . .

The golem stood before Eric, its foot rising in preparation to crush him . . . when suddenly the giant stone being was tackled, flying backward into the gate that thankfully the archers and knights had vacated before it was crushed.

What had tackled it?

Eric stared in confusion, unsure if he was hallucinating.

However . . . as it turned out . . . it was the first golem.

The first golem that had arrived with the first witch was pummeling the other one that had come through the portal.

The prince was too stunned to comprehend what in the world was going on, when a large pair of boots thudded to a stop at his side.

Despite the pain racking Eric's body, he managed to look up and see Sir Cleophus Miller with Pina on his shoulder, who was in the process of casually grooming her tiny white paw.

"W-What—"

"It likes Pina," Cleophus explained simply as though that answer should've made perfect sense.

It took Eric far longer than it perhaps normally would've to figure out what the Troivackian knight meant.

"The golem . . . that first attacked . . . is now on our side . . . because of—"

"Because of Pina," Cleophus confirmed once more with a nod.

"Huh . . ." Eric turned, then coughed, which just about made him pass out from the agony.

He vaguely wondered what was happening with the rebel army, and the other sirin, but really, his eyes were glued on the line of light that barred him from Kat.

"She'll be fine," Cleophus grunted down at the prince.

Eric felt his hand grip into a fist. "How can you be so sure?"

From just outside the gates a series of shouts and orders to retreat echoed over the thunderous crunching noises from the fight between the two golems.

"Those are the rebels. I had my unit hang back to ambush them in the event of a retreat. They'll take care of them," Cleophus announced calmly. "And I'm sure she'll be fine, because look." He pointed to the kitten on his shoulder, whose eyes were closing sleepily.

Eric stared at the knight blankly. Perhaps he had died. That would make the most sense right in that moment. For one, Cleophus was talking more than he had ever heard before, and for another, two giant ancient beasts were brawling because of a kitten.

When Cleophus realized the prince wasn't processing his words, he grumbled loudly, "Princess wouldn't be purring if her witch wasn't going to be fine."

Sitting up straighter despite the pain in his ribs, Eric snapped out of his daze and looked at Pina with keen interest.

Cleophus was right.

If Kat were dead, surely her familiar would be in distress!

Eric attempted to push himself to his feet but nearly fainted as his wounds screamed at him.

A hand appeared before him.

The prince looked up, already knowing who he would be staring at.

Fin regarded his son-in-law soberly.

They shared a meaningful moment of eye contact.

Eric opened his mouth to ask what happened to the last sirin but found he didn't need to bother, as a fluffy black cat fell from the sky onto the head of the last sirin that was barely managing to stay conscious amidst the cloud of birds.

Clasping Fin's hand and cradling his ribs, Eric had just about risen to stand perfectly straight when Fin's eyes suddenly glowed . . .

They didn't fill with lightning or even white light, but their blue depths shone . . .

Fin straightened, and at the same time, Eric felt his energy levels rise and his pain dim . . .

Rounding back, Fin looked at the closed mouth of the portal.

"She's still alive." Fin's words warbled. "Thank the Gods . . ."

Both he and Eric stepped closer to the crackling light where Alina, Kezia, Rebecca, Annika, and Likon already waited.

On what remained of the castle walls, the archers were still peppering the occasional rebel soldier that tried to get closer. Aside from that, the only threat before them . . . was the devil.

He was gagged, blindfolded, and bound on the stones.

The first witch made gurgling sounds on the ground, and her appearance kept shifting to the forms of different women from various kingdoms as her body struggled to heal. But her attempts were unsuccessful due to Eric's sword being lodged where it was.

They all ignored her and instead looked at the devil.

"What are we going to do?" Alina asked Fin, her eyes filled with fear. "How can we open this gate and get Kat out?"

"What about stabbing the devil?" Eric volunteered, his darkened hazel eyes falling to the son of the Gods coldly.

"It could work. Maybe stabbing both of them will absorb enough power to open the gate again," Likon agreed eagerly.

"If that was the case, she would have just opened a gate right after getting her hands on the devil. She needed magic from all four elements . . . Or something needs to come back through. I honestly don't know what is required to bring balance back at this point," Fin lamented irritably.

"I saw that the first witch used something else . . . She had a vial," Eric recalled slowly before crouching down by the daughter of the Gods and pulling free an empty vial from an inside pocket of her coat.

Uncorking it, Eric handed it to Fin, and the house witch took a sniff.

He wrinkled his nose. "It smells . . . a little like Witch's Brew and . . . blood?"

The devil started making a series of noises as though trying to form words . . .

Everyone looked questioningly at one another, but in the end, it was Likon who removed the gag, though he remained standing behind the devil with it at the ready just in case.

"Lady Katarina is a mutant witch, is she not?" the devil mused after clearing his throat indignantly.

"So what?" Eric demanded tonelessly.

"This means my sister already had the four elements, but because Lady Katarina had very little power when she was stabbed, Aradia relied on the death of the Troivackian soldiers to fuel it and also act as the payment for an ancient beast. She most likely saved Lady Katarina's blood to get the most out of it. My guess is Aradia was also hoping to steal some other witches' powers to bolster herself, and of course, bring in reinforcements." The devil gestured with his chin toward the ruckus the stone golems were still making.

Fin frowned in their direction. While the golems hadn't crossed the border ring of fire yet, it wouldn't be long until they did, which meant the civilians may start being placed in harm's way.

"Think of the soldiers' deaths as the force to push the door open, but the blood carrying magic of the four elements the key," the devil concluded while sounding annoyed that the group before him wasn't as swift in figuring things out as he would've liked.

"In other words, we need the blood of witches with each element, and we might need to get one or both of the golems to open the gate without them necessarily passing through? Kraken, is there any way you can maneuver that?" Fin turned toward his familiar, who was licking his lips and sauntering toward them having just finished off the last sirin.

"House witch, believe it or not, you are *also* a mutated witch," the devil announced sarcastically.

He then tried to stand up, but the edge of Annika Ashowan's blade touched his throat, stopping him.

Fin faltered as the obvious answer dawned on them.

"Eric, give me the first witch's blade."

"Now, now, house witch, you might be the key, but the Forest of the Afterlife owes this realm another life. Do you think you have the power to open the door and pull her out? You aren't a stone golem." The devil's voice had grown louder as he sensed this was a rather precarious position. "If *you* promise to release me, *I* promise to tell you how to get everything back to rights."

Everyone exchanged glances.

It was a terrible option.

Really, what they all wanted was to chuck the first witch and devil in the portal, grab Kat, and be done with the children of the Gods. But it was true they weren't sure if they could open the portal on their own . . .

However, it was Pina who mewed and snapped everyone's attention to her.

Cleophus had joined the group as they brainstormed.

Everyone turned to look at the kitten, who was staring at the wrestling stone golems with her head tilted.

"*I KNEW YOU WERE MOCKING ME!*" Kraken meowed loudly.

Fin jumped at his familiar's shout. "What is it?"

"*THAT LITTLE RAT JUST TOLD ME PERFECTLY CLEARLY THAT A GOLEM CAN HOLD OPEN THE DOOR WITHOUT CROSSING IF WE USE YOUR BLOOD TO OPEN THE GATE!*" Kraken was livid. He growled up at the kitten accusatorily.

Ignoring the feud between the two familiars, everyone perked up hopefully as Fin repeated what he had heard.

"Well, of course none of you know how you can defeat a golem or convince one to help!" the devil declared, though he was sounding more antsy . . . as though he had lost his leverage . . . "It also seems as though my sister had made this portal using a certain kind of spell—which makes it more complicated."

Ignoring the devil's attempt at convincing them all he was still valuable, it dawned on Eric that he didn't seem to have his powers while blindfolded . . .

The prince recalled how, back when Kat had rescued him and she was overwhelmed with power, she had tried to gouge the devil's eyes out.

Eric smiled ominously down at the devil (though the son of the Gods couldn't see it) and held out a hand toward Annika Ashowan.

"Your Grace, might I borrow that?"

Annika looked at her dagger and then at Eric, but as she opened her mouth to ask the reason why, he looked over his shoulder at Cleophus Miller. "What are the odds that you think the other golem will help Pina because he thinks she's cute?"

Cleophus looked at Eric as though he had just insulted the beloved kitten. That was enough of a confirmation to the question that he needed.

"Great. Mind walking over there and seeing if she can convince the golem to give us a hand?"

The knight reached up, scritched Pina's cheeks, and stomped indignantly toward the golems as though he were heading out for a leisurely stroll . . . or . . . his version of a leisurely stroll at least . . .

The devil hadn't been aware that one of the golem's had already fallen under the charms of Katarina's familiar.

"What do you need the dagger for?" Fin asked intently as he sensed that Eric had an idea.

"I'm taking the devil's eyes, but I don't think I should do it with the first witch's blade in case that makes things more complicated."

The devil stilled, and a black eyebrow arched up past his blindfold. "How depraved of you."

"Well, it's one way to make sure you don't give us any more problems." Eric accepted the blade the duchess offered him.

Alina held her hand out in front of her brother, halting him as he started to move forward.

"I want to do it."

The prince turned in alarm toward the Troivackian queen.

Then he saw the darkness in his sister's eyes, and remembered who was responsible for it.

He handed over the blade without another word.

Fin stared at Alina in horror. "Wait—"

But the queen had already seized a fistful of the devil's hair and plunged the blade through the blindfold.

The devil screamed, but he shocked Alina by grasping her hand and pushing himself farther *into* the blade before she could stop him . . .

And then . . . he fell over. Dead.

"*That*—" Eric started to boom furiously, when the glowing seam of the portal brightened substantially, cutting him off.

Everyone backed away as the opening started to widen. It snapped and hissed and roared again much as it had the first time . . . But as the portal stretched, there was a gleaming figure inside it, pushing back its opening . . .

Whoever it was did not look human as it stood there, but rather like human-shaped coal. The portal started to hum, and red and gold magic started to flow from it into the fiery being.

Eric stared through the glaring brightness with a squint and saw that sure enough . . .

It looked like Kat.

He didn't care what would happen next, he bolted toward the portal, his eyes watering against the brilliance, the magic making his hair stand on end. Sweat poured from his face, and it felt as though time had slowed almost to a stop, but he dragged his limbs through the power, pushing against the pain in his side until he reached into the scalding, blinding light, seized what he believed to be an arm . . . and pulled.

A deafening explosion blasted and echoed across Vessa in such a way that it sounded as though the world had ended in a final moment of magical combustion.

Eric closed his eyes as he was thrown into the air for a second time that day, his ears ringing.

But . . . he felt power searing through his being. He had known Kat had inadvertently sent him power before, but this was so much more potent, he could even feel it streaming from her to others around them.

He didn't have a chance to think about the sensation anymore as he braced himself to hit the courtyard stones.

Instead . . . he felt his back land against something surprisingly soft.

And to make matters even better . . .

He felt the unmistakable shape of his wife against his chest, where his heart was thundering.

In the deathlike hush that followed, Eric wondered if they'd all died . . . not particularly caring too much just yet as he could still feel Kat . . .

But then he heard a weary, groaning moan . . .

"Godsdamnit . . . Please . . . tell me . . . that it's over."

Kat opened her eyes and found herself in her husband's arms. His face was smudged with soot, and blood stained various parts of his body, but he was alive. She knew he was alive despite him lying relatively still because he was smiling and staring at her even though they were, interestingly, completely encompassed . . . in magical lightning.

In fact, the entire courtyard with the soldiers, golems, and flying debris appeared to have been caught and held in place by Finlay Ashowan's shield, preventing everyone from being killed by the blast. Luckily, he had also received a healthy surge of redistributed power from his daughter.

Sighing in relief, Kat dropped her head to Eric's chest, relishing in a moment of rest and enjoying being back in the realm of the living.

"Oh no. You don't get off so easily."

Kat lifted her head to stare back up at Eric, though it took a good deal of effort.

The effort as it turned out happened to be worth it as he dragged her up and kissed her soundly on the mouth.

From a distance, someone laughed . . .

Then another person whooped.

Eventually everyone was gently placed back on the ground as the cheers rose to a roar, but Eric kept hugging and kissing his wife over and over, not caring that she was lying on top of him on the courtyard stones, or about anything else.

It seemed as though, against all odds . . .

They had won.

CHAPTER 61

IN THE WAKE OF WAR

Kat huffed irritably as the physician disinfected her numerous wounds. It was already a frustrating time, as she had to lie topless on her stomach as he tended to the scratches and bites she'd received from the sirins.

Eric grinned from his seat on the stool in front of her, his broken ribs and stab wound already bandaged, leaving him free to pull on his tunic while his wife finished being tended to.

"I said I'm fine. It was just a few scratches," she grumbled.

"These scratches along your shoulder and waist will scar," the physician informed her patiently.

Eric stared at her, unable to stop smiling.

"You being in a good mood makes this more annoying," Kat bit out, though she could tell she was starting to blush as Eric brought his stool closer to her.

"Don't be a brat," he chided while reaching for her hands and grasping them. "I get to be happy that we survived a war involving supernatural beings, *and* I can now take you on a honeymoon where no one— Not a single. Person. Is allowed. To bother. Us," Eric enunciated through his smile while leaning a little closer with each point.

Kat pretended to glare. "So what happened with the . . . mercenary . . . leader's . . . body?" she asked awkwardly while trying not to explicitly mention the devil in front of the physician.

Thus far, the supernatural appearances had been explained to the general public by saying that a mage and a witch had worked together to seek revenge for how the witches had been treated in Troivack.

The only reason this narrative was approved was because Katarina and her father had fought against them, which provided a valid argument that not all witches were awful.

At least they hoped that would be the consensus . . . It would be hard enough with the preexisting bias against magic users . . .

Eric didn't respond to Kat's question as he eyed the physician, who was still tending to the back of her legs. So they waited in silence until the man finished, and then with a polite, quiet bow, the physician left to tend to the other wounded soldiers that had returned.

Once alone in the small room that prior to the war had been a storage closet, but had since had its shelves full of dishware pushed to the side to make room for tables for the physicians to work on the battle-injured, Eric kissed Kat's fingers that he had been clasping and stood to retrieve her tunic.

"The devil's body turned to ash."

Kat frowned while accepting her tunic, carefully covering herself before rolling over to slip it over her head and bandages. "What do you mean?"

"I mean your father went to investigate after I took you inside the castle, and there was nothing but a pile of ash. Sir Cas says that he had guarded the first witch and the devil's body with Lady Kezia, but neither of them can explain what happened. Lady Elena's familiar, Reggie, picked up a handful of ash and ran off with it . . . Not sure what that was about yet, but yes, the devil is now a harmless pile of soot. We aren't sure if he is going to be reborn from that pile or appear elsewhere . . . As for the first witch, they are locking her in the castle dungeon for now, but His Majesty is working on finding another prison for her where no one can find her while also having people study the tool Likon stole."

Kat nodded along to the news. "What happened to Mr. Levin and your assistant?"

Eric's good mood at last dimmed.

"Mr. Levin disappeared with his wife and daughter sometime during the fighting. We think he fled toward the west given that that was the only gateway not properly guarded during the conflict. As for Thomas Julian . . . I don't know. I need to speak with Likon about him."

Kat fidgeted uncomfortably.

Seeing this, Eric let out a disappointed sigh.

"Listen, I know you care about Likon, but planting a spy who tampers with my correspondence? I'm going to have to arrange a formal investigation and arrest."

"But—"

"Kat, you know I can't ignore this."

After a moment of staring earnestly at her husband's stern face, Kat's shoulders slumped forward in defeat, though she gave a minor wince as the deep cuts along her waist protested.

"I understand what you're saying, but can you just promise me you will talk to him about it first? At least figure out the whole situation. I mean, obviously Likon isn't the only one Thomas Julian was talking to, otherwise we would've received the ransom letter the first witch sent."

Eric opened his mouth but could tell by the desperation in Kat's face she wasn't going to concede on this point, and well . . . it *was* the right thing to do to ensure there was a proper punishment assigned, even if Eric still wasn't entirely too fond of the man.

"Now that we've been patched up, shall we go see how my sister and His Majesty are faring?"

Kat gave a dip of her chin to signify her assent before she slid off the table.

"So . . . Did Alina really shoot the first witch in the arse?"

Eric grinned once more as they proceeded toward the door.

"She did indeed. Real pity you missed it . . . If only you hadn't *tried to sacrifice yourself*, you could've seen it."

"Oyy! That's the thanks I get?! There's no chance you would've survived what I did! Did you see the bite marks? I tell you, sirins are nasty birds . . ." Kat shouted at Eric indignantly as they made their way down the bustling corridor.

Eric rounded on her, locked eyes with her, and grasped her face in both his hands, making Kat instantly burn red . . . until he smooshed her cheeks.

"Never. *Ever.* Do that again. No amount of you being sneaky or adorable will save you in this argument. Got it?"

Kat tried to find a way to avoid making such an agreement, but sensing this, Eric squished her cheeks an extra amount until she double tapped his forearm into releasing.

"Fine! Fine, I won't . . . sacrifice myself for your old arse. Do you need a cane by the way?" Kat asked while only partially jesting as she noticed Eric's shuffling steps thanks to his ribs.

"I'll be fine. I'll drink some willow bark tea later—I promise I will this time. Don't go dosing my coffee again," he retorted sternly.

Kat smirked but held her tongue as they continued down the corridor.

As was usual between the couple, their attentions were completely fixed on each other, which meant they missed the amount of gawking and awe-filled whispers that trailed after them . . .

⁎   ⁎   ⁎

Brendan's fist pounded his desk, making the furniture creak ominously.

Faucher had just informed the king that there was no sign of where Mr. Levin and his wife had fled to. Apparently, the ever-thorough assistant had prepared an escape plan should the first witch lose. The military leader bowed and excused himself to see to the other knights that were still returning.

To make matters even worse, they had no idea when the prince's assistant had disappeared, though Lady Katarina's maid Poppy said she received a sweet note from Thomas Julian apologizing to her, saying that things were complicated but that he hoped to see her again one day.

Likon had also received a letter from his nephew. It had been left with the innkeeper of the establishment where he had first been abducted. After learning the missive was waiting for him there, Likon had gone to retrieve it with several knights who were to guard him. In the meantime, Brendan was apprised of everything that had transpired in his absence from the castle.

Fin was slumped in his chair, the exhaustion lines in his face dark, and any pretense of acting as a nobleman long gone. His wife sat at his side, though she was able to maintain her cool composure as was her norm, albeit she did have blood and soot spattering her own attire as well . . .

"What were you saying before Leader Faucher came in? Something about the devil turning to dust?" Brendan rounded on the house witch after taking a breath to compose himself.

"It's just that. I think he is in the process of being reborn somewhere as we speak, but what is especially interesting is that Lady Elena's familiar, Reggie, brought her some of the ash, and we think *that* was the missing element from when she was trying to re-create the mold on the mushrooms."

Brendan straightened, his previous ire forgotten in light of the startling discovery.

"With a bit of water, apply the ash to a mushroom, let it decay a little, and it has the ability to suspend someone in a state between life and death, where they see magic, half fey, imps . . . The mushrooms, we think, are what is anchoring the teleportation through the portal. Both Kat and Kraken said they saw the mushrooms in a stone circle in the Forest of the Afterlife."

"Fin?" Surprisingly it was the duchess who interrupted her husband.

Both men looked to her. "You told me that when you ate the mold, it was able to separate your soul from your body and transport you . . . Why did you appear in our home in front of Tam?"

Fin balked.

He had completely forgotten about his impromptu spiritual journey . . .

"Maybe it's because that was where I had the most pull to? I didn't eat the mushroom with it, so my soul didn't have an anchor summoning it. So with our home in Austice, and Tam being there, maybe that is simply where I had the strongest connection?"

Annika and Brendan each considered this theory, and after a time, both seemed to agree it did make the most sense though it really was nothing but a speculation.

"Your Majesty, I can stay until we are certain the first witch is imprisoned, but would you maybe like help finding where the devil has respawned?" Fin asked as he mentally sifted through all the work that needed to be completed following the battle.

"I will consider your offer, Your Grace. However, I am intending to send Mr. Kraft and Mage Sebastian to search for him with the assistance of a Coven of Aguas member who volunteered. If we do not find hide nor hair of him in a few months, I will send word to Daxaria's court for you."

Fin didn't look fully convinced that this was the best plan of action but decided not to argue the point any further . . . He didn't have the energy for a battle of wills after the recent days he had lived. Instead, he reached for his wife's hand, startling her with the casual display of affection in the presence of the Troivackian king.

"You know . . . I think if you aren't requiring our assistance . . . after another two months, I'd like us to head home. Kat and Eric included. Your Majesty, I understand that this ends Katarina's time here a good deal earlier than planned, but frankly speaking, we all knew they both would need to return sooner than later after their marriage."

Brendan tilted his head and let out a sigh.

"I'm aware. However . . . I will request your assistance in a matter that is going to be a bit of a problem before then."

Fin barely resisted moaning in exasperation.

He really just wanted to make some fresh dinner rolls, his famous potato soup, and relax with Annika . . .

"What matter is that, Your Majesty?" Annika jumped in, sensing her husband's patience and ability to behave properly had expired.

Brendan cleared his throat and leaned back on his desk. "Well . . . Sir Cleophus Miller . . . wants to swear his fealty to your duchy and move to Daxaria."

Fin snorted before he could stop himself, then leaned forward, his eyes gleaming humorously. "He wants to follow Pina, doesn't he?"

The king gave a mildly irritable grumble. "Yes, he does. But he is a knight sworn in service to me, and if he leaves without my permission, he will be charged with treason. I don't think I need to expand on the fact that he is our most talented and notable knight, and for him to wish to change the nobility he serves—"

"Wait . . . Isn't he also supposed to inherit Lord Milo Miller's earldom?" Annika interjected.

"He . . . wishes to surrender the position—"

"But Broghan Miller is already set to serve our daughter for the remainder of his life," Annika finished.

Brendan let that development rest over the duke and duchess. Fin still looked like he was about to start laughing, but Annika's mind was racing . . .

"During our initial confrontation with the devil and first witch in the throne room, the first witch said something to Lady Sarah Miller, Sir Cleophus and Broghan's sister, before disappearing. I was concerned and suspicious about what she was talking about, but it now makes sense. I've since learned from Lady Sarah that the first witch had believed it would be Lady Sarah herself who would inherit Lord Milo Miller's house. The first witch seemed incredibly confident about it as well."

Annika didn't hide her shock, and Fin's humored expression dulled at the mention of the first witch.

"I'm reluctant to say this would be a great opportunity to leverage more equal rights for Troivackian women given it was our enemy who supposedly sparked this development."

"Going back to the matter with Cleophus . . . Hypothetically, is there a way he could remain as a part of Your Majesty's army but be dubbed a diplomat that stays on our grounds in Daxaria when he visits? Will Lady Sarah even be approved as an heir by her father?" Fin wondered aloud.

Brendan raised an eyebrow. "If we pressured Lord Milo Miller to support the decision, he has a number of noblemen already indebted to him which could sway the vote in favor of naming Lady Sarah as the next head of her house. It is . . . possible that your suggestion of making Sir Cleophus a diplomat could sway him . . . Again, I suspect I will need your help with this, and . . . possibly Lady Katarina's familiar."

Annika and Fin shared a look that the king couldn't quite determine the meaning of, but afterward, Annika lowered her chin respectfully. "We'll do what we can."

After the Ashowans left his office, the king made his way back to his own chamber, doing his best to quickly handle those that approached to congratulate him on the successful win . . .

However, while relieved, Brendan couldn't be entirely happy.

Upon entering his quarters, he found Alina sitting on their bed, her back to the door as she blindly stared at the wall in front of her.

She didn't even turn to see who had come in.

Brendan wasn't sure she had even heard him.

Instead of calling out to his wife, he started undoing his armor.

He had just about succeeded in taking most of it off himself, when at long last he felt Alina's gentle hands undoing the final trickier parts from around his shoulders.

"I heard you killed the devil," Brendan said quietly as he watched Alina's flat gaze fix itself to her task.

"I didn't mean to. I was just trying to blind him."

Brendan felt his chest ache . . .

He thought back to the sweet, whole, happy young woman he had fallen in love with back in Daxaria . . . back when he was simply focused on helping her lungs grow stronger . . .

What have I done to her? He stared sadly at his wife as she worked, wishing that Troivack wasn't such a brutal, harsh place for a woman as good as her . . .

"Brendan, stop staring at me like you're the guilty party." Alina's quiet voice was firm, but she still didn't look at him before she moved over to his other side. "The violence in this kingdom . . . I expected it. I am making a difference, and that is what I wanted."

"The cost is higher than you thought it would be." Brendan continued to watch her. He stared at her fine thin nose and marveled at how she could still look so delicate after having tried to gouge the devil's eyes out and having shot the first witch with a crossbow. Twice.

"I think this battle was unique, and to be honest . . ." she trailed off and turned around to set down the final plate of armor on the nearby table. "What's difficult is that everyone has every right to be happy about winning. About being safe once more and overcoming this threat. But no one is going to properly grieve or even think much about our child, and . . . it isn't fair. To anyone. While they should be happy, our child has a right to be mourned. There is no perfect solution."

Brendan stared at his wife's back as she lingered at the table, not wanting to show the expression she was making . . .

The king stepped over to Alina, and from behind, he wrapped his strong arms around her in an embrace and held her.

Alina allowed herself to break down again. She allowed herself to grieve without feeling the need to force herself to carry on through her next duty, to be strong in order to help others . . .

And Brendan did the same as he lowered his head and wept into Alina's hair for their loss.

While he knew that there would be a time in the future when things wouldn't be as hard or painful . . . he also knew that both he and Alina needed a little bit of time before everything felt right again. And that was alright.

CHAPTER 62

HOMEWARD BOUND HEROES

K raken glared at the kitten, who was in the process of having a leisurely stretch in front of the fire while yawning.

He lowered his head and padded closer.

"Now that the battle has ended, little familiar, you have much to explain."

Pina turned her head so that she stared at Kraken upside down, her ears flattening against the carpet.

Kraken could tell that if a human were nearby, they would be helpless to her charms.

Seating himself in front of her, the empurror waited, his air of disapproval palpable.

"I will not simply let you be should you pretend not to be able to speak again."

Pina rolled back over to rest on her belly, shook her head, licked her lips . . . and purred.

"I wasn't sure what kind of cat you were." Her voice was young, but sweet . . .

Kraken's tail twitched. *"Speak plainly."*

"Well . . . My witch kept talking about how great you were—"

"Naturally."

"How you are the empurror of Daxaria—"

"All this is true, yes."

"And how you could relay what I say to my witch."

The fluffy empurror huffed. *"I have yet to glean the reasoning for your deception."*

"What if you decided you wanted to be the only powerful familiar? You could lie about what I said. You could turn me into a villain."

"*Your age is apparent. Don't you know it is a familiar's sacred duty to serve their witch well? I am the familiar to the mighty house witch. It would not be appropriate for me to interfere with the harmony of our family,*" Kraken scoffed.

"*That may be true for your relationship with your witch, but . . . What if I want my own land? Will the great empurror share his kingdom?*"

Kraken stilled, and Pina started to smile.

"*What do you need with such power? My witch's destiny is to create a harmonious home for those he cares for. It is best that I offer my influence to help him achieve that.*"

"*My witch is prone to trouble. I need to help her escape those situations. Her destiny is to burn away the darkness and the bad. I bring out the good in people, and that makes her calling that much easier to fulfill.*"

Kraken fell silent.

Pina stood while slipping into another languid stretch as she flexed her claws. "*I am charm, sweetness, and soft as the Goddess's touch. I rule the hearts of the good, and I needed to be sure that you, Empurror Kraken, were one of the good.*"

The empurror stared down at Pina and lowered his chin.

A charged moment passed between the two felines.

Kraken then abruptly tackled her to the ground, kicking her back legs, and smothering her face in his chest fur.

Pina tried to squirm her way out of his hold, but there was too much fluff to battle against.

She was about to start yowling for help when a low rumble sounded in her ear.

"*Not bad, little familiar, but we're going to have to train you up.*"

Pina paused in her struggle, realizing that this impromptu wrestling was better intentioned than she had originally interpreted.

After a moment of scuffle, Kraken eventually released her from the hold, though he reached out a large paw and rested it on her forehead.

"*It was good of you to speak up during the battle and that you were able to convince the golems to help.*"

Pina sighed and ducked out from under Kraken's paw. "*The first witch and devil will come back.*"

Kraken chirped. "*Yes. After all this, I'm beginning to suspect what my witch heard foretold from the Goddess decades ago is not about our dear burning witch . . .*"

Pina squinted. She had no idea the prophetic words the Gods had uttered back when Finlay Ashowan had died . . .

Sensing her confusion, Kraken purred mightily. *"The Goddess declared that a child of my witch's would help a being she cares about . . . We can surmise the being is either the devil or first witch but . . . I am starting to suspect that it may in fact be Tamlin Ashowan who is destined to help the Goddess's offspring."*

The kitten listened, sitting primly.

His dramatic announcement weighed down the mood of the darkening room as his musings rang with truth . . .

However, the moment was ruined when Pina then took it upon herself to get even with the empurror and flung him to the ground with a flying leap.

The rest of the evening was spent engaging in races around the castle to see who was fastest (Pina), and who was strongest (Kraken), but after a while, they both forgot about the more serious matters and instead enjoyed having what some might call the starting of what could be a long friendship blooming.

Three months after the battle with the first witch . . .

Kat stared at the nearing shore with a beaming smile, her hands gripping the railing as she leaned her head back and let out a long breath.

"I. Can't. Wait. To. Be. HOME!" she crowed loudly without a care in the world.

At long last, she was almost back in Daxaria.

While her father had tried to arrange for them all to leave at least a month earlier, the poor weather conditions and Kat wanting to stay longer to help Alina solidify her position in the council took more time.

However, after the battle, not much really needed to be done to promote Alina's image as a hardened Troivackian woman, as several powerful men had seen her violent acts during the attack.

What had actually wound up being a significantly larger amount of work was managing all the new responsibilities that the council felt she could handle—and of course hiring new handmaidens.

Lady Kezia had been officially appointed as the Royal Court Mage, and Lady Sarah had begun the process of taking over as the next head of her household—she begrudgingly admitted Katarina had given her the courage to do so. This meant every handmaiden position had to be filled.

Dana was hired as Alina's handmaiden, though she was known to antagonize Sir Cleophus Miller a great deal whenever they crossed paths. Faucher permitted Sir Cas to continue teaching the women who wished to learn to fight, though he still hadn't come around to allowing his daughter to join.

Despite this, by the time Kat set sail, she knew it was only a matter of time. Especially as Alina had sternly informed the military leader he was to stop giving Dana new dogs, meaning he had no other means of placating his daughter's displeasure.

Mage Sebastian and Mr. Kraft had departed a fortnight after the battle to try to find any mysteriously appearing infants who could be the reincarnated devil . . .

The first witch's invention, Chronos, was to remain in Troivack to be studied, but her dagger was to return with Finlay Ashowan to be kept safe with the Coven of Wittica.

Piers, Conrad, and Dante gave a tearful farewell to their father's best student—though Kat was already well aware that the only reason for Dante's upset was that he had to say goodbye to Pina . . .

Lady Rebecca Devark didn't find poop in her shoes again, though she *did* find an unfathomable amount of cat hair in her food and beverages. Despite this, even the impenetrable former queen had started softening a little over the recent months as well.

When asked about her short hair style, she admitted to having had cut it when her boys were young, shortly after her husband's death, as it seemed more efficient, but she knew it was unladylike . . .

A fact that Kat teased her endlessly about.

Suffice it to say, the former queen had eagerly helped Kat pack for her trip back to Daxaria.

Caleb Herra had taken over as the head of his house given that his father had been a part of the coup and his older brother was dead. The poor man barely had time to come out and grunt whenever Kat had taken it upon herself to visit, as he was flooded with new responsibilities.

And while Joshua Ball was not being considered for taking the place of his half brother, he had started visiting Elyse Ball more frequently while he started preparing to take his knight's exam the following year.

Best yet, by the time of Kat's departure, Alina found that she was once again feeling more like herself, though she had her good days and bad . . . It helped that for the first time since setting foot on Troivackian soil, she felt genuinely welcomed and as though she was making a difference in a relatively safe environment.

Yes, everything had more or less wrapped up, save for the fact that the devil was out there somewhere . . . and he may have a small vendetta against them all . . . While the first witch lived in her new prison, far underneath the city of Vessa, where only a handful of people knew how to find.

A hand clasping Kat's shoulder distracted her from her thoughts and had her turning around to see Eric wearing a white tunic and loose trousers that fluttered in the fair sea wind.

She reached up and gripped his hand in return, then leaned back and gave him a quick kiss.

"Are you happy that we're finally back? And please don't talk about the honeymoon again. You know we can't leave for another two months at the earliest after we tell everyone about our marriage, and I have to go through the stupid coronation . . ."

Eric laughed a little and proceeded to wrap his arms around Kat's waist and rest his chin on her shoulder.

"I am excited to be back, yes."

Kat nodded her head. "Good."

Eric nuzzled her neck, making her squawk in response.

"By the way, I kept forgetting to ask, but back when we first told your father—and he was angry with us—you said you had a plan. I don't think I ever heard what that was . . ."

Tilting her head back and letting out a laugh, Kat enlightened her husband. "Ah, that! I was thinking of baking him a pie and talking about emotional things . . . Maybe while Pina was on my shoulder."

"You can cook?" Eric asked without fully hiding his skepticism.

"Oh, I'm terrible at both baking and cooking. I tend to burn things. I was just hoping that between my sincerity and him never wanting me to make him anything ever again he'd choose to forgive us a little."

Eric chuckled. It had been a fantastic plan, though in the end they didn't need it.

"Are you really okay with leaving Likon in Troivack?" the prince asked suddenly.

Though he had been checking in regularly ever since Likon's punishment had been decided, Eric could sense his wife's unhappiness, and so found himself repeatedly asking the question.

Kat sighed and proceeded to turn around to face Eric more directly. "Of course I wish he could come home, but . . . I recognize he still had Thomas Julian reporting your activities, and that's illegal. Even if it was to make sure I was safe . . ."

Eric raised an eyebrow, sensing that his wife was needling him.

"Plus, he wasn't the one telling Likon to tamper with your correspondence!"

"We still need proof of that. Hence the duration of his punishment," Eric reminded her seriously. "If he can find his nephew while serving as His Majesty's assistant before the ten years of his term is up, then he can be released and come home."

"Yeah, yeah . . . At least I know Brendan and Alina will bring him when they visit in the next three to five years . . ."

Kat's eyes fell to Eric's chest glumly.

Her deflated mood was unacceptable to the prince, and so he picked her up and sat her on the railing of the ship, making sure to hold her steady, though he knew she wouldn't fall overboard so easily.

"Come on, you know we still have the absolute best event of our lives coming up."

Kat smiled shyly and looked down at her lap.

"Do you . . . Do you think it'll help things . . . ?"

"We both know the answer to that," Eric affirmed while dropping his forehead to hers, then kissing her. "Alina already wrote to Reese Flint to have the painter ready for when we tell Mr. Howard the news that we're married and your father is my in-law. Now let's finish packing below deck. Also, can you please remind Sir Cleophus about boundaries when it comes to our chamber? I don't care if he thinks Pina needs to be guarded while napping."

Kat laughed and after grasping her husband's hand followed him back below deck.

Meanwhile, from the upper deck of the ship, Fin and Annika watched their daughter, wearing content smiles.

"I admit it . . . I did *not* predict anything that happened for Kat in Troivack," Annika lamented with a sigh.

Fin grinned and kissed his wife on the side of the head. "Things turned out even better for her, right?"

"She really has given up wearing dresses though."

"What is the big deal about her wearing trousers exactly?"

"I just think she looks nicer in dresses . . . And I always had to dress while keeping everyone else in mind for how I wanted to manipulate them or to hide myself . . ." Annika explained quietly, looking ever so slightly as though she were pouting.

Taken aback by this new detail about his wife, Fin felt himself somehow fall even more in love with her as he realized just how much she had wanted to give their daughter a better life than her own . . .

After overcoming his surprise, Fin laughed softly. "Well, who knows? Maybe you'll have granddaughters you can dress up as you please. I'm sure Kat won't mind until the children express otherwise."

The duchess's brown eyes flew up to her husband. "She shouldn't have children for at least another year! She needs to prepare for taking on more responsibilities for the crown, and amidst that, His Highness is adamant about the long honeymoon, and—"

"You and I both know trying to make Kat follow any sort of plan that is not her own won't go well." The duke sighed with a smile, his blue eyes lowering thoughtfully.

Annika's gaze, on the other hand, narrowed.

"You know something."

Fin jolted in alarm.

"You should retire from the spy business; you're starting to get far too suspicious of everything I say—"

"Fin, I swear to the Gods, did she tell you that she's—" The duchess wielded her finger up into her husband's face as he held up his hands in surrender.

"She doesn't know herself yet! So don't be mad at her."

Annika froze. Utterly shocked.

She had thought her husband had been teasing her.

"Fin . . . are you . . . serious . . . ?! Kat is . . . She . . . I'm going to be a *grandmother*?!"

Fin couldn't help it—hearing Annika say the word *grandmother* had his face splitting into the biggest smile his cheeks could hold.

"I sensed it two days ago at dinner. Kat was craving lamb, but there was another little someone craving honey cakes . . ."

Annika's lips pressed together, her eyes widened and watered.

At first, Fin didn't know what she was going to say or how she would react. Would she be angry that their daughter was getting herself into a new world of trouble that would last a lifetime?

But then, as only she could do, his wife surprised him for a second time that day and let out a shrieking cheer before leaping into his arms.

"Gods, you really want a girl to dress up, don't you?" Fin laughed but relished in the happy embrace as they celebrated the news that they would be grandparents in the near future . . . not that their daughter or her husband had any idea just yet . . .

Ah well. It was one of the perks of being a house witch.

EPILOGUE 1

TROIVACK'S TURNAROUND

Likon stared out of his new chamber window, feeling the warming breeze on his face and letting out a sigh of relief.

It had been a chaotic few months as he had frantically searched for his nephew. Though while many thought it was because it would clear his debt and charges against himself, it was because the uncle was incredibly worried for the lad. His sister Dena's eldest son had been selected as the crown prince's assistant for three reasons back when it had been decided Eric would be going to Troivack.

First, Thomas was incredibly bright and capable. He had impressed all his tutors and showed a real interest in administrative work. Though he had dreams of being a knight like his father, when he failed his squire's test, that option for his future dimmed.

The second, there weren't many qualified people the king could trust available for hire at the last minute, which led to the third reason . . .

Likon had vouched for his nephew to Annika Ashowan.

Shame, pain, and hurt broiled in Likon's gut when he had found out that Thomas had been doing more than simply keeping tabs on the prince's self-indulgent and self-destructive propensities.

He felt as though he had failed and hurt the Ashowans . . . The family that had taken him in and introduced Dena to a knight who instantly fell in love with and married her despite her time at Madam Nonata's brothel. Her husband, Sir Kenneth Julian, provided her with a good, comfortable life and gave her four beautiful children.

Likon dropped his head as his mind roved over such thoughts for the thousandth time . . .

Even though both Annika and Fin had adamantly insisted there could still be a reason the young man had done what he had, Likon couldn't hold on to any hope. Particularly, as all the letter from his nephew had said was:

> Uncle Likon,
>   I'm sorry for what I've done . . . Thank you for everything. Please send my love to my mother and siblings, and maybe one day I'll see all you again.
>   Love,
>   Tommy

Likon pinched the bridge of his nose and did his best to force thoughts of his nephew aside. Though he knew in the darkest moments of the nights ahead he would be helpless against pondering the unanswered questions . . . What did the first witch offer innocent Tommy that would make him turn his back on his family, whom he loved? Was he threatened into it? Were Dena and the rest of the family in danger?

A knock on his chamber door snapped Likon from his spiraling thoughts.

"Come in," he called. At first his heart leapt in excitement, thinking it was Kat coming to visit him, until he was reminded that Kat was probably already in Daxaria . . .

The door opened, and in stepped Eli.

The Zinferan boy, who had enough secrets that he could compete with Tamlin Ashowan.

Only the Troivackian king, Daxarian prince, and Finlay Ashowan knew some of the more intimate details about him, but even then, it allegedly wasn't much . . .

"His Majesty says that he's decided not to hold a council meeting tonight after all, so you're free to rest."

Likon nodded at the top of Eli's bowed head.

"Thank you. How're you settling in?"

The young man straightened, but as usual kept his eyes downcast and his hands clasped in front of himself.

"Fine, sir. I—"

"I'm not 'sir,' nor am I 'lord,' or even 'mister.' Just call me Likon. You and I probably come from a similar background." Likon turned from the window.

Eli didn't say anything in response.

"Look, I know you wanted to go to Daxaria, but it'll be a little while before matters of Duke Icarus's estate are settled. In the meantime the Ashowans are going to make sure you can join their coven and kingdom as soon as possible. But until then, let's work well together, alright?"

The young man merely inclined his torso in response.

Likon dropped his head to his chest. "Right. Come on. Let's grab dinner."

"As you please . . . Likon."

At least this small win made Likon smile.

He would wear the lad down eventually through subtle kindness and trying to present himself as an older brother figure.

The king and Daxarian prince had arranged it so that Eli would be able to work and make some kind of income while the matters of the deceased duke settled, though he was not permitted to travel around Vessa freely, and so Likon had been placed as his supervisor . . .

And the only reason Likon had even been afforded the temporary position of the king's assistant? Well, that was because he not only had the education for the role after serving the Ashowan household, but he also happened to have a number of joint investments in the Troivackian brothels, which Brendan Devark had wisely seen as an opportunity to leverage himself into the information veins.

Compared to being imprisoned? It was a charitable deal, though Likon knew that especially in the wake of Mr. Levin's betrayal, he would not be afforded much flexibility or trust . . . But, the king and queen would take him when they'd visit Daxaria, so he would at least be able to visit his family.

"Do you have any brothers or sisters?" Likon asked Eli over his shoulder as the two descended the castle stairwell.

"Stepsiblings. We aren't close."

Likon nodded along, feigning disinterest.

"Do you have any friends you used to sail with who wound up in Daxaria?"

"Not that I'm aware of."

"Ah . . . It smells like we're having pheasant tonight."

"Yes. Pheasant, roast vegetables, and I believe there is grilled salmon as well."

"As a Zinferan, you must like seafood a great deal."

"I enjoy it time to time."

Likon conceded defeat on trying to get the young man to open up for the time being as he and Eli touched down on the main floor of the castle, only to have to come to an abrupt halt as four dogs happily trotted around the corner.

"Nickel, you need to stop stealing your sister's food, you know she's too lazy to—" Lady Dana rounded the corner while speaking in a chiding tone to one of the dogs that padded along at her side.

"Ah, pardon us, Lady Dana." Likon bowed.

The young lady blushed scarlet and jolted when she realized she was not alone. "Ah . . . N-No, it's alright. I thought everyone was already in the dining hall."

Likon smiled reassuringly before kneeling in front of her dogs and holding out a curled hand to let them smell him.

"Have you spent much time with dogs?" Dana wondered curiously as she watched the deft way the Daxarian man handled her beasties.

"I have indeed. My brother-in-law always has two hounds at home, and I've spent a month every year with them for the past fifteen or so years. They're brilliant animals. Much smarter than many people give them credit, and they're better behaved than even some knights," Likon mused while getting a surprise cheek lick from a brown-eyed pup with caramel-colored fur.

Dana perked up excitedly. Which Likon did not see, but Eli did.

"W-Well, I . . . I better go check on my other dog . . . Pork Chop . . . He . . . He still is a little confused since coming back from the Forest of the Afterlife."

Likon looked up and would have perhaps seen the telling shyness in the young woman's face if it weren't for the fact that two more dogs tried to lick his face.

"I heard that His Grace Finlay Ashowan's familiar was able to arrange for one of the stone golems to make an exchange for him," Eli volunteered, subtly saving the young woman from exposing her budding feelings.

"Yes, though I do feel a bit bad . . . They both wished to stay to serve Lady Katarina's familiar . . . He just happened to lose the competition."

Eli nodded sagely, even though he had already heard the story from several people how there had been an incredible strength competition between the two ancient beasts. They competed in boulder chucking in the desert, wrestling, and distance jumping.

The earth had shaken horribly for three days, but in the end, it was the golem Tak who had won.

Meaning his brethren, Jor, had to return . . .

While it wasn't certain whether Pork Chop would even be able to return, the high price of a stone golem traveling back to the forest thankfully made up for dear Pork Chop.

"Ah, yes, I believe Mr. Kraft said something about Pork Chop now being able to see the imps and half fey?" Likon asked while standing back up.

"Yes. He spooks easily now . . ."

"Have you created a dark den for him to have a place to hide?"

"I-I haven't yet. Would you"—Dana cleared her throat—"maybe be able to help me with that?"

Likon smiled and bowed. "Of course, Lady Dana. Now, if you will excuse us, I think we should try to get some supper while we—"

"DANA!"

The roar of Leader Gregory Faucher echoed up the corridor.

Instantly, Dana's shy, sweet countenance hardened to that of a soldier preparing for battle.

Likon blinked rapidly at the dramatic shift in the noblewoman, and even Eli raised an eyebrow as Dana proceeded to fold her arms.

By the time Gregory Faucher stood in front of his daughter, the young woman was tapping her right foot against the stones.

"You are never to bring those dogs into the dining hall again, understood?" He bore down on Dana. Most knights under his command would cower at such a face.

His daughter only scowled back up at him.

"Well, you won't let me learn to defend myself, so I need them with me at all times. For protection."

"Dana, I told you, *I* will protect you and—

"You can't be with me all the time, and we did just have a war where multiple nobles betrayed the king! Why is it a terrible idea for me to have their protection?"

"At least two nobles were urinated on, and one noblewoman had her shoe stolen during dinner."

"Maybe she lost it somewhere else!" Dana retorted indignantly.

"I swear to the Gods, did Lady Katarina put you up to this?"

"Why? Because I could never think of doing such a thing on my own?" Dana accused hotly.

"Not before you met her, you couldn't! Dana, I will not concede to you learning how to fight, so you should—" Faucher started to rumble, but then belatedly realized he and his daughter had an audience.

Likon quickly bowed, as did Eli, then the two quietly sidled around the crowd of dogs and the family feud toward the dining hall.

However, just as they had cleared the circumference of dogs, Dana called out.

"Likon, thank you for agreeing to help me. I'll send a note to you soon to build the den."

Turning back around to awkwardly wave to the young woman, Likon was caught off guard yet again by her when he saw the genuine warmth in her eyes as she smiled at him . . .

"Of course, my lady." He cleared his throat and did his best to mask his reaction.

Faucher stared with a mixture of incredulousness and fury at Likon, then his daughter.

"What invitation did you issue?" the military leader ground out.

Likon and Eli hastily made their escape.

Once safely out of earshot, the Zinferan lad slid a quick look at Likon but was unfortunately caught, as Likon noticed.

"Is there something you'd like to say?"

Eli's eyes snapped forward. "Not at all."

Likon sighed while shaking his head . . .

He was starting to suspect that not only was Eli going to be difficult to get to open up, but also that the Ashowan family had influenced the Troivack-ian court more than the foreign nobility were aware. He was observing more and more instances of outrageousness and just a little bit of lighthearted silliness that had that familiar undercurrent of good-hearted magic. After all, Likon had heard from Kat how Lady Dana used to be painfully demure and soft-spoken, and there used to be an awkwardness between her and her father. But ever since the father and daughter had started fighting each other regularly in battles of wills . . . They'd never been closer.

Maybe Troivack won't be as lonely a place as I thought it'd be . . .

With a half smile, Likon decided then and there that while his fate hadn't always been kind, he would make the best of it, and hopefully, one day, he could find happiness and a place where he belonged all on his own. If he ever got a little downtrodden along the way? He knew he could always rely on the Ashowans to have his back.

EPILOGUE 2

AN ASHOWAN ANNOUNCEMENT

Fresh green buds dotted the trees, balmy winds carried the smell of the earth readying itself for farmers to plant their spring crops, birds trilled in the mornings, adding notes of brightness . . .

And on that sunny, spring day, the castle in Austice of the kingdom Daxaria bustled with excitement that the enticing weather only complemented.

It was the day the prince of Daxaria and the Ashowan family returned from Troivack!

As King Norman Reyes discussed with Hannah, his newest Head of Housekeeping, the details of the feast they were to serve that evening, several excited shouts rang out around him.

"The carriages are coming up the hill, Your Majesty! They are almost here!"

Norman perked up excitedly.

He had missed his son and friend a great deal, and in light of the onslaught of news from Troivack, he had lain awake more nights than he'd slept as he worried for their safety . . .

After all, a battle with the children of the Gods . . . It was hard to even try to imagine. Of course, it also made sense that after such an ordeal Katarina Ashowan would return to Daxaria, and so Norman didn't question her early return for an instant.

The king was also worried about news of his own daughter . . . He had heard of her miscarriage and had wept, wishing she did not have to endure such hardship while in a foreign, harsh land. Though Norman was immensely grateful that at the time Eric, Katarina, and Duchess Annika Ashowan had at least been there. At the very least Alina's most recent missives had been upbeat and hopeful.

Upon hearing that the duke's family and prince were almost returned, the king seated himself on his throne while his courtiers filed in, all aflutter with excitement.

Captain Taylor talked and jested with his knights off in the corner—the man seemed to be in better spirits than anyone had seen him in in months. Lord Dick Fuks was rambling in great detail to Mage Keith Lee about some peculiar dreams of his involving a nobleman named Lord Harry Ball. And last but certainly not least, Mr. Kevin Howard entered the throne room, his head hidden behind a scroll he was reviewing. The paperwork was most likely from the Coven of Wittica, discussing the refugee witches that wished to come from Troivack.

"Mr. Howard!" Norman called over the many heads.

The assistant proceeded up the aisle not raising his gaze until before the dais.

"Your Majesty?"

"You've heard the news that His Highness and Duke Ashowan have returned?"

"Indeed, Your Majesty." Mr. Howard bowed, then climbed the stairs to stand beside the king.

Norman's hazel gaze moved knowingly across his assistant's lined face.

While he may have appeared composed and indifferent to the return of the duke, the king was well aware that the assistant had polished off two bottles of wine the night before, and a maid or two had reportedly heard him muttering to himself about such things as "He's going to give me a wildly inappropriate gift in front of everyone again, isn't he?" And "I swear if he tells me Kraken has organized another kind of rodent that I have to keep track of, I'm going shove that cat out on a rowboat . . . Gods . . . but knowing him, Kraken would enslave the fish next, wouldn't he? That fluffy bugger . . ."

Norman chuckled to himself.

It was true that whenever Fin returned from a diplomatic mission, there was almost always some new small aggrievance he would bestow upon the assistant. Though Norman had seen to giving Mr. Howard raises around the same time these events took place just to be on the safe side, it didn't bode well that there was a mysterious artist who had taken up a prime viewing spot in the throne room's front row that was sent as a gift from Alina . . .

Norman straightened his rust and emerald patterned vest and sat taller in his throne as the room filled completely save for the aisle.

While it simultaneously felt like a long and short time had passed, eventually there was a gesture from one of the guards at the doors to Mr. Howard, who, with a faint grumble at the back of his throat, held up his hand silencing the crowd.

"Announcing the return of Prince Eric Reyes of Daxaria!" Mr. Howard shouted, as the doors to the throne room swung open once more.

Eric strode in, nodding his thanks to the guards as he passed the nobles. Several young women whispered excitedly to their parents.

Norman beamed at his son, who looked significantly healthier than the last time he had laid eyes on him. Even his hair was well kept, although he did have a stoic seriousness about him that told Norman there was bad news to come, or that perhaps he had simply become too accustomed to Troivack's severity . . .

Whatever the reason, the king couldn't ask about it just yet.

When Eric reached the dais, wearing a simple white coat with a black tunic underneath and black pants, he proceeded to bow to his father.

"Welcome back, my son," Norman declared, his smile warm.

Eric straightened. "I am pleased to be back, Father."

Norman nodded and gestured to his right, where Eric could stand at attention while he continued to greet the Ashowans.

However, shortly after this exchange, a squire whispered something to Mr. Howard that had the man blinking in surprise. After overcoming whatever news he had just heard, the assistant gave a brief shake of his head.

From the sidelines, Eric barely stifled a smile.

"Lady Katarina, head of her peers as a student of Leader Gregory Faucher and daughter of Duke Finlay Ashowan, has returned."

Eric chewed on his tongue.

He had come up with the idea of how best to introduce Kat to the nobility without lying . . . And judging from the look of subtle disgruntlement on Mr. Howard's face, he had chosen the perfect wording, as the man obviously thought Katarina's status as a swordswoman to be problematic . . .

When Kat appeared in the doorway to the throne room, the nobles broke out in whispers.

She wore an official uniform.

Not all the nobility even recognized the gravity of the symbolism of it either, but they did notice the sword at her side and the severity of her expression as she made her way down to the king.

With a ceremonial stop, Katarina swept into a bow, further shocking not only the audience, but the king himself.

"Lady Katarina at your service, Your Majesty. I am pleased to have returned home, and I am happy to report that my studies in swordsmanship were a success. I have letters from my teacher, Leader Gregory Faucher of Troivack, as well as from His Majesty King Brendan Devark, recommending me to be knighted in Your Majesty's court."

Norman's mouth dropped open a fraction as the room fell into a stunned silence once again.

He had known that Katarina Ashowan would be learning how to wield a sword theoretically in the name of self-defense, but had she really excelled to the point of earning knighthood recommendations from two powerful men in Troivack?!

Mr. Howard let out a soft whimper. Norman knew the man was imagining the chaos she would bring to their own men-at-arms.

"I shall take these recommendations into serious consideration, Lady Katarina, and we can discuss this at length in the near future. For the time being, however, I hope you take time to settle yourself back home. I also wish to thank you for your service to my daughter. It was a great comfort to know she had a loyal friend at her side."

Kat bowed formally once more and stepped over to stand beside the prince, her head held high.

Freeing themselves from their shock, the nobles couldn't resist gossiping with one another about how Troivack seemed to have changed the troublesome Lady Katarina, and whether she truly was good enough with the sword to be worthy of being knighted . . .

The king studied the redhead and his son carefully. What was it exactly that seemed so different about them?

Certainly, they both looked stronger, and they both stood straighter, but there was something else . . . A presence about them that had completely changed . . .

"His Grace . . . Duke Finlay Ashowan and Her Grace Annika Ashowan!" Mr. Howard almost sounded as though he were going to weep.

Norman wondered for what felt like the thousandth time whether his assistant ever put effort into being so dramatic.

He didn't spare it any more consideration though, as Finlay and Annika swept into the room, looking as striking as ever. The duchess wore a sharp navy blue dress while her neck was adorned with glittering diamonds, and a small clump of her hair waved by her face. Finlay wore a navy blue coat with silvery lining and pants that matched his wife's dress.

As always for formal events, the two matched beautifully.

A feat Norman knew without a doubt was the duchess's machination.

He smiled as the duke and duchess bowed and curtsied gracefully before him.

"I hear thanks to the Ashowan family, my daughter, Her Majesty, can live in a much safer land. I am grateful for all your efforts." Norman lowered his chin. "I look forward to hearing about your travels."

"Yeah," Fin started informally before his wife subtly elbowed him in the side, making him clear his throat. "Yes, Your Majesty, though . . . there is something of the utmost importance that we must tell you today."

A low, prolonged groan began to sound from Mr. Howard. Fortunately, Norman was the only one who could hear it.

"Yes, Your Grace? What might this news be?"

Everyone in the room leaned forward interestedly. They wondered with what new surprise the house witch could spring on the king's assistant . . .

Fin and Annika bowed and curtsied again.

Norman frowned. Were they asking for forgiveness . . . ?

"Actually, Father, it is my news they are referring to." Eric stepped in front of the duke and duchess while giving another bow to the king himself.

Norman shifted forward in his seat with a concerned eyebrow raise.

"What is this news?"

Eric lifted his face and took a steadying breath.

"While in Troivack . . . I fell in love and was married by His Majesty King Brendan Devark with witnesses. This happened before His Grace arrived."

The quiet that crushed the room bordered on supernatural.

Norman tried to speak twice.

But he did not have a voice.

"Wh . . ." He licked his lips and tried again. "Who . . ." He wheezed, then swallowed. "Who did you marry?"

The corners of Eric's lips twitched as his gaze slid to Mr. Howard.

The assistant's eyes bulged. "Gods . . . No . . ."

"I married Lady Katarina Ashowan. Though she is now Lady Katarina Reyes. My wife."

Kat made her way over and stood beside Eric before bowing once more before the king and then looking at the king's assistant.

Norman stared dumbly at his son, then at Kat.

Mr. Howard whimpered, let out a ragged breath, gagged a little, and then . . .

Fainted.

"Oh . . . dear. Kevin." Norman was up from his chair and kneeling at the assistant's side while waving forward the Royal Court Physician earnestly.

The man hustled up the stairs while everyone in the room abandoned any former attempt at whispering.

It was during this time that Eric and Kat locked eyes with the artist and gave simultaneous thumbs-up gestures in silent affirmation.

The man nodded to confirm he indeed would capture the moment perfectly.

Kat and Eric then looked back at each other and finally grinned as brightly as they had wanted to the entire time as the room fell into utter disarray.

"Oh . . . by the way . . . I had this made for you back in Troivack." Eric said the words loudly enough that they drew even more attention as he proceeded to procure from his pocket a small silvery band. "I had this made out of the blade that you had on you when you were stabbed."

"Which time?"

"The second time. You know I can't melt down the first witch's blade." He scoffed.

Kat beamed as he slipped the ring onto her finger, then produced the matching band that was to be his own for her to do the same.

Kat did so as her father and mother smiled happily at them from behind.

By this time, Mr. Howard was thankfully coming back to the world of consciousness.

He sat up, taking slow, deep breaths.

Eric leaned back toward Fin, and while lowering his voice said, "I guess neither of us won the bet."

"Oh, just wait. You just finished your announcement; I have one myself," the house witch retorted innocently.

Eric reared back. "We agreed that it'd be about this news! You can't just add news. That wasn't—"

"Your Majesty!" Fin called out over Eric while Annika delicately lifted her hand to cover a smile of her own.

Norman looked at the house witch as Eric and Kat moved aside so the two could stare at each other clearly.

"My daughter happens to have a bit more to add to His Highness's announcement. She has given me permission to share it with you."

Mr. Howard, who was already accepting a goblet from a nearby steward, held up his hand, stopping the house witch as he drank. Even though it wasn't Mr. Howard's place to do so, Norman decided the poor man needed a bit of pity . . .

"Your Grace, I . . . I do think we should maybe try and hear a bit more about His Highness's marriage before any other details are shared."

Fin stared at the king with a mysterious half smile, then shrugged.

The nobility collectively stared at Norman pleadingly. They wanted to know what it was!

"It's fine, Your Majesty, I know you are caring about my fragile state of mind, but it may be best to get this all over with at once," Mr. Howard informed the king charitably.

"Kevin, this is as much about my mental well-being as your own," Norman muttered.

However, when he stared at the room full of courtiers, he admitted that he did indeed wish to know what else could possibly compare to the news that Katarina had married his son . . .

"Oh, very well. Out with it."

Fin's smile turned perfectly devious as he stared at his daughter who gave an affirming nod then at his son-in-law before gazing up at the king.

"I happen to have the great privilege of informing you that Katarina is also expecting the next ruler of Daxaria."

"Come again?" Eric's voice had jumped a pitch as he turned to his wife, utterly baffled, and staring at her as though expecting her to announce it was a prank, but instead she leaned in a little closer with a glowing smile.

"I wanted a picture of your reaction and Mr. Howard's, and let's be honest . . . It's far better for Mr. Howard to hear it from my father for dramatic effect. It was Alina's idea back before we left. She must have had a sixth sense about the pregnancy because that was weeks ago, and Da just told me this morning!"

Eric dumbly looked over at the artist who proceeded to nod toward Kat while furiously scribbling on his notepad. The prince then half collapsed into a sitting position on the stairs. "I think . . . I'll just . . . sit . . . here . . . for . . . a moment . . ."

It was then in the absolute chaos of the room, that a lone figure broke free from the crowd and stared at the scene.

"Well . . . Kat . . . I really think you've outdone yourself this time."

The Ashowan family members turned to find Tamlin Ashowan, who was staring at his twin sister with a mixture of utter disbelief and humor.

Kat put her hands on her hips and beamed at her twin brother. "You know I always like to make an entrance. Good to see you, by the way!"

Luckily, Eric at least overcame his shock enough to look over his shoulder and discover that Mr. Howard had, in fact, fainted again, making him nod and smile in appreciation as he idly thought it was worth being caught off guard to capture such a moment.

While this carried on, Fin looked back up at Norman. The Daxarian king gazed back at him. His thoughts and feelings indiscernible . . . Until after a moment, he shook his head slowly, let out a long breath, and stared at the house witch. Looking a mixture of defeated, happy, and maybe just a little bit amazed by the Ashowan family, who yet again, threw his entire life into a whirlwind of wonderful mayhem.

Tam closed the office door behind him and let out a breathy laugh while reaching up to rub his eyes.

"Godsdamn . . . I knew she'd get into trouble, but she really pulled a whole kingdom into her nonsense . . ." He shook his head while slipping his hands into his pockets and leaned with his back against the door.

"I guess I'll have to wait to ask her about anything strange involving her powers in Troivack . . ."

The young man's jovial expression dissipated as he then lifted his gaze to the scene he had been trying to hide ever since his sister did something in Troivack that he had felt all the way back home in Daxaria . . .

The entire wall of the office overlooking the Alcide Sea was gone along with part of the floor and the large heavy desk that had held innumerable stacks of important paperwork.

Tam hadn't been able to find a way to explain what had happened and so had barred everyone from entering the office.

Outside, gulls cried over the water, and the peaceful sound of waves lapping the cliff below echoed up . . .

Tam wasn't even sure he understood how it had come to be, but what he did know was that one day he was sitting, working on the mountain of paperwork his father and Likon had left him with, and then a rushing jolt of power had suddenly thrust his magic out of him for the first time since he was a child.

Sighing, Tam reached up and rubbed the back of his neck.

"I . . . don't think my family is just going to let this go . . ."

ABOUT THE AUTHOR

Delemhach is the pseudonym of Emilie Nikota, author of the House Witch series, which she began in order to share with readers some of the warmth, fun, and love of food she experienced while growing up. Born and raised in Canada, she discovered her love of fantasy and magic at a young age, and the affair has carried on well into adulthood. Recently, Delemhach has started work on several all-new stories while simultaneously writing the next books in the House Witch universe, and she can't wait for readers to dive into these forthcoming adventures.

Get whiskered away

with updates on your favorite
magical hijinks, the coziest
content, and all things
Delemhach!

Visit

mailchi.mp/podiumaudio/delemhach

*to sign up for
Delemhach's newsletter!*

Podium

DISCOVER MORE

STORIES UNBOUND

PodiumEntertainment.com

www.ingramcontent.com/pod-product-compliance
Lightning Source LLC
Chambersburg PA
CBHW031340180325
23662CB00026B/55

9 781039 448490